A MEMORY OF
Elephants

An Inspector McLean Mystery

By DAVID W. RUDLIN

ISBN: 1512353337
ISBN 13: 9781512353334

A memory: the collective noun for elephants.

CHAPTER 1

"McLean."

"Hello, Inspector. The chief would like to see you now."

Even after more than two moderately successful decades at Scotland Yard, these words still made Inspector Ian McLean's blood run cold. Chief Franklin loved the chaos, the noise and even the vulgarity of the pit where his detectives worked. He would take just about any excuse to leave his mammoth wood-paneled office, walk down three flights of stairs, pick his way through the maze of desks covered with unsolved cases dating back to the Victorian Era, and immerse himself once again in the constant frustrations and occasional joys of being a copper. Therefore, a summons to his office could mean only one thing: someone was about to get a thrashing too severe to be done in public.

As Ian trudged up the dimly lit staircase he thought about how he might have sinned. The internal investigation into the death of the Home Secretary concluded that Ian had acted appropriately when he gunned the man down in his own conservatory. His next two murder cases had been solved in a reasonable amount of time, and prosecutors were confident of gaining convictions in both. He had not spoken to the press for months, which he'd learned – the hard way – was the best way to avoid saying something he'd later regret. All of his paperwork had been turned in, much of it on time. Ian McLean had been, by any reasonable standard, an exemplary constable.

So it was with a combination of trepidation and confusion that he knocked ever so gently on the chief's highly polished oak door.

No response.

McLean knocked again – a little louder this time.

Still nothing, which was odd. Why would Chief Franklin order him to come up immediately, and then not be there when he arrived? His birthday was weeks away, so there was unlikely to be a crowd of people hiding just behind the door, waiting to shout "Surprise!" And if Chief Franklin had ever been involved in a prank of any kind, he'd kept the matter a well-buried secret.

Thinking his boss might have dozed off after a liquid lunch, McLean closed his fist and banged as hard as he could without hurting himself.

"I'm tempted to wait this out just to see how deaf you think I am, McLean," came a booming voice only slightly muffled by the thick door. "But since neither of us is likely to be happy with the outcome of that little test, why don't you just come in and take a seat."

Slightly embarrassed, McLean did exactly that.

Chief Franklin was flipping through a huge pile of documents, scribbling his signature in the bottom right corner of each without bothering to read the contents. "Does the name Brian Cahill mean anything to you?"

Ian made a rapid inventory of his memory banks and was delighted to find something that might fit the bill. "Isn't he the former Secretary of State for Work and Pensions?"

"Close, but no. That's Robert Cahill. Brian is his son."

"Oh."

"You certainly have a way with word. But I'm going to assume you had no idea that Brian Cahill died five days ago while on a business trip to Thailand."

McLean was about to shake his head, but at the last second salvation arrived. "Wasn't the father on TV recently demanding an inquest?"

"Very good! That means you know as much as the average punter walking past an electronics store with TVs in the window – do they still do that? – and considerably less than the average London cabbie. Shall I fill in the sizeable gaps in your knowledge? Hmm? I'll take your stupefaction to mean 'yes sir, please sir.' Until five days ago Brian Cahill was an investment banker. He worked for Cooper, Littleton & Hall in the City, specializing in corporate finance in Asia. The role required a considerable amount of travel, including nearly monthly visits to Thailand. On the most recent of those visits, Cahill came back home in a box."

"Natural causes?"

"If you believe the Thai authorities."

"But the minister doesn't?"

"He did – at least at first. Like so many obscenely overpaid young bankers, Brian liked to eat well and drink even better. He was at least three stone overweight, had cholesterol at the high end of the danger zone, and the blood pressure of a driving instructor. Believe it or not, all that is just a preface to what supposedly killed him: symptomatic tachycardia."

"Which is?"

"Irregular heartbeats. You'll know that sort of thing when you get to be my age. Anyhow, Thai police called to the scene found a bottle of Propafenone on the night table, and no signs of foul play. They put two and two together and determined that Brian's heart just stopped. Given the lad's medical history, the family was saddened but not hugely surprised."

"But...?"

"But then there was a funeral."

"Usually is, sir."

The chief's eyes narrowed. "Get that sort of thing out of your system now, before someone affiliated with the grieving family hears your inappropriate attempts at wit."

"Sorry, sir."

"As you should be. Cahill is no longer in government, but he still knows where all the bodies are buried. He is one man you do *not* wish to run afoul of."

McLean dropped his head in mock penance.

"That's better. Now, I believe we'd reached the funeral. Minutes before the doors of the local church were to be thrown open to guests, mother breaks down and demands to see her only son one last time before they seal the casket forever and lower it into the ground. Sir Robert tells her to buck up, and she becomes abusive – rather creatively, I'm told, using vocabulary she must have learned from a man who spent his life at sea. Horrified by the thought that she might be overheard by the hordes massed outside, he acquiesces to her demand. The lid on the coffin is raised. His wife bends over to see a pale, lifeless replica of her son lying in front of her, and becomes completely hysterical. At one point she's halfway into the damn coffin, trying to hug her son, while

Sir Robert is pulling on her legs. She grabs the first thing she can, which turns out to be Brian's shirt. Sir Robert pulls even harder, and suddenly there's a ripping sound that – according to one of the altar boys – caused everyone inside the church to freeze. Several of them said they thought Lady Cahill had torn her clothes, which would have added humiliation to the already present horror. And then they heard a shriek."

"Which was...?"

"Lady Cahill, seeing her son's bare chest."

"So the ripping sound was his shirt?"

The chief took a surprising amount of time before replying. "Yes, Ian, it was. But the important thing is not the garment. The important thing is what Lady Cahill saw when it was removed – namely the fact her son had been sliced open, from just below the collar bone all the way down to the navel, and then sewn back up by someone who clearly had no idea what he was doing."

"Oh my God."

"Precisely. As if the poor woman didn't have enough to deal with. Anyhow, a proper British doctor was called to the scene, and asked to do a cursory investigation of the body. His attention was immediately drawn to the way the gash had been closed."

"And how was that?"

"With fishing line." For the first time Chief Franklin consulted his notes. "A rather inexpensive monofilament, apparently. The doctor also noted that the cut lacked the precision you would expect of a trained professional. It looked, in his colorful description, 'like someone had hacked Brian open with a meat cleaver.'" The chief pulled an 8 x 10" photo out of the file, and placed it in front of McLean. "As you can see, there are a series of slashes approximately eight inches long, which led to the cleaver theory."

"Jesus."

"There it is again: your admirable manipulation of the complexities of the English language. But in this particular case I'll concede that's possibly the only sensible reaction. However, there is more. The fishing line was removed, and it instantly became clear that an inability to maintain a steady rhythm was not the only problem with Brian's heart."

"Oh? What else was wrong?"

"Cahill's heart also suffered from multiple puncture wounds. Eight of them, to be precise. Care to venture a guess as to what caused them?"

Ian knew the question was more of a test than the casualness of the chief's tone might suggest. He took his time before replying. "Maybe the meat cleaver? If someone was wielding it with enough force to crack open Cahill's chest, it would have been hard to pull back once the cleaver reached the internal organs."

Franklin nodded in admiration. "A sensible guess. Wrong, I'm afraid, but not a bad go." He pulled out another photo, this one showing a side-by-side comparison of two clearly different knife wounds. "The one on the left was made by the cleaver. You can see that it's deeper at the base than at the top, which is consistent with an overhand motion."

"And suggestive that the killer was shorter than Cahill."

"Just so. But given that Cahill was a large man, and the Thais generally aren't, I don't think that's tremendously helpful. Now, as I was saying, the wound on the right looks more like a puncture. The surrounding tissue is intact, suggesting it was made with an up and down motion by someone standing over the heart."

"After Cahill had fallen to the ground."

"Again, true but not illuminating. There are no such puncture wounds in the skin, meaning the damage to the heart was inflicted after Cahill had been sliced in half. I very much doubt he was able to stand by that point."

"What sort of knife was it?"

"Now *that* is a good question! Tell me, Ian: Have you ever been to Thailand?"

"No, sir."

"Ever seen Thai women of infinite patience carving elaborate designs in watermelons?"

"Why do they do that, sir?"

"I haven't the foggiest. To please the eye, I suppose. In any event, the puncture wounds were made with a fine-tipped knife used exclusively for fruit and vegetable carving."

The two men let that statement sit in the air for a bit.

McLean blinked first. "No chance the heart was damaged post-mortem, maybe during the autopsy?"

"According to the official report we received from the Royal Thai Police, no autopsy was made. It was felt to be unnecessary given that" – the chief opened a folder and rifled through a few pages before finding the passage he was looking for – "'the deceased obviously died of natural causes.'"

Ian always found it difficult to kill off a failing theory when it was his own. "Maybe they did conduct an autopsy, or started to.

But then they botched it and lied to save face. Avoiding embarrassment is very important in Asia."

The chief stifled a smile. "Good to see your Open University course in International Studies has taught you to be so sensitive to cultural differences. And I will admit that a similar idea occurred to me, which is why I asked the coroner, Dr. Benjamin, whether what looked like a crime could simply be a criminal lack of the requisite skills. His response was classic." Franklin cleared his throat, and began speaking in an even deeper rumble than his usual baritone. "'Based on my centuries of experience in the medical profession, I can say without fear of correction there isn't a chance in hell that's what happened. A coroner removes the heart – along with the liver, lungs, stomach, pancreas, kidneys and brain – for weighing and examination. He does not poke it with a fruit knife just to see if anything pops up. Moreover he has better options for closing a body than... *fishing* line. I can therefore say without an instant's hesitation that this wasn't incompetence or a poor set of tools. This was an act of violence.'"

McLean raised his eyebrows. "I've never heard Benjamin be that certain of anything. Cause of death. Time of death. Even time of day, for that matter."

"I was as surprised as you are."

The two men sat in silence for a bit, considering the implications of Dr. Benjamin's assertions. It was Ian who said what both men were thinking. "So there's obviously something the Thais aren't telling us."

Chief Franklin nodded.

"Moreover, having tried to cover it up, they're now stuck with defending the indefensible."

Another nod.

"In which case there's no point in emailing them a series of questions they couldn't or wouldn't answer honestly."

The faintest trace of a smile appeared at the corner of the chief's mouth. "No point at all."

"That means the only way we're going to make any progress is if someone gets on a plane, flies to Thailand, and sticks his head into the lion's mouth."

"I'd say that's a fair assessment."

"Fair, but still incomplete. Dispatching one of our own to double-check what the Thais have done sends a very blunt message that we don't believe what they're telling us. They're going to find that insulting; I would, if the roles were reversed. And they're going to respond to that insult by slamming all the shutters closed, making it impossible for the unfortunate chap who gets burdened with this job to come back with anything more than a suntan."

"I agree that's a distinct possibility."

"But that's not the end of it, is it? Because when the bearer of no news returns to Britain empty handed, Lord Cahill will start raising hell. Someone will have to be held responsible, and no one fills those shoes better than the man who failed in Thailand. Loss of job? Without doubt. Loss of pension? Two-to-one on."

"Indeed."

"So which marked man gets to wear the target on his back?"

"I'm disappointed you think you can sit there pretending you don't already know the answer and expect me to buy your amateurish performance."

"Why me?" McLean was surprised by how whiney he sounded and quickly shifted from crankiness to self-deprecation. "You know I'm terrible at this sort of thing. I got thrown out of Beijing less than three hours after arriving. I admit I'm arrogant enough to think I'm a pretty decent copper, but I'm a terrible diplomat."

"And yet despite leaving China in cuffs, you eventually got a result which the Home Office found highly satisfactory. And let us not forget you survived a terrorist bombing in Mumbai *and* managed to recover a stolen blue diamond. It was that latter case which the prime minister mentioned with great admiration when he asked for you to be assigned to this case."

That caused McLean to sit up. "The prime minister asked for me personally?"

"Don't waste your false modesty on me, McLean. This is the second time the leader of Great Britain has called your number. You may be as clumsy as a drunken bull in a china shop – pun not intended but owned up to – yet somehow you manage to find your way home in the end."

"But those two cases were different! They speak English in Mumbai."

"And in China they speak Chinese. What's your point?"

"In China I had Sally to translate and explain how the culture works. The only thing I know about Thailand is that the red duck curry is excellent."

"That's more than you knew about Botswana when you went there."

Ian was on the verge of pointing out that he came back from Botswana without a conviction – or even enough evidence for a trial. But one look at the chief's face told him this topic was not up for debate. The decision to send McLean had already been made at a level well above the chief's. Debating it with the messenger was a waste of breath.

"Yes, sir," Ian said with forced meekness.

"Oh stop feeling sorry for yourself," Franklin admonished. "Your country is offering you an all-expenses paid trip to sunny Thailand. You should be pleased!"

"A free trip would be lovely if the only thing on the itinerary was lying on the beach drinking cold beer and eating *pad Thai*. Somehow I suspect accusing the Thai police of a cover-up is going to be significantly less satisfying for all involved."

"Well, the good news is you won't be on your own. Thomas will be there to carry your bag, and I'm sending Sally along in case things get rough and you need protection." This attempt to lighten the mood failed to get off the ground, so the chief shifted gears. "You should be flattered, Ian. The PM doesn't know the names of very many people at your pay grade, and most of the names he does know are of attractive women who do their best to avoid being caught alone with him at the Downing Street Christmas party. Visibility counts as you climb the greasy pole. The PM says something nice about you over breakfast and by lunch every toady in town is repeating it. What's more, he said you were both capable *and* discreet. I should have argued with him on both counts, but once he's made up his mind about something he doesn't listen to reason."

Ian had to admit that he *did* feel flattered. And he felt positively giddy when he imagined how his wife Edith would react to learning her husband was "the prime minister's right hand man" – which is how she would tell the story to her friends at the beauty parlor.

And then it hit him. "This is a murder case, right? What has discretion got to do with it?"

Chief Franklin actually looked embarrassed. "Ah, yes, about that. There's one complication I haven't had a chance to mention."

The chief waited for a helping hand that Ian declined to offer.

"As you may know, Thailand has a bit of a reputation for, well, the willingness of some of its young women to make themselves available, in a sexual way, for tourists willing to pay for their services."

McLean tried to suppress a smile but failed. "You mean prostitutes."

"I mean this is the part of the conversation where I talk, you listen, and then you keep this information to yourself in case it proves to have no relevance to the case. Have I made myself clear?"

He hadn't, but Ian nodded anyway.

"A few items have been removed from the case file at the request of Lord Cahill. These relate to an item that was discovered amongst Brian's personal belongings, which were returned with his body. It was a small photo that got stuck between two credit cards, which is probably how the Thai police overlooked it. This picture shows a smiling Cahill together with a Thai woman who looks to be in her very early 20's. He has his arm around her in a manner that suggests the two were... intimate."

"Why assume she was a sex worker rather than a colleague or a friend or even a proper girlfriend?"

The chief gave a Gallic shrug. "Fair point. Let the record show that she *might* have been a proper young lady from a good family that the Cahills would have happily treated as one of their own. But given Thailand's aforementioned reputation, there is at least the *possibility* the young lady was motivated more by lucre than love. If that does prove to be the case, the family is keen to see that information never goes beyond a small group of people on a need-to-know basis."

"And if it does turn out that the woman in the photo had something to do with Brian's death?"

"We cross that bridge when we get to it."

McLean couldn't disagree. The tabloids would have a field day with "Son of Secretary In Saucy Thai Sex Romp." "So given this added... *complexity*, is this an official mission, or am I expected to fly below the radar?"

"This one's on the books. Given what happened in China – when you didn't fly below the radar so much as crash into it – the Foreign Office wants you going through formal channels. You are to make contact with the Royal Thai Police the instant you arrive in Bangkok and keep them posted of any significant developments. They have assigned an English-speaking officer to meet you at the airport, and accompany you at all times. Before you ask, 'at all times' means exactly that: I do not want to hear you've given him the slip so you can stick your nose where it doesn't belong. You can ask questions of whomever you like, but you can't compel Thai citizens to answer. You have no legal authority, meaning you're more private detective than cop. You are to tread softly, speak gently, and otherwise do whatever you can to remain inconspicuous."

"Do I have a curfew and a bedtime, too?"

"Another question like that and you most certainly will. Are we clear?"

McLean nodded, stood, and headed for the door.

"Oh, one more thing," the chief added. "If you come back with a tan anywhere but your face, neck and hands I will have your guts for garters."

CHAPTER 2

Bangkok
Two Years Earlier

Brian Cahill thought he'd died and gone to heaven. As his eyes shifted from the bright lights of the Patpong night market to the smoky interior of a girlie bar called Lady Go Go, he was able to make out a raised platform dotted with half-a-dozen stripper poles. On this small stage were at least 40 raven-haired beauties, not one of whom looked to be older than twenty. Most wore a skimpy bikini sagging under the weight of a circular badge with numbers so large even a blind man could read them in the dark. They gyrated in defiance of the beat, at least until the DJ sent Beyoncé's *Single Ladies* blasting through the bass-heavy sound system. The girls screamed in delight, and for the first time danced with something approaching genuine enjoyment.

Greg Underhill, the managing director of Cooper, Littleton & Hall Thailand, looked at his visiting colleagues like the father of unruly young boys eager to start ripping open their presents on Christmas morning. "Okay, lads, let me explain how this particular game is played. There's no cover, no minimum – but you are expected to order a drink at regular intervals. Those drinks are 120 baht, which is about £2.50."

"Is it a proper drink?" the portly Andrew Cummings asked without taking his eyes from the stage.

"I can guarantee it's free of date rape drugs, and contains some form of alcohol. Whether or not that alcohol is what you asked for, or any smoother than gasoline, is a different story. Now, to continue with your education: While you're drinking and enjoying the show on stage, the girls will try to make eye contact."

"How?" the still-transfixed Andrew asked. "It's dark in here. You can't see anything."

"Nothing escapes you, does it?" Greg replied with a shake of his head. "Trust me, Randy Andy: When a girl tries to make eye contact, you'll know it. And since that will probably be both the first and last time a nearly naked girl is going to express an interest in your fat ass, shut up and let me explain how this dance plays out. First, she will ask you three questions."

"Like in *Monty Python and the Holy Grail.*"

"Yeah, Brian," Greg said. "Just like that. Very helpful reference. Now if I may continue, the first question will be: 'Where are you from?' She's asking this because she knows Brits and Yanks usually have money and a guilty conscience, which means a good tip."

"And what if we were from – I don't know – the Ukraine?"

"You'd be left holding your own, Andrew, a situation with which I'm sure you're intimately familiar. Now shut up so I can tell you about the second question, namely: 'What hotel are you staying at?'"

"Again to ascertain our economic attractiveness?" Brian asked.

Greg wiggled his hand in a yes-and-no gesture. "Partly. But it's also because most of the five-star places won't let bar girls through the door. They figure it makes them look like a brothel rather than a classy establishment."

"So we're out of luck since we're staying at the Four Seasons?"

"Fortunately for you, there are other options," Greg continued. "There's a little love hotel around the corner you can rent by the hour, even though 57 minutes of that time is wasted on you."

"Not me!" Andrew said proudly. "I bought a bunch of Viagra at the chemists today."

"Women all over Bangkok are shuddering at the thought. Anyhow, you're better off with the short-term option. I can guarantee you that no matter how beautiful she appears to you tonight, she's going to look pretty rough in the morning. Plus the three questions are likely to have exhausted her English ability. Take it from me: there's nothing worse than trying to make chit-chat with a bar girl who neither knows nor cares what you're saying while all the married couples in the breakfast room look at you with contempt."

"I suspect the men will be looking at me with envy, but I'm used to that so go ahead and reveal the final question."

"The final question is: 'How long you stay Thailand?' It sounds innocent enough, but the last thing these girls are is innocent. They know there's nothing better than a repeat customer, particularly one who will be here over the weekend."

"Why's that?" Andrew asked while continuing to scan the stage.

"Because then there's a chance you'll take them to Pattaya for a few days on the beach. There's good money in that, and it beats dancing with most of your clothes off. But we're getting well ahead of ourselves. I was saying that even ugly wankers like you lot are going to have girls giving you the eye. If she's not bad looking, give her a little nod of the head to let her know she can come sit with you."

"'Let her come sit with me.' God I love this country!" Brian affirmed.

"What sort of nod?" Andrew asked while making a gesture than was more a nervous tic than an invitation.

"Anything will do," said an increasingly exasperated Greg. "Guys, get this through your thick heads. Unlike every other encounter you've ever had with the opposite sex, this girl actually *wants* to sit close to you. So relax. And shut up so I can finish."

Both Brian and Andrew nodded eagerly.

"Once she sits down she'll ask you your name, and give you one of hers."

"What does that mean?" Brian asked.

"Thai names are impossibly long. To make life easier, almost everyone has a one-syllable nickname. The girl may give you her real one, which is unlikely. Or she may give you the name by which she's known in the club. Chances are extremely high it will be either 'Lek' or 'Nan', so keep your ears open for those.

"Then she will say, 'You buy me drink?' If you say no, she'll be gone within the next 60 seconds. If you say yes, she'll be served a tiny little glass of juice that may or may not have any alcohol in it."

"And that's where they screw you on price, right?" Andrew's head looked like it had been bolted in place, and that place was facing the stage.

"Not really. Sometimes they're more than customer drinks, but often they're the same price. They're just a lot smaller."

"So why don't I get her a customer drink?"

"Because she makes a commission on the lady drinks, but nothing at all on the customer drinks. May I continue?"

Andrew gave a little squeak of acquiescence.

"Now, if you're enjoying the girl's company you can just keep on ordering drinks at a reasonable pace and have a pleasant evening. Tell her your life story. Put your arm around her. Let her put her hand on your knee. Just don't start groping her. It's embarrassing for the girl, and bad for business."

"A girl who's dancing in her bra and pants is going to be embarrassed by a little light snogging in the dark?" Brian asked.

"Strangely enough, yes. Even in Thailand, some things remain behind closed doors. You won't see couples slobbering all over each other here like you do back home."

"What if I don't – you know?"

"What if you think she's ugly when you see her close up?"

Brian shuffled his feet as if trying to stamp out his embarrassment.

"You replace her. Repeat the eye contact process. Or if you want to save time, just find someone you *do* like, and give her number to one of the waiters."

"Won't the girl sitting next to me be offended?" Greg asked.

"Of course she will. She may be a bar girl, but she's still human. However all the girls know this is how the system works. They'll move on to another customer the same way you move on to another girl."

"That's pretty harsh."

"If you don't like it we can leave, Brian."

"No, I'm just saying, that's all."

"Eloquent point noted. Now, if the girl thinks you want her – which in Andrew's case will always be true – she will ask you to pay her bar fine. That 's about 500 to 600 baht, which is ten to twelve quid."

"What's a bar fine?"

"Glad to see you're still paying attention, Andrew. It's the price you pay to the mama-san for taking one of her girls out of the bar and therefore out of commission for the night. Think of it as compensation for lost revenue."

"What do we do with her once we've taken her out of the bar?"

"Well, Andrew old chap, there are birds and there are bees and sometimes...."

"You know damn well what I meant!"

"Of course I did. But you can't hand me a straight line like that and not expect to get mocked. Anyhow, all the bar fine gets is her release from work. Everything else is a direct deal between you and the girl."

"And she can't say no?"

"Once she sees your hairless chest and prodigious love handles I have no doubt she will. But there must be a sum of money for which she'd agree to deflower even a revolting specimen like you. You just have to use those vaunted negotiating skills of yours to find a price for which she'd sell out everything she's ever believed in."

"Ha! She'll be paying me by the time I'm done."

"Of that I have no doubt," Greg replied. "I'd happily pay to get rid of you right now!"

CHAPTER 3

British Airways Flight 9 landed at Bangkok's Suvarnabhumi Airport nearly an hour late. Ian had been expecting a little of the chaos – and the stench – that greeted his arrival in Mumbai a few years earlier, but Suvarnabhumi turned out to be modern and organized to the point of soullessness.

However the destination quickly took on a human face. At the end of the Jetway stood a Thai policeman dressed in a crisply pressed uniform and holding a sign that said – in English – "Mr. I. McLean." Ian raised a finger to indicate the officer had found what he was looking for, causing the man to quickly slide the sign underneath his left armpit, bring his hands together in the prayer position, and bow his head in a *wai*.

Ian and Sally stood there dumbfounded. Thomas attempted to copy the greeting, but succeeded only in looking like a robot whose battery was rapidly wearing down.

Despite the traditional Thai greeting, the policeman spoke impeccable English with a distinct American accent. "Welcome to Thailand! My name is Nattapong Kadesadayurat, but please call me Nat."

Inspector McLean extended his right hand and said "I'm Ian McLean. These are my colleagues Sally Chan and Thomas McMillan."

The officer did another *wai,* and then shook hands with all three detectives. "How was your flight?"

"Not too bad," Ian replied. "But 11-plus hours in an Economy Class seat is never an enjoyable experience, especially when you're my height."

"You're making me feel good about being a short, scrawny Asian," Nat replied.

"Your English is really good," said a visibly surprised and relieved Thomas.

"You have the University of Iowa to thank for that. That's where I got my undergraduate degree."

Sally smiled. "There are plenty of nice places in the US for a young man to spend four years. Why did you choose Iowa?"

"It was either that or the University of Minnesota Duluth. I figured a Thai boy like me wouldn't survive the first winter."

Sally threw back her head and laughed without restraint. "A wise choice, Nat. I only went to that part of the country once, and I've got the frostbite scars to prove it."

The policeman's smile conveyed genuine warmth and amusement. "Follow me. I know a shortcut through Immigration."

Nat proved as good as his word, which was fortunate: the lines for ordinary passengers looked to be at least an hour long. However most of the time saved by the shortcut was used up waiting for bags, especially Sally's oversized Samsonite. "A girl's got to look good," she said more than once when the men stole none-too-subtle glances at their watches.

Eventually the detectives were reunited with their luggage. They flew through the unmanned green channel at Customs, and into the arrivals area. With its soaring ceilings, 7-Eleven, and Starbucks, Ian felt he could have been anywhere in the world. But that international feeling disappeared the instant they stepped out into the heat and humidity of mid-morning Bangkok. The pickup zone was chaotic, but passengers were being packed into small Toyota taxis with reasonable efficiency. The rapidity of movement was in contrast to the sounds of the Thai language, which seemed to require that all sentences end by fading off into the distance like an echo. The smells were a strange mix of cigarettes, diesel fuel, and a sweet floral note that Ian soon discovered was coming from the jasmine bouquets almost every car had hanging from the rear-view mirror.

Thomas took in the scene with wide eyes and an open mouth. Sally appeared to be scanning for potential threats. What she discovered was truly shocking.

Taking up a space large enough for at least three taxis was a white, late-model BMW 5 series. The writing on the sides of both front doors was completely illegible, but the light bar across the top made it clear this was a law enforcement vehicle. While news reports swore the UK police also had a few flash cars, none of the detectives had ever seen one. Their rides were far more likely to be in a clapped out Ford or a Vauxhall with a back seat that doubled as a rubbish dump.

"I'm liking this place already," Sally said as she hopped in.

The driver was also in a police uniform, but no introductions were made. And while Nat had been downright chatty inside the airport, he fell silent as soon as seatbelts were buckled and the driver navigated through the very heavy traffic of the access road and onto the elevated highway. Ian found the sudden change in conversational style a bid odd but wrote it off to cultural differences.

Freed from the need to talk, the inspector pressed his nose against the window as his first glimpses of the Bangkok suburbs flashed past. What he saw bore only a slight resemblance to what he had expected. While there were occasional patches of dense vegetation that looked like what passed for Asia in Hollywood movies, the overall impression was that jungle and concrete had waged a fierce battle for dominance– and concrete had recently emerged victorious. There were buildings everywhere, many of them only a few stories high, but some were skyscrapers that could have been refugees from Manhattan. Giant billboards grew like weeds by the side of the road, advertising Sony TVs, Johnnie Walker Scotch, Emirates flights to Dubai, and every imaginable kind of medical tourism.

Modernity triumphed on the highway as well. German luxury cars determined the pace of traffic, fighting their way around aging trucks overloaded with fresh pineapples, green mangoes, just-picked corn, and a huge range of unrecognizable green vegetables. Some of the trucks were carrying people squashed together like sardines in a can and often with the same lack of seating. Ian noticed they all kept one hand pressed against the roof, presumably to keep from banging their heads against the uncovered metal every time the truck encountered a bump.

Colorful taxis were everywhere. Most were either hot pink or a green and yellow combination that reminded Ian of India. There were also red and yellow and red and blue combinations. Ian assumed each represented a different company, though he couldn't be certain as the only word in English was "TAXI." Everything else was either a number or a flowing script that looked like a cross between Arabic and the scribblings of a toddler. "Do foreigners learn how to read Thai?" he asked, in a half-hearted attempt to restart the conversation with Nat. "Rarely," was the only response he got.

Ian's contemplations were periodically interrupted by the blinding light bouncing off what he guessed – correctly – were Buddhist temples. From a distance the long, thin structures looked like they were covered in gemstones, but traffic slowed as they were passing one situated unusually close to the highway, and he was able to make out that the walls had been coated with shards of mirrors and colored glass. Up close it looked cheap to the point of tacky. But from a distance they – like the towering steeples of old European churches – must send a compelling message about the power of faith to peasants living in ramshackle structures not much taller than they were.

About 40 minutes after leaving the airport, the car finally descended from the elevated highway and turned right onto Ploenchit Road – the stream in a canyon comprised of modern shopping malls, imposing banks, international hotels, and glitzy eateries. Finally Nat broke his long silence.

"We're coming up on Erawan Square. Erawan is the Thai name for the elephant god, bringer of rain and therefore of life. According to our legends, he has 33 heads, each of which has seven tusks."

"Sounds lovely," Sally said to a disapproving glance from Ian.

Nat, however, laughed. "And that's just for starters. There are a couple more calculations, and Erawan ends up with nearly four million angels and more than 27 million ladies-in-waiting."

"All of that in such a small temple?" Thomas asked.

"Most of it is left to the imagination. For artistic reasons Erawan is usually shown with just three heads, and that makes all the numbers that follow more manageable."

"So that's what's under the golden roof in the middle of the square – an elephant?" Sally asked as she leaned across Ian's lap to get a better view.

"Actually, no. That's a statue of Brahma."

"Wait a minute: isn't Brahma a Hindu god?" The question caused Sally to pull away from Ian and gawk in surprised admiration at Thomas. Even Nat turned around to face the young man before answering his question.

"He is. But there are a lot of Buddhist deities who originated in Hinduism. This particular statue has four sides, and we Thais believe that each side of it offers different benefits to the person praying. It's particularly popular with people looking for wealth, success and power."

"Why is that?" Ian asked.

"It's partly the stuff of legend. Back in the 1950's they were building the Union Thai Hotel right over there, where the Grand Hyatt now stands. Everything seemed to go wrong. There were fatal accidents and parts of the structure collapsed. It got so bad that eventually the workers put down their tools and refused to budge until the site's luck changed. An astrologer was consulted, and he said the name Erawan came to him in a dream. He insisted the project needed protection from Brahma, who rides on Erawan. This shrine was built, the hotel became an enormous success, and Thai people started thinking that what worked for the hotel could also work for them."

Just then the detectives saw the driver of the car in front of them take his hands off the wheel, put them in the prayer position, and bow towards the statue – *while the car was going around the corner.*

"Isn't that dangerous?" Thomas asked while pointing at the daredevil ahead.

Nat smiled. "Maybe he's praying he doesn't have an accident."

"What are all those people selling?" Sally asked, eager to change the topic to something less life threatening.

"Mostly offerings to the Buddha: garlands of flowers and incense sticks, that sort of thing."

"What's in the cages?"

"Sparrows. You buy a cage full of them, then open it and set them free. It's supposed to bring good luck."

"Seems counterproductive. Aren't you just incentivizing the sellers to go catch some more sparrows?"

Nat laughed again, but this time it felt a bit forced. "I suppose you could see it that way."

"How about that old lady selling booklets of paper. Do you burn those, like incense?"

"You might as well, for all the good it does you. They're lottery tickets. I guess the woman felt it best to set up shop where there are always a lot of potential customers."

The light changed, and the BMW rounded the curve to enter a very broad street topped with an elevated train line. The broad sidewalks were covered with vendors selling bags of sliced pineapple and papaya, corn on and off the cob, noodles in soup covered by a thick layer of chili oil, stir-fried meat and vegetables served over a small mountain of rice, and fried chicken that smelled so good the detectives were reminded they'd missed breakfast on the plane. The hot food stands had a single gas flame, on top of which was a cauldron of boiling soup or a wok that appeared to be in constant motion. Nearby most of the carts were half-a-dozen stools that looked like they'd been taken from a children's tea party, organized around a rickety table. The food must have been good, as most of the seats were occupied despite the fact it wasn't yet lunchtime. The customers ranged from well-dressed young women in skirts to hopefully off-duty security guards in uniforms at least two sizes too big for them.

Nat noticed what the detectives were looking at. "We Thais are constantly hungry. You're never more than a few feet from a hot meal in this country."

"Is it safe to eat on the streets?" Thomas asked meekly. "I mean, in terms of hygiene and all."

The Thai shrugged. "It's fine for us, as we grew up eating street food. For you it's probably... reasonably safe. There's no refrigeration, despite all the heat. But the ingredients are purchased fresh each morning, with anything that goes unsold being thrown out at the end of the day. In fact, a few years ago there was a TV program that found there's less bacteria in Bangkok street food than there is in a meal from McDonalds. However if you're not used to eating on the street, it's probably better to stick to indoor restaurants."

"Excellent advice," Ian said with finality, "advice we plan to follow to the letter. Right, Thomas?"

"Uh, right, sir."

Just then the car pulled into a semi-circular cobblestone driveway that led to a stately whitewashed building. Lotus ponds flanked the broad entrance. All of the hustle and bustle of the street vanished as the BMW came to a stop underneath a roof large enough to cover a four-bedroom house. "We have reached our final destination, gentlemen and lady. Welcome to The Four Seasons Bangkok."

At the mention of the name, Sally glanced at Ian. "Business must be good for the Thai police department. Usually we stay at places that make jail look like the lap of luxury."

"Speak for yourself," Thomas said as he jumped out of the car.

A tall Thai man in a light green uniform and pith helmet gave the detectives a snappy salute. "Welcome home!" he said.

Sally smiled again. "Oh, Ian, dear, you do know how to treat a lady."

"And don't you ever forget it, even though you've forgotten how you normally speak and are now channeling some sort of southern belle."

A Thai woman in a traditional long skirt and silk blouse appeared out of nowhere. "Welcome to the Four Seasons Bangkok. We'll take care of the check-in process in your room, so if you'd like to follow me...."

"Most impressive," Sally judged.

"Nothing I haven't seen before," Thomas replied with a snobbishness that Ian found surprising – and felt compelled to explain to Sally.

"When we went to Mumbai, the owner of the missing blue diamond paid for us to stay at the Four Seasons there – in suites, no less."

"And then you almost got killed by a terrorist bomb." Sally looked up at the elegant hotel surrounded by lush gardens. "Seems like a reasonable trade-off."

The huge glass doors of the hotel swung open, liberating a blast of cold air that felt so good all three detectives closed their eyes and savored the escape from stickiness. Once those eyes re-opened they saw a wall covered in a two-story painting in the traditional Thai style, a highly detailed combination of vibrant colors and what Ian suspected was actual gold leaf. It was stunning, and soothing, and distinctively oriental all at the same time.

Sally nodded her approval. "Not too shabby."

A silent elevator took the group up to the fifth floor, where the receptionist – whose name was so long it barely fit on her nametag and was clearly unpronounceable by anyone without a Thai tongue – said "We have you in adjoining rooms. Inspector McLean, we've upgraded you to a Junior Suite. Detectives Chan and McMillan, you're in our deluxe rooms."

Sally feigned disappointment, but not for long. The second she walked into her room and saw the bed was even wider than it was long, she couldn't help smiling. "Now *that's* what I'm talking about."

Nat looked a little embarrassed to be standing in Sally's room. "I'll let you get settled, and have a shower or a nap if you like. Whenever you're ready I can brief you on the case."

Ian spoke for the group. "We can be ready to go in 20 minutes." Sally grimaced. "How long is the ride to the station?"

Nat swallowed surprisingly hard and then said "I thought it would be more convenient if we met here. Bangkok traffic can be a nightmare. And our station is run down even by Thai standards. I've booked a conference room on the 2nd floor, and arranged for coffee and snacks to be served throughout the day. The business center has printers, copiers and all clerical services. Fast Wi-Fi is also available. I think you'll find it much more comfortable than the station."

Ian spoke quickly, before Thomas could ask a question. "That sounds perfect – and very thoughtful. Thanks. Shall we meet you downstairs at" – he paused briefly to look at his watch – "11:45?"

Nat's relief was palpable. "Perfect. See you soon."

As he walked away the three detectives looked at each other with expressions of puzzlement on their faces. "You'd almost think he didn't want his colleagues to know we're here," Sally said as she threw open her capacious suitcase and began digging through it in search of a change of clothes.

CHAPTER 4

"You pillocks made up your minds yet?" Greg asked his gob-smacked charges.

"Why make a choice and risk hurting some poor girl's feelings? I'll have them all," said Andrew hopefully.

"Just one for me," Brian added. "Number 32."

Greg stood up to get a better look, then nodded approvingly. "A good choice. Thai men wouldn't like her because she's too dark, but you two have more than enough blindingly white skin at home. Lovely hair, though that's pretty common here. No scars or visible wounds. Looks to have most if not all of her teeth. You have my blessing."

Andrew suddenly looked panicked. "How do I know they haven't got AIDS?"

"Unless you went to medical school during your lengthy lunch breaks, you probably don't. But the girls are checked once a week, and they're told to use condoms. If you've got even half a brain you'll insist they follow that order."

Andrew's concern didn't last beyond yet another glance at the stage. "Right. Then let's get this party started." He raised one finger to get the waiter's attention."

"Yes?"

"I'd like to entertain #47, #53, and #77. Plus I'd like another round of drinks for my friends, and Lady Drinks for my three girls."

Greg shook his head in disappointment. "Pace yourself, lad. The last thing I need is for you to bang yourself to death on my watch."

Brian sat down on the faux-velvet bench cushions, and laid his arm across the back. He felt something slightly sticky, and instantly put his hand back in his lap. It was probably just a little spilled beer that had been overlooked by the cleaning crew in the blackness of the seating area – and if it wasn't, he didn't want to know about it.

Just then #32 walked up to Brian, a packet of Marlboros and a disposable lighter in her left hand. She held out her right. "What you name?"

"I'm Brian. What's your name?"

"Me Nan." She dragged out the vowel in her name for what seemed an eternity.

Brian took her hand, but instead of shaking it he gave it a kiss. "I'm very pleased to meet you, Nan."

"Can I sit down?"

"Yes, please. Would you like a drink?"

"Okay for you?"

Brian called for a waiter, then wondered if that really answered her question. Once again the server appeared almost instantly, and Nan said something in Thai, in a voice far harsher and more guttural than the one she'd used when introducing herself in English. The waiter went running back to the bar.

"Where you from?"

So far the story was unfolding exactly as Greg had foretold. "I'm English."

"You England?"

"No, my country is England. I am English." Jesus Christ, Cahill: save the grammar lesson for another day.

"Where you stay Bangkok?"

"At the Four Seasons." From Nan's response it was impossible to tell if she'd ever heard of the place.

"When you go back England?"

"Wednesday morning. We're on BA 10." *Far* too much information. You've really lost your touch, assuming you ever had one to begin with.

Nan's drink arrived, and she raised her glass. Brian clicked his to hers. "To you, the lovely Nan." In the dark of the bar he couldn't be sure, but he thought she might have smiled demurely.

"You how old?"

"How old do you think I am?" Now I sound like one of those women who think their age should be a state secret.

Nan gave Brian a slow and thorough head-to-toe inspection before concluding "You 27."

"Thank you, but no. I'm actually 32."

"You young man!"

"Well, I work out whenever I can, and try to watch what I eat." Brian hoped none of his friends could hear him now, especially since neither of those statements was the least bit true.

Though he wouldn't mind if those friends were able to *see* him. Up close Nan was, if anything, even more beautiful than she'd looked from a distance. Her skin was flawless, the dark caramel color set off by thick red lips and dazzling white teeth. Her hair – which she kept tossing back in what Brian was hoping was a suggestive gesture – was straight and smooth and shiny. She was trim without being thin, and had long, well-toned legs. When she crossed her right leg over her left knee, he found the contrast between the brown skin on the top of her foot and the pinkish skin underneath irresistibly sexy.

"So, Nan. How old are you?"

"You guess."

"Okay. I'd say... 21."

"Nooooo! Me 27." It sounded like *tuwentee sebbennnn.*

"You certainly don't look it. How do you keep your skin so smooth?"

The confusion was evident in Nan's face, so Brian dragged his finger down one cheek. "So smooth."

That one clearly scored. Nan put down her glass, and put her hand on the inside of Brian's left knee.

"You've just been claimed, mate," Greg said into his opposite ear.

"Meaning what, exactly?"

"Meaning she's sending a signal to her competition to stay the hell away from you."

"So now no other girls will talk to me?"

"Not unless you make the first move." Greg finished his Johnnie Walker Black Label and soda, and signaled for a refill.

"It's rather funny, really. These girls would tear each other's eyes out over a bit of fresh meat, which is, I hesitate to say, exactly what you are to them. But once a man's been marked, you become invisible, you're off the field, you're no longer in play. It's a strange sort of code, but the girls follow it religiously."

"But what if I decide I don't like the girl who marked me?"

"Then you order someone else. That's all it takes to lift the restraining order, and you'll be getting Come Hither looks from half the girls on the stage. But why are you asking me all this? Already in the mood for a change?"

Brian reacted as if someone asked him if he was cheating on his wife. "Absolutely not! I'm just trying to understand how the system works." He then refocused his attention on Nan. "So, where do you live?"

"Bangkok."

"Well, yes, I assumed as much. But whereabouts in Bangkok?"

Nan looked confused.

"Sukhumvit? Siam Square? Klong Toey?" The first is a major road that runs all the way to Cambodia, the second a tourist spot, and the third a massive slum, but they were the only Thai place names Brian knew. And the helping hand worked: Nan nodded her head eagerly, and said "Din Daeng."

Brian hadn't a clue where that was, so he just smiled. "How do you get to work?" Blank expression. "You come taxi? *Tuk-tuk*?" He turned to Andrew, who had a look of sheer bliss on his face. "I haven't even finished my first drink and I'm already speaking without the benefit of prepositions. Another 10 minutes and I'll be talking very loudly because that's the only thing that makes the natives understand the Queen's English."

He needn't have been so harsh on himself. Nan understood the question, and answered it with pride. "Me *motosai*."

"*Motosai*? What's that? Like a bonsai?"

"*Motosai*. 125cc." Nan twisted her hands as if changing gears.

"Oh, a motorcycle!" Brian bellowed in triumph.

It wasn't a particularly important piece of information to have gained, but it was his first conversational breakthrough – and it led to a burst of over-confidence. "I'm from London. I have a hired car that picks me up each morning at 6:30. In the evening I'm usually out and about with friends, so I just grab a cab when I'm ready to go home."

Brian watched the words soar over Nan's head. Hiding his disappointment, he reverted to speaking like an ill-mannered tourist. "Me taxi." That got a big smile, probably – he realized later – because it suggested he had money to throw around.

Suddenly Andrew's large frame was blocking Brian's view of the stage. His colleague and occasional friend had one girl under each arm, both of whom seemed to be struggling under the weight. "That's me set," he said. "I've chosen the best two out of three and paid both bar fines. I know where the short-stay hotel is, and as far as the rest of it goes, I've never had an unsatisfied customer."

"Nor a satisfied one," Greg added. "Brian, if it's okay with you, I'm going to head home. You'll be okay on your own, won't you?"

Brian stole another glance at Nan, who smiled radiantly. "I'll be fine," he replied.

CHAPTER 5

The entrance to the meeting room was obscured by tables on either side that groaned under the weight of the food piled on top of them. Five different varieties of fruit – two of which the detectives recognized – all sliced and picture-perfect. A tray of finger sandwiches: salmon, cucumber, and tuna salad. Mini scones with clotted cream and raspberry jam. Three different salads. A tray of cold and smoked meats and fish that in other circumstances would have made a filling dinner for 20. Bite-size pieces of charcoal-grilled chicken accompanied by a sweet chili sauce. And half a dozen different desserts – including two metal containers of ice cream nearly buried in a mountain of ice.

Nat stood off to one side looking anxious.

"It looks beautiful, Nat" Sally offered. "And I'm famished. Would you be offended if we nibble while you brief us?"

"Not at all," the policeman replied, clearly relieved his prepa-rations had met with approval. "I've got everything ready to go inside, so load up your plates and let me know when you're ready to start."

The detectives wasted no time grabbing enough food to last them for a week of hurried meals at their desks back at Scotland Yard. A waiter in a black bow tie appeared out of nowhere, silently poured coffees, and then vanished. Ian picked up his cup and said, "Nat, we're all set."

The lights lowered. A slightly nervous Nat stood next to the screen, laser pointer in hand, and began his PowerPoint presentation. The first slide showed a photo of a landing card. "Brian Cahill arrived in Thailand for the first time on April 13, 2012. As you can see from the information on that card" – Nat swiveled and then pointed at the relevant portion of the image on the screen – "he arrived on the same BA flight as you did and was also given a visa exemption. His stated purpose for visiting was listed as 'Business.'" Nat moved the pointer. "His hotel is listed as the Four Seasons, and we have confirmed that this is indeed where he stayed."

Sally raised her hand. "Is that why you put us here?"

"Partly," Nat admitted. "But it really is a nice hotel."

"That it is," Ian agreed. "Please continue."

"Immigration records show he left the country four days later, on BA 10 to Heathrow. He did not engage in any activity that resulted in a report being made to the police. The Assistant Manager of the hotel described his stay as 'ordinary.' His company – Cooper, Littleton & Hall Thailand – confirmed he came to the office the first three days of his stay, and worked until after the secretarial staff had gone home. On the fourth day he went directly from his hotel to the airport, using a hotel car."

"So a straightforward business trip."

"Yes, Ms. Chan."

"Please, Nat. Call me Sally."

"Sally it is, then. Over the next two years Mr. Cahill returned to Thailand a total of 17 times." Six eyebrows rose in unison as the PowerPoint slide showed an array of landing cards. "In each case the purpose was listed as 'Business.' However a careful analysis of the timing and duration of his visits suggests that business may not have been his only objective." The slide changed again, this time showing a spreadsheet listing the 17 arrival dates down the left side, with days of the week across the top. "As you can see, his trips increasingly occurred – deliberately or otherwise – over a period that included the weekend."

"Is that unusual for foreign businessmen?" Ian asked.

"No, Ian, it is not." Nat paused briefly. "Thanks to the efforts of the Thai Tourist Board, the beauty of our beaches is well known. It's common for visitors to mix a little pleasure with their business."

Sally bit her tongue.

Nat invited additional questions with his eyes and, when none were asked, clicked for the next slide. "On both his third and fourth trips, Mr. Cahill spent Friday and Saturday night in Pattaya – that's a beach resort about two hours from Bangkok by car – at the five-star Dusit Thani hotel."

"Same question as previously," Ian said. "Is that unusual?"

"And I have the same answer: not at all. Most tour packages include a side trip there – especially the budget ones."

"Because...?"

"Because unlike most of our island resorts, you don't have to fly or take a boat to get there. That makes it cheap, fast, and easy to reach. As a result, it tends to attract backpackers and – ever since the visa requirement was waived in 2007 – Russians with cash to burn."

"Doesn't sound like the most romantic of spots," Sally said coyly.

Ian made a mental note to compliment Sally on this rare display of tact. She'd created an opening for Nat to talk about any love interests Brian Cahill may have had, and she did it without her usual full-frontal confrontation. Alas, her diplomacy failed and she came away empty handed. If Nat got the hint, he chose to ignore it and take the question at face value. "It's not. It's fine for a boy's weekend away, but most people tire of it pretty quickly and move on to nicer destinations. And that's exactly what Mr. Cahill did. On his fifth trip he went to Hua Hin, which is very popular with rich Thais and foreigners looking for a healthy retreat. It's much quieter than Pattaya, though it does have bars and" – Nat developed a sudden interest in the pattern on the carpet – "other attractions. I don't think Mr. Cahill liked it too much, as on his sixth trip he went to Phuket. That's an island off the southwest coast, facing the Andaman Sea."

McLean cocked his head quizzically. "I thought Phuket had its share of girlie bars as well."

Although the cat was now halfway out of the bag, Nat refused to pick it up and pet it. "Thailand strives to cater to all types of tourists. For those looking for excitement we have sports bars and pool bars and – as you call them – girlie bars. But not everyone who comes here is looking to get drunk and disorderly. Parts of Phuket are very quiet, with elegant hotels that cater to the world's rich and famous. Aman Resorts – the ultra-luxurious hotel chain – chose Phuket as the site of their very first hotel."

"And that matters because...?"

"Because that's where Mr. Cahill stayed."

"Aha," said Sally.

Nat smiled, clearly eager to make his next revelation. "And he didn't stay alone."

"Aha!" Sally repeated in a very different tone of voice.

"His registered guest was Kanokwan Supitayaporn, born in 1985 and a resident of Bangkok. Her profession was listed in the register as 'hair dresser.'"

"I know I'm starting to sound like a broken record, but is that significant?" Ian asked.

Nat looked somewhat embarrassed. "It's often what bar girls use on official documents to avoid... complications."

"Aha," Sally said for a third time.

"Miss Supitayaporn accompanied Mr. Cahill on all subsequent domestic trips within Thailand. These included weekend stays in Koh Samui, Koh Karon, Koh Lanta and Koh Phangan. All of those are beaches; 'koh' is the Thai word for 'island.' They also went to Chiang Mai and Chiang Rai in the mountainous north – twice to Chiang Rai, in fact."

"Sounds like love," Sally said.

"That's one possibility," Nat said while avoiding Sally's gaze.

Ian looked troubled. "I'm impressed you know so much about not only where Brian went, but who he went with. How is that even possible?"

Nat's embarrassment was quickly replaced by pride. "In Thailand, for the safety of our overseas visitors, everyone who spends the night in a hotel must register – not just the person paying the bill. Foreigners must show a passport, and Thai residents must produce their identity card so that we can verify the name and birthdate supplied. That makes it relatively easy to track the movements of someone staying in paid accommodations. When necessary, we can cross-check the registration information with credit card usage details."

"I'm envious," Ian said generously.

Sally was eager to get back to the juicy details. "So, can we assume from this very comprehensive information you've provided that Brian and this girl whose name I can't pronounce were an item?"

"You mean, were they romantically involved?"

Sally nodded.

"I couldn't say. It's not uncommon for male visitors to Thailand to bring a... guest along for company. No one likes to lie on the beach alone, and traveling with a local who speaks some English can make the journey easier."

Sally looked at the policeman with motherly affection. "Then there's that other thing...."

Nat's eyes returned to their intimate study of the floor. "Yes, there is that, I suppose. However I cannot say with certainty whether or not intimacy played a role in this relationship. What I *can* say is that on all but three of his subsequent visits to Thailand, Mr. Cahill and Miss Supitayaporn registered for the same hotel room."

Ian arched an eyebrow. "And you don't think that's reasonably solid evidence there might have been more between them than just a, um, business relationship?"

Nat cocked his head like a dog that thinks he heard the word "walk." "That's certainly a possibility. Maybe even a likelihood. But there's no *evidence* the relationship was more than casual."

"Come on, Nat," Sally chided. "Do you think they shared a room so they could eat popcorn and watch in-house movies together?"

"I think that Mr. Cahill came to Thailand on business, and by all accounts he worked very hard. Unlike tourists who can devote most of their waking hours to the search for companionship, Mr. Cahill may have decided that the best use of the limited time available to him was to maintain a relationship with one person."

"That's sweet, Nat, and on behalf of all women I thank you for assuming the best. But I struggle to see the combination of bar girl, non-working weekends and lavish beach resorts as anything other than a fling – an extended fling, but nothing more than a fling."

"Perhaps you're right, Sally. And I'm not trying to argue that the relationship was purely platonic. But there's a big difference between what my friends in Iowa call a roll in the hay with a drunken stranger and spending an entire weekend away. Traveling together is arguably more intimate than sleeping together. You see each other first thing in the morning, when your hair sticks up and your breath smells like your feet. You have to use the toilet in front of each other. Other people will see you together. You have to make polite conversation over breakfast. And then lunch. And then dinner. What happens if you wake up the first morning and decide you can't stand the person lying next to you in bed?"

"So you're saying maybe she was just the path of least resistance, a known entity, a comfortable traveling companion – but with benefits?"

"I'm saying that's possible." Nat flashed a winning smile. "And it's also possible the two were romantically involved."

"Did you contact the staff at any of the hotels where the couple stayed and ask about their behavior?" Ian asked.

"Of course. But no one remembered them, as a *farang* with a bar girl is a pretty common sight, and unless they get out of control no one pays them much notice. After three or four dead ends we simply gave up."

"And *frung* means what, exactly?" Sally asked with only a touch of menace.

"It's pronounced *farang,* and it's how we Thais refer to foreigners."

Thomas had a flashback to their trip to Hong Kong, where he learned that the Cantonese word for foreigners – *gweilo* – translates as "foreign devils." Thinking the Thai word might be similarly revealing, he asked Nat what it meant.

"Strictly speaking it just means someone white, a European or American."

"So it doesn't apply to me," Sally said cheerfully.

Nat shrugged. "Technically, I suppose not. But the word does get used with pretty much anyone who isn't Thai."

"Well then, put me down for Mortally Offended, but please carry on." Sally punctuated the statement with a grin.

"Right, sorry. Anyhow, after we discovered this pattern, we tracked down Ms. Supitayaporn, or at least tried to."

"Meaning?"

"Meaning that by the time we found her she was already dead."

CHAPTER 6

Brian Cahill was 15 minutes late for breakfast. As he ignored the hostess and made his way straight to the table where his colleagues were already seated, Greg and Andrew stood in unison and pretended to applaud wildly.

"Very funny. So I'm a little late. Get over it."

"How was it?" said Andrew with a lascivious grin. "Or should I say, how was *she*?"

"She was fine. It was fine. End of discussion."

"'Fine'? You're barely able to walk this morning and all you'll say is 'fine'?"

"A gentlemen doesn't kiss and tell."

"So leave out the kissing part. It's everything else I'm interested in."

Greg held up both palms. "Enough, Andrew. Give him a break."

"I'll bet that's what she said!"

Both Greg and Brian groaned. "Can we talk about something else, like how we're going to play the meeting that starts in" – Brian looked at his Panerai diver's watch – "a little less than three hours?"

But Andrew wasn't ready to throw in the towel. "Jesus, Brian. She's just a bar girl. It's not like you have to protect her honor or anything."

Andrew remained oblivious to the effect his words were having, but Greg saw Brian's jaw clench. Determined to avoid a confrontation, he jumped in between the two men with both feet. "I spoke to their financial advisor early this morning, and he's still insisting we undervalued the control premium by $28 million."

Andrew snorted. "That's bullshit and they know it."

"Of course it is and of course they do," Greg replied. "But they want more money and figured this was their best excuse for getting it."

"So what's our play?" Brian asked.

"We say the offer on the table is more than fair. And if they can get more money from somewhere else, show us a firm offer and we'll match it."

Andrew grew serious. "But we're not going to walk away if they don't buckle and accept our offer as is. London gave me approval to go as high as another $5 million, and I've got that in writing."

"$5 million is a lot of money, but it's also a lot less than $28 million," Brian pointed out.

"Yeah, but this isn't about the money. It's about saving face. They're not going to say yes just because we tell them to. They need to salvage a victory – no matter how tiny – here at the end."

"I understand all that," Brian said. "But any little gifts we give them today will come back to haunt us at bonus time. I'm not saying we can't bend a little, just that we need to stay well clear of reckless generosity."

Andrew pushed away his plate, which he had scraped clean. "The negative impact of a few million extra dollars pales in comparison with what will happen if we don't close this deal. I spent 18 months getting us to this point, and our legal bills are at $3 million and climbing. We're going to close this bastard if I have to start threatening people with a knife."

Greg smiled. "I'm here to follow your lead. But let me say this: there's a lot more business I could be doing with these guys, so I need to come out of this meeting with the relationship intact. If this deal goes south, I'm blaming the two of you. Not in London, but here."

Brian nodded. "That's fine. We'd do the same if the roles were reversed. So, just to confirm: our first response is the offer stands. Second is an additional – what? – million. Then three million. Then five. Then we walk. Everyone okay with that?"

Cahill's two colleagues inclined their heads in agreement.

"Good," Andrew announced. "Now that we've got the day sorted, what are we doing tonight? Wait: I've got a crazy idea. There's this bar I heard about in a place called Patpong. I think it's called... Lady Go Go. Maybe we should check it out."

His colleagues groaned. Then Greg said, "If we close this deal, tonight we're going to be out celebrating with the client."

"So we'll take them with us!"

Greg shook his head. "You don't say thank you for a $256 million deal with watered-down drinks in a girlie bar. Andrew, these guys live here. If they wanted to – which they don't – they could go to Lady Go Go every night. What you're suggesting is the equivalent of holding a closing dinner at the pub round the corner."

"If the pub round the corner had beautiful half-naked girls willing to dance on my face, I'd hold all my closing dinners there."

"Forget it. It's just not up to the expected standard."

Andrew actually looked offended. "You weren't quite so dismissive last night."

"That's because last night I was entertaining you two virgins. For you guys, a girlie bar is a treat. It's something new. But it's for tourists. Not even the foreigners who live here go to that sort of place. Well, not often. It's kind of embarrassing."

With eyes narrowed in concentration, Brian rejoined the conversation. "Why embarrassing?"

"It's sort of an admission that the only way you can pull is to pay for it."

"No it's not," Andrew replied with indignation. "It's a bit of fun. The girls get what they want, and we get what we want – without all the fuss and day-after nonsense."

"And you think what they want is *you*?"

"Of course not. They want my money. I want their sweet, sweet loving. It's a commercial exchange, no different than any other. The only time it gets messy is when one side forgets it's a business transaction and nothing more."

Greg massaged the back of his neck. "I suppose that's one way to look at it. But it's a transaction in which only one side has a choice. Those girls do it because they need the money."

"And the only reason I do what I do is because *I* need the money," Brian insisted.

"But it's different. You're chasing *more* money. The girls are after *some* money." Greg folded his napkin and dropped it on the table. "Most of them come from a place in the northeast called Isaan. It's farm country. It might look bucolic from a distance, but life there is really, really hard."

"So why don't they go to school, and learn to be a secretary or a tour guide or some other profession where you get to keep your clothes on?"

"Because that costs money, and money is one thing that doesn't grow in Isaan. Most farmers, if they're lucky, harvest enough rice to keep their families fed and have a little left over to trade for meat, cooking oil and other essentials. But the problem with a barter economy is that it doesn't generate any cash. And if that weren't enough of a barrier, there's also a language issue."

"Which is?" Brian asked.

"Laos is next door, and they speak a local dialect that's very similar to Lao. It's called 'Thai language', 'Lao language' or 'Isaan language', which highlights the fact it's a mongrel that doesn't travel well to places like Bangkok where the better paying jobs are."

"Okay, so why don't they stay on the farm and live like they always have?"

"That's fine if you're the eldest male in the family – or married to one. Otherwise you're expected to make your own way in the world."

"And the only way to do that is to become a whore? Come on, Greg. Life on the farm is tough everywhere, but people manage," Brian objected.

"They manage if they don't have any debt. Or dad doesn't drink or gamble too much. Or there's never a bad harvest. Or no one gets sick. Everyone in Isaan is walking a tightrope, and if they fall there's only a threadbare safety net to catch them."

Greg poured himself another coffee, clearly trying to decide whether he'd said enough to make his point. He concluded that he hadn't.

"I'm not talking about having to skip a few bills to make ends meet. I'm talking about sheer desperation. Sometimes, when a family gets deep into debt, they have no choice but to sell a daughter to a brothel broker."

"Surely not," Brian said.

"But that's slavery!" Andrew protested.

"I wouldn't disagree, though technically it's probably closer to indentured servitude. The daughter agrees to work until the debt is paid off, which it never would be if she stayed on the farm. But that's probably not the most common route to the big city."

"What is?"

"The girls volunteer."

"They volunteer to get banged by strangers? Whatever for?"

"Think about it. Your whole life you've had maybe two changes of clothes and a school uniform. One day a village girl comes back from Bangkok. When she left two years ago she was just like you. Now she's walking down the muddy main road in six-inch heels.

Her long nails are manicured and dotted with small gemstones; yours have been chewed down to the quick and most likely have pig shit under them. She's wearing lipstick and smells of flowers; you smell of sweat. She's got a gold necklace and an ankle bracelet with a ruby in it. You look at all that wealth and think 'why her and not me?'"

"Sounds to me like she looks like a whore," Andrew said.

Greg ignored him. "This girl has been coached on her sales pitch. 'If I did it, so can you. You're a beautiful girl; men will like you. Come back with me to Bangkok. I'll introduce you to a place where you can make more money than you ever dreamed of. We'll live together for the first few months so I can show you the ropes. We'll travel around the city in air-conditioned taxis and go to the best restaurants and clubs. Would you like that?' And this little farm girl, who has never been to a restaurant with indoor seating and only has the faintest idea of what a club might be, can't wait to go."

"But she's a kid who doesn't know any better. Her parents must be smart enough to realize what's going on. Surely they object?"

"Chances are they have even less education than their daughter. And there's a pitch for them, too. They're invited over to the girl's house for a lavish meal. They notice the fake marble floors, and the hand-carved furniture, and the flat screen TV. They notice there's running water in both the kitchen and the bathroom. And they notice when the girl from Bangkok hands her dad a huge pile of cash.

"On the way home they think about what they could do with all that money. And it looks so easy. Enough money to take a family that's been dirt poor for generations and turn them into the neighborhood gentry – all for sending one daughter to work in Bangkok. How bad could it be? The girl who invited them over to dinner looked *very* happy, didn't she?"

"But they're preying on the poor and ill-informed," Brian said.

"That's certainly one way to look at it. But I suspect if girls and their families knew exactly what they were signing up for, most of them would still go. Happily. Sons here are more highly valued than daughters. But Bangkok gives girls the opportunity to transform themselves from burden to savior of the entire family. All they need to do is close their eyes and think of England once or twice a night, six or seven nights a week. I'm sure they're very proud of what their sacrifices make possible for their loved ones. But no one with half a brain thinks any of these girls enjoy what they have to do to survive."

"All of which is a very long-winded way of saying Lady Go Go is not an appropriate place to celebrate a multimillion dollar deal that will generate bonuses for each of us that are more than those girls could ever dream of."

"That's it exactly, Brian."

Andrew rubbed the sleep from his eyes, partly to hide his emotions. "I've gotta say: that was a sad story and all, but I actually admire those girls."

"You realize that 'admire' doesn't mean the same thing as 'lust after', right?"

"Yes, Brian Smart Arse Cahill, I do. I'm just saying that there's a certain nobility in what they're doing. If the roles were reversed I suspect I'd take the easy way out and jump off a bridge."

Brian wasn't persuaded. "Maybe, *maybe* if a girl works until the family is out of debt, and then goes home to a simple life on the farm, I'd believe all this bullshit about having no choice. But think about what Greg just said. That girl in the heels was long past the point where she *needed* to screw strangers for money. She kept on doing it because she wanted to. I'm not saying she actually likes the work, though for all I know she very well might. I'm saying that – just like the rest of us – she found a job where what she's asked to do and the money she's paid to do it are in balance. She made a choice, and her choice was to be a whore."

Andrew looked at his colleague with disappointment. "Once we get our bonus checks, you ought to invest in some empathy. It'll change the way you see the world."

"Here's something I never thought I'd say in public: I'm with Andrew on this one," Greg said. "And it's not just the work that's tough. These girls have made a choice that takes them out of the mainstream of Thai society forever. Most Thai men won't touch them. There's something about the way they dress or speak or carry themselves that makes them easy for other Thais to iden- tify, and they're shunned. Neighbors turn the other way when they pass on the street. Shopkeepers will take their money, but won't say anything more than is necessary to complete the trans- action. These girls have sacrificed any hope of having a normal life in order to make a little money."

"So what happens to them?" Brian asked.

"Some of them go home and live in destitution on the farm. A few get normal jobs; hair salons and house cleaning companies are popular. The lucky ones end up married to an aging *farang* with a drinking problem and a genuine belief that a girl 30 years his junior loves him for his personality."

"You're proving to be a bit of a killjoy this morning," Andrew said flippantly.

"Sorry. Certainly wasn't meaning to. All I really wanted to say is that it would be better to go to a steakhouse for the closing dinner."

"Fair enough," Andrew agreed, "as long as we have dessert at Lady Go Go."

CHAPTER 7

"Dead?" Ian asked in amazement.

Nat's eyes focused on a point above and to the right of Ian's head. "I'm afraid so."

The inspector counted to ten. "Nat, I'm not blaming you or anything, but put yourself in my shoes for a second. The report we received from the authorities here made no mention of a girlfriend or travel companion or whatever it was that Miss Sappa... Miss... whatever was to Brian Cahill. Now we learn that almost every time he came to Thailand the two of them traveled together in considerable style, which to me, at least, seems worth mentioning. As does the fact that this person of interest is now dead." McLean crossed his arms and leaned on the table. "When did she die? And what did she die *of*?"

Nat's face reddened. "She died the same week as Mr. Cahill. Of a drug overdose. And I'm truly sorry you were disappointed in the report provided to you. Since Mr. Cahill died of natural causes it seemed unnecessary and possibly inappropriate to mention the details of his social life."

"And were you involved in that decision?" McLean asked.

Nat refused to meet his glance. "I haven't reached the level where decisions are made."

"You lost me."

The Thai detective took a deep breath, held it for several seconds, and let it out slowly. "I was assigned to this case after my boss learned that you were coming to... look into the circumstances of Mr. Cahill's passing. I'm still very junior, and the only reason I'm involved at all is that I'm one of the few English speakers on the force."

"So you have no idea why your superiors decided to omit a number of significant details?"

"As I said, my understanding is they felt those weren't relevant to death by symptomatic tachycardia."

Ian felt his blood pressure rise. Back home he would have attenuated his anger by dumping it on a subordinate – usually Thomas – who had the misfortune to be within shouting distance. But Nat wasn't Ian's to abuse as he saw fit. Nat was on his home ground, with the ability to either open doors or slam then shut. Moreover he might very well be the only person on the Thai police force who was both familiar with at least some the details of the case *and* able to speak about them in fluent English. Better a helping hand you're not sure you trust than no hand at all.

"I'm sorry Nat," Ian said as Sally and Thomas gaped in surprise. "I'm not accusing you of anything, and if it sounded like I am, I apologize. It's just that both this woman's existence and her death are critical pieces of the puzzle, and we're just a little surprised to be hearing about them for the first time."

The Thai policeman found himself at a crossroads. The American part of his brain – which tended to dominate when he was in an English-speaking environment – demanded that he stand his ground. The far larger Thai portion counseled the avoidance of interpersonal conflict if at all possible. In the end, it was the frontal lobe that carried the day, arguing that falling out with the visitors from Scotland Yard before he'd even finished his PowerPoint presentation was a turn of events he could not easily explain to his superiors. So he forced the tension from his face and replaced it with a smile. "There's nothing to apologize for. I'd feel the same way in your shoes. And I really wish I could do a better job of explaining why my colleagues handled this information the way they did. But all I know is what they told me: they didn't think it was relevant."

McLean had been running a similar risk/reward analysis and reached the same conclusion. "Whatever the reason, it is what it is. Let's focus on what we can do now that we have this additional information." A relieved Nat returned to his presentation, but Ian's mind didn't follow him. There could have been a lot of reasons for withholding the information about Brian's companion. Maybe Nat's superiors were worried it would portray Thai women in an unflattering light. Maybe they wanted the 'natural causes' explanation to fly through without being dragged down by complicating factors – and a dead Thai hooker was definitely a complicating factor. Maybe they were trying to spare the Cahill family a post-mortem scandal that would cause them to rethink the son they thought they knew. Or maybe they expected the Brits to conduct an investigation of their own and wanted to keep some information in reserve they could use as a bargaining chip.

Ian was so wrapped up in his own thoughts that he didn't hear Nat asking to see a copy of the report the Yard received from the Thai authorities. It wasn't until Sally kicked him under the table that his brain registered Nat justifying the request with, "That way I can identify any gaps between the earlier report and my own presentation and focus on filling in the holes."

Now that *was* odd, McLean thought. Why hadn't Nat's superiors given him a thorough briefing before sending him out to defend the home team against a delegation from London looking for someone to blame?

Another kick from Sally brought Ian back into the here and now. "Of course, Nat. Why don't you take us through your deck, and then we'll go to the Business Center and make a copy of the report for you to read at your leisure."

Disappointment made a fast dash across Nat's face, but the young man quickly regained his composure and clicked the next slide. "Of course, Inspector. As I said earlier, our first assumption was that Miss Supitayaporn was a bar girl, as that sort of short-lived relationship is not uncommon with visiting businessmen. However an inter-office romance was also a possibility, so we asked Mr. Cahill's Thai office for a list of all employees, both full- and part-time. In this way we were able to confirm that Ms. Supitayaporn was not working for Cooper, Littleton & Hall in any capacity."

"And from that you concluded that she was a bar girl?" Sally challenged.

"We concluded that it was a possibility deserving further investigation." McLean grinned. Nat definitely got his money's worth from the University of Iowa; he could non-answer like a career politician. "There are a number of bar areas in Bangkok, but the one that is both the most famous and the closest to Mr. Cahill's office is called Patpong."

"I thought that was a night market," Sally said.

"It's that, too." Nat said, "But the stalls are a relatively recent addition, put there to take advantage of all the foot traffic."

"By which you mean drunken men on expense accounts looking to get their jollies with underage hookers." Ian hoped that Sally was being playful, and not starting to mount her high horse. A careful examination of her body language revealed absolutely nothing.

Fortunately, Nat chose to take the statement at face value. "Businessmen are a big part of the clientele, but there are many tourists as well. Some locals go, though usually they're guiding overseas visitors. And some of the women who come for the market end up poking their heads into the bars, just to see if it's all it's cracked up to be."

"And is it?" Thomas asked, a tad too eagerly.

"I suppose that depends on the individual making the judgment. There are definitely a lot of scantily clad women – that's my favorite phrase from four years learning English in Iowa – dancing on stage. But it's not like a strip club. The girls never take their tops off. And their dancing isn't all that erotic. Most of the time it's not even very good. Usually they just kind of shuffle."

McLean chuckled. Sally did not. "I suspect they find it hard to muster much enthusiasm for their performance when the true purpose of the exercise is to display what's for sale."

"You could well be right, Sally. But I think there's another explanation. Thai girls aren't like American girls. They don't like to – can I say 'strut their stuff'? It may be hard to believe, but Thai girls – even Thai bar girls – are very shy and proper."

"Yet they're willing to have sex with perfect strangers in exchange for money."

"I know it sounds like a paradox, at least to western sensibilities. But 90% of Thais are Buddhists. Unlike Christianity, there's no concept of a good Buddhist or a bad Buddhist. Everyone is striving for enlightenment in his own way and his own time."

Sally shrugged. "I read *Zen in the Art of Archery*, too, Nat, but this just sounds like a good excuse to do whatever you want, whenever you want."

Ian was about to intervene, but Nat got there first. "Or maybe just a realization that we've all got our own paths to travel."

"And that makes prostitution okay?" Sally snapped.

"It recognizes sometimes people have to do things they don't want to if they hope to survive," Nat said in an attempt to soothe the waters.

"What about the ping-pong balls?" Thomas asked, bringing looks of bemused confusion to the faces of his colleagues.

"I don't think the Buddha had anything to say about table tennis."

"No, I mean, you hear stories about those girls, and how they, you know, shoot ping pong balls and bananas and stuff. From their, well, their... *parts*."

Thomas reddened with embarrassment, the color deepening when Sally burst out laughing. "Their... *parts*? Do you want me to teach you what they're called?"

"It doesn't really matter."

"Oh, I think that you'll find it does, Thomas. It matters quite a lot." By now both Ian and Nat were trying – unsuccessfully – not to snicker. The Thai policeman recovered first. "Let me see if I can address Thomas' question. Yes, there are bars that offer what are called 'sex shows', even though you'll never see anyone having sex. Instead you'll see women doing a variety of tricks involving... their 'parts.'" This time even Thomas laughed. "It's for tourists, the sort of thing most men go to once and only once."

"Well then," Sally said with determination. "We will definitely have to go. Maybe not tonight, as I can feel jet lag taking over my brain, but tomorrow for sure. Far be it from me to stand in the way of Thomas' hitherto unknown love of women's table tennis."

Ian seized the opportunity to shift the conversation onto less hazardous ground. "Why don't we save the planning of our evenings for later and let poor, besieged Nat get through his presentation. I believe that before we got sidetracked he was telling us about the investigation of Miss Supi… Cahill's girlfriend."

The Thai man brushed out an imaginary wrinkle in his shirt, and continued his talk. "According to the case file, a detective was dispatched to Patpong with a photo of Ms. Supitayaporn. He spent 12 hours over three nights asking mama-sans, bar girls, waiters, and staff of nearby convenience stores and restaurants whether anyone recognized the girl in the photo. They all said no."

"From which you concluded she did not work in Patpong?" Sally asked.

Nat nodded. "As you'll see when we go there, Patpong is basically a small side street connecting two larger thoroughfares. There are a few back alleys, but even with those thrown in we are talking about a geographically small area. Moreover when the girls come to work in the late afternoon it's still light out, and there are very few customers around. It's probably best to think of it as a small neighborhood where everyone knows everyone else, or has at least seen them."

"So the fact that no one recognized our girl's picture is pretty good evidence she didn't work there," Ian clarified.

"That's what we thought. So after the first night drew a blank, additional teams were sent to Soi Cowboy and Nana Plaza. Soi

Cowboy is a smaller version of Patpong, but many of the expats who live in Bangkok prefer it because it's much less crowded and a lot friendlier. Nana Plaza is said to be the largest sex complex in the world, a sort of shopping mall for the pleasures of the flesh. But the results were the same as in Patpong: no one recognized Miss Supitayaporn."

With that all talking stopped, and the sound of cups being picked up or returned to saucers became distracting. Sally sipped her now-cold coffee. "And that's it? In a city as big as Bangkok there are only three places where working girls congregate?" A waiter appeared out of the ether, refilled their cups, and disappeared again. "I spent six years in Vice, and know for a fact that wherever there are men, there are women looking to take their money. I realize Bangkok isn't London, but some things are the same the world over."

"You're right, Sally, those aren't the only places. There are massage parlors in between office buildings, and on the main streets in residential areas. There are high-end hostess clubs that are based on the Japanese original but have the same take-out system as the girlie bars. You can find girls for hire in karaoke joints and – very, very rarely – on street corners."

"So did you check all those places?"

"No, we did not."

"Why not?"

"Because, as I mentioned earlier, the official judgment was that Mr. Cahill died of natural causes. Miss Supitayaporn was a loose end, but an irrelevant one. We covered the most obvious bases, but we simply couldn't justify the financial and human costs required to mount a full-scale manhunt. Or should I say womanhunt?"

Nat's attempt at levity fell flat. "We all have budget constraints," Ian said with forced calm. "And perhaps if Cahill and the girl were only together once or twice, I'd agree that it looked to be a casual hookup and therefore not an area of focus. But – and I apologize in advance if this is offensive – Bangkok is known for the, um, range of options available to a young man with money. If Cahill's wallet had been stuffed full of snaps of him with a dozen different girls, I would have said boys will be boys and let the matter drop. But that's not what happened. Cahill chose the same girl on at least a dozen different occasions. That's got to mean something."

"It means he enjoyed her company. That's not so unusual, is it?" The three visitors tried without success to plumb the depths of Nat's defensiveness.

McLean pressed on. "You tell me. Do visiting businessmen tend to settle down with the first bar girl they meet?"

"We don't know that she was the first, just that she was the first to spend the night in his room."

"In fact, we don't even know that," Ian admitted. "All we know is that she was the first girl he signed in. He could have been having orgies every night before that trip to Phuket."

"Not to mention during and after," Sally muttered.

McLean gave her a stern look. "The important thing is not *what* Cahill was doing but who he was doing it with. And every time he registered an overnight guest, it was the same woman. Surely, Nat, you'll agree that's significant?"

"I would agree that the combination of these visits and Miss Supitayaporn's death does raise a few red flags."

"Duh," said Sally with more aggression than Ian thought appropriate.

"And there was nothing about the bar girl's death that might have indicated foul play?" Ian asked.

Nat shook his head. "Unfortunately, overdoses are pretty common here. There are over 1.2 million drug addicts in this country, and the number of casual users is much, much higher. The biggest problem is something called *ya ba*, which means 'madness drug.' It's a mixture of methamphetamine and caffeine, and it's rampant in the entertainment areas. A lot of girls start taking it the first time they have to go with a customer and never stop. I guess it numbs them to what they have to do."

"Did you conduct an autopsy?" Ian asked.

"There was no need to. There was an open bag with nearly 100 pills lying right next to the bed."

"Jesus," Sally responded. "That's a lot of drugs. How does a bar girl afford a habit like that?"

"*Ya ba* used to be cheap. Up north you could buy a pill for 10 baht, which is about 30 cents. It's gone up quite a lot since the government started cracking down – under Prime Minister Shinawatra more than 2,000 suspected drug traffickers were killed – but even during times of peak demand the price rarely goes beyond $3."

Sally did the math. "That's $300 worth of drugs. How many guys did she have to sleep with in order to pay for that?"

"A woman as beautiful as Miss Supitayaporn could easily make that much money in a couple of nights."

Perhaps, thought McLean. But why keep such a large stash? Why leave it in plain sight of any first responders? It would be one thing if the overdose had been accidental, but that was far from certain. For that matter, so was the alleged overdose. The existence of pills outside a dead body suggests – but doesn't prove – the existence of pills *inside* that body. Without some sort of post-mortem examination it was equally possible the pills were added after the fact as a way of shouting "DRUG OVERDOSE!" so loudly that it would pre-empt any other explanation for the girl's demise.

Not unlike the bottle of heart medication that was cited to shift attention away from the fact that Brian Cahill's chest had been cracked open and his heart filled with holes.

Sally seemed to be exploring similarly suspicious territory. "Were you able to talk to any of her family or friends? Find out why she may have wanted to take her own life?"

"You're assuming that she did," Nat replied. "It may have been an accidental overdose or some sort of poison in the drug. You wouldn't believe the things we find in *ya ba*."

"Actually," Sally said after pretending to consider the matter for a moment, "I not only believe it – I expect it. With prices that low you'd almost have to add fillers. And that's why I share Ian's surprise that no autopsy or tox screen was performed. At the very least, send the bag of pills to the lab and have them analyzed."

"To what end? Even if we found evidence the pills had rat poison in them, what could we do with the information? We've got no idea who sold her the pills, much less who made them. If we knew that, we'd arrest them for manufacturing methamphetamines, not for selling an impure product."

Sally had to admit he had a point, but she was still bothered by the fact that two possibly connected and potentially suspicious deaths had both been packaged up and dismissed without even the most cursory of inspections.

A thought popped into Ian's head from an unexpected direction. "Earlier you showed us a picture of her ID card. Can't you cross-reference that with employment or tax records? If we knew where she worked it would be easy to find friends and coworkers we could ask whether she had a drug problem, or had shown previous signs of self harm."

Nat shook his head. "Two-thirds of the people in this country work in the informal sector, where record keeping is considered an unnecessary luxury. If Miss Supitayaporn worked pretty much anywhere except inside an office building, she'd be almost impossible to track down."

There it was again, Ian thought. *If.* Why had the Thai police been so quick to jump to conclusions rather than running the victim's name through the computer just to see if anything popped up? It was as if they didn't *want* any alternative theories of the case to emerge.

"Did the teams who went to the entertainment districts show Cahill's picture as well?" Thomas asked.

"Why would they do that?"

"I don't know. Maybe someone had seen the two of them together."

Nat looked angry but tried to keep his voice under control. "I don't know how else to say this. We didn't do a murder investigation on Brian Cahill because Brian Cahill died of natural causes."

"Except he didn't," Ian said softly.

"Excuse me?"

"I said he didn't. Or perhaps it would be more accurate to say that's not the only thing that killed him."

"Excuse me Inspector. Either my English has suddenly failed me or you aren't making sense."

"The existence of Miss" – McLean checked his notes – "Supitayaporn wasn't the only thing missing from the official report. So was the fact that Cahill's chest had been cracked open with what was most likely some sort of meat cleaver. His exposed heart was then stabbed multiple times. And to finish his body was sewn shut using a cheap monofilament fishing line."

Nat's eyes were the size of saucers; his mouth hung wide open. "Are you serious?"

"I'm afraid so. Now, it's possible that the proximate cause of death may indeed have been an irregular heartbeat, with the mutilation taking place post mortem. But if that were the case, the hotel cleaning crew would have walked into a room awash in blood. Yet there was no mention of them finding anything out of the ordinary in the report your colleagues sent us."

McLean paused to let all this new information sink in, taking a few sips of coffee to fill the interval. "We'll obviously need to determine the order in which these events occurred, not least so we can work out whether the charge is murder or desecration of a corpse. But right now I'm less interested in the *when* than I am the *who*. Clearly Cahill didn't split his own body in half. So who did?"

Nat's forehead was covered in sweat, his color an unhealthy shade of green. "How did you find all this out? And when?"

"At Cahill's funeral, unfortunately. It was his mother who noticed he'd been cut open. A coroner was called in. He noted the violent way in which the body had been opened, the damage to the heart, and the use of ordinary fishing line as a rough closure."

"So why didn't you tell us?"

Ian considered a number of responses that would echo the growing anger he felt but rejected them all. "That's one of the reasons we're here now."

"I really don't know what to say. I'm shocked, well and truly shocked." Nat poured himself a glass of ice water and quickly drained it. If asked, McLean would have said he thought it was a delaying tactic used by a young man who suddenly found himself on a tightrope with no net.

"So this is the first you've heard about the mutilation?"

"Of course! I would have told you if I knew."

The inspector filed that away for another day.

"No rumors around the station? No one behaving oddly or pages missing from the case file?"

"Are you suggesting the Royal Thai Police knew all this and covered it up?"

"Nat, I'm just trying to understand how this could have happened. We're on the same side here." As soon as the words were out of his mouth, McLean wondered if they were true.

CHAPTER 8

"That's five hours of my life I'll never get back," Andrew grumbled once the clients had been bundled into their chauffeur-driven Mercedes amidst mutual declarations of undying love and affection. "Is Lady Go Go still open?"

Greg looked at his watch. "For another 45 minutes."

"Then what are we standing here for? Let's go spread the love!"

"You're not going to find much to spread it on. By this hour the only girls left will either be too ugly to look at, or recycled goods from earlier in the evening."

"Then I'll close my eyes and hold my nose. Come on, Greg. I just sat through a three-hour lecture on Thai politics. I've earned a reward."

Greg rolled his eyes. "It was more like 15 minutes, and if you'd paid attention you might have learned something for a change." Andrew was champing at the bit so hard it was in danger of breaking. "What do you say, Brian?"

Cahill feigned a casualness he did not feel. "If it makes Andrew happy, it wouldn't hurt to check it out. After all, the only thing we've got to do tomorrow is get on an airplane."

"Fine," Greg said as he signaled for his car. "But don't say I didn't warn you."

25 minutes later they walked through the open door of Lady Go Go. "Hello, ladies. Andrew's here!"

The only response came from two very drunk Germans in shorts, hiking boots and white calf socks. They raised their glasses in a Sleazy Man Salute, which Andrew met with an actual salute of his own. Meanwhile, Brian's eyes were focused on the stage.

"I don't see her," Greg said as softly as was possible in a room still being shaken by the pounding bass. Brian briefly considered pretending he didn't know what was being suggested, but concluded there was no time for games. "Think she might be on break? Maybe went out for something to eat?"

Greg knew the chances of either were close to zero, but said only "We can ask." And he did. In Thai, so Brian had no idea what was being said, or why a simple yes or no question merited such a long response. "Mama-san says she went home already. And, for what it's worth, she recommends #158."

Brian looked to the stage, where only five girls remained. #158 appeared to be in danger of falling asleep on her feet. Or, more precisely, on her stiletto heels, which she seemed unable to steady. Her skin was dark brown, her face pockmarked. Only her long, silky hair kept her from being just plain ugly.

"Pass," said Brian.

"Good call," Greg agreed. "Physical attributes aside, she's clearly stoned out of her mind."

"Who's stoned?" Andrew asked as he wiggled his way into the conversation.

"#158," Brian answered unenthusiastically.

"Then I'll have her, and one of her friends. Lady's choice. After all, if we're going to be having a threesome, it's important that everyone gets along."

"I'm going home," Greg announced.

"I'll join you."

"What's wrong with you, Brian? This is our last night in Bangkok. And as the song says, one night in Bangkok makes a hard man humble." Andrew scowled. "Actually, now that I think about it, I've got no idea what that means."

"I suspect you're about to find out," Greg said as he headed for the door. Brian tried to follow his blocking but felt Andrew grab his arm from behind. "What's with you? I thought you liked to party."

"I do, but it's late, and I've had a lot to drink, and the options here aren't all that appealing."

"Then you're not drunk enough," Andrew replied.

Brian shook off the hold on his biceps. "Next time, I promise."

"You got it wrong, mate. It's *every* time."

The next morning Brian found himself alone in the breakfast room. And at the cashier's desk. As the appointed departure time crept closer, he began to worry about his colleague. Leaving his bags with one of the seemingly omnipresent bellboys, he returned to the fifth floor and banged on Andrew's door.

And then banged some more.

Eventually he heard the sound of the door being unlocked, and a haggard face with eye bags the size of billiard balls appeared in the crack. "What?"

"Crikey. What time did you crawl in?"

Andrew looked at his watch, and discovered he wasn't wearing one. "Dunno. Sometime after four, I think. What time is it now?"

"Five minutes after we were supposed to leave for the airport."

"Shit."

"That about sums things up. How long do you need to throw your crap in a suitcase and stumble downstairs?"

"15 minutes, tops."

"You've got 10 and then I'm leaving. The traffic is supposed to be terrible during the morning rush, and I'm not missing the flight simply because you don't know when to call it a night." And with that, Brian went back downstairs.

Much to his surprise, Andrew joined him with a minute to spare. He looked terrible, smelled worse, and had a luminous green color that made Brian think that – despite the heat – they should open the windows in the hotel car.

Standing next to the hangover victim was a Thai woman wearing a jean skirt and a t-shirt that said "Jay-Z Cray-Z." Her hair was pulled back into a tight bun, and her face was free of makeup. Brian guessed her age, added three years because Asian women always look young to western eyes, and decided that on a good day she might be 21. He assumed this was one of the girls Andrew bought out of Lady Go Go; what happened to the second was a mystery probably best left unsolved.

Andrew leaned over to give his new friend a goodbye kiss, but missed when she pulled away. Instead she brought her palms together in a traditional *wai* greeting, and then walked out of the hotel without looking back. "Another satisfied customer," he said with a grin as he picked up his bag and marched out the front door of the hotel.

"I could see she was having trouble containing her excitement – about finally being able to escape from under you."

"Ha ha. So, Judgmental Mr. Cahill, what did you get up to last night?"

"About seven hours sleep. You should try it some time."

"I'll be back in the office tomorrow. I can catch up on my sleep then. There are better things to do in Bangkok, as I thought you knew."

Cahill shrugged.

"Don't tell me you're a one woman man, especially when that woman is a bar girl you've met once and never spoken to in complete sentences."

Brian wasn't sure why, but he felt compelled to defend his choice to go home alone last night. "I don't feed from the bottom of the barrel. Unlike you, I don't have to."

"Alas, I have been struck! I fear it is a mortal wound. My pride draineth like, like, whatever drains quickly." Andrew laughed. "Don't be such a girl's blouse. I'll grant you last night's selection might have been sub-optimal, but that doesn't mean it should have been ignored. In the words of the immortal Plutarch, 'when the candles are out all women are fair.'"

"I don't think there were nearly as many STD's back in 100 AD."

"I notice you weren't worried about health issues two nights ago."

Cahill turned to look out the window.

"Just as I thought. You're smitten. With a bloody bar girl. Christ, Cahill: you're a living, walking, breathing, stinking cliché."

"You clearly haven't had a whiff of yourself this morning. You smell like a urinal."

"Ah, but I can shower and you'll still be blouse-y."

Brian started to speak, changed his mind, and then changed it back again. "Doesn't it bother you?"

"Doesn't what bother me? My stench?"

"No, you know: paying for it."

Andrew smiled indulgently. "A man *always* pays for sex – either directly, as I did last night, or via an expensive meal in a pretentious establishment one would never patronize for the food alone. You may think that extra layer of complication makes traditional dating somehow more moral or acceptable or – God help me – romantic, but at the end of the day – and I mean that quite literally – it's the same transaction."

"You can be a real cynic."

"And you're not? The only difference between you and me is that I have the good sense to enjoy my pleasures."

Brian knew there should be a snappy, argument-clinching response to that statement, but for the life of him he couldn't figure out what it was. And that worried him. In the office he could run intellectual circles around Andrew. Yet this morning in Bangkok, with Andrew clearly suffering from both a bad hangover and a near-total lack of sleep, Brian was unable to keep up. Surely that didn't mean that Andrew had a point?

While Brian pondered that possibility, Andrew nodded off. By the time the hotel Mercedes reached the highway, Andrew was snoring loudly enough to rattle the windows – which Brian had raised once it was clear his colleague wasn't going to throw up over the side of the well-polished car. And Andrew remained in the land of dreams until the car pulled up to the entrance of Suvarnabhumi Airport.

"We there?"

"Yup."

Andrew looked at his watch. "It only took us 45 minutes to get here. We're early! I could have had another 30 minutes' kip."

"You slept all the way here!"

"Doesn't count unless you're in bed. And that, my friend, is true of many things."

Brian shook his head, tipped the diver an excessive 300 baht, and headed for the First Class check-in counter at British Airways. Less than 15 minutes later the two colleagues were in the lounge. Andrew surveyed his surroundings.

"Verdict: not bad. However I'd be a whole lot happier if we didn't have to share with the kangaroo-huggers heading home on Qantas."

"I hope you noticed they have showers. I suspect that's a hint from the Almighty."

"You aren't even the tiniest bit mighty, my friend. So be a good lad and grab me some hair of the dog while I mentally prepare myself to bid adieu to all evidence of last night's favorably reviewed performance."

Brian thought about a snappy retort, but decided that a short trip to the bar was a cheap price to pay for not having to sit next to an unwashed Andrew for the next 12 hours. And Andrew kept his part of the bargain: after downing the beer in worryingly little time, he stumbled off to the showers. 20 minutes later he was back, still unshaven, but now smelling of Molton Brown body soap.

"That's a significant improvement, thank you."

"We aim to please. Until now I had no idea you liked to sniff me so much."

"I slow down for car wrecks, too. Just because I find something fascinating doesn't mean I like it. Or even tolerate it."

"You not only tolerate me, mate. You worship the ground I walk on. I am a sort of god to you: omniscient, omnipresent, and omni-bloody-potent."

Brian rolled his eyes. Nibbled at the fried chicken and ginger rice he'd taken from the buffet. Found an article in *The FT* that looked worth pretending to read.

"Let me ask you something, Ms. Blouse. Did you enjoy yourself the other night?"

Brian feigned nonchalance. "It was all right, I guess."

"Something you'd be up for doing again?"

"Probably wouldn't go out of my way for it, but if it was there in front of me, yeah, I might."

Andrew nodded. "While you were pretending you knew something about the labels on the wine list, Greg and I were talking with our clients about the impact of the street protests on the business environment. Everyone agreed there's likely to be lots of upheaval ahead. The Thais seemed rather nervous about that, but Greg was salivating at the prospect."

"As they say, the best time to invest is when there's blood in the streets."

"Greg actually said that! Didn't go over too well, probably because that blood is more likely to be Thai than tourist. But I think they agreed with the sentiment."

"And your point is?"

"That if there are a lot of deals to be done, they're going to need a lot of people to do them. And that's where you and I come in."

"Go on."

"We've proven we can close here. We get along fine with Greg and his team. It would be a mistake *not* to send us here on a regular basis."

"Which would allow you to spend your nights at Lady Go Go."

"It would be a crime to limit the wonderfulness that is me to a single establishment. But yes, these trips that are being made entirely for the company's benefit might also have a certain upside for the individuals involved."

Brian shook his head, partly in disgust, partly in admiration. "You are incorrigible, you know that?"

"I take that as the compliment that was no doubt intended. So: are you in?"

"Well, it's true there's a lot more happening here than there is in London at the moment. And international exposure would look good on my CV. It's certainly worth thinking about."

"Stop thinking all the bloody time! Act! Seize the day! More important, seize the night! After all, what's the downside?"

"Sylvia, for starters."

"Don't tell me she's already got you whipped. 'Oh dearest, I cannot bear for us to part, not even for a fraction of a sliver of a second. Without you there is no me.' Did you happen to notice whether the buffet has a knife suitable for slitting my wrists?"

"It's not like that. She's supportive of my career. But there's a big difference between going to, say, Berlin on business and going to Bangkok."

"That's because you suck at selling. 'I really don't want to go, dear. It's hot and dirty, and the traffic is terrible. But it's an investment in our future, so I must do my duty.'"

"You don't actually say that shit to anyone, do you?"

"Don't need to. I'm not stupid enough to play house with a quote unquote *nice* girl before all of my wild oats have been sown and well watered."

Brian held up his hands in mock resignation. "It's not like I had a choice. The girl worships the ground I walk on."

"Probably checking to see whether you tracked mud onto her freshly cleaned floors, which are undoubtedly some sort of recently invented color like eggshell or Irish linen." Andrew leaned back over his chair, and heard a satisfying crack as his spine shifted into place. "Are you going to marry that girl?"

"I don't know. Maybe."

"Which also means maybe not. What are the obstacles to a successful conclusion of the negotiation?"

"There's no negotiation. She's keen. I'm just not sure I'm ready."

"Because?"

Brian looked at the orchids in the planter next to his seat. The flowers were outrageously expensive in London, but they grew like weeds in Bangkok. "Because I'm not sure I'm ready to settle down and – as you so delicately put it – play house. I mean, I'm sure it would work out just fine. She's smart and she's sweet and she'll be a good mother."

"Christ, I'm getting a hard-on just listening to all that."

"Which is precisely the point. There's no passion, no excitement. For that matter, I'm not sure how much she really fancies me."

"She wouldn't be proposing to play house with you if she thought you were as horrible as your mates know you to be."

"I wouldn't be too sure about that. I come from a good family, we've got money, I've got a high-paying job, and we get invited to the right parties. I'm sure her parents are thrilled."

"But this isn't the 18th century. Even if her parents thought you'd make a good match, she wouldn't be wasting her time with you unless she found you at least a tiny bit tolerable."

"I'm increasingly of the view that I might want to hold out for just a bit more than that."

Andrew shook his head with surprising violence. "I told you no self-respecting man should ever watch a romcom. Life ain't *Romeo and Juliet*, which is fortunate, because if it were, both you and Sylvia would end up dead. You find someone who doesn't make you want to hurl, and you learn to repress your annoyance at all the dumb things they do. If you get good at it, you'll have a long and reasonably pleasant married life. If you don't, you'll get divorced and lose half of everything you ever had. I'd say you and Sylvia are off to a pretty good start."

"You're a bleak bastard, you know that?"

"I've been called worse."

"Fortunately they're calling our flight."

"Right on cue. Hey: didn't you say you needed to get a gift for Sylvia?"

"Shit. I completely forgot. I'll have to find her something on board."

"Yup, nothing says 'I love you' like a plastic In-Flight Duty Free bag."

The two colleagues boarded the plane, and accepted their sleeper suits from the Chief Purser herself. Andrew handed his bag to Brian and disappeared into the men's room for a quick change into his jammies. He emerged with a demand: "The second the seatbelt light goes off my seat goes flat and I go to sleep. Don't wake me until the wheels are on the ground. If I snore, put on your headphones."

"You're nearly as much fun to travel with as you are to work with."

"Brian wants to have a conversation, does he? Fine. Let's chat. I've been thinking about your situation."

"What situation?"

"The one with Sylvia."

"And in the time it took you to change you've sorted out my life, have you?"

"Yes. Now shut up and listen to my sage advice. What you should do is... nothing."

"Great. That's most helpful, really it is. I can see why it took three whole minutes to come up with that."

"Shut up and listen, would you? You spent one night with a hooker. Big deal. If you listen to Wise Old Andrew, you will spend many more nights with many more hookers, and none of those will be big deals, either. It's just sex."

"You've just demonstrated one of the many reasons you're still single, and probably will be for the rest of your life."

"I'm not saying you should go home and tell Sylvia all about it as if you're describing a trip to the gym. I'm saying that Lady Go Go and Sylvia are in two separate worlds that never have to overlap if you don't want them to."

"What happens on the road stays on the road. Is that it?"

"Partly. But mostly it's a simple observation: this and that are not the same. Sylvia is about a shared life, growing old together, raising a family. Lady Go Go is about taking the beast out for a ride. The two are completely different."

"But Greg said some of the girls end up marrying *farang*. So maybe, at least for some guys, what starts off as being purely physical turns out to be something more."

"Some guys are fucking idiots. And if you really believe a 60-year-old man marrying a 20-year-old Thai prozzie is about intertwined hopes and dreams, you're too naïve to live." Andrew saw an attractive stewardess, and called her over. "Could I get a Bloody Mary and your phone number please?"

"One out of two is the best you can hope for," she replied with well-practiced calm.

"In that case I'll take the phone number."

"You're relentless," Brian said. "Have you ever met a girl you *didn't* make a play for?"

"Why not give it a shot? Sure, 99 times out of 100 I get shot down, but that 100th time makes it all worthwhile."

"And to think: a few minutes ago I was almost convinced you are capable of saying something sensible."

"I am and I was. I may be a reprobate, but at least I know my specialist subject."

Brian just shook his head. "Let's wrap it up, shall we? What are you advising me to do?"

"I'm advising you to relax. Render unto Sylvia what is Sylvia's, and give everything else to the lovely ladies at Lady Go Go. Accept it for what it is, and keep it well clear from what it isn't. And with those words of wisdom, I bid you goodnight."

Andrew pulled the sleeping mask over his eyes, and curled up in his still upright seat. 30 seconds later he was fast asleep.

CHAPTER 9

Sally's hair was still wet and her face flushed when she joined her colleagues for breakfast. "I had a good night's sleep, a refreshing swim in the pool – which is simply splendid; you should check it out – and a relaxing shower with some lovely smelling amenities. My brain is working as well as it ever does. And I still can't make sense of what happened yesterday."

"Did you buy his Oh-My-God-I-Had-No-Idea routine?" Thomas asked.

"I take it you didn't," Ian replied.

"Surely you're not saying you *did*?" Sally challenged. "They see a dead businessman lying on a bed in a 5-star hotel, and determine a cause of death based on nothing more than his weight and a bottle of prescription medicine on the night table. They package him up and put him on a plane to London without noticing he's been gutted and therefore weighs a tad less than someone who still has all his blood on the *inside*. They see a dead girl and a bag of *ya ba* and instantly conclude overdose, without checking whether any of those pills were actually inside her. They send us a report saying 'nothing to see here' and don't ask a single question when we announce we're coming to look for ourselves. And then when we start pointing out the blindingly bloody obvious, they pretend to be shocked, just shocked, that there's gambling going on in this establishment."

"You've ruled out incompetence, have you?" McLean asked.

"Pretty much, yeah."

"On what basis?"

"Even the Keystone Cops weren't this bad at their jobs."

Thomas frowned. "My question wasn't about whether the Thai police were covering something up. My question was about whether Nat is in on it. Less than 30 minutes from now he's going to walk into that conference room. We need to have a game plan."

"He's right," Ian admitted. "The problem is, Nat's been a mystery to me from the minute he held up that sign at the airport. I can't even figure out how old he is. Asians always look young to me – sorry, Sally, I hope that wasn't racist – but Nat can't be more than 25."

"As my distant ancestor Confucius once said, yeah, that sounds about right."

"If the roles were reversed and the Royal Thai Police were sending a delegation to Scotland Yard, would we assign a single detective with only a few years' experience and no direct involvement in the case to look after them? It's as if they're saying they don't take us seriously."

"Could be a language problem," Thomas suggested.

"Or maybe they just don't like foreigners flying in and commenting on how they do their jobs," Sally added. "Chief Franklin is usually above that sort of pettiness, but there are a number of our colleagues who would get a kick out of putting jolly foreigner in his place by assigning him a minder who's still in diapers."

Ian grunted partial acceptance of the arguments. "Then there's Silent Sam who drove us from the airport. He was in uniform, so I'm pretty sure he's a cop rather than a chauffeur. But Nat wouldn't say boo in front of him. Is that because he's very junior and Nat doesn't want him listening to the grown-ups' conversation? Or because he's a superior officer, and Nat doesn't want to screw up in front of him?"

"Maybe he's just there to listen in and report back," Thomas suggested.

"Maybe," Ian admitted. "But if you're right, what does that say about Nat's position in the hierarchy? Then there was all that stuff about calling off the search for the girlfriend after just three days. Either she's a person of interest – in which case you keep going until you find her – or she's not, in which case you don't start looking."

"Probably not Nat's call," Sally pointed out.

"But when he was told what happened, why didn't he ask a few questions? We would have, and not just because we're good at our jobs. We would ask the questions we expected *to be* asked so we didn't end up standing at the front of the room with our tongues hanging out while our distinguished visitors tut-tutted about how stupid we are."

"Maybe Nat now realizes that," Sally said, though this time there was little conviction in her voice.

"On the other hand," McLean continued, "it could be the typical bumbling of the bureaucracy. Word comes down that detectives from England will be dropping in for a few days. Some desk sergeant two years from a pension is told to assign someone who speaks English. Nat gets the job, and a last-minute, half-assed brief from whichever detective happened to be closest when the sergeant took a quick look around the squad room."

"So more incompetence?" Sally asked.

"It would be in good company," Ian replied. "On the other hand..."

"You're out of hands, boss," Thomas said. Ian ignored him.

"... if you did want to stonewall the visitors, fronting Nat is a stroke of genius. He can't give away something he shouldn't because he doesn't know anything. His surprise over each revelation looks genuine because it is. And by keeping us locked up in what are admittedly extremely nice surroundings, there's no way for us to talk to anyone *but* Nat. His ignorance becomes ours."

"So what have you concluded?"

"That's just it: I don't know."

Sally picked up her glass, and had a sip of juice. And then another. And then one that suggested she had just crawled out of an arid desert. "Damn. That's really good! I thought it was regular orange juice, but it's sweeter and – for lack of a better word – softer."

"The sign said it's Mandarin orange juice," Thomas offered.

"Well there you have it: one mystery solved. Let's try to keep the streak alive." Sally finished her juice, then theatrically wiped her mouth with the back of her hand. "As for Nat, I say we just ask him, straight up. First thing this morning."

McLean shook his head. "Too risky. We can't afford to cross swords with the only person in this entire country who we both know and can talk to."

"Don't be such a wimp, McLean. I'm sure the hotel can find us a translator."

"No doubt. But that's only useful if people are actually talking to us. They're unlikely to do that if Nat goes back to the station, tells his bosses we think they're hiding something, and they stick a 24/7 tail on us just to be safe. Hell, for that matter we might find ourselves getting thrown out of Thailand, just like we did China."

"At least we got a chance to check into the hotel this time," Sally said with a smile she hoped was endearing.

It must have been, since Ian smiled back. "And we have yet to be either beaten or gassed. I'd say we're getting better at this." He signaled for the check, and was pleased to discover breakfast was included in the room rate.

"Unless either of you have a better idea, here's how we play it. We open with an apology for not giving him the report as soon as the briefing session started yesterday. Swear we weren't withholding anything, at least, not intentionally. Blame it on jet lag. Deliver a few platitudes about the importance of total transparency if we're going to work together to solve this crime. If he responds by sharing something of his own, we can assume we're on the same side."

"And then what?" Sally asked. "We braid each other's hair and promise to be best friends forever? Thomas, would you go online and find us some pony pictures to put us all in the mood?" Laughing, the detectives made their way to the conference room.

An hour and a half later, there was still no sign of Nat.

CHAPTER 10

A little less than three weeks later, Brian and Andrew were back on BA 9 to Bangkok.

"So here's the plan," Andrew said. "Three glasses of shampoo and a Valium for dinner, followed by as much sleep as we can possibly manage. Take a shower upon arrival at the airport, and go straight to the office. Work like men possessed until six on the dot, then claim jet lag is making us sloppy with our maths and head back to the hotel. Tell Greg we're too knackered to accept his hospitality. Have a quick burger at the hotel and be out the door by seven at the latest."

"Why the rush?"

"I want to hit Lady Go Go while there are still choices to be had."

"You're in serious danger of becoming obsessed."

"So you're going to stay in, maybe watch CNN while you catch up on email?"

"No, I'll join you. Wouldn't want to be rude."

"Of course not."

The day went almost exactly as Andrew had envisioned. The meetings were surprisingly productive, the work plan for the next few days readily agreed, and Greg managed to suppress his smirk a few seconds after his visitors claimed they needed a night in.

"Do you think he knows?" Andrew asked.

"Of course he knows, you idiot. You were drooling most of the afternoon." Brian put his 13" MacBook Air back in its travel case, and tossed the whole thing into his Porsche Design briefcase. "By the way, did you know that when you're lying you overexplain things? It's a pretty obvious tell, one you should get rid of before out next meeting with the client."

"I get a bit sloppy when I'm tired. For the record, I can lie with the best of them. At least, that's what the girls tell me."

"That one was so bad it hurt."

"See previous statement."

"Let's hurry up and get to Go Go so I can hand your leash to some poor girl who has no economically viable choice other than to take you out for a walk, leaving me in peace and quiet."

Which is exactly what he did. Rush hour traffic was horrendous, but when Andrew complained about lost time to the driver he was directed to a room service menu in the pocket behind the front passenger seat. The driver promised to alert them when they were 20 minutes from the hotel, timing their orders so the food would arrive when they did.

Andrew beamed. "That's the sort of service I shall now expect to have for the rest of my awe-inspiring life. Thank you, my good man."

The colleagues were a bit disappointed to walk into their rooms and find them empty, but Brian had no sooner put down his briefcase than the doorbell rang with his dinner burger. He wolfed it down together with an ice-cold Singha beer, gave his teeth a cursory brushing, and was pacing excitedly around his large room by the time Andrew came to pick him up.

"Took you long enough," he said as he opened the door.

"For someone who joined this mission under duress, you suddenly seem very eager to see it underway."

"Just trying to make efficient use of my time," Brian muttered unconvincingly.

It was just past 7:30 when the two men walked out of the light of Patpong Market and into the dark interior of Lady Go Go.

Brian saw Nan almost immediately.

He smiled.

She smiled back, but in a way that left it unclear whether she recognized him or was just being nice to a potential customer.

"Isn't that the love of your life?" Andrew asked.

"If you mean the girl I was with last time, yes, I think it might be."

"You think it might be? Talk about needing to improve your lying skills. You know damn well that's her. Why don't you call her over?"

"No need to rush."

"Wrong! Any second a German tourist slash senior citizen wearing Birkenstock sandals with effin' socks could walk in here, slap some money on the bar, and steal that lovely lady right out from under you. Literally. So stop pretending you're not all lathered up, and invite her over here. Hell, I'll even do it for you." He signaled for a waiter. "Number 32, my good man. That and two of the coldest beers you can find."

Nan arrived before the drinks. "What you name?" she asked Andrew. He shook his head, and pointed at Brian. "That's the man you should be talking to."

She turned her head ever so slightly. "What you name?"

"I'm Brian. Don't you remember me?"

Nan cocked her head but said nothing.

"I was here three weeks ago. We... I... um... we...."

"He bought you out," said Andrew. "I'm sure the sex was just as forgettable as he was. But this time, try to remember his name. Brian. Bry. Un."

"Say again?"

Andrew laughed. "She's all yours, mate."

Brian took Nan's hand. "Don't you remember me?"

The girl just smiled.

"We went to the hotel together."

"What hotel you stay?"

"The Four Seasons. But we didn't go to that hotel. We went to the one around the corner."

The girl just smiled.

Frustrated, Brian decided to try another approach. "Would you like something to drink?"

This she understood. Nan nodded her head, signaled for the waiter, barked something unintelligible to him, and then sat quietly until her drink arrived. She picked up the glass and tapped it to Brian's beer. "Cheers," she said.

Brian found himself both confused and frustrated. If she didn't remember him, no big deal. Or it wouldn't have been if he were able to start afresh in a language Nan understood. Reduced to hand gestures and simple declarative statements free of prepositions and multisyllable words, he wasn't sure where to begin.

In the end, he didn't have to. "You no first time come Bangkok."

"No, that's right. I mean yes, right. I was here three weeks ago."

The girl nodded. "You like Nan."

"Well, yes, very much, actually. You're very pretty."

"Thai men no like me. Skin too dark. Me, mostly *farang*."

"Maybe *farang* have better taste," Brian said chivalrously.

Nan cocked her head in confusion.

"Anyhow, I'm here now. You're here. We're having a nice drink together." He raised his beer again. "Cheers."

Brian could hear Andrew snickering.

"Last time, you, me, go hotel?"

"Yes, that's right!" Brian knew it was ridiculous to get so excited about so small a breakthrough, but he couldn't help himself. He had suddenly become fifteen years old again.

"Tonight, we go hotel?"

The feeling of triumph disappeared nearly as quickly as it had arrived. It was possible, Brian told himself, that what those few words were really saying was that she liked him, she enjoyed the time they spent together before, and wanted to do it again. But the logical fragments of his brain insisted that all Nan was doing was drumming up business.

"If you like."

No response, physical or verbal.

"Yes, we go hotel."

That brought a smile. But Brian felt like an idiot. He couldn't talk to this girl. She was more interested in his wallet than his personality. She was no better than a coin-operated robot.

Then again, look at who was paying whom.

"You like Bangkok?" came a soft voice in his ear.

"Yes. I haven't seen much of it. I'm here on business and usually in the office 10 or 12 hours a day. That's a lot, but it's pretty typical in investment banking."

Listen to me, he thought. I sound like a teenager on a first date, trying to impress a girl who's out of my league. Except as long as I've got the cash, she's very much in my league. Plus she can't understand a word I'm saying.

And there I go again. I'm having the internal monologue of a lunatic on the verge of a nervous breakdown.

Inspiration struck. Brian suddenly remembered a seemingly unimportant part of Greg's introductory lecture on Thailand. He turned to Nan and asked "Are you hungry?"

For the first time, the smile wasn't forced. It was genuine.

And it was dazzling.

CHAPTER 11

Sally looked up from her iPhone. "I am now officially bored. And 99% certain that Nat is not going to show up. So we can either sit here snacking ourselves to a weight problem while you boys listen to me whine, or we can get off what in my case is a truly lovely ass and go do some detective work."

"How are we going to do that without Nat to translate?" Thomas asked, not unreasonably.

"We interview someone who speaks English," Ian replied. "What was the name of the company Cahill worked for?"

"Cooper, Littleton & Hall," Thomas said after a few seconds of massaging his iPad. "I've got an address and phone number right here."

"MD's name?"

"Greg Walsh."

"Sounds English. Excellent. Let's give him a call."

Thomas pulled out his iPad and started searching for the firm's phone number. McLean held up his hand. "Do we know what this company does?"

"Investment banking, I think," Sally answered.

"Thomas, look them up on that gadget of yours and tell the assembled what sort of investments they bank in. On. Whatever."

Thomas' hand stretched and crunched and swiped. Finally: "Looks like a lot of different things. Construction. Banking. Corporate M&A. But all that's in the UK. Let's see if the list is any different for Thailand."

Ian actually had an early model iPad, but he'd never felt comfortable with it and rarely took it out of the house. For him a tablet was more TV than computer, something for watching the occasional rented movie. He envied Thomas' ability to coax information out of the damn things, but not so much that he was tempted to learn how to master them himself.

"Thailand seems more focused on M&A. There's an article here from the *Bangkok Post* saying they were number two in terms of acquisitions in 2013." Thomas scrolled down what was apparently a very long article. "Oh, look: there's a short profile of Walsh. Says he's been here almost a decade. Thai wife. Speaks Thai fluently. On the board of the British Chamber of Commerce. And he's an Arsenal fan."

"No one's perfect," McLean quipped.

"Did the Thai police interview him?" Sally asked.

"Officially they didn't interview anyone, remember?" Ian reminded her. "What with the death being due to natural causes and all. But yesterday Nat said they checked to see if his girl-friend was on the payroll there – she wasn't – so while they may not have talked to Walsh himself they must have spoken to someone in his office."

Sally beamed. "Not a bad memory for someone of your advanced years."

Her boss pretended not to hear. "I'd be interested to know what the investigators *did* ask, particularly whether they mentioned the connection between Supita...Supi... hell, you know who I'm talking about... the connection between her and Cahill."

"While we're there can we also ask for a primer on the Thai police?" Thomas asked. "You know: how corrupt are they, who really calls the shots..."

Sally completed Thomas' sentence. "And what are the odds Nat is being set up to take the fall."

"We can ask," Ian said sternly, "but carefully. For all we know Walsh lunches with the chief of police. Or maybe one of the secretaries is sleeping with him. Keep your questions general, and don't let on that we have our suspicions."

Sally leaned back in her chair and put her hands on her hips. "Have you got any idea how sexist that was?"

"What? Don't tell me I'm about to get a lecture about mansplaining."

"I'm fine with the 'splaining. It's your thinking that's troubling. You assume that the guy is a power broker who dines with the chief as equals, while the only way the females can get near the man is to sleep with him."

"It's you who are unaware of your own prejudices," Ian said with a smug look on his face. "Unlike you, *I* did not assume that the secretaries were female."

"Wow," said Thomas, "you can practically smell the repressed sexual tension in the room – and it's making me ill. You two can keep doing whatever... *this* is, but I'm calling Walsh to see if he's accepting visitors at the moment. Are you in or out?"

Ian and Sally looked at each other, their faces identical pictures of shock and embarrassment. "Of course we're going," Ian managed to say as Thomas exited the room at top speed, his iPhone pressed tightly to his ear. Three minutes later they were stepping into one of the hotel's Mercedes Benz E350's and being offered a cold towel and a bottle of mineral water by their uniformed driver.

"Walsh is there and able to meet us," Thomas reported. "He said the trip could take anywhere between 15 minutes and an hour, depending on traffic. He recommended we – quote – 'enjoy the view.'"

So Ian did exactly that. As the car progressed at a snail's pace, he saw two completely different worlds. One was the modern elegance of the St. Regis Hotel and Apartments, which had huge billboards advertising apartments for sale starting at "just" $3 million. The other was life lived on the teeming streets. There were food stands and fruit vendors and old women with sewing machines doing clothing repairs. The were a dozen men straddling motorbikes and wearing bright orange vests who sprang to life the instant a passenger hopped on behind them. There were shops where the merchandise flowed out over the sidewalk and onto the street. There were girls in tight miniskirts sitting outside shops with the words THAI MASSAGE written by hand on signboards. There were racks and racks of clothing – everything from baby clothes with the customer's choice of designer logo to brilliantly colored polyester dresses that claimed to be made from "REAL THAI SILK."

And there were people everywhere – mostly Thais, but also tourists, foreign businessmen wearing wool suits they should have left at home, and saffron-robed monks who looked to be a few years away from hitting their teens.

Presiding over this throbbing mass of humanity was an oasis of green the driver identified as Lumpini Park. Judging from the non-stop flow of irritatingly trim men and women dressed in fluorescent shorts and t-shirts, it was the destination of choice for joggers. But Ian remembered it had also been a key staging point for demonstrations by the "yellow shirts" – mostly affluent Bangkok residents looking to overthrow Prime Minister Yingluck Shinawatra, claiming they were being unfairly taxed so the government could buy rural votes and pay for a disastrous program of rice subsidies.

"Is it safe to go there?" Ian asked the driver.

"Now okay. There were bombs before, but just a little. All gone now."

McLean made a mental note to visit the park if they found themselves with any free time and the protests hadn't started up again. They'd have to do it first thing in the morning, though; a digital clock atop an office tower announced the current temperature was 37 degrees centigrade.

And it wasn't even noon yet.

The car slowed down as it approached an impressive marble and glass tower that was at least 30 stories high. A cobblestoned ramp took them to a belowground entrance where a small man in what appeared to be parade dress snapped to attention. He yanked open the back door on the left side, and saluted while Ian squeezed his large frame out of the car.

The two other passengers were left to fend for themselves.

After a quick security check they were handed electronic visitor cards that automatically summoned an elevator with their floor preset.

"Nice!" Sally said admiringly.

"Also a very good way to ensure you go only where you're supposed to," a more suspicious Thomas replied.

The elevator climbed 850 feet in a few seconds – and total silence. When the doors opened there was a receptionist standing by the Cooper, Littleton & Hall sign. She brought her hands together in a *wai* and bowed her head.

"That's a truly beautiful gesture," Sally said. "It's at least as relaxing as a vodka tonic, works faster, costs nothing, and contains no calories. Ian, think we can create a new tradition at the Yard?"

McLean's answer would remain a mystery, since the receptionist immediately led them into a large conference room with a stunning view of Lumpini Park and what looked like all of Bangkok.

"It's flat as a pancake," said an unfamiliar voice coming from behind the detectives. They turned around to see a sharply dressed man in his late thirties walking towards them with his hand extended. "Hi, I'm Greg Walsh. I'm the manager of this office." With a nose well trained to sniff out the center of power in a room, Walsh made a beeline for the inspector.

"Ian McLean. Thank you for taking the time to see us, especially on such short notice," the inspector replied as the two men shook hands.

"Not at all. I hope I can be of service to Scotland Yard, though I'm not exactly sure why you're here."

Ian nodded. "I'll get to that in just a minute. First, these are my associates, Sally Chan and Thomas McMillan."

"It's a pleasure to meet you. Please sit down; anywhere you'd like is fine. Can I arrange coffees? Water? Juice?"

"Water would be fine," Ian said quickly, knowing that Sally was on the verge of ordering an endless supply of Mandarin orange juice, and Thomas was imagining a coffee that would require a trip to the nearby Starbucks.

Greg pressed one of the many buttons on the phone in the middle of the conference table, said something quickly in Thai, and smiled. "So, to what do I owe the honor of a visit from Scotland Yard?"

"It's about Brian Cahill."

McLean watched Walsh's reaction carefully. His smile evaporated almost instantly, but what emerged in its place wasn't fear or guilt. It was sadness.

"A terrible thing, that. He was such a young guy. I was really shocked when I heard the news. Do they know whether his heart problem was hereditary or lifestyle related?"

"That's a question best left to the doctors," McLean said evasively.

Walsh shook his head. "There are a lot of bad hearts in investment banking. Most people think it's because of the stress. But I'd be willing to bet the real problem is all the money."

"You lost me on the turn there," McLean said.

"We probably consume twice as many calories as the average Brit, most of it in the form of well-marbled steak. We can drink as much as we want and charge it to the company. We don't walk anywhere because we've got either a chauffer or a car service. We say we want to exercise but it's hard to fit in a session if your day starts with a breakfast meeting and ends in the wee small hours when you shove a very drunk client into a limo. Most of us would do very little of that stuff if we were paying for it ourselves; the fact that it's free just seems to suck us in."

McLean was surprised by the very un-British descent into introspection in front of three people who had been total strangers minutes earlier. Perhaps Greg was experiencing a moment of *there but for the grace of God go I.*

"You could be right," Ian allowed. "But Brian knew he had a problem. He was on medication for an irregular heartbeat. There was a bottle of prescription pills next to the bed where they found him. In fact, that's how the Thai police were able to settle on a cause of death so quickly."

Greg tented his hands over his mouth while he took in this new information. Then, all of a sudden, his hands fell to the table. "Wait: if Brian died of an irregular heartbeat, what is Scotland Yard doing here?"

McLean was impressed. He'd known it wouldn't be long until they had to place a few of their cards on the table, but that moment had come about 20 minutes faster than he expected.

"There are some irregularities in the official reporting that we're looking into," he said.

But Walsh was not to be put off. He picked up the card McLean handed him during the introductions, and stared at it. "You're in Homicide. Do you think Brian was murdered?"

McLean said nothing, wanting to know where the banker's quick mind would lead him.

"Jesus. Who would want to kill Brian?"

"That's one of the things we wanted to ask you. But first we need to gather some background. Is that okay with you?"

"Of course," Greg said as he pulled his chair very close to the conference table. "I'll help in any way I can."

"We appreciate that. Now, when and where did you first meet Brian?"

Walsh took his time before replying. "I think I met him when he joined the London office about 10 years ago, probably at some sort of social event to welcome new recruits. But we were in different sections, and I never spent any time with him before being transferred here in late 2004. Two years ago, when I was informed he was coming over to work on the Global Gourmet business, I recognized the name but was unable to put a face to it."

"What's Global Gourmet?"

"It's a holding company for seven different QSR chains."

"And what's QSR?"

"Quick Service Restaurants. Fast food joints to you and me. Brian specializes" – Greg caught the error, and had to swallow hard several times before regaining his composure – "*specialized* in the food and drink industry. Thailand has always been a huge player, but for years they were focused further up the pipeline. They used to be the largest supplier of shrimp to the US. Thai Union Group is the biggest canned tuna company in the world. But then lower cost production sprang up in China, Vietnam, Cambodia and even India, so Thailand had to start adding value. QSR was one way to do that."

"And Brian came over to acquire some QSR companies?"

Walsh shook his head. "Originally he was targeting just one. The biggest one: Global Gourmet."

"Why now?" Sally asked.

"Even before the coup, investors were getting edgy. There were street protests as early as 2010, and it was clear that the underlying political issues were long-term and not easy to address. Foreign money started heading out of the country, and even the locals decided to hedge their bets by moving a bigger share of their portfolios overseas. For someone with a high risk tolerance, it was – and still is –a great time to buy in Thailand."

"That's very helpful, thank you," Ian said as the drinks arrived. He took advantage of the quick break to look around the conference room and take in the antiques that were displayed against the back wall, each with its own perfectly placed spotlight. "If you don't mind my saying so, it seems like the team here has been very successful."

"London always wants more, but personally I agree with your opinion wholeheartedly." Greg punctuated the statement with a smile.

"So why couldn't you handle the Global Gourmet acquisition on your own? Why fly someone in from London?"

"We don't have Brian's specific expertise. We know nothing about Global Gourmet's foreign competition, its overseas markets, sector trends and so on."

"I see," Ian said without looking up from his note taking. "And was Global Gourmet the only acquisition Brian made?"

"No. He'd completed three and was working on a fourth when he... passed away."

"Is that a lot or a little for a two-year period?"

"It's enough to get him bonus checks comfortably in the seven figures."

Thomas dropped his iPad.

Ian glared at the young man, and the continued the questioning. "What was his style like?"

"What do you mean?"

"I'm guessing that investment bankers come in as many models as policemen. Some come on strong, trying to intimidate the other party into submission? Others pretend to be your best mate, getting a suspect to lower his guard and reveal more than he planned?"

"We generally don't think of our clients as 'suspects,' Inspector, but I know what you mean. Brian was" – he paused to re-evaluate his initial response – "he was a networker. He was constantly calling people, trying to find that little bit of information that would give him the edge."

"So he did a lot of wining and dining?"

"He certainly did his share. But he was never into winning clients by charming them. He was too rational for that. I'd say he was about doing his homework. When he walked into a meeting he knew the target company's business better than they did. Clients were both impressed and intimidated. Several told me the reason they sold out is they'd rather work with Brian than against him."

Sally and Thomas exchanged glances.

"So he was rather scary?" Sally asked.

"By the standards of normal humans, perhaps. But by the standards of this industry? He was a sweetheart."

McLean decided to leave the point – for the moment. "I would have thought it's pretty traumatic for the company being bought out, especially if the acquirer is foreign. Do companies ever get sellers' remorse, or complain that you took advantage of them?"

Walsh's expression changed from pleasantly helpful to mildly irritated. "I could answer that question a number of different ways, though I'm not sure you'd accept any of them."

"Try me."

"Okay. One is, if they think we aren't offering enough money, they don't sell."

"Maybe they're in such bad shape financially they have no choice."

"In which case they should be thanking us for saving them."

"Do they?"

"Rarely," Walsh acknowledged. "Most of these companies are still run by the man who started them. Founders have an emotional attachment to their creations that defies all the logic of business. I understand that, I really do."

"Okay, that's Answer One. What's next?"

"Some of them figure they made out like bandits. Thanks to the uncertainty following the coup, we could probably close some of our 2012 deals for 30-40% less if we did them today. So they're grateful."

"Is there a third answer?"

Greg's enthusiasm fed on the detectives' curiosity. "In most cases I suspect it's a bit of an emotional roller coaster. Selling something you've built with your own hands is always tough, whether it's a business or a house or a boat. Ultimately, though, the latter two are just *things*. What hurts when you sell a business is losing the people who helped you along the way, the people who stood by you when success was far from assured. Some of them have been there since the very beginning, and remember the days when you were all just a couple of hustlers trading cheap goods out of a run-down warehouse. That core group knows each other better than they know their own spouses – and they should, given that they spent a lot more time together. How do you look at your wife of 20 years and say you're leaving her, not for love but for a better offer?"

"Bosses leave all the time. Companies recover."

Walsh shook his head. "That's how it works in public companies, when the boss is just the current occupant of the seat at the head of the org chart. Family businesses – and that's most of what we deal with here, even if they're listed on the stock market – are different. It's a much more emotional connection."

McLean nodded. "Any of those people ever get so emotional they ask you to unwind the deal?"

"It happens, but not often. And we always talk them out of it."

No surprise there, McLean thought. "What do you do with the companies once you acquire them?"

"It varies. In some cases we bring in new management to turn the company around. In a few cases we manage them directly until we think the company is on the right track. Sometimes we split the company into parts, keep the bits that are working, and either sell or scrap the bits that aren't."

"Meaning there's a lot of restructuring taking place?"

Ian tried to make the question sound casual, almost an afterthought. But Greg Walsh hadn't risen to MD by missing any tricks. "If you're thinking Brian got killed by someone he put out of a job, you're wrong."

"How could you possibly know that?" Sally asked.

"We are on very good terms with current and former management of all three companies Brian acquired. And management of the fourth company is devastated that Brian isn't around to close that deal."

"A company is more than its management," Sally pointed out.

"Of course it is. But unemployment in this country is less than 1%. Until recently you could walk out of one company in the morning and join a new one in the afternoon."

"But as you just said, that was 'until recently.'"

To his credit, Walsh accepted the point. "True. But the only people who ever heard of Brian are in middle-to-upper management. A factory worker who gets the chop is more likely to go after the manager who gave him the bad news."

Fair enough, McLean thought as he decided to take a different tack. "With this sort of acquisition, is there usually only one buyer?"

"There are as many variations as there are deals. If I had to generalize, I'd say we probably faced a less-than-usual amount of competition with Brian's deals. Most of the local players don't fully understand the global potential for domestic companies, and as we've been discussing, overseas investors have been wary of Thailand ever since the colored shirts started closing down the streets."

"So there were no defeated competitors who might have held a grudge?"

Walsh shook his head. "They might have been disappointed. But that's the business. Some deals you get, some you don't. You can't get emotionally invested."

That was all very sensible, McLean thought – and then wondered if anyone actually put the philosophy into practice. "No chance a rabid nationalist got upset by foreign firms acquiring Thai assets at fire sale prices?"

Walsh took his time with this one. "I doubt it. The Thais are as nationalistic as anyone else. But foreign money has played a huge role in this country for at least the last 50 years, and generally people are happy about the jobs and opportunities it brings." Greg brushed an imaginary piece of lint off his perfectly pressed trousers. "Do you really think one of his deals got Brian killed?"

McLean stared back. "We don't think anything at this point. We're just trying to gather information."

Walsh noticed that the detective didn't debate his use of the word *killed* – and he'd used it twice, the second time just to make sure. "Look: they were Brian's deals, and my involvement was limited to providing local expertise, if and when it was needed. I was not in every meeting. I was not on every conference call. But I was copied on every single email, both internal and external. I reviewed all documentation before it was sent out. I was in regular contact with both Brian and Andrew Cummings about the progress they were making and the issues they were facing. We had meals together and went out drinking together. If there had been friction that might have led to someone wanting to do harm to Brian or anyone else in this company, I would have known about it. And I tell you: there was nothing."

"Assuming the threat came from someone involved in the deal." All eyes turned to look at Thomas.

Walsh smiled for the first time since the introductions were made. "Well spotted."

Sally twisted the plastic cap off her bottle of mineral water and stared at the underside as if she'd expected it to announce she'd won big money. Without looking up she began to speak. "Help me understand something. I thought a big part of being an investment banker was having balls the size of watermelons. But from what little I've seen of this country, everyone is soft and gentle and as completely unlike me as it's possible to be. What happens when those two cultures collide?"

This time Walsh's smile was broad and genuine. "The short answer is that I get paid, and rather well. One of my key responsibilities is bridging the cultural gap before someone falls in."

Only after the words were out of his mouth did Walsh realize their relevance to Brian Cahill. The color drained from his face.

Sally rode quickly to his rescue. "Don't let that thought take root in your mind. We still have no idea what happened, much less whether it was work-related. And the only person truly responsible for a murder is the murderer."

She meant to be reassuring, but the temperature in the room seemed to drop a few degrees. An old hand at navigating the twists and turns of a difficult conversation, Walsh quickly regained his color. "You're absolutely right. In most parts of the world, bluff and bluster are key weapons in a banker's arsenal. But this is Thailand. Thais don't like conflict. They think it makes you look childish and lacking in self-control. I explained all that to Brian when he first arrived."

"And did he understand and adapt?" Sally asked.

"Hard to say, since I never saw Brian at work in the UK. My sense was that he was a very patient listener, but he didn't respond well when he thought people were trying to cheat or manipulate him. Whether either of those characteristics was more or less pronounced when he was back in London, I cannot say."

McLean made a note. He wasn't yet ready to write off a business bruising as a possible motivation for murder, but the more he learned about Brian Cahill the more unlikely that scenario seemed. "Brian came here quite a lot over the course of just over two years – 17 times if our information is correct."

"I'm not sure of the exact number, but yes, he came often. As I said, there's a lot of business to be done here, and Brian was good at it. I was happy to see him whenever he was here, and would have loved to have him here more often."

"So who decided when he'd visit – and for how long?"

Walsh shrugged. "The decision about whether to come at all was usually dictated by the needs of the business. But Brian determined all the details based on his own schedule, his commitments in the UK, and so on."

"Did there come a point at which his visits were extended?"

"Meaning what? That he stayed longer than was originally planned?"

"No, I was thinking more of the scheduled duration of each trip getting longer over time."

Greg looked puzzled for a moment, then understanding flooded across his face. "You're asking about Nan."

"Nan?"

"I believe her real name was Kanokwan, but most Thais go by a nickname – especially when there are foreigners involved."

"Because?"

"Because Thai names are almost impossibly long. And until you get used to the sounds and intonation of the language, they fly past you in an incomprehensible buzz. Most of the people in this office go by their nicknames for everything except legal documents."

"And the girl Brian was seeing went by Nan."

Walsh smiled. "So you know about that."

McLean gave the faintest of nods. "Do you know where they met?"

"At a Patpong bar called Lady Go Go."

Well, well, well, McLean thought. The Thai police had spent three days trying to track down the girlfriend's place of employment and – supposedly – failed. Had they even bothered to interview Walsh? Or was the whole story about searching for her a lie?

"Did you ever meet Nan?"

"As a matter of fact, I did – the same night as Brian."

"Tell us about that."

Greg smiled at Sally, as if in apology for what he was about to say. "When blokes visit Bangkok, they want to see the legendary nightlife for themselves. As manager of this office, and the only *farang* here, it usually falls to me to take them out and explain how the system works."

"The system?"

Walsh's smile evaporated, replaced by a look of discomfort, and he was obviously trying to evade Sally's sightline. "I never know quite how to explain this."

"I used to work Vice," Sally stated. "I suspect I know how the story ends."

"Yes, I suppose you do." Walsh took a sip of coffee, then daintily wiped his lips while stalling for time. "But it's not what you think. Well, it is, in that sex is for sale pretty much everywhere in Bangkok. But it's not just about prostitution. A lot of guys go just to sit at the bar, drink some beer, listen to music and" – Greg finally met Sally's eye – "look at girls dancing in skimpy clothing."

"And they only read *Playboy* for the articles," was Sally's rejoinder.

McLean silenced her with a stare. "So you took Brian there."

"Brian and Andrew. They showed up together on that first trip."

"And you remember that detail because...?"

"Because it's hard to forget the look on a man's face the first time he sees the bright lights of Patpong. Over the years I've taken a lot of people there, but I'm pretty sure I could describe each and every visit in an incredible amount of detail. Quite honestly, it's pretty funny."

"Seeing otherwise intelligent, successful men standing there with their tongues hanging out," Sally quickly supplied.

"Exactly."

"So you take Brian and..."

"Andrew. Andrew Cummings. He accompanied Brian on some of the early trips to help with the numbers."

"Right. So you take Brian and Andrew to Lady Go Go. Why there?"

"It's probably the best bar in Patpong. It's big, which means there are lots of girls. The mama-san doesn't tolerate any nonsense. The drinks aren't watered down. And the music is usually pretty good."

"Okay. You take them there, and then what happens?"

"I explained how the system works – you know, the various charges for drinks, calling girls over, and so on."

Sally mouthed the words "and so on" to the far wall.

"Anyhow," Walsh said with an excessive emphasis on the first syllable, "I took them there. Andrew met up with some girls I don't believe he ever saw again."

"And Brian met Nan."

Walsh nodded.

"Then what happened?"

"I told them they were on their own and went home."

"So you don't know what happened next?"

"I don't *know*, but I think we both can guess."

"Did Brian say anything the next day?"

Walsh looked at the ceiling for a bit, and then shook his head. "Andrew tried to drag some details out of him, but Brian refused – which I think speaks well of him. Plus, we were in the final stages of a deal, and the company to be acquired was adding some last-minute demands. That sort of thing tends to focus the mind."

"Yet you still had time to go to a strip bar the night before," Sally pointed out.

Walsh, wisely, said nothing.

"Okay," McLean continued. "You go through the next day without talking about what happened at the bar. What about that night?"

"We were able to close the deal, fortunately, so that night we went out to dinner with the clients to celebrate. That's standard stuff, and no different here than in London."

"Meaning huge steaks, expensive red wine, the whole nine yards."

"Exactly."

"And when you finished?"

"I put the clients in one car, me in a second, and told Brian and Andrew to knock themselves out."

"Did they?"

"I wouldn't know. They left early the next morning."

"And you didn't ask them about the night? Either over the phone, or the next time you saw them?"

Walsh looked uncomfortable, a feeling Sally's unblinking stare did nothing to ameliorate. "I'm not quite sure how to say this without sounding like a pimp in a £2,000 suit, but in this town a night in the bars isn't anything special. At home I wouldn't ask a colleague 'how was the pub last night?' Same thing here."

"And a gentlemen doesn't kiss and tell," Sally said as she began to thaw.

Walsh smiled in return. "Actually, a large number of them do. Or try to. I find the best way to discourage them is to ask no questions and show no interest."

"Unfortunately we at the Yard don't have that option," McLean said primly. "So, Brian meets Nan the first time he comes to town. What happened next?"

"That's probably a question you should ask Nan."

Now *that* was interesting, Ian thought. If Walsh knew the girl was dead, he could have a career on the stage when his days in investment banking were over.

"Let me rephrase. You have no idea how their... *relationship* developed?"

"Not really, no."

"But you knew they were spending weekends together?"

"Yes, that I knew."

"How?"

"Because Brian had my secretary make all the arrangements."

"Classy," Sally snapped.

"I wasn't thrilled, especially since Brian likes to see a costing for every conceivable option, and my secretary ended up spending far too many hours getting him sorted. Plus, Brian only went to very nice places. I'm sure my secretary didn't enjoy seeing bills larger than her monthly salary being spent on a mere bar girl."

"Did his little adventures bother you?" Sally asked as she caught the faint note of disdain in Greg's voice.

"I didn't think it was my place to judge. He's... he *was* a single guy, and how he chose to spend his time was his decision."

"Did you ever ask him about their relationship? After all, they spent a lot of weekends together. Didn't you wonder if they were getting serious?"

Walsh took his time before answering. "To be honest, until this moment I never considered the possibility that their relationship was anything more than a commercial exchange of sex for money."

"On maybe 15 different occasions."

Greg smiled and drank some water. "Let me explain something to you. Men are stupid. Really, really stupid."

"Preaching to the choir on that one," Sally said with a short laugh.

"They come to Bangkok and for the first couple of nights in town they can't believe their luck. It's like they're getting to rewrite their teenage years, except this time Penthouse is in charge of casting. They walk into a room certain they can leave with any girl they want. And while during the cold light of day they know it's a commercial transaction rather than true attraction, it takes surprisingly little time before they start seeing themselves as God's gift to women. Sally, you're absolutely gorgeous, so you're undoubtedly used to having every man in the room try to make eye contact with you." Walsh was so caught up in his speech he didn't notice that both Sally *and* Thomas turned a bit red. "But for guys that just doesn't happen. Especially not overweight, prematurely bald investment bankers who were most likely social outcasts growing up. Suddenly everyone – or everyone who counts – is looking at you like a rock star. And little by little you find yourself thinking, 'hey, maybe I am one.'"

"And that's when the trouble starts."

Walsh nodded vigorously. "They think they've suddenly got license to treat women like crap and get even for all those times when they were rejected as a spotty teenager drowning in Axe Body Spray. They walk into a bar and completely ignore the girl they took home last night and ostentatiously buy out her best friend instead. A few nights of unpunished boorish behavior, and they start believing they're God's gift to women. They hear the flattery and convince themselves that it comes from the heart, forgetting that the girl has said exactly the same thing to the hundreds of men who had her previously. They stop hearing the falsity in the moans and genuinely believe that this woman who has sex for a living is being driven to the point of uncontrolled ecstasy by a drunken plodder with one move he learned on holiday in Ibiza." Greg smiled sheepishly. "Sorry. I got a bit worked up there."

"No need to apologize. It was all very interesting – though rather sad," McLean said. "But I'm not sure I see the relevance."

"Perhaps because it's not there. I do tend to go on a bit. The point I was trying to make is that men and their bar girls is an area I prefer not to enter, not least because I don't trust myself not to tell them they're being total idiots."

"So you know nothing about Brian's relationship with Nan, other than that they were together on most of his visits."

Walsh nodded.

"What about this Andrew?" asked the nearly forgotten Thomas.

"Andrew Cummings."

"Right. Would he know more?"

"Almost certainly," McLean said under his breath while making a note to question the young man as soon as they returned to London.

CHAPTER 12

Nan led Brian down a series of dark side streets until they emerged on the side of a four-lane road. There were food carts set up as far as the eye could see, each lit by a single bare light bulb and the flashy neon signboards of nearby businesses. None had a name, or a menu on display, or anything that would differentiate it from the competing cart two feet away. Yet Nan headed directly to the stand closest to the corner, and dropped onto a rusty stool so small it looked like it had been made for a three-year-old. She screeched something at the man with a large ladle in his hand; gone were the soft, slow, elongated vowels Brian had come to associate with the Thai language.

"What would you like?" he asked in what he immediately realized was an impractical attempt to take charge of the situation as he would at home.

"Me order already. You same same, ok?"

"Same same? Oh, right. Yes, I see. The same is fine. Thanks." Cahill suddenly remembered why he had found dating so difficult as a teen. "What did you order?"

Nan scrunched up her face in concentration. "Mmm, no English! Only Thai name."

"Okay. I guess I'll find out soon enough. Did you get *pad Thai*?

"No, no *pad Thai*. Noodles."

"I though *pad Thai was* noodles," Brian mumbled.

The two sat in uncomfortable silence, watching the traffic fly by. Despite the fact it was nearly midnight, the air was still hot and almost unbearably humid. Add the smell of exhaust fumes and the slightly oily feel of all the eating utensils, and Cahill wasn't sure he had much of an appetite.

That changed when the food arrived. The colors were so vibrant, so different than the grays and browns of British food, that he found himself suddenly eager to dig in. Nan served him a massive helping of rice, and then placed daintier portions of all the other dishes around the side. "Bon appétit!" he announced as he dug in with both anticipation and a touch of anxiety.

The pain was almost instantaneous. His mouth felt numb and on fire at the same time. Tears started pouring out of his eyes. Then the hiccups arrived. Sweat raced to the spot on the top of his head where hair was at its rarest. The thought briefly crossed his mind that he might die right there and then.

Nan was laughing uproariously.

In desperation, Brian reached for his water – only to find his hand slapped. "No water. Make more hot." Nan shouted at the cook, who quickly brought over a small container with a spoon. "Sugar. You take."

He did. Much to his surprise, the flames began to flicker, and then die. The pain subsided to the point where it was merely horrible. "Wow. What in the hell was that?"

Nan pointed her spoon at a tiny green chili. "Very hot. No good for you. Only Thai people."

Brian picked up the small pepper with his chopsticks – after only two failed attempts – and peered at it. "It looks so innocent. Usually green things don't have a kick. Lettuce isn't spicy. Peas, beans, cucumbers – they're all pleasantly bland. Jalapeños can pack a punch, but at least they have the decency to be large enough to suggest caution is in order. But this little bastard is like a stealth bomb."

He gently laid the dangerous pepper on his plate next to a much larger, bright red chili. "Now this one's red. Red means caution. Red means hot. This chili carries a proper warning label."

Nan picked up the red chili with her fingers, and popped the entire thing into her mouth. "Red chili no hot. For baby. Even *farang* can eat."

Brian stared at her in disbelief, and then turned his attention to the choices on the table. He immediately eliminated the two dishes that were covered in a thick layer of oily red spice, and focused on a stir-fry that seemed to be mostly meat and vegetables – plus a few red peppers large enough to be picked out with a spoon. He also took a generous helping of a cold salad containing tomatoes, bean sprouts, beans, shrimp and crushed peanuts which he thought would cool his mouth between bites of the stir-fry.

He decided to start with the salad, and by the time he noticed that Nan had put down her eating utensils and was watching him intently, it was already too late.

"Jesus Christ!" he shouted, and began filling his mouth with sugar, water, rice, beer, ice, and anything else that might smother the fire.

Nan was laughing so hard she had tears in her eyes. "*Som tam* very hot! Make no spicy for you. Next time."

"At this rate there's not going to be a next time," he choked. "I'm going to die right here, right now." With that he pushed his plate halfway across the table.

Nan shook her head, and pointed at the stir-fry. "You eat." With extraordinary dexterity she used her chopsticks to pick out even the tiniest pieces of red chili, then pushed the plate back to Brian. He used his spoon to take a baby-sized bite, and discovered he could just about tolerate the level of spice.

"That's actually good." He pulled out his handkerchief to wipe the sweat off his forehead, giving Nan another fit of the giggles. Sitting on the side of the street in a strange but exotic city, eating food he'd never seen before, listening to a beautiful girl laugh unreservedly, Brian realized that for one of the few times in his life he felt truly happy.

After Nan had devoured enough food to feed a family of four, literally without breaking a sweat, Brian asked her about her life. He learned that she was from Isaan, the farming area in the northeast of Thailand that Greg had described the morning after their first trip to Lady Go Go. She had either three or four brothers and sisters, one of whom may have died as a small child. Nan herself had come to Bangkok about 18 months ago. Her hobby was "eating."

Brian also talked about himself, but he wasn't sure how much of what he said she understood. In listening mode Nan seemed to be getting more than just the gist, but when she spoke her English was so limited it seemed unlikely she understood as much as he gave her credit for. Nevertheless, the time passed quickly, and he found it impossible to say goodnight.

So he snuck her into his room at the Four Seasons.

As soon as the door was locked and the Do Not Disturb sign switched on, Brian began pulling off his shirt. He had the garment inside out and upside down – but stuck around his head – when his mobile rang.

Brian decided to ignore it.

It didn't stop ringing.

"Why you no answer?"

"Because it's probably the office. Whatever they want can wait. The work day is long since over and I have better things to do at the moment," he said with a lecherous grin that his half-off shirt hid from Nan's view.

A few more rings and two things became clear: the mood was broken and it was never coming back unless Brian answered the damn phone.

He opened with "Do you know what time it is here?"

"Don't know, don't care," said the voice of Brian's boss in London. "I need you on the morning flight back here."

"What the hell for?"

"The Huddleston deal is turning to shit faster than you can say 'there goes my bonus,' and the client is not at all happy about you – to use their words – 'farting around in bloody southeast Asia when there's work to be done here.'"

"Everything was under control when I left."

"And now it's not."

"How could it get so screwed up in just three days?"

"That's what you're going to look into the second you get back here. And that, according to my infallible secretary, is 5:20 P.M. Get a quick shower at the Arrivals Lounge, don't bother to shave your girlish face, and get your ass *here*."

"But I'm in the middle of a deal *here*," Brian protested.

"Oh. That changes everything. I thought you were lying on the beach somewhere, taking advantage of our Got Nothing To Do – Go To The Fucking Beach At Company Expense policy."

"It's two in the morning. I'm not in the mood for bloody sarcasm."

"And I'm not in the mood to see our second biggest client fuck off to somewhere else because you don't like having your beauty sleep interrupted. I don't care if you've got to hang onto the landing gear the whole damn way. I want you on that flight tomorrow morning."

"It's already today over here."

"And you said you weren't in the mood for sarcasm. Now: are we clear?"

Brian knew further resistance was futile. "Yes, yes we are. I'll be there."

His boss hung up without another word.

Brian looked at Nan, who was lying across the huge bed, still wearing everything except her shoes. Five minutes ago his desire for her was uncontrollable. Now, much to his surprise, it was undiscoverable.

Rationally he knew there was plenty of time for a satisfying roll in the silky smooth sheets. After that all he needed to do was leave the hotel by 7:30, and stay functional long enough to get on the plane. He would then have 13 hours and a full-flat seat on which to catch up on his sleep.

But the fact the client was not happy worried him. Huddleston had been his ticket to both promotion and obscene bonuses. If he lost the account due to circumstances beyond his control, his career would probably survive. But if he lost it because he wasn't around when the client needed him, it might be game over for Brian Cahill at Cooper, Littleton & Hall.

As those thoughts bounced around in his head, Brian didn't even hear Nan calling to him. He only noticed when she stood up, walked to within six inches of his face, and waved both hands in front of him.

"Sorry. That was the office. I have to go back to London."

"Why you go?"

"The client insisted."

Nan's face was a blank.

"The customer wants me."

That was a concept a Bangkok bar girl understood perfectly well. Nan slung her handbag over her shoulder, stepped into her heeled sandals, and put her hands together in what Brian realized with both shock and disappointment was a reminder that he owed her for her time – regardless of how little he ended up doing with it.

He pulled out his wallet, and took out a handful of bills without looking at the denominations. Nan took the money, bowed her head slightly, and left without another word.

Brian opened the mini fridge and pulled out a beer. He stared at the golden lion on the label. "Why is it that everyone got what they wanted tonight – everyone except me?"

The lion didn't answer.

CHAPTER 13

"Well, that was a complete waste," Thomas complained as soon as the hotel car had left Cooper, Littleton & Hall behind. "Everyone loved him. No one would have hurt him. The girl-friend was just a phase that foreign men go through."

"We did get one thing out of it," Sally said.

"What's that?" Ian asked.

"We can now call her Nan instead of trying to pronounce 'Supitayaporn.' Hey, I finally did it!"

They rode for a while in silence. It wasn't until the car pulled onto Ratchadamri Road and crawled past the racetrack of the Royal Bangkok Sports Club across from the hotel that Thomas asked the question that had been on everyone's mind.

"Think Nat's waiting for us in the conference room?"

"I don't," Ian replied. "If he was still talking to us, he would have called and asked where the hell we were."

"He might be sitting in the conference room thinking the exact same thing about you," Sally countered.

And so he was.

"What happened to you guys?"

"We thought you must have been held up, so we struck out on our own." McLean was pretty pleased with that answer, since it gave away nothing.

Unfortunately, Nat wasn't buying it. "Oh, yeah? Where'd you go?"

Ian knew he couldn't hesitate, and the truth is faster than a lie. "We went to Cooper, Littleton & Hall to speak with Greg Walsh. We figured it was the only place we could go where we could get by in English."

Nat smiled, but his eyes remained skeptical. "Learn anything?"

"Just that Brian Cahill was widely loved and respected." McLean found himself starting to resent being questioned by a cop many years his junior. He decided to flip the script. "How about you? What did you get up to this morning?"

"I suspect you can guess. I reported back about yesterday, including the fact there is reason to believe that Brian Cahill did not die of natural causes."

"Bet that went over well," said Sally, apparently positioning herself as the Good Cop.

Nat ignored the proffered helping hand and said nothing.

"What did they say when you told them?" Ian asked as he slid into Slightly Bad Cop mode.

"They said it was impossible, that they couldn't have missed something that obvious. They asked for proof, preferably photographs. I had nothing to show them. They asked why I believed this story despite the absence of evidence of any kind. I told them I neither believed nor disbelieved; I was just reporting what I'd been told."

"Which probably didn't help much," offered the ostensibly sympathetic Sally.

"No, it didn't. It was then suggested that the mutilation took place *after* the body left Thailand. I said I thought that was unlikely. They asked how I could be certain it hadn't happened that way."

"Who's they?" asked Ian.

"My superiors," was all Nat would reveal.

"Why would *we* cut Cahill open and puncture his heart?" Thomas asked.

"Why would *we*?" Nat snapped.

"So where did it all end?" Ian asked, eager to short-circuit a standoff. "Are you still assigned to the case, and to us?"

"I'm here, aren't I?"

That left a lot of questions unanswered. McLean would have liked nothing more than to take his colleagues somewhere private and agree a strategy for dealing with this latest twist in the tale. But leaving Nat alone would increase his already strong sense of alienation. And unless they wanted to spend the rest of their time talking only to Greg Walsh, they were going to need him.

Ian searched his pockets for an olive branch.

"Okay, then," he said with false bonhomie. "I made a copy of the report we received about Cahill's death. You can read it at your leisure; it won't take long. And you'll see there is no mention of the mutilation, and no mention of Nan."

Nat's radar went on high alert. "How did you know Miss Supitayaporn's nickname was Nan?"

And how did *you*, McLean asked himself silently. Out loud he said, "Walsh told us. Apparently he met her the same night as Cahill."

"I don't find that information to be particularly useful."

"That's because you can pronounce her actual name," Sally said as light-heartedly as she was capable of being. "For those of us who can't, the shorter moniker is a lifesaver."

There was a boom loud enough to rattle the windows. "What in the hell was that?" Thomas asked.

"Thunder," was the one word reply.

The heavens opened up, and rain pounded the pavement like a jackhammer. "I didn't know it was rainy season," Sally said.

"It's not," Nat replied without further elaboration.

Just then the doors to the conference room flew open, and a tuxedoed waiter entered bearing a coffee pot in one hand and hot water for tea in the other. All four policemen nodded listlessly at their cups, which were quickly filled.

The short break gave Ian time to think, and when they were once again on their own, he shifted into high gear.

"Let's be honest, Nat. We've got some questions about whether your side is being straight with us. And you – or at least your superiors – have some questions about whether we're being straight with you. We can either give each other the evil eye for a couple of days and then crawl back to our respective offices having failed in our missions. Or we can work together to figure out exactly what is going on. I much prefer the latter option. What about you?"

It took Nat a very long time to answer, and what he had to say clearly pained him. "It's different for you. Your worst-case scenario is you don't find an answer." He took a sip of coffee, swallowing with great difficulty. "My worst-case scenario is, I do."

CHAPTER 14

Brian Cahill woke to the sound of elephants. When he'd checked in at the Anantara Elephant Camp & Resort the night before, the deliciously soft-spoken clerk at the front desk had mentioned there were more than 25 elephants being cared for on the far reaches of the property and warned him that the animals tended to get a little boisterous early in the morning when their breakfast was served.

She'd also suggested he check out some of the resort's more unusual offerings, including elephant yoga and private dining in the baby elephant encampment. He'd assured her he would "most definitely think about it."

There was something about starting the day to the sound of trumpeting elephants that made a man want to sample the exotic. Brian rolled out of bed and peeked through the curtains. To the left was Burma. To the right, Laos and the muddy Mekong River. Beneath his feet, the Thai region of Chiang Rai. "I'm in the goddamn Golden Triangle," he said to himself.

A groan from the bed caused him to turn around. "Too early. You come back me."

He smiled. That was an invitation that didn't need to be issued twice.

An hour later he opened his eyes to see the curtains were now wide open. Nan had just stepped out of the shower, a towel wrapped around her middle. She was fit in the way only someone who has never seen a gym can be, her rich brown skin taut and smooth.

"You're beautiful, you know."

Nan tried unsuccessfully to suppress a smile. "You talk crazy. Have breakfast first. Then maybe not crazy."

Brian spread his arms wide. "Come here."

She shook her head. "Hungry. Thai people eat when hungry."

"No you don't," he said as he pulled on some drawstring pants he bought at the night market for $10. "Thai people eat constantly. You should weigh as much as... that elephant."

"No elephant."

Brian looked at her in mock disbelief. "Then what is it?"

"Two elephant!" Nan threw back her head in laughter, and headed out the door. "Come or I eat everything!" was her parting shot.

It wasn't going to be easy. The breakfast buffet at the Sala Mae Nam restaurant had dozens of different Thai and Chinese delicacies on display, as well as a menu for more complex dishes that taste best served straight from the kitchen. Brian downed a large plate of fruit and some dim sum, and pronounced himself pleasantly full.

Nan laughed at the announcement. "You eat like baby!"

As she went back for thirds, Brian smiled to himself. The last two weekend trips – both to Pattaya – had gone reasonably well. But when the plan for the day was "lie around the pool getting slowly drunk on overly sweet cocktails," the language and cultural barriers between them were almost irrelevant. Meal times, on the other hand, were painful, and Brian noticed himself skipping courses at dinner in order to finish more quickly – although Nan flatly refused to miss dessert. But this trip would require them to act like a real couple, passing time together in the airport waiting for their flight and doing touristy things once they reached their destination. It had been a gamble, but so far, Brian thought, it had paid off.

Last night, of course, had helped.

Nan had fallen into conversation with the chef managing two skillets at once behind the omelet station, so Brian picked up a nearby pamphlet about elephants and began to read. His initial objective was just to remind himself what English sentences looked like when grammatically correct and structured into a larger narrative. But against expectation, he found himself getting drawn into the subject matter.

He learned that Thais originally used elephants in warfare, but in the modern era the beasts earned their crust in the logging industry. Thais consider white elephants to be particularly auspicious, as Queen Maya, the mother of the Buddha, was able to conceive only after dreaming of a white elephant finding its way into her belly.

Dr. Freud would have a field day with that one, Brian thought as he turned the page.

By law all white elephants belong to the king. The English expression "white elephant" is thought to come from the days when Thai kings would give the rare animals as gifts. Favored recipients would be given both the elephant and the land on which the elephant could live. Recipients who needed to be taught a lesson would be given just the elephant, with no food or place to keep it. Since royal elephants cannot be sold, the gift of a white elephant could break a man, financially and emotionally.

"That's some evil-genius-level shit," Brian said as an ebullient Nan returned with yet another plate piled high with food.

"What shit?" she asked innocently.

"Oh, just this thing the king used to do."

Nan's eyes doubled in size as she looked nervously around the open-air restaurant. "No say bad thing about king. Go jail, long time."

"You've still got lèse-majesté laws in this country?"

"Have king. All people love. Good man."

"So why does he need laws to protect him?"

Nan's only reply was a frown.

"In any event, I wasn't talking about him. I was talking about old kings."

"He 85."

"No, before him. A different king. Anyhow, forget it. It was just something to do with elephants."

Nan looked at him as if he were a blithering idiot, and a dangerous one at that.

Brian quickly scanned the rest of the pamphlet in search of firmer ground. And he found it. "It says here that if you walk under an elephant it brings good luck. Is that true?"

Nan nodded solemnly. "Must walk three times."

"But isn't it dangerous? What happens if – I don't know – the elephant sits on you or takes a shit while you're still underneath?"

He'd been aiming for the funny bone but hit a raw nerve instead. "Why you no believe? Why you think Thai custom no good?"

Brian held up his hands in self-defense. "Whoa! I never said any of that."

"No need say." She tapped her head. "I know."

"Look: if you want to walk under an elephant, we'll walk under the damn elephant. Or you can walk and I'll take pictures. Or I'll walk and you take the pictures. Whatever makes you happy."

Nan folded her arms tightly across her chest and gave Brian a death glare.

"Fuck me," Brian said in a voice too small to be heard. "We should have gone to the damn beach."

CHAPTER 15

Nat said he needed the afternoon to think. Sally was on the verge of saying absolutely not, but Ian held up his hand. "Do what you need to do. We'll see you in the morning."

Sally fumed until the policeman had gathered his things and left the room. She pointed at the exit, which Thomas correctly interpreted to mean, "Make sure Nat's not standing outside the door listening."

"You're getting a tad paranoid, you know."

"No, Ian, I'm getting careful – and it's pretty evident we should have been doing that from the moment we landed." Sally got up, stuck her head out the door to ensure Nat had gone, and than waved her hand violently until her colleagues followed her out into the hall. "For all you know that room is bugged so Nat's unnamed 'superiors' can keep tabs on everything we say and do."

"See previous statement," Ian declared.

But Sally was not to be put off. "Think about it: we didn't get a say in where the meetings were held. Nat already had this place set up."

"With food and drink. That hardly counts as a conspiracy."

"Don't be daft. We know about the buffet table because you can't miss it on the way into the room. But the only way we'd see listening devices and cameras is if we went looking for them – and we didn't. I doubt the hotel cleaning crew dusts the ceiling and inside the light fixtures every single day. And even if they did come across the devices, what are they going to do? Tell the Thai police they need to remove the bugs from the room they're renting at presumably considerable expense? No hotel manager is going to shoot himself in the foot like that."

"I can't tell if you're serious," Thomas declared.

"I'm definitely serious." Sally took a calming breath. "Whether I'm right is a different matter."

"So what are you proposing?" Ian asked. "Want to go back inside and have a look around all the nooks and crannies? Take apart the phone and check it for bugs? And what do you propose we do if the search *does* turn up something? File a formal complaint with the Thai police?"

"Of course not. What I want to do is get out of this hotel so we can talk freely without my inner paranoid taking over."

"Fine," Ian agreed. "Anyhow, it's time for lunch. Let's go out into the real world and see what we can find."

The detectives wandered down Ratchadamri Road until they reached Erawan Square. Drawn in by the music and overpowering smell of incense, they stopped to watch a group of traditional dancers. They wore what looked like tiny golden temples on their heads, forcing them to remain perfectly centered and upright, no matter how deeply they swayed.

In the center of the square was the four-sided statue of Brahma they had seen on their way in from the airport. It was surrounded by vases of light pink and green lotus blossoms, their petals still tightly closed. Nearby tables were covered with orange, yellow and white flowers. Reverent Thais prayed while holding handfuls of joss sticks, the smoldering tips filling the square with fragrant smoke. "England's got nothing like this," said a transfixed Thomas.

"Makes you think they know something we don't," agreed Ian.

"Which is precisely our problem," said Sally, shattering the mood with her characteristic contempt for solemnity. "So let's go eat and figure out what we're going to do next."

They ended up in a Thai restaurant called Nara in the basement of the shopping center that towered above Erawan Square. After a brief debate about who knew the most about Thai food, the three novices agreed that each would choose one dish, a task made easier by the fact the menu came with color photos. Sally quickly chose *kao tang na tang*, rice crackers served with a pork and prawn coconut dip. Ian opted for a red duck curry ("typical," Sally commented). Thomas was unable to choose between *tom yum kung* – the fiery soup Thailand is famous for – and *gai hor bai toei*, chicken wrapped in pandan leaves. It was quickly agreed to get both.

"So," Sally said as soon as the waiter was out of earshot. "You think Nat was telling the truth?"

"I don't know," Ian replied honestly. "I find his body language very hard to read. Between the Thai tranquility and the American false optimism he's a junk heap of conflicting signs. Throw in the modesty – false or otherwise – and I can't tell if he's oblivious to being caught between the rock of the Thai police and the hard place of Scotland Yard's finest, or a very skilled manipulator who's laughing at us behind our backs."

Sally sniffed. "Jesus. If he really is a pawn in all this, I feel sorry for him. Talk about being in over your head."

"Where do you think he's really going this afternoon?" Thomas asked.

"What, you don't think he's going to take a long walk on the beach and think deep thoughts?" Sally teased. "Here's a better question: what are *we* going to do?"

"I thought we might lie out by the pool," Ian replied.

"I will admit I was not expecting that answer," Sally said with a bemused glance at Thomas. "Worn out, are we?"

"Not yet. But it could be a long night."

Thomas was about to ask why, but the food arrived and conversation was suspended as two waitresses placed huge green bowls of food in the center of the table, then returned with plates and a giant bucket of rice from which they served helpings the size of a baby's head. The instant the waitresses turned away, Thomas started furiously shoveling huge helpings of each dish onto his plate.

"Were you from a big family?" Sally asked. "You've got that self-protective way of eating one usually sees with kids who had to fight older siblings for the serving spoon."

Thomas was too busy chewing to answer.

Ian unwrapped one of the pandan leaves, popped a piece of chicken in his mouth, and smiled as the complexity of the seemingly simple dish revealed itself. The first sensation was the aroma of grass and flowers. Next came the creamy taste of the coconut marinade. That was followed by the sweet crunchiness of caramelized sugar. And to finish, a distinctively nutty aftertaste.

The inspector shook his head in admiration. "I don't know how they do it. Everything is just so... *layered.* At home we'd toss a whole chicken in the oven and call it cooking. We don't have the patience to make something like this."

Sally appeared skeptical. "That's an awful lot to take out of one bite of chicken. But if you're suggesting that British cooking sucks, I agree completely."

McLean pointed at the rice cake Thomas had just smothered in pork dip. "See how it's curved like a cup so the sauce doesn't drip over the sides?"

"Crisps are curved, Ian, and I don't hear you waxing poetic about them."

"Maybe that was a bad example, but you know what I mean, right? The Thais just seem to be in less of a hurry than we are. They make the effort to do things right."

"Except when it comes to getting rich," Thomas said before swallowing. "For that they just pray to the elephant god on the corner."

"Steady, Thomas," Sally cautioned. "I'm nominally Buddhist, you know."

In the uncomfortable silence that followed, Ian helped himself to the red duck curry. "That's bloody brilliant!" he announced.

Sally shook her head in disappointment. "You men really are simple creatures, aren't you? We get jerked around all morning, and all it takes to cheer you up is a couple of bites of spicy food. Throw in a beer and you'll be moaning in ecstasy."

"Sounds like a plan," Thomas said as he called for the waitress.

"I don't know what you're so down about," Ian added. "Despite all of the smoke blown our way today, we did learn one thing – well, two actually. One is the name *Nan*, which will make life a lot easier. The second is her place of employment."

"Yeah, about that," Sally said. "How come when the Thai police did their three-day canvas of Patpong they were unable to find a soul who knew our girl?"

"And why did no one mention it when they asked Cooper, Littleton & Hall whether she was on staff?" Thomas added with his mouth still half full.

"Second question first. It's possible the only people who knew about Nan were Greg and his secretary, and the police spoke to someone else. HR, maybe. Or maybe people knew, but didn't volunteer the information because they thought it might bring further grief to Brian's family.

"As for the first question, I have no idea. Did the search really take place? Did the uniforms assigned actually do what they were supposed to, or did they spend three nights looking at half-naked girls at the taxpayer's expense? Or maybe it was the people of Patpong who lied. After all, not much good comes from cooperating with the police, especially on a murder inquiry."

"Remind me not to let you do the community outreach program next year," Sally said as she tried to put out the fire in her mouth with a cold beer.

"In any event, I was thinking that tonight we do a search of our own. We've got the picture of Nan that Cahill kept between his credit cards, and now we know both her full name and her nickname."

"What we don't know is Thai," Thomas pointed out.

"That could be a bit of a handicap," Ian admitted, "especially if someone says 'yes.' But if the Thai police are telling the truth, all we're going to get is heads shaking 'no.'"

"So why bother?" Thomas persisted.

McLean shrugged. "With any luck I'll be proved wrong."

The trio ate in silence for a bit. "Plan to tell Nat what we're up to?" Sally asked.

"If he asks. But am I going to call him up and volunteer information when he couldn't be bothered to do the same for us this morning? No fucking way."

Sally smiled. "My sentiments exactly."

CHAPTER 16

The need to be in the UK for the Christmas holiday and – far more important – the cutthroat interoffice battles over shares of the year-end bonus pool meant it had been nearly two months since Brian last stepped out of BA 9 to be smacked in the face by the hot, humid, fragrant air of Bangkok. He walked rapidly up the Jetway, pulling his wheeled suitcase so quickly that both wheels were rarely on the ground at the same time. At first he thought the quivering in his arms and legs was the result of increased blood flow, now that he was no longer trapped in a giant tin can. But then he realized the true cause of his unusual condition: he couldn't wait to see Nan.

Getting her to meet him at the airport had not been easy. Neither had the conversation, the first time he called her from the UK.

"Hello."

"Hi, is this Nan?"

"Who this?"

"This is Brian. Cahill. From London."

Silence.

"You know, we went to Pattaya and Chiang Rai together. Remember?"

Click.

The next two calls went unanswered.

A Google search for her email address came up empty.

So finally he sent a text, and got a reply in English far better than Nan was capable of. That was a topic he'd explore in depth at a later date. For now what mattered was that she had agreed to meet him at Suvarnabhumi Airport, and from there they would check in as a couple at the Four Seasons Hotel.

Brian couldn't remember the last time he'd felt this giddy about a girl. Maybe in his early teens, when women were a source of endless fascination and complete inaccessibility, but certainly not since he'd gained a little experience and learned how to do what Elvis Costello so aptly called "the mystery dance."

He definitely never felt that way about Sylvia. Not even in the beginning. Sure, he loved Sylvia and thought it highly likely they'd end up married. But he never *wanted* her the way he did Nan.

Brian broke into a run.

On his last trip he had signed up for the Thailand Elite program, largely because it allowed him to sail through Immigration. Today he thought that was some of the best money he'd ever spent. He flew past the poor sods waiting for checked bags, yelled "thank you" in mangled Thai to the customs inspector who waived him through, and burst out into the arrivals area.

No sign of Nan.

Brian's shoulders slumped, and he stood frozen in place while annoyed travelers with carts full of luggage struggled to navigate around him. Maybe she was stuck in traffic. During rush hour, the city was effectively a parking lot. But she was coming *from* downtown, and should have been fine.

Maybe she was sick, and tried to call him while he was on the plane. He whipped out his iPhone, tapping his thumb impatiently on the Gorilla Glass while waiting for the magic of software to find a local carrier.

Brian became excited as the number of reception bars suddenly rose, but the feeling only lasted a few seconds. His phone informed him he had no new messages, and no missed calls.

So he called Nan, and let the phone ring 20 times before hanging up in disappointment.

"Khun Brian?"

And there she was. Demurely dressed in well-worn jeans and a collared shirt, with her hair pulled up in an elegant chignon. She put her hands together in a *wai* and slowly lowered her head.

Brian ran to her, arms wide open. And they stayed open. Nan was keeping her culturally acceptable distance.

"I thought you hadn't come."

"You call me. You say come."

"Yes, that's right. I *wanted* you to come. But when I didn't see you I thought you weren't here. But you are, so that's good. I'm really glad to see you, you know." Christ, I sound like a moron, said Brian's inner editor. "There's a hotel car here to pick us up. Shall we go?"

He found the driver holding a sign with "Cahill" on it. The uniformed man made a *wai* and reached for Brian's bag. "Welcome back to Bangkok!"

"Thank you."

"How was your flight?"

"Long, but survivable."

The smile never disappeared from the driver's face, but a sudden narrowing of the eyes made it clear that he'd noticed Nan, and was none too happy about the fact she was following them. He shifted his body closer to Brian, as if trying to physically separate the couple.

The hotel Mercedes was waiting right outside the exit, a uniformed driver at the wheel. The designated greeter opened the car door, indicated Brian should enter, and bowed stiffly when he did. All Nan got in the way of service was a sharp nod at the opposite door.

As the car pulled away, Brian jerked his head in the direction of the man they'd left behind. "What's wrong with him?"

"He no like."

"He no like... what doesn't he like?"

"Me."

"You? He doesn't even know you."

Nan shook her head furiously. "He know me bar girl. No like."

Brian felt his blood pressure rising. "Well, fuck him. I couldn't care less about what he likes and doesn't like. *I* like you, and I want you here. That's all that matters."

Nan turned towards the window to hide the smile on her face.

"Are all Thai men like that? They don't like bar girls?"

"Thai men like bar girls. Don't like bar girls with *farang*."

Pretty much the way Londoners feel about rich Middle Easterners with runway models hanging off their furry arms, Brian thought.

During the hour-long ride, Brian made several attempts to start a conversation, most of which died on the vine. Strangely, that failure didn't make him feel uncomfortable. There was something inordinately calming about Nan's presence, and he found himself enjoying just sitting in silence and looking out the window as the Bangkok suburbs flew past.

He was greeted by name as the Mercedes pulled up to the whitewashed hotel exterior, first by the doorman, and then by the receptionist who walked them up to their room for check-in.

"Welcome back, Mr. Cahill. We've upgraded you to an Executive Suite." She was the very essence of polite efficiency.

"Thank you very much."

"We have a copy of your passport on file. Will your" – the pause was momentary, but nonetheless awkward – "companion be staying with you?"

"Yes, she will."

"Then I'll need a copy of her national ID card." At that point, the conversation switched to Thai.

Brian wondered what the perfectly presented clerk thought about what she was seeing. After all, there's a world of difference between stumbling home with a drunken bar girl hanging on your shoulder, and coming directly from the airport with a clean and sober young woman at 10:30 in the morning. For all the clerk knew, Nan could be a medical student at Chulalongkorn

University or a resident of the UK who was living together with Brian in their cozy suburban home.

In which case she should have had a suitcase of her own.

Speaking of which, why *didn't* she have a suitcase of her own? They were going to be together for the next five days. Shouldn't she at least have a toothbrush?

Brian waited until the clerk left, full of smiles and gentle wishes to have "a most enjoyable stay." Then: "Where's your stuff?"

"I need?"

"Well, yes. I assume so. I mean, you're going to be here for five days."

Nan nodded her head as if hearing something for the very first time. "You no say. Just say 'come airport.'"

"Sorry about that. I thought it was implied."

Puzzlement.

"You know: inviting you to meet me meant an invitation to stay."

Still blank.

"You're right. I should have said."

Triumphant smile.

"So, now that you're here, what would you like to do?"

"Shopping."

Brian laughed. It was only when they reached the elevator that he began to wonder whether he'd just been expertly played.

CHAPTER 17

The Patpong Night Market was packed. Overweight, badly sun-burned tourists wearing t-shirts and shorts with far too many pockets fought their way through the maze of stands piled high with pirated DVD's, knock-offs of famous clothing brands, fake Rolexes, cheap elephant-themed souvenirs, and jagged-edged knives that looked like something out of a horror movie. Backpackers who had gone too long without a shower negotiated for another 10 cents off a $5 cotton shoulder bag as if their very lives depended on it. Women in their 30's and 40's carried half-a-dozen plastic bags full of purchases in each hand while never letting their husbands out of their sight, for the real business of Patpong was not the trinkets sold in the middle of the *soi*; it was the flesh for sale in the girlie bars on either side.

Huge neon signs with a contempt for euphemism called out to lonely men – and the occasional adventurous woman – with names like Pussy Galore, Hot Spot, Devil's Delight, The Strip, and Queen of Hearts. To ensure there was no misunderstanding about what wonders waited inside, three or four young women were posted outside each entrance, wearing hip-length flashy polyester bathrobes that looked like they'd been purloined from a boxing gym. Whenever a group of guys or the rare unattached male walked by, the girls in robes burst into a chorus of welcome. If their prey slowed for even an instant, the girls pounced – locking arms and escorting him into the club to a high-pitched chorus of "Hello, sir!"

Thomas found the sudden attention to be both wonderful and unsettling. Sally took one look at the confused emotions written across his face, and burst out laughing. "Not used to being noticed by the opposite sex?" she asked teasingly.

"Noticed, yes. Solicited, no."

"Aren't you making a rather heroic assumption?" When Ian replied with arched eyebrows, Sally continued. "How do you know those are women?"

"Well, look at them!" Thomas exclaimed. "I mean, there can't be much debate about *that.*"

"Don't be too sure. Patpong is famous for what the Thais call *kathoey* or *ladyboys.* Most of them have had operations so that they're anatomically correct. Breast implants. Surgical reduction of the Adam's apple. They can even turn outy genitalia into the inny version you like so much."

"But you can still tell, right?" said an increasingly uncomfortable Thomas. "What about the voice?"

"Raised using hormone pills."

"Come on. Men and women are just... different. There's got to be some way of knowing which is which."

"Does it matter?" asked Ian with a grin. "After all, if you can't tell, no harm no foul."

"Of course it matters! I don't want to have sex with a *guy,*" Thomas protested with an air of panic.

"But you *are* planning to have sex with one of these women?" Sally teased.

"No! You know what I mean. It's just... not right."

"I think it's all rather wonderful, and perfectly understandable," said Sally. "If all men converted to women this world would be a kindler, gentler place."

"For one generation until the human race died out."

"I'll give you that one, Ian. I guess you lot can stick around, but for reproductive purposes only. And try to cut down on all that war and violence stuff while you're here, won't you?"

Thomas was clearly discomfited. "You two can laugh about it, but it's not funny. My whole life I thought I knew the difference between men and women, and now you're telling me I don't?"

Sally laughed, but a quick look at Thomas' bewildered face moved her to pity. "I suggest you look at the hands."

"Why the hands?"

"Men usually have broader palms. It's not a hard and fast rule, as women who grew up working the fields may have wider shoulders and stronger hands than a man who sits at a desk all day. But it's a good early warning sign."

"Great," said Thomas dejectedly.

"I must have missed part of the discussion on tonight's mission," Ian said with mock solemnity. "I was under the impression we came here to investigate a murder, not help Thomas determine whether the bar girl reaching for his wallet is actually a girl."

"Ha ha," Thomas said flatly. "I'm just curious."

"I bet you are!" Sally teased.

"All right, children, that's enough," Ian barked. "How do we want to play this?"

"Same way we would at home," said Sally. "Walk in, order a drink, and have a look around."

"You don't think you might stand out a bit more than usual?"

"Why, Ian? Because I'm a girl with her clothes *on*?"

The inspector blushed. "Well, yes."

The artlessness of the answer pleased Sally no end. "At least you're honest. But look: there are women going into that bar two doors down. And there's a mixed group negotiating entrance at the place next to that. We'll fit right in."

"Maybe we should buy a few things from the market so we look like real tourists," Thomas suggested.

"Got your eye on some pirated DVD's, eh?"

"I can get those later. I'm just trying to blend in."

"Good thought, Thomas, but I think it's unnecessary," Ian announced. "As long as we spread a little money around, I'm sure Lady Go Go will be happy to welcome us. *All* of us."

"Fine," the young man replied. "But if the girl who takes our money has big hands, I'm legging it."

The detectives stepped past the curtain, and gave their eyes a moment to adjust. A waiter – who couldn't have been more than 5'2" – approached them. With a silver tray tucked under his left arm, he pointed at some open seats with his right.

"Wonder what would happen if we ran a Polilight around this place," Sally mused.

"It would look like a teenage boy's bedsheet," Ian said graphically. "Probably best not to think about it. Or the STD's that are making the jump from the seat cover to the back of your legs even as we speak."

"That is simply disgusting, McLean, as well as being a veiled attack on my decision to wear a skirt tonight because it's too damn hot for slacks."

"Drinks?" the waiter asked.

"Two gin & tonics and a vodka tonic, please."

"You're really on a roll tonight, McLean. No need to ask the little lady what she wants to drink, much less allow her to order it herself."

"Did you want something else?"

"No, but that's not the point."

"Then what is?"

"That you managed to be insulting and sexist in two consecutive sentences. That's a pretty aggressive pace. Sure you can keep it up?" Sally groaned. "Yeah, I heard it."

Both men smiled.

The waiter quickly returned bearing three identical drinks and a bill for 360 baht. "We're looking for a girl," Ian said, shouting to make himself heard over the din of a song that consisted almost entirely of the words "bitch, bitch, bitch."

The waiter pointed to the stage.

"No, not those girls. A girl who used to work here." The waiter shook his head again, and pointed at the bill. Ian pulled a purple 500 baht bill out of his wallet, and told the waiter to keep the change. The waiter picked up the money, made a quick *wai*, and disappeared.

"You think he didn't know or didn't understand?" Sally asked.

"Hard to say. Maybe both."

"So let's ask one of the girls. Thomas, here's your chance: have a look at what's onstage – a brief look, mind you – and choose the girl who looks chatty."

"How am I supposed to know whether she's chatty?"

"You can start by looking at the part of her body that's *above* her breasts."

The young man knew this was a question that must be answered quickly. "Number 187," he said before finishing off his entire drink in one slightly embarrassed gulp.

"Why her?"

"Why not?"

Sally nodded in agreement, and signaled for the waiter. He pretended not to see her. She quickly found another – there were half a dozen in sight – and waved. "You drinks?" he asked.

"No, number 187 please."

The waiter's face revealed no surprise whatsoever. "Bet he's seen just about every perversity known to man," said the former Vice cop.

#187 may have had a little less experience with the weirdness of the world than her colleagues; she looked surprised to be requested by a woman traveling with two men. But she made her way over to the table and extended her hand.

"What you name?"

"I'm Sally. This is... oh, they don't matter. Would you like a drink?"

#187 nodded, and gave what sounded like a one-word order to the still hovering waiter.

"We're looking..." Ian began, but was quickly cut off by Sally.

"What's your name?"

"Me Lek."

"Melek. That's an unusual name."

The girl shook her head. "Lek."

"Oh I see!" Sally said. "Sorry."

"Okay. How long you stay Bangkok?"

"Just a few days. How about you, Lek? How long have you been working here?"

"Yes, *ka.*"

Sally groaned, and wondered if it had been a mistake coming without Nat. "Here. How long? One month? One year?"

Comprehension blossomed on Lek's face. "Me, three month."

"I see. Three months. So did you know a girl named Nan?"

"Many Nan. All girl name Nan."

Thomas pulled out his notebook, but struggled to read it in the dark. The waiter was hovering nearby, and helpfully pulled out a flashlight. Perhaps Ian had been right to tip generously.

"Right. Thanks. Very helpful that. Did you know a girl named Kanokwan Supitayaporn? I'm not sure I pronounced that right."

The name had no impact on Lek, but it caused the waiter to flee. Ian gave each of his colleagues a gentle kick under the table to ensure they noted the departure.

"Me, no. Some other girl, maybe."

"Could you ask for us please? See if any of the girls know...."

"Kanokwan Supitayaporn," Thomas said, this time with noticeably greater fluency.

Lek said nothing.

"We'd really appreciate it," Sally added. Still no reaction. So she reached into her purse and pulled out the first bill she found – which happened to be 1,000 baht, or nearly 25 pounds.

Lek pocketed the bill in a flash, then got up and left.

"I have a feeling I just wasted 1,000 baht," Sally said while punctuating the remark with a long pull on her drink. "There's actually alcohol in this," she said approvingly.

"Right idea, wrong level," Ian said as he signaled for another waiter. "Another round of drinks – same again – and we'd like to speak with the mama-san."

Sally tapped her temple with her right index finger. "Good idea."

"Not sure it's going to work," the inspector replied as he gestured towards the bar counter with his head. The waiter was talking to an attractive but forbidding woman who looked to be in her early 50's. While she listened the woman stared directly at the detectives.

"Doesn't look real happy, does she?" Thomas asked.

"I'd call that look closer to 'furious,'" McLean replied.

But she did come over, drawing surreptitious glances as she moved slowly but confidently through the crowded room.

"I help you?" she said.

"I hope so. Please, sit down. We'd like to buy you a drink."

The woman shook her head. "No sit. Working."

"Okay. We really just have a quick question. Do you know a girl who used to work here named..."

Thomas supplied the name. "Kanokwan Supitayaporn."

The mama-san stared at Thomas like she was looking into his soul. "No. No Kanokwan here."

"No, I know she's not here *now*. But we were told she used to work here."

"Who say?"

"Just someone who used to know her."

Mama-san shook her head again. "No here. You want more drink? Or now you finish?"

McLean looked at the three barely touched drinks, their ice cubes rapidly losing a battle with the Bangkok heat. Next his eyes traveled up to the mama-san's resolute expression. Finally he scanned the room and noticed that all of the waiters, many of the girls, and even a significant percentage of the customers were raptly watching the drama unfold, maybe hoping for a little violence to add color to an otherwise stock-standard evening. "I think we're done," Ian announced.

As he stood up to leave, he noticed a Thai man in a superfluous warm-up jacket doing the same thing. There were no empty glasses on his table.

CHAPTER 18

Brian tried to remember when was the last time he'd taken Sylvia shopping, and was surprised to realize the answer was, in all likelihood, never. There was something about the idea of holding a woman's purse while she tried on endless outfits she didn't need that made watching paint dry sound like a vastly preferable way to spend the day.

But this was different. Yes, he was holding Nan's tiny handbag while she popped in and out of dressing rooms. But when she emerged wearing something for which she wanted his approval, she looked like a little kid on Christmas morning. It made him feel – it took him a moment to settle on the right descriptor – powerful.

Also thrifty. Nan navigated past the sparkling brand boutiques on the ground floor of the Siam Paragon mall, and headed upstairs to tiny shops with names he'd either never heard or – in many cases – couldn't read. Two and half hours later Nan had three massive bags stuffed with new clothes, and he'd spent less than the cost of Sylvia's birthday meal at Heston Blumenthal's decidedly overrated *Dinner* at London's Mandarin Oriental on Hyde Park.

Plus Nan looked *great* in proper clothes. Gone was the hard edge of a bar girl. In its place was the soft confidence of a woman just beginning to understand how truly beautiful she was.

"My life has turned into a remake of *My Fair Lady*," he muttered with no small amount of pleasure.

But the enjoyable afternoon came to a disagreeable end when Nan noticed it was nearly 5 P.M. "Must work," she said without preamble.

"I thought perhaps you could take today off so we can have some dinner together."

She shook her head violently. "Can't. Lose job. Every day, must go."

"But that's just silly. Why go all the way to work, just to leave as soon as you get there?"

Nan beamed. "Yes."

"I'm not making myself clear. Your plan is a waste of time. Just call mama-san and tell her you're taking the night off. In fact, tell her you're taking the next five nights off, and that I'll pay the bar fines for all of them. Plus tip. We'll drop by maybe tomorrow or the day after to give her the money."

It was unclear how much of that speech was actually intelligible to Nan, but judging from her cocked head, the answer was probably "not much."

"No can. Everyday, must work. All girls."

Brian inhaled and exhaled slowly. "Fine. We'll go together, and I'll pay everything. In advance. Would that make you happy?"

Clearly it would.

"Go hotel first."

"It's nearly rush hour. That'll take ages! Why do we have to go there first?"

Nan pointed at all her bags. "Can't take to work. Other girls see. They jealous me. No good."

Now it was Brian who smiled. Thai women weren't all that different from English women after all.

The taxi made a brief stop at the Four Seasons – just long enough for Brian to hand the bags to a nearby bellman, shout his room number, and hand him a fistful of unexamined bills from his right pants pocket. Nan then instructed the driver to take them to Patpong, resulting in a few overly long glances in the rear view mirror.

It was still light when they reached the *soi*, and most of the girls were in their come-to-work clothes. Many were perched on the high stools outside their respective bars, hunched over a plate of spicy stir-fry or a bowl of noodles covered in chili. Some were nattering away as they made their selections from one of the three carts selling a wide variety of insects.

"What do they do with those?" Brian asked, his face contorted in disgust.

"Eat. Snack. Very good. Isaan girls like."

"Surely you're not serious."

"You want try?"

"Oh good God, no! They look revolting."

"I buy for you."

"That's quite all right."

Possibly deliberately, Nan didn't understand. She happily pointed at four different types of deep-fried bugs, which were handed to her in a small paper cone. She reached in, grabbed a handful, and popped the crispy creatures in her mouth as if she were eating popcorn.

Brian would have sworn he heard the shrill stridulation of a grasshopper's legs as they grated between Nan's teeth. When she offered him the bag, he nearly lost his lunch.

"What don't we save that for *after* dinner," he said diplomatically. "For now let's focus on finding mama-san, paying your bar fine, and getting ourselves to a nice restaurant for a proper dinner."

Brian started to move forward, but found his way blocked by a barefoot child who couldn't have been more than five, holding up loose cigarettes for sale. "You buy?" the boy asked in surprisingly unaccented English.

"No, um, I don't smoke. But thank you."

The kid didn't move.

"Can you tell him I'm not interested?" he asked.

Nan looked down at her chest before responding. "Give him five baht or ten baht."

"But I don't smoke."

"Don't take cigarettes. Just give money. This child very poor. No can eat. We help."

Of course we help, Brian thought. Five baht is the equivalent of ten pence. Surely a man who had just blown several hundred pounds on fancy dresses for a bar girl could afford ten pence so an obviously malnourished kid could eat.

He pulled out twenty baht, and handed it to the boy – who pocketed the money immediately and began counting out the equivalent in loose cigarettes. When Nan told him the money was his to keep, he flashed a blinding smile and then ran off before his benefactors had a chance to rethink their generosity.

And that made Brian Cahill – an investment banker who usually considered anything less than five figures to be a rounding error – surprisingly and utterly happy.

CHAPTER 19

"Think he'll show today?" Sally asked as the three detectives walked into the empty conference room for the start of Day 3.

"Yes," Ian and Thomas said at the same time.

"Not even a moment's hesitation. What makes you boys so sure?"

"The Thai police can't simply abandon us. That's tantamount to admitting that there *has* been a cover-up. And what good would it do to send someone new – assuming they even have a second detective who speaks fluent English? Sure, he'll start the game knowing more than Nat did. But he'll still be left struggling to explain a few inexplicable things," Ian concluded.

Thomas turned to Sally. "But you don't think he's coming?"

"I wouldn't if I were him," she replied. "What sacrificial lamb puts himself on the grill?"

"Certainly not me," said Nat. "I always find the smell of roast lamb revolting."

While the three detectives looked at each other in embarrassed surprise, Nat walked purposefully to the head of the room, plugged in his computer, connected the projector, and cleared his throat. "I have a presentation to make. I would ask that you hold all questions until I'm finished. There will be time for discussion at the end."

The contingent from Scotland Yard nodded in bewildered unison.

"Thank you. Page 1. Page 2. Page 3. Page 4."

Nat continued to flip through the slides at a rate of one every two seconds. Not only were they impossible to read; it was barely possible to tell if there was anything on them at all.

Except for slide 79. It said "thank you!"

"That completes my presentation. Are there any questions?"

"Yeah," said Sally. "What the hell was that?"

"That was the presentation I worked on all yesterday afternoon and most of last night."

"A follow up, if I may."

"Go ahead, Sally."

"What was in it?"

"Data about the incidence of heart attacks among males in high-stress occupations, broken down by age. Charts showing that most foreigners who visit Thailand each year *don't* die. Some hard-to-read spreadsheets showing the time spent on this case, by detective, by day. And those were the interesting bits."

"And you prepared all this... why?"

"Because I was instructed to do so."

Sally threw up her hands. "Hell if I know what's going on."

Ian, however, did. He circled his finger around the room, pausing briefly at each corner.

"I don't think so," said Nat. "We asked before you arrived, but the hotel said no. They said they wouldn't permit anyone – including the police – to electronically eavesdrop on their guests. However they may have changed their mind between then and now, under pressure from my embarrassed superiors."

"But you obviously don't think so, or you wouldn't be speaking so openly."

Nat smiled. "Either that or I'm eager to start a new career. Also, if they *had* bugged this room, they wouldn't need the guys outside."

"What guys outside?" Sally asked, her eyes narrowing.

"There are two guys in uniform standing at the railing overlooking the lobby. They positioned themselves between this room and the only ways off this floor – those being the elevator and the staircase to the lobby. To avoid courting suspicion they will swap places in about 20 minutes with two guys in plain clothes who are currently having a coffee in the lobby lounge and wishing policemen got paid a lot more than they do so they could make a return visit to these lovely surroundings when they don't have to work."

"Are they here to arrest us?" Thomas asked.

"No, they're here to make sure I force you to sit through the presentation, and don't let you escape to do any investigating on your own. My superiors were not happy about your visit to Cooper, Littleton & Hall yesterday."

Sally was not happy with their unhappiness. "So what were we supposed to do: sit here all day waiting for you to call? Take a Thai cookery class? See if any of the Patpong bars have a lunch buffet? We're detectives; hitting the street and asking questions is what we do."

"It's what you do in London. Here you have no jurisdiction," Nat reminded her.

"We never pretended otherwise. We merely asked questions, which people were free to answer or ignore as they pleased."

"Besides," Thomas added, "Greg Walsh is an English citizen."

"I don't see how that makes any difference," Nat replied, "but I'll give you that one as a professional courtesy. However Cooper, Littleton & Hall wasn't the only place you visited yesterday, was it?"

"I feel like I'm being interrogated, Nat, and I don't like the feeling one bit," Sally snapped.

"I'm only asking questions. You are free to answer them or ignore them as you please."

"So that's how you're going to play this?" Ian asked. "Treat us like suspects? Have us followed? Post guards outside our room? I have to say, none of that strikes me as the behavior of an organization with nothing to hide."

"That's a bit much, don't you think?" Nat's tone was calm, but he was clearly reaching the limits of his forced patience. "After all, you didn't see fit to mention to your hosts that you were popping out to interview Greg Walsh. Or that you were spending the evening at Lady Go Go."

Ian shrugged. "We'd heard about Patpong and wanted to see what all the fuss was about."

"And it's just coincidence you walked into the bar where Nan used to work and started asking questions?"

The words were still echoing through the conference room when Nat realized he'd made a major strategic error. Ian attacked the exposed flank with vigor.

"How did you know that's where we went?"

"I already told you. We've had a tail on you since your unannounced trip to see Greg Walsh."

McLean was certain the tail had been there *before* the trip to Cooper, Littleton & Hall, which was why Nat was so quick to ask them how they spent the morning yesterday. But he decided to leave that for the moment and focus on last night.

"And how did this so-called tail know we were asking questions inside the bar, rather than – oh, I don't know – having a couple of drinks and enjoying the excellent DJ?"

Unexpectedly, Nat smiled. "You're very good at this, Inspector. So I won't insult you by trying to concoct a cover story on the fly. We had a two-man team on you last night. One man stayed outside the bar, waiting for you to leave. The other was inside. As soon as you left, he had a chat with everyone you spoke to – including the waiters."

Now that was curious, Ian thought. There had indeed been a man in the bar last night but he exited *before* the detectives. Perhaps he was Mr. Outside, and had come inside just to rest his feet? Maybe there was a third man who Nat failed to mention?

McLean filed these questions away and aimed to match Nat's tone of forced friendliness. "Well, I suppose all those minders have saved us some time since there's no need to brief you on what we learned yesterday. That gives us plenty of time to hear your thoughts on a couple of things that have us stumped."

"Such as?"

"For starters, Greg Walsh is certain that Nan worked at Lady Go Go. Yet the mama-san there swears otherwise. How do you explain that?"

"I don't," Nat said. "What did the mama-san say when you asked her?"

"She said there was 'no one here' named Kanokwan Supitayaporn."

"That seems pretty definitive, doesn't it?"

McLean shrugged. "If you take her statement at face value. But then there's another question that needs to be answered."

"And what is that?"

"Just a second ago you asked us whether it was a coincidence we went to the bar where Nan used to work. But earlier you told us you'd tried and failed to discover her place of employment. So how did you know about Lady Go Go?"

Nat had a decent poker face, but a tightening of the jaw muscles gave away his growing panic. "I've already admitted we followed you."

"The tail just told you where we went. It wouldn't tell you why."

"Which is why we spoke to the mama-san."

"But she told *us* she didn't know anything about Nan. So either she told you something very different, or...."

"Or what, Inspector?"

"Or you already knew about Lady Go Go and have been pretending you didn't."

Nat's teeth were now clenched so tightly McLean could practically hear them grate. "Okay," the Thai policeman said. "You want to know? I'll tell you. As soon as you left Cooper, Littleton &

Hall, I went in and retraced your steps. I asked Walsh what you talked about, and he told me exactly what he told you."

"See? That wasn't so hard. It must feel better to have that off your chest and out in the open." McLean's tone was playful, but there was no mistaking the anger that lay just below the surface. "Unfortunately it's another one of those answers that carries its own questions. Specifically, I can understand the mama-san's reluctance to cooperate with three random Brits, especially when the subject of their inquiries is a dead girl." Nat nodded encouragingly. "But since we now all agree that Nan worked at Lady Go Go, I don't understand why your colleagues were unable to find anyone who would admit to knowing her – assuming, that is, they actually tried."

"You're suggesting they didn't, Inspector?"

"I'm saying Patpong has a lot of temptations that might cause a man to lose focus on his assignment."

After a short internal debate, Nat decided that it was time to de-escalate. "I thought the same thing. So I spoke with every single policeman who was assigned to the search, separately and privately. They all swore they did exactly what they were supposed to do."

"Of course they did," said Sally sarcastically.

"You're right that they could all be lying, and undoubtedly would have if their bosses were asking the questions. But I kept my tone as casual as possible, and avoided doing anything that felt like an interrogation. It was just two colleagues chatting about a few nights out at company expense. I even asked them to include me the next time they got a sweet assignment like that."

"And?"

"Everything I heard and saw indicated they were telling the truth."

"That leaves the possibility no one in Patpong wants to get involved with police of *any* nationality," Sally pointed out.

"Nat, do you know whether your colleagues mentioned they were investigating a murder?"

"Well, since until yesterday we didn't think there had been one – and still haven't seen proof that there was – I think we can safely assume they didn't." Nat switched off his laptop and the projector. "I know where you're heading, Ian, but it could cut either way. If civilians think you're looking for a girl to tell her that her mother is sick, they'll help you. But if it's a murder investigation? Suddenly nobody knows a thing."

"True enough," Ian admitted before deciding to test the fragile bridge that he and his Thai counterpart were rebuilding. "Walsh told us that the reason Cahill came to Thailand so often was that there's a lot of business to be done here. One of the reasons is that investors, both domestic and foreign, have been nervous ever since 2010 when the red and yellow shirts first took to the streets. Would you agree with that?"

"To be honest, Walsh probably has a better handle on business confidence levels than I do. I can tell you about the mood on the streets, but if you want to know what's happening in the boardrooms, talk to someone who spends time there." McLean's silence made it abundantly clear he wasn't satisfied with the answer, so Nat tried again. "My personal opinion is that while 2010 made some money men uncomfortable, it was the coup d'état of 2014 that really scared people off."

"We asked him whether the acquired companies would feel like Cahill had taken advantage of them in a moment of weakness. As expected, Walsh said no, that if anything those companies appreciated the rescue. Do you buy that?"

"Again, not really my area," Nat replied. "But if Thai companies really do think foreign investors are preying upon them, it hasn't made the papers."

"Is it safe to assume the unrest has been bad for tourism as well?"

Nat laughed, but his heart wasn't in it. "Trust me: you wouldn't be staying at the Four Seasons if the price was still as high as it was before the coup."

Sally and Thomas had been closely watching the chess game. They knew their boss well enough to realize he was going somewhere with his seemingly casual questions, but like Nat they had yet to figure out his destination.

That was about to change.

"So it would be in the government's interest to keep a lid on any news regarding crimes against overseas visitors?"

The bridge collapsed. "If you're suggesting the Thai government is covering up a murder simply to get a few more backpackers staying at cheap hotels, you're wrong," Nat bristled.

"What makes you so sure?" Ian asked.

Nat locked eyes before speaking. "Because if we wanted to hide what happened to Cahill, we would have set fire to a flophouse, tossed his body in, and let it burn until the only way to identify the remains was with dental records."

CHAPTER 20

"I've got to go to work today. I'll try to get back as early as I can, but it might be close to 8 P.M."

"No shopping today?"

"I'd like to, Nan. But I can't. This is a business trip, so I've got things to do."

"Why you work but me no work?"

"It's different."

"Why different?"

"Well, you can get someone else to cover for you."

"I no understand."

"Another girl can work for you. Take your place."

"Other boy can work for you. Same same."

Brian tried to laugh, but what came out sounded like he'd just been punched in the stomach. "I have a very important job, Nan. Not just anyone can do it."

"My job not important? Anyone can do?"

"I didn't say that."

"You did."

"Well, that's not what I meant."

"Why you tell me no work, then you go work. Should be same."

"I can't believe we're fighting about this. Look: go to the spa, have a facial, get your nails done. Lie around the pool and drink cocktails. Get a hotel car and tell him to take you wherever you want to go. Do you want to do more shopping? Fine, though I wish you told me over breakfast so I could have arranged for some cash. Tell you what: choose whatever you like today, and then tonight, after I get back, we'll go and pick it all up. I'll buy whatever you like, I promise."

"What I like?"

"Yes, whatever you like."

"I like go work."

"But why? Why would you want to go fuck some stranger for money?"

And there it was: the six-ton elephant in the room.

"You think I no good girl? Just fuck men all time? You no like Nan. You just like fuck. Same customer."

Brian reached out to take her hands, but Nan pulled them away angrily.

"Nan, you know that's not true. I like you, and I want to spend time with you."

"But you go work. Nan just sitting all day, waiting, waiting. Waiting no good. Need money."

"I'll give you all the money you want! Didn't I do that yesterday? Did I say no to anything you wanted to buy? You bought – I don't know – six or seven dresses. Three handbags. Four pairs of shoes. That costs a lot of money."

"But no give money. No can buy food with shoes. No can pay house."

"So I'll buy you food and I'll pay your rent and I'll give you cash to spend on whatever you like."

Nan looked both suspicious and hopeful. "You buy all?"

"Yes! That's what I keep saying."

"Nan no work, you pay?"

"Yes!"

Nan nodded, but then suspicion returned. "No fuck, you pay?"

Brian wondered how he'd gotten himself so tangled up, and how could he get out – quickly, before he was inexcusably late for his 8:15 meeting with Greg. "I'll pay everything. Nan no work. Sorry – that was rude. You don't need to work. I'll take care of you. I promise."

"Promise," Nan echoed, and headed off to have a long hot bath with lots of bubbles.

CHAPTER **21**

"Wow," Ian remarked. "One can't get much more honest than that."

Nat couldn't hide his embarrassment. Dental records! How in the world did he let that slip out? "That was disrespectful to the dead, and I shouldn't have said it. I'm sorry."

"No, I'm glad you did. It was certainly harsh. And heartless. But it's also probably true."

Silence descended as the four policemen got lost in their own thoughts. It was Sally who led the way back to normality. "So, now that we're all in a strange sort of agreement, where do we go from here?"

"Let me think out loud for a moment," Ian said, hoping to dispel some of the tension in the room by replacing it with the deliberate calm of his voice. "I think we all agree that some aspects of Cahill's death have been hidden – by someone."

Nods all around.

"If we rule out the police, who does that leave?"

Thomas raised his hand before realizing the gesture was unnecessary and letting it fall slowly to the table. "What about interference at the level of Lady Go Go?"

187

"Meaning?"

"The mama-san. The owner. Anyone who thinks it might be bad for business if word got out that a customer, a *European* customer, had been killed in horrifying fashion."

"But how would this word get out?" Sally asked. "Until yesterday even we" – she gestured to include Nat in the plural pronoun – "didn't know about the connection with Lady Go Go, and we were actively looking for it."

"Sounds like a pretty effective cover-up to me," Nat said. "If Greg Walsh hadn't mentioned Miss Supitayaporn's nickname and place of business, the link with Lady Go Go would still be hidden."

Except it wouldn't, McLean thought. The Thai police knew about Cahill's relationship with Nan from the travel records. Scotland Yard had her picture. It would have been easy to connect the dots. Why was Nat so keen to suggest otherwise?

Yet it was true the police had failed to find a trace of Nan, despite spending three days looking for her. If that wasn't incompetence, was it an indication that Lady Go Go had successfully sealed lips throughout Patpong?

"But Greg volunteered the information freely," Thomas pointed out. "If there is a cover-up going on, nobody told...."

McLean was so caught up in his own analysis he started speaking without realizing that Thomas was already talking. "Say Thomas is right. Who in the management structure of Lady Go Go has the clout to get everyone in Patpong – bar girls, waiters, restaurant and convenience store staff – to pretend they never heard of Nan?"

"It may not be *in* the management structure," Sally suggested, "at least, not the one that shows up on paper."

"What do you mean?" Nat asked.

"I know men, especially of the rich and powerful variety."

"You do, do you?" Thomas broke in, irked at being cut off by McLean and taking it out on Sally.

But Sally had yet to meet an interruption she couldn't ignore. "If there's money being made – and girlie bars usually do well financially – they want a piece of the action. If there are women to be exploited... they want a piece." McLean frowned at Sally, but failed to slow her down. "If there's a chance to get information about and therefore leverage over a rival – whether it's money problems, a hidden mistress, or simply falling down drunk in the street – they want a piece."

"So you're saying that Lady Go Go might have connections with, and leverage over, someone who's not part of the bar *per se.*"

"If Bangkok is anything like London, it's a possibility bordering on a likelihood."

Ian turned to Nat. "Let's assume for a second she's right."

"For a whole *second?*"

Ian growled at Sally and continued. "How do we find out how Patpong girlie bars really work?"

Nat had just opened his mouth when a waiter arrived with fresh coffees. It took him several agonizing minutes for him to put the tiny spoons on the saucers just so, pour the coffees with a flourish, and then offer fresh cream from a pitcher that was clearly not going to be left behind. The thought briefly crossed

McLean's mind that Nat had summoned this perfectionist in order to buy some time, but if he had, he'd done it in a way that escaped detection.

Finally there was nothing more for the waiter to arrange. He made a small bow and quietly left the room.

"You're going beyond my area of expertise," Nat said. "I get called to Patpong a fair bit, but always to sort out a problem with a drunk tourist. I know a lot about the men who go to girlie bars, but very little about the bars themselves."

"Do you know anyone who does?"

Nat looked up at the ceiling, crossed his arms, and did a mental inventory of his address book. "I do know one guy who might be able to help. He's *farang*, but he's been in Thailand longer than I've been alive, and most of that time has been spent in Patpong."

"Sounds ideal," Sally said with a heavy lashing of sarcasm.

"Oh, you'll hate him," Nat said with inexplicable enthusiasm. "His attitudes toward women come straight from the 60's, as do most of his clothes. Let me just make a call to let him know we're coming, and we'll be off."

"Are you sure he's available?" Sally asked.

"Oh, he's available," Nat said with a confident smile.

Sitting in the back of the police BMW, Ian again let his mind go to a dark place. If Nat was so certain his contact had time and an inclination to meet with the visiting detectives, why did he have to call him? And why did he step outside the conference room to make the call? Was Nat briefing the man on what to say – and more importantly, what not to?

While McLean mused, Sally got her bearings. "Isn't that Patpong?" she asked as she pointed across the road.

"Well spotted," Nat said. "It looks a bit different in the daytime, huh?"

"Actually, not a whole lot – except the market's closed."

The car pulled to a halt beneath a pedestrian overpass, and Nat led the team on a death-defying dash across the four-lane road before heading down a side street to an establishment called Pat's Sports Bar. It had a large veranda with a standing bar that could prop up eight Thais or five Americans.

The area inside was surprisingly spacious, and thankfully well air-conditioned. Except for three 50-inch flat-screen TVs each showing a different Champion's League soccer game, Pat's Sports Bar looked like a relic from the 1960's when American soldiers fighting in Vietnam came to Bangkok for a little R&R. The tables were plastic that, once upon a time, was probably white. There were as many chairs with three legs as with four, and Sally was seriously tempted to demand somebody wipe them down before she would sit on one. The bar offered a choice of four kinds of beer, half a dozen whiskeys, and two generic vodkas. The establishment's only redeeming features were the two promotional girls in green Heineken mini-skirts and life-threateningly tight white t-shirts.

Seemingly unfazed by the rundown character of his surroundings, Nat walked over to Pat's lone customer. He was a white man who looked like all his 50+ years had been hard ones. The few hairs that remained on his head were pulled back into a greasy ponytail held together by a green rubber band. He had a scraggly mustache decorated with a few reminders of what Sally hoped was lunch, the alternatives being too disgusting to consider. He wore a Grateful Dead t-shirt and knee-length shorts that made his thin legs look bird-like. His horn-rimmed glasses were held together in two places with white adhesive tape. His pale skin showed all the signs of excessive exposure to the sun: wrinkles, moles, sagging. His nose had the prominent red veins of a habitual drinker. Yet he looked to be at peace with himself, and when he turned to wave at Nat, the smile on his face was warm and genuine.

"Officer Nattapong Kadesadayurat, as I live and wheeze."

"Hello, Marey" Nat said as he pulled up a chair.

"Mary – as in the girl's name?" a surprised Sally asked.

"No, Gorgeous. M-a-r-*e*-y, as in Your Mother's Worst Nightmare," the old man replied before a coughing fit bent him in half. "Someday I'm gonna give up the cigs. And do you know when that day is?"

"The day you fucking die?"

"The day I fucking die. Thank you, *Khun* Nat. It's good to know that someone around here is listening to me."

It was clear that Marey had a repertoire of badly overused lines and was thoroughly enjoying the all-too-rare opportunity to perform them in front of a new audience. While McLean was no fan of this particular show, he sensed that audience participation was critical if they hoped to get anything out of Marey.

"That accent sounds Australian."

"Too right, mate! And you sound like a bloody Pom."

"Guilty as charged," Ian replied.

"Nah, mate. That's us Aussies! Convicts to a man, we are."

Sally groaned, but Ian provided the hoped-for smile. Marey, meanwhile, was looking Thomas up and down in a way that made the young man feel distinctly uncomfortable and frighteningly exposed.

"First trip to Thailand?"

"How did you know?"

"Wool pants when it's nearly 40 fuckin' degrees Centigrade. Long sleeves. Pasty face that hasn't seen the sun – I'm thinking *ever*. A horrified expression when you look around the estimable Pat's Sports Bar. Yeah, you're a newbie alright."

That got a smile out of Sally, which Marey acknowledged with a wink that was just on the safe side of the line between friendly and lascivious. "So, *Khun* Nat, to what do I owe the honor of a Happy Hour visit?"

Nat took the hint, and ordered Marey another beer. "A man hates to drink alone," he said.

"I think we'll all have a beer," Ian said to the Heineken girl, winning a dazzling smile in return.

Sally checked her watch. It was 3:15.

Nat pulled out a picture of Nan, and put it on the table.

"Nice looking bird."

"Know her?"

"I may have seen her around from time to time, but I never took her out. With a face like that, I would have remembered." Marey picked up the picture and stared intently. "Might have managed a surreptitious squeeze of her love jugs when the mama-san wasn't looking, but that's as common as farting for a geezer like me."

Ian looked over at Sally, worried she was about to say something involving the words "sexist pig." Much to his amazement, she was grinning and shaking her head in amusement.

"Maybe you heard her name?" Nat suggested. "Kanokwan Supitayaporn, but she went by Nan."

Marey shook his head. Looked at the picture, and then at Nat. "Missing or dead?"

McLean folded his arms across his chest and looked hard at Marey's well-lined face. It would have been easy to dismiss him as just another ne'er-do-well who moved to Southeast Asia as an alternative to growing up. But Ian sensed that once you got past the tired jokes and pre-fab patter, there was a mind that missed very little and eyes that had seen quite a lot.

"Dead," he replied.

Marey nodded. "Where'd she work?"

"Lady Go Go."

The reaction was extremely subtle. But McLean had spent a life reading the body language of men asked questions they didn't want to answer, and he could feel in his bones that Marey's guard had just gone up.

"Is that significant?"

Marey turned to Nat, and locked eyes. Nat nodded. Marey said nothing, as if waiting for competing voices in his head to reach a decision. Finally he sniffed loudly, and signaled the prettier of the two promo girls to bring him another beer. "Lotta girls go missing from that place."

"Why is that?" Ian asked.

It was clearly not a story that Marey wanted to tell. "It's important, Marey," Ian assured him.

"Dead girls usually are. But you'll forgive me if I've got no desire to join her."

Nat started to give reassurances... but thought better of it and stopped talking. He leaned back in his seat and folded his arms behind his head. Marey beamed.

"You're learning, boy – you're learning. Your father – whichever drunken one night stand he might have been – would be proud."

Nat grinned. The detectives look baffled.

"Six months ago this whelp would have launched into a bullshit story about how he can protect me, even though we both know he can't. But he's wised up a bit, and now knows if you're going to yank on Old Marey's crank, it had better have a happy ending."

"And does it?" Ian asked while his three-legged plastic chair suddenly lurched to the right.

Marey didn't answer the question directly. "Does the budget stretch to a nice piece of steak with a mountain of fries on the side?"

Nat nodded.

"In that case I'll tell you everything I know, and a lot of shit I just made up. Right. The first thing you gotta understand is that girls disappear from Patpong all the bloody time. Most of these girls come from up north, where their best friend was a pig and a night out meant exactly that: sitting in a fucking field looking up at the stars and asking yourself if this is as good as it gets. Then they come to Bangkok and it scares the shit out of 'em. Everything's too fast, too loud, too expensive. The food's different. They haven't got a clue how to ride the bloody subway. They've never seen a *farang*, much less spoken with one. They're used to having a momma, not a mama-san, and they've never met a cop who expects a free handie on demand. It's fucking terrifying, mate. Some of 'em just can't take it and go home.

"Then there's that clause in their contracts – which, remarkably, no one ever reads – saying they've got to work on their backs. Almost all the girls are virgins when they get here, and those who aren't pretend otherwise. Now, for some reason Asian men are convinced sex with virgins cures what ails 'ya *and* gives you eternal life. For a while there most of 'em were convinced that sex with virgins could prevent – and possibly even cure – AIDS. So they're willing to pay top dollar for a little girl with her hymen still intact."

"How much are we talking," Sally asked, her eyes narrowed.

"Depends on the girl, but 40,000 baht isn't unheard of."

Thomas pulled out his iPhone, and banged on the glass. "Nearly £800," he announced.

"And what would a non-virgin go for?" Sally asked.

"1,500 to a resident *farang*, maybe 2,500 to a tourist who doesn't know the going rate."

"Do the girls get to keep the money?"

Marey smiled. "You know the answer to that one, don't you, gorgeous?"

"Who buys these girls?" Ian asked.

"Depends. Sometimes she's made available to a VIP customer" – Ian made a mental note – "but sometimes it's just an auction."

"Jesus Christ," Sally muttered.

"Don't think he's got a lot to do with it," Marey replied. "Anyhow, after that the real education begins. Walk into any bar a half hour before closing time, and you'll see there're still a lot of girls left. The funny thing is, it's not just the ugly chicks. You'd be amazed at some of the things men are into. Old chicks. Fat chicks. Nasty-looking chicks. Chicks with tats in weird places. Girls that look like butter wouldn't melt in their mouths, but are downright nasty once their clothes come off."

"Is there a point to this?" Sally asked in irritation.

"Just enjoying the diversity that is the human race." Marey said it with a straight face, but burst out laughing when he saw Sally's expression. "Yes, darling, there is. You'd think any woman willing to trade her body for money would have her choice of willing buyers, but it's just not so – especially in a place like Bangkok where there's so much competition. These girls have to learn how to get noticed, and then how to get noticed by the right sort of guy."

"Meaning?"

"Meaning there are sickos in this world that girls need to stay away from. Not as many as you'd think, but they exist. And there are a *lot* of guys who are into kinky stuff. If that's your thing, fine. But if it's not, you do *not* want to walk out of the bar with some guy who is. If you're lucky the worst that will happen is he gets mad and doesn't pay you. But if you're not lucky, well...."

"How does one tell what a potential customer is into?"

"How the hell should I know? I'm the guy all the girls are trying to avoid!" Marey laughed at his own joke, but Ian, Sally and Thomas all wondered if it didn't contain more than a grain of truth.

"The point is, these girls need to learn how to spot the weirdos. If they don't, and something bad happens, they're not going to get much sympathy from either management or their colleagues. Combine a frightening sexual experience with alienation from your co-workers, and running away seems like a smart career move.

"Then there's all the shit that goes on between the girls – and I'm telling you, it's *nasty*."

"Details, please," Sally requested in her "I-used-to-work-in-Vice" tone.

"Knew you'd be into that!" Marey drained about half his beer with obvious enjoyment. "Say a reasonably young, reasonably good-looking guy walks in with one of those watches on steroids that tells you he's both overpaid and a total wanker. The girls *live* for that sort of customer. And as soon as they spot one, the battle begins. A couple of girls will move to the front of the stage, and position themselves to block the view of the sexier, better-looking girl behind them. A few will trot out their patented moves: holding one leg straight up in the air is a perennial favorite. Some will start dirty dancing. Others will suddenly turn lesbian and put on a little show. But the ones with a bit of class and some experience will run their hands through their hair with their heads thrown back. That one always seems to work. It's sexy without being tawdry.

"Now, all that's happening on stage. You've also got girls on break. There's nothing to stop them from walking right up to Mr. Right and saying hello. Some of the more experienced girls don't waste time with subtlety and just plop themselves down on the guy's lap. I'm telling you: this is a blood sport."

Marey's steak arrived, and he looked at it with glee. He carved off a huge piece, popped it into his mouth, and closed his eyes with pleasure. Sally found herself wondering what he'd been before he devoted his life to propping up the bar.

After what seemed an eternity, Marey swallowed. He stared at the remaining steak with an expression best described as lust, considered his next move, sighed, then put down his knife and fork and returned to his story.

"As policemen and women you have seen the darker side of human nature. You will therefore have anticipated that when women start trying to top one another, things often turn ugly. I've seen some bar fights that could make millions on pay-per-view. The best I've ever seen ended with a wicked right cross, followed by a left slap, three kicks to the midsection, and a beer mug on the crown of the head. Great stuff.

"It's not always that physical, of course. There's lots of yelling and name-calling and saying shit about people to their faces as well as behind their backs. But when the same two girls clash repeatedly, it's only a matter of time before one of them tries to scratch the other's eyes out."

Ian turned to Sally. "I thought you were supposed to be the fairer sex."

Sally snorted. "Even you aren't that dumb."

"But all that is just the warm-up act," Marey said. "The real show begins when one girl takes another's customer."

"How does that happen?" Sally asked. "I thought it was always a free-for-all."

"In theory, yes. But go back to my example about the young, handsome rich guy. Let's add that he's decent in bed and an excellent tipper. When he comes into the bar a second time, the girl he took the first time feels she owns him. And if another girl tries to move in before he's spotted his first course? Knives come out."

"Literally?" McLean asked.

"Nah, mate. Just a figure of speech." The tenor of Marey's voice made it impossible to tell if he was kidding.

McLean decided it was now or never if he wanted to move the conversation from a primer on Bangkok bar life to something that might actually help them with this particular investigation. "I wasn't thinking that someone gets stabbed right then and there. But what if one girl made a habit out of stealing the other girls' men, to the point that it started costing the other girls a lot of money. That sort of thing could come to blows, couldn't it?"

Marey shrugged, doused a French fry with ketchup, and lowered it into his mouth. "Might do."

"Okay," McLean persisted. "Say it did. And now it's the entire bar against this one girl. Does she fight or flee?"

Marey took another bite of steak, which he savored as if he had never tasted anything so delicious. "Probably flee. But in all likelihood she goes no further than the bar two doors down."

For the first time since he made the introductions, Nat spoke. "But rivalries aren't the only thing that causes girls to leave. Tell them about the drugs."

"It'll probably surprise you to hear that Thailand is actually pretty strict about drugs." Marey finished his beer. "But that doesn't mean they can't be had if you know the right people."

"And these girls..." Sally began.

"Know the right people. Or maybe I should say the wrong ones." Marey sniffed. "No matter what you may think of it from a moral and legal perspective, hooking ain't an easy job. Sure, there are some girls who can't believe they're getting paid to do something they enjoy anyway, but they're maybe one in a hundred. For the other 99 it's like cleaning up pig shit back home: something to be endured.

"Some of the girls drink their way through it, but customers get pissed off when their slapper throws up on 'em. Worse still is when the girl passes out, giving the guy a chance to escape without paying. From what I hear, a lot of the girls think drugs are a better way to go."

"*Ya ba*?" Sally asked.

"Aren't you full of surprises?" Marey replied. "Yeah, that's a popular one. Anyhow, as you know, wherever there are drugs there are overdoses, some of them fatal. These days a lot of the *ya ba* comes in from Myanmar, and even God doesn't know what sort of crap they're putting in the pills. You might as well grab a random bottle of cleanser from under the sink and take your chances."

"But you're talking deaths rather than disappearances."

Marey gave McLean an admiring glance. "You're pretty sharp – for a bloody Pom. So let's talk about the disappearances. The girls have to pay for their habit, which is easy when they start out but it gets progressively harder as their intake increases and their willingness to put in an effort at the bar starts dropping. Eventually they owe their dealer more money than they can possibly pay, and drug dealers the world over are not known for being creative when it comes to restructuring debt."

The team from Scotland Yard smiled in unison.

"Some of the girls, the smarter ones, realize they are fucking their lives up big time, and they quit cold turkey."

"You mean they quit drugs?" Thomas asked.

"Drugs, the life, Bangkok. Sometimes they just take off, leaving everything behind except what they can fit in a suitcase or two."

"And where do they go?" Sally asked.

"Some go back home, which is usually upcountry. But many of them think they're damaged goods, and that their return would be an embarrassment to the family. Those girls just... disappear to God knows where.

"And then you've got my favorite variety of bar girl: the one who thinks even old farts like me have got piles of cash simply because we're foreign."

Sally looked at the old man sitting in front of her, stuffing his face with French fries like a six-year-old. "Don't take this the wrong way, Marey, but your appearance doesn't exactly scream 'money!'"

"Ah, that's where you're wrong, my pretty. The only *farang* who dress respectably in this town are newbies like young Thomas here, and the bloody Japanese. Everyone else looks like a sex criminal on a beach holiday – not least because some of them are."

"You're saying the girls know you can't judge a book by its cover?"

Marey nodded. "The randy old man trying to put his hand between your legs could be the former CEO of a global corporation on a seven-figure pension. And even if he's just a cog in someone else's machine, as long as he's from the West he's likely to be sitting on a bank balance that would go a long way toward luxury in this country."

"So some of the girls marry their way out of the business, is that what you're saying?" Thomas asked.

"Precisely, young man. And sorry I made that crack about your trousers. We lifers get our jollies out of mocking recent arrivals."

McLean's mouth smiled, but his eyes did not. "That's all very useful, Marey. It certainly helps us get a better feel for the world we're entering. But at the risk of sounding ungrateful, everything you told us applies equally to most or all of the bars in Patpong. But when we started this discussion you said – quote – 'a lot' of girls go missing from Lady Go Go, suggesting that particular bar has seen more than its fair share of sudden disappearances."

It was hard to tell in the subdued lighting of Pat's Sports Bar, but Ian was pretty sure Marey flinched.

"Just a figure of speech, mate. I've never done a tally to see which bar has the most girls taking off."

"Of course not." Ian's tone was friendly, but there was no mistaking the increase in pressure. "But is there something about Lady Go Go that would make it *more* likely to lose girls?"

Marey cut himself another piece of steak, and chewed it very, very slowly. It was all McLean could do to keep himself from laughing. Talkative guys *always* had the worst delaying tactics.

Finally Marey had no choice but to swallow the overly masticated meat. "It's a big place, so they've got more of everything. Plus more girls means more competition. And it's a tightly run ship, so girls can't get away with some of the crap that's ignored elsewhere."

"But no particular problem with drugs?"

"Not that I know of."

"And the mama-san isn't a lunatic or anything?"

To Ian's surprise, Marey laughed. "Dude, *all* mama-sans are lunatics."

"Why do you say that?" Thomas asked.

"'You'd have to be to do that job. You've got competitors trying to steal your best-looking girls. Customers trying to get the girls' phone numbers so they can arrange dates without paying the bar fine. Bartenders skimming from the register. Cops looking for payoffs. Thugs demanding protection money. Teenage girls from the countryside being forced to grow up in a real hurry and crying on your shoulder when they crack under the strain. And when you're not dealing with all that crap, you're trying to make a profit in a very competitive business. It takes a special type of insanity to sign up for that."

Nat signaled for the bill, indicating that he thought the interview was over. But McLean wasn't quite ready to leave.

"In that long list of horribles you mentioned the police," he noted, turning his body ever-so-slightly so that he didn't have to see the angry look Nat was sending his way.

"What about them?" Marey asked cautiously.

"In most places they come to some sort of an arrangement with the entertainment districts. Maybe they get to drink for free. Maybe they get something else for free on their birthday. In exchange they make sure the club doesn't get hassled, and they respond quickly if trouble breaks out. Does the same sort of thing happen here?"

Marey swallowed hard. "Not really my area. But like you say, it happens everywhere so I suppose it happens here, too."

"But you can tell if someone is a cop, right? You ever see them in the bars, maybe throwing their weight around a little bit?"

"I'm usually too focused on the girls to worry about stuff like that."

Ian nodded as though Marey had said something profound.

CHAPTER 22

The room's three phones rang at once: on the desk, next to the bed, and in the toilet. It took Nan a moment to decide which one to answer.

"Hi! It's me. Brian. I'm really sorry about this, but I have to go out to dinner with the client. I'll try to get back early, but you never know with these things. Just order yourself some room service, watch TV, get a massage if you feel like it. I'll be back as soon as I can."

"You no come back?"

"No, I will. But not for a couple of hours."

"You work?"

"Yes, work. Then dinner with the client. We have a lot of business to discuss."

"No go Patpong?"

"I don't think so. I mean, we might hit a bar or two. It depends on what the client wants to do."

There was a long silence.

"But maybe you go Patpong, get girl?"

"I can't promise you we won't go to Patpong. Like I said, it's all up to the client. They're in charge. It's work."

"Nan work too."

Jesus. Not this again. "Anyhow, I've got to run. I'll be back as soon as I can." And with that, he hung up.

"Trouble at home, squire?" Greg asked with a knowing smile.

Brian groaned. "I thought it would be easier this way. Have her meet me at the airport, and then check into the hotel together. That way she's around…"

"…whenever you're ready for her."

"Exactly."

"And what about when she's ready for you?"

"What's that supposed to mean?"

"It means she's a woman, not a dog. Like you, she's willing to put up with some shit in order to make a living. Unlike you, she has to put up with a lot of shit in order to make a not-very-good living. But that doesn't mean she has to like it."

"You make it sound like she's my girlfriend."

"Isn't she?"

"Of course not! She's just a bar girl."

"But she's not *in* the bar, is she? She's in your hotel room, waiting for you to come home. Now tell me: what does that sound like?"

Brian couldn't think of a suitable answer, despite continuing to ponder the question throughout dinner. And then for two painful hours of karaoke at a high-end membership club, the exterior of which bore a striking resemblance to the White House.

It was nearly 1 A.M. when he finally walked through the huge doors of the Four Seasons and headed up to his room. He was 90% convinced co-habitation had been a mistake, a step too far too soon. Maybe the best thing would be a sort of compromise: Nan could go to the bar as usual, talk to her friends, sit with a few customers, make a commission on her lady drinks. The one thing she *couldn't* do was walk out of the bar with anyone but him.

As he got out of the elevator he realized that in his eagerness to escape from Nan's accusations that morning he'd forgotten to take his room key. His first thought was to go down to the front desk and get another, but that would be a waste of time if Nan were still awake. He knocked gently on the door.

The response that came back, in Thai, was anything but gentle.

"It's me, Nan. Sorry I'm late."

He heard footsteps, and then the sound of the door being opened just far enough for her to stick her head through.

"You go Patpong?"

"No! I went to karaoke with the client."

"You get girl?"

"What? No, I didn't get a girl. What sort of a guy do you think I am?"

Nan's hand shot out and grabbed him between the legs. Expertly she ran her hand up and down, softly, until she felt him harden. Then she smiled and threw the door wide open.

Brian started into the room, then froze in his tracks. Nan was wearing a cream-colored corset that laced up the back – and nothing else. It took his breath away.

"I waiting you," she said, as she led the way to the bed.

CHAPTER 23

The detectives thanked Nat for the very useful introduction, said they would fend for themselves for dinner, and headed back to the Four Seasons in a taxi.

"Well, that was weird," Sally opined. "Marey was certainly interesting, but I don't think he told us anything Nat couldn't have."

"Maybe Nat doesn't think we trust him," Thomas suggested.

"We don't, so he gets full marks for perceptiveness."

"How much of Marey's speech do you think he prepared in advance?"

Ian turned his back to the car door so he could see Thomas while he spoke. "Based on content I would have said all of it, but there wasn't enough time to set it up."

"Unless Nat did that yesterday," Sally said. "In which case, nice job manipulating our conversation until we were exactly where he wanted us." She paused for a few beats. "What was with your last question, the one about the police? Just trying to stir the pot?"

"Maybe a little. What I really wanted to see was whether he'd admit to something that is almost certainly true but wouldn't look good for Nat."

"And he didn't," Thomas pointed out.

"That might be a bit harsh. He ducked."

Sally grunted. "Meaning what?"

"Meaning that old Marey has a scruple or two. He's willing to evade a tricky question but not tell a flat-out lie."

"That doesn't mean he's got a conscience, just that he knows better than to start telling porkie pies to an audience of cops."

"You could be right."

Sally's head snapped in surprise. "You never give in this easy on anything. If there's something on your mind, spit it out."

McLean smiled. "And I thought my poker face was one of my most admirable qualities. I was actually thinking about what you two were saying: what was Nat's motivation in setting up this meeting? I think there's one other possibility we haven't considered."

"Do tell."

"There are things Nat wanted us to hear, but he needed plausible deniability if the shit ever hit the fan."

Sally leaned back against the headrest and considered the implications. "You're saying it's possible that Nat is trying to do the right thing, but in a way that doesn't get him fired. Or killed."

McLean nodded.

"And that means he's worried about the people he reports to."

"It does."

"Senior police officials."

"Exactly."

"So our little Nat is treading the fine line between the devil and the deep blue sea, sending out coded messages in hopes we'll be able to solve the case without too much input from him."

"That's the theory."

"Do you believe it?"

"You first."

"Let me respond by quoting that legendary detective inspector, Ian McLean. Inspector McLean – 'Mackers' to his friends – was fond of asking one question: What would we need to believe in order for that to be true? In this particular case, we would need to believe that Nat is a lot smarter and more politically astute than his youth and inexperience would suggest is probable."

"And is that believable?"

Sally looked to Thomas to take the first swing. "It's *conceivable*, though it hardly seems likely. His disappearing acts the past two days struck me as somewhat immature."

Both Ian and Sally burst out laughing.

"You asked." Thomas said the line as a throwaway, but it failed to hide the hurt.

"For the sake of argument, let's say Nat is trying to do the right thing. The question then becomes: when did he start trying? Did he walk in on Day One thinking this was a straightforward death by natural causes – only to discover that he'd been lied to by his own people?"

Sally took her time before her replying. "I think that's more likely than the possibility he's been stage-managing this thing from the start."

"Because?"

"Didn't you see that first presentation? He was just ticking off the boxes."

Traffic had ground to a halt. "Next time we go by bicycle," Sally grumped.

Thomas pulled out his phone, and checked Google Maps. "We could walk it in about 25 minutes."

Sally shook her head. "Inside is air-conditioning. Outside is a steam room. I ain't moving."

Ian said nothing.

"Still alive there, guv?" Thomas asked.

"Mmm. Just thinking."

"About what?"

McLean grabbed the handle above the door, and pulled himself upright. "I'm still bothered by the fact that nobody in Patpong admits to knowing Nan, even though first Walsh and then Marey confirmed she worked there."

"I thought we agreed the *demi monde* wasn't overly fond of cops."

"Exactly."

"Exactly what?" Sally asked.

"First the Thais went in, asking the same question of everyone they saw. That marked them as cops. Then we go in, and before we've even finished our first drink we start asking about the same dead girl at the place she used to work. We might as well have stuck our warrant cards on our foreheads."

"Have you got an alternative?"

McLean's devilish smile filled the back of the cab. "I most certainly do."

"Go on."

"Thomas goes in..."

The young detective cut his boss off mid-sentence. "But the mama-san already knows I'm a cop!"

"Thomas goes in, by himself, as a customer. Has a few drinks. Chooses a girl. Pays her bar fine. Takes her to a hotel where no one can see her, and there he..."

This time Sally provided the interruption. "He bangs her senseless!"

"For queen and country," McLean agreed.

Thomas was stunned. The color drained from his face.

"*Or*, McLean continued, to Thomas' extreme relief, "he asks about Nan. With money on the table."

Sally crossed her arms and hugged herself. "I dunno, boss. I get what you're thinking, and I'll admit it's clever. But what happens if something goes wrong? What happens if Nat has still got a tail on us, and when they see where he's heading, they send some uniforms to knock down the door and bust him for solicitation? We'd have no choice but to get on a plane and go home. And Thomas' career – not to mention his reputation – might not survive the fallout."

"I'll do it."

"There *are* risks," Ian admitted. "But remember what we've been hearing all along. These girls are doing something they don't want to do because they need the money. This is no different, except instead of buying sex we're buying information. Unless Nat's managed to have every room in every short-stay hotel in Bangkok bugged, there's no way anyone will ever find out what she tells us. It's a safe environment for a straightforward business transaction."

"I'll do it."

"Under normal circumstances you might be right. But if the Thai police are looking for a stick to beat us with, this hands them a goddamn log."

"I said I'll do it!"

Brian Cahill walked through the sun-drenched corridors of Suvarnabhumi Airport feeling like a free man. Having learned a valuable lesson from his previous trip, the only person waiting for him in the Arrivals Hall was the unfailingly cheerful driver from the Four Seasons Hotel. Nan was lined up for the weekend, starting with a 9 P.M. flight to Phuket on Friday. If he got lonely before that, he could always pay an unannounced visit to Lady Go Go or any of its many competitors in Patpong. In fact, a little variety might be nice. Might find someone even hotter than Nan.

During dinner with Greg and Andrew at the Seafood Market, Andrew made clear he wasn't buying it. "So let me get this straight. You're finished playing house. Now you're free as a bird, eager to sample widely from the buffet that is Bangkok."

Brian calmly liberated the meat from a very large prawn. "That's it exactly."

"Good thing you got a job in banking, because if you were an actor you'd starve."

Brian washed down the shellfish with a surprisingly nice Chenin Blanc from a winery two hours north of Bangkok. "I'm not sure which of the voices in your head is telling you that you can see into the depths of my soul, but it's lying to you."

Andrew put down his fork and spoon, relishing the challenge. "Then tell me this: If you're such a free spirit, why have you booked a weekend at the Aman Phuket with Nan's name on one of the tickets?"

"Greg, care to comment on that one?" Brian asked with a surprisingly sharp tone.

"I mentioned it in passing when we were talking about schedules. Andrew suggested we take the client to dinner Friday night and I told him you weren't going to be around. I didn't realize that it was meant to be secret."

"It wasn't. But there was no need to mention Nan."

"Sor-ry. But come on, Brian: Last time you were here the two of you shacked up in the Four Seasons like newlyweds. It didn't seem like you were trying to be discreet then."

Andrew smelled blood. "What happened? You couldn't satisfy her sexually? She snores? *You* snore? You couldn't agree which religion to raise the kids? Don't make us beg; Daddy wants details!"

"Then Daddy is going to be severely disappointed." Brian looked up from his plate and realized he was investing the situation with an unnecessary and uncomfortable level of seriousness. "Look, guys. We had a great time together the last time I was in town. But you may remember we were really busy with the Thai Tuna presentation, and she ended up sitting by herself in the hotel most of the time. I figured everyone would be happier if we kept our... *thing* to the weekends."

Greg was ready to let the matter rest, but that was not Andrew's style. "So you two are still an item – Friday through Sunday at least."

Brian saw an escape route. "But this is Wednesday, so none of that matters. What are we going to do after dinner?"

"Hallelujah! The prodigal son has returned!" Andrew shouted, causing the surrounding tables to stare at him disapprovingly. "And this time it's... well, not the least bit personal. More of a rape and pillage sort of thing. But it shall be legend! Where we gonna go?"

"I'm going home," Greg said, "which I'm sure will be a surprise to neither of you. But I'll take a taxi so you've got my car and driver, provided you agree to send him home by 7 A.M. so he can pick me up for work."

Brian turned to Andrew. "Your call, mate."

"Unlike you, my friend, I am nothing if not loyal. There is only one girl for me, and her name is Lady Go Go."

It was nearly 9:30 by the time Greg's driver dropped them off at the entrance to Patpong. The market was packed, as always, with bargain hunters gingerly stepping over puddles of water in the unevenly paved streets. Smells of chili, overused cooking oil, car exhaust, sweat and fermenting garbage combined forces into an olfactory assault that left the head spinning. Street urchins weaved their way in and out of the shoppers, their nimble fingers looking for an open purse or exposed wallet. A shoeless woman sat on the stairs to the pedestrian overpass, holding a dirty baby in one hand and a paper begging cup in the other. Young men carrying piles of fake shirts in cheap plastic bags worked their way between the stands, moving inventory to wherever customers happened to be at the moment. It was chaotic, oppressive, overwhelming, and pulsating with life.

Brian and Andrew had to fight their way through a group of unnaturally chipper men and women all wearing identical lime green polo shirts with the slogan "Building Excellence 2013" on the back. "Nothing brings people together like a trip to a whorehouse," Brian said as he shook his head in bemusement.

Andrew didn't bother responding. Or waiting for Brian to catch up. He forced his way through the crowd and past the curtain at the entrance to Lady Go Go. He gave his eyes a minute to adjust to the darkness, then walked straight over to the stage to review his options.

Brian tried to find Nan, but the bar was dark and very crowded. He thought about a walk-through, but after getting bumped three times in 10 feet by what looked to be a rugby team several hours into an highly competitive drinking session, he decided it would be easier simply to ask for her.

"Can I get a Singha beer and number 32, please?"

The waiter shook his head. "No free."

"You mean she's not here at the moment?"

"No free. Pick different girl."

Brian's attempts to decipher the underlying message were interrupted by Andrew's arrival. "Thanks for deserting me like that. I will remember your disappearing loyalties once the tables have turned."

"Admit it: it took five minutes before you even noticed I wasn't behind you."

Andrew laughed. "I was engaged in serious study of the local culture." He pointed at Brian's beer, and then at his own chest – hoping the simple gestures made his order clear. "So, where's the lovely Nan?"

"Good question. The waiter kept saying she's not free, but I don't really know what that means."

And then he did. Nan was walking out of the bar, holding hands with a man who must have been at least 60. Without thinking, Brian jumped out of his seat and ran after her.

"Nan! Hang on! It's me, Brian."

She turned towards him with an expression that conveyed surprise, confusion and anger in equal measures. Then she turned away.

"What? Where are you going? I just want to talk to you for a second."

He got the old man instead. "Sorry, but she's spoken for."

The words hit Brian like a punch in the gut. "Nan, listen, I was going to call you, but things got really busy at the office. We're still on for Friday, right?"

Nan stood silently, glaring.

The old man grinned. "You heard her. She and I got better things to do."

"Her name is 'Nan.' Not 'she.' Nan."

"Right, mate. Whatever. Now bugger off and let me rock her world."

Brian stood there silently as Nan walked out, her hand now clutching the old man's elbow as if she were afraid he'd fall if she let go. Brian stumbled blindly back to his table. Andrew was sitting between two girls, both of whom had their hands on his inner thighs. Without saying a word, Brian picked up his drink, drained it, threw a few bills on the table, and walked out.

Andrew turned to the girl on his right. "*Farang*, eh? They can act like such children sometimes. That's why you were lucky to be chosen by a real man like me."

The next morning the two men met for breakfast, as always, at 8 A.M. They walked to their table in silence. Brian ordered an espresso for himself and a latte for Andrew, and then turned away to dismiss the waiter. "I do not want to talk about it. No cracks. Nothing. Everything to do with Nan and last night is a No Go Zone."

Andrew thought about making a joke, and realized that it was a very bad idea. "Whatever you want, my friend."

"Good. Let's get something to eat. I'm starving."

That was either a lie, or a severe misreading of his hunger levels. Although Brian piled his plate high with eggs and chicken sausage and smoked salmon and mind-numbingly fresh fruit, he ended up consuming just half a *pain au chocolat* and most of his coffee. Everything else remained on the plate, untouched.

At the office Brian thought he did a passable job of appearing normal, smiling whenever the tea lady brought food or drinks to the conference room that was serving as Mission Control. He even managed to be chatty on an extended conference call with the client. But inside and alone with Andrew he remained nearly as furious as he had been last night, repeating the words "that bitch" so many times they became a mantra.

It was close to 8 P.M. when Andrew shut his laptop. "I'm knackered and hungry enough to eat a horse, provided it comes in a green curry. What do you want to do for dinner?"

He expected Brian to beg off and was therefore surprised by his answer. "I'm in the mood to drink. Let's go to one of those places where you can sit out in the garden, have a couple of curries and an excessive amount of beer. Greg, you must know somewhere that fits the bill."

"Indeed I do," said Greg, even though he'd been hoping to leave the visitors on their own tonight. I'll give them a call from the car."

The restaurant was down one of Bangkok's many dimly lit side streets that were as much pothole as pavement. The garden was draped with fairy lights, giving it a Christmas-y feel despite the fact Brian started sweating the instant he stepped out of the car. There was an extensive menu – complete with photographs – but Greg recommended they choose from the fresh fish, meat and vegetables piled up on beds of ice around two huge barbecue grills. "You guys go ahead, and order whatever looks good. I'll be in charge of the drinks."

Despite having said that he was in the mood for beer, Brian quickly ordered three Johnnie Walker Black Label and sodas – "blaak sodaaah" as the locals called it. When the drinks arrived he pronounced them too weak and requested a bottle. He added as much whisky as the glasses would hold, and started knocking them back as if the drinks were no stronger than water.

He had finished two and was about to start the third when Greg and Andrew returned. Greg looked at Brian with concern. "Should I get them to bring us something quick – like fish cakes or noodles – just to coat your stomach?"

"I *know* how to drink."

"Of course you do. Just offering."

Greg and Andrew exchanged looks, and Greg shrugged in resignation.

Brian said very little throughout dinner, leaving his colleagues to share a meandering conversation filled with long pauses and worried looks in Brian's direction. While a huge amount of food had been ordered, only a fraction of it got eaten. After 20 minutes during which no one even picked at the lobster, grilled pork, squid, chicken curry, stir-fried vegetables or pineapple rice, Greg declared the meal to be over.

Two bottles of Johnnie Walker lay on their sides like dead soldiers, their contents completely drained.

Brian had to be carried to the car.

CHAPTER 25

Ian and Sally wished Thomas good luck and insisted he "*not* have a good time."

"This is work, you know," he said somewhat testily.

"Make sure it stays that way," Sally said. "Four feet on the floor at all times. And if she tries to do something yucky like kissing you on the lips, call and we'll send in a rescue team."

"How delightfully droll. What are you two going to get up to while I'm working undercover – and before you make a crack, Sally, I said 'undercover', not 'under the covers'?"

"Ian offered to take me somewhere very beautiful and expensive."

"I did?"

"Well, not out loud, perhaps, but I know you were thinking it."

Thomas bid them farewell, and Ian and Sally started walking down Rajadamri Road. They ended up at a Chinese-influenced seafood restaurant recommended by the hotel. At the waiter's near-insistence they ordered grilled *pla kapong*, a type of Asian sea bass. Filling out the meal were a spicy beef salad, morning glory stir-fried with garlic, and rice noodles with shrimp. Ian tried to order beer, but was overruled by the shockingly confident waiter.

"In Thailand drink whisky soda. Mekong."

"I have no idea what that is, but fine. Two of those, please."

The water smiled radiantly, and then rushed their order to the kitchen.

"I thought Mekong was a river," Sally said.

"Maybe that's where they get the water for the whisky. Or the soda. Perhaps both."

The waiter magically reappeared at their table, presenting what looked like a hip flask with an indecipherable Thai label more suggestive of obscure Oriental herbal medicine than a 40-proof beverage. Sally unscrewed the cap, took a sniff, and made a pained face. "Christ. Smells like they brought you paint thinner by mistake."

"No drink from bottle," the waiter insisted. "Soda."

"Make mine a full glass of soda with just a dusting of that crap, please," Sally instructed Ian. But when she took a sip, she had to admit it wasn't quite as bad as she expected.

McLean was next. "It's a bit harsh, but I guess that helps it stand up to the heat of the chilies. A smoother whisky would be overpowered."

"The Russian army couldn't overpower this stuff," Sally said as she took a second, equally minuscule sip.

But when the food came, Sally realized that Ian was right. The mixture was a bit too potent for the simple grilled fish, but with spicier dishes like the beef salad the combination seemed just about perfect.

"I'm not going to be taking any of this river water home with me," Sally clarified, "but I will admit it isn't as revolting as I initially thought."

"We aim to please," Ian replied.

"About that," Sally said with sudden seriousness. "What is it with you guys?"

"Could you be just a little more specific?"

"I don't understand this whole fascination with hookers. I mean, you *know* what she does for a living. You *know* hundreds of guys have been there before you – maybe even just a few minutes earlier. You *know* it's all about the money and any sweet nothings she whispers in your ear are coming off a script. What's sexy about that?"

"Well, I'm a happily married man, so I can't speak from personal experience." Sally ignored the gaping hole in Ian's logic. "But my guess is evolution is to blame."

"You're pinning this on Charles Darwin?"

Ian smiled and had another bite of the beef. It was perfectly cooked: slightly charred on the outside, medium rare on the inside. Combined with the coolness of the cucumbers and the heat of the ubiquitous red chilies, the dish was delicious and memorable and addictive. "We're programmed to propagate the species. So when we see a... potential partner in propagation, our hormones take over from our brains."

"Which implies that you have some – brains, that is. I tend to doubt that, given your apparent inability to comprehend the difference between a potential mother for your children and a hooker who – with luck – you'll never see again."

"I'm not defending it; I'm just explaining it."

"I mean, look at Thomas. He couldn't wait to head over to Lady Go Go tonight."

McLean took another generous serving of the beef salad. "You're being unfair. It's not often he gets to fly solo in an investigation, and I think he's eager to prove himself up to the task."

"So he'd be equally chuffed about, say, going to the Public Records Office and searching for mortgage information – as long as we let him go by himself?"

"Fine. I grant you this is a more exciting assignment than most, and he's undoubtedly looking forward to taking a short walk on the wild side. But I don't see that as evidence of the failure of men as a species."

"Men are a sex."

Ian simply frowned.

"Talk to me, Ian. I'm not trying to beat you up or embarrass you or anything. I really am trying to understand."

"Well let's switch the shoe to the other foot for a second. What goes through your mind when you watch the Chippendales guys or someone invites a male stripper to a hen night?"

"I appreciate the beauty that gyrates before me, thank the Lord for giving them such great bodies, and wish that at least one of them was straight."

McLean frowned. "You're not getting off that easy. If they weren't gay, and you had the opportunity to sleep with one of them – for money – would you do it?"

"Depends on how much they paid me."

Despite himself, Ian laughed. "Still waiting for an honest response."

"Do I get turned on? Maybe a little bit. Do I think about what it might be like to hang onto a body like that for an evening? Sure. Despite rumors to the contrary, I'm human. But would I pay money to have sex with someone who does it for a living? Absolutely not."

"Why not?"

"It's just... icky. And that's why I can't understand why you guys are so into it."

"Who said I am?"

Sally's eyebrows paid a visit to her hairline. "Ian. I saw you at Lady Go Go last night. You were staring at those girls so hard I thought you were going to get a cerebral aneurysm."

"That's worryingly specific. But be reasonable. I'd never seen anything like that before."

"You should have worked Vice."

"If I'd known that's what it's like, I would have."

Sally took a small chunk of pineapple out of the fried rice and threw it at her boss. "But you know what I'm saying, right? When you look at those girls, is your mind going through the same" – Sally waved her right hand as if skimming through words until she found the right one – "*processes* as when you see someone attractive at the Yard?"

"There's no one attractive at the Yard."

"Present company excepted, I'm sure" Sally said as she batted her impossibly long eyelashes.

"Of course."

"Let the record show you repeatedly dodged my question." Sally helped herself to the remains of the fish. "So let me ask you a different one. Do you think guys ever fall for those girls? You know, it starts off being about raging hormones and somehow turns to love?"

Ian shrugged. "I'm sure it happens. Maybe not love in the way we normally think about it, with flowers and chocolates and poems and so on."

"Poems?"

"So I'm told." Ian refreshed their drinks. "Anyhow, I guess I'm saying that maybe love doesn't always come before sex. Maybe the other way around is just as good."

"Spoken like a man."

"As it should be. But you're not seriously telling me you've never slept with a man you weren't already romantically involved with?"

Sally developed a sudden interest in the contents of her fried rice. "I might not go that far. But we seem to have strayed off topic. I'm saying that it's different when there's money involved."

McLean knew he should leave it there, but he couldn't help himself. "But isn't money *always* involved? Sure, some times it's hidden behind an expensive dinner or a present when it's not your birthday. But isn't the objective the same?"

"So now you're *defending* prostitution?"

"I don't think so. I'm just saying that their world and ours are not really all that far apart." Ian scraped what was left of the beef salad onto his plate. The dish was painfully hot, but the instant his mouth cooled from one bite he was eager for another. "Why did you bring this up? Are you worried Thomas is going to... you know... go beyond the call of duty?"

"Do I think Thomas is screwing his brains out when the only thing he should be mounting is a gentle interrogation? No, I do not. Do I think he might want to? Yes, I think that's a distinct possibility. And that's the bit I was trying to understand."

"So what bothers you the most? The money, the number of partners, or the fact it's all with strangers?"

"Hunh. When you put it that way, I'm not actually sure." Sally leaned back in her chair and interlaced her fingers behind her head. "The more I think about it, the more I think it's *not* the money. I mean, if men are stupid enough to pay you, you'd have to be stupid not to take it."

"You don't think that's demeaning?"

"Of course I think it's demeaning, but so is appearing on *Britain's Got Talent.* No, I think what bothers me most is seeing what it does to these girls. They start every evening with men telling them how beautiful they are. An hour or two later they're lying on a filthy bed somewhere while the guy hurriedly zips up his pants and heads the hell home just as quickly as he can. That's got to mess with your sense of self-worth."

"You saw a bit of that in Vice, I'll wager."

Sally nodded sadly. "Yeah. Throw in a substance-abuse problem as a kicker, and it gets really messed up."

"Does anyone ever get out of that world intact?"

Sally started picking the best bits out of the fried rice with her fingers. "Surprisingly, yes. Not many, but some. But even hookers who come across as centered and sensible are actually very, very fragile. A few things go the wrong way and they're standing in front of the bathroom mirror with a razor blade poised above their wrists."

"Do you think that's what happened to Nan?"

Sally took her time before replying. "Could be. But there's another possibility. You'd be amazed how many of these girls still believe there's a Prince Charming out there waiting just for them."

"Despite all the evidence to the contrary?"

"It's illogical, I know. But it's real. These hard, hard women suddenly fall like a little schoolgirl. And when they find out their prince is actually an accountant from Manchester with two kids and a Volvo, they're crushed. They take everything reality can dish out, but when their dreams are destroyed, so are they."

McLean let that thought wander around his brain for a bit. "Men whose hormones do their thinking for them. Women who still believe in fairy tales. Throw in sex, money and drugs, and it's hard to see the story ending in anything but tragedy."

CHAPTER 26

Thursday night Brian had a room service dinner while working his way through the more than 350 emails that had piled up while he focused on the Thai project. Friday's meetings went well, and as Greg's driver took him to the Don Muang domestic airport he felt reasonably at peace with the world.

His sense of serenity was quickly shattered when he got to the agreed meeting point and Nan was nowhere to be seen. "That stupid bitch," he said under his breath. "If she wasn't going to show she could have just called."

No sooner were the words out of his mouth than he realized they might not be fair. The few times they had spoken on the phone it had always been him who did the dialing. Maybe she didn't know how to make an international call?

Then she should have asked someone. Or looked it up on the internet. She's not stupid, is she?

Is she? Brian wasn't exactly sure. Very little of their time together had been spent in conversation, and even that was colored by her limited understanding of English. For all he knew she could be brilliant in her native tongue, well versed in culture, history and politics.

Or she could be thick as a plank. He just didn't know.

And that was what finally brought home the stark reality of what he was doing. He was about to spend yet another weekend with a girl he still barely knew, a girl who – the last time he'd seen her – was walking away on the arm of a man old enough to be her father. Maybe even her grandfather. A man she was with simply because he was paying her. How idiotic was that?

Then again, easy for him to judge. Maybe she really needed the money. After all, no one becomes a whore because they like the work. Poor kid.

Then why didn't she just ask him for money? His salary bordered on the ridiculous, plus he would inherit a country estate and three smaller houses once dear old dad left to rejoin his maker. A sum of money that meant nothing to him was probably enough to live a life of luxury in Thailand, particularly if Nan went back to her home in the rice fields, far from the costly temptations of Bangkok.

What if she asked him? Would he give her money? No questions asked? No stipulations made?

The internal debate was raging so fiercely he didn't notice that Nan had arrived and was standing in front of him, a small wheeled bag to her right. When he finally did see her, she brought her hands together in a perfunctory *wai*. Brian couldn't decide if he was pleased to see her, relieved, or still angry about Wednesday night. And so he said nothing.

After an awkward period of silence, Nan grabbed her bag and headed towards the check-in counter. 15 minutes later they were sitting in the Bangkok Air lounge, facing one another, still silent. Ultimately it was the ridiculousness of their face-off that forced Brian to speak.

"I wasn't sure you were coming."

Nan looked slightly offended. "You say. I come."

"I know. But with the other night...."

"Why you care?"

"Why do I care? Because... because you were with another man."

"No mind. You with other girl."

"No I wasn't! I went straight back to the hotel."

"Not Thailand. Your country. You have girl your country. Customer tell me."

"How would he know? I never met the man."

Nan was unmoved. "He say young man, rich man, always have girlfriend. No need Thai girl."

Brian rolled his eyes. "Fine. You want to know the truth? I'll tell you the truth. Yes, I have a girlfriend. But we've been together for several years. That's a relationship. It's... different."

"No different. You butterfly."

"Butterfly?"

"Butterfly."

"I don't know what that means."

"Butterfly fly from girl to girl. No care. Just...." Nan made an obscene gesture.

"I can't believe you'd say that to me after I saw you with a man old enough to be your father."

"No choice. Must work."

And there it was. He had chosen to go away for the weekend with a prostitute while his almost-fiancée sat at home in London none the wiser. Nan, on the other hand, was just doing her job. Who had the moral upper hand in this scenario?

"You're right, Nan. I'm sorry. Can we start over?"

Nan said nothing, but Brian sensed that was because she wasn't entirely sure of what he said – or meant. "Forget before. Start now. Hello, Nan! It's good to see you."

She smiled. And suddenly all of the moral questions were completely irrelevant.

CHAPTER 27

Thomas' stomach was doing somersaults. At first he thought it was the vague air of menace that hung over Patpong market. It was a giant, open-air trademark infringement, one that couldn't exist without both the criminals who pirated the goods and the police who looked the other way.

Then he thought he was nervous about being seen by someone from home. It would have been different if he were with a group of friends, but going into a girlie bar on your own earned him far too many Possibly a Pervert Points.

After exhausting all the other possibilities, Thomas realized he was excited. He'd never been with a prostitute, much less in a foreign country. And while technically that might continue to be the case even after tonight – depending on your definition of "with" – at least he'd have a story he could tell his mates for years to come.

Provided they didn't ask too many questions about how the evening ended.

Bugger that. He could make up any ending he chose. This was more an exercise in creative writing than sexual adventurism.

As he neared the entrance to Lady Go Go two girls grabbed him and tried to guide him to another club.

"Thanks, but I'm going to Lady Go Go."

"Go Go no good! You come Pussy Galore. Many girls! Beautiful girls!"

"I'm sure there are. They are. And you're both very beautiful." Giggles. "But I have a friend waiting at Lady Go Go."

"Your friend girl?"

Thomas had to think quickly. "Um, yes."

The girl on his right swung around so she was facing him. "She have nice body like me?" And with that she pulled open her robe, revealing all she had on were bikini bottoms.

Thomas had never found it so difficult to swallow. "Well, that certainly is a very nice body. I'd like to see more of it – I mean, more of *you*. But I can't tonight. Maybe another night."

"Noooo," the girls said in unison. "You just talking. You no come back."

"I will, I promise!"

The second girl pushed herself against Thomas' body, and whispered in his ear. "You like two girl? Thai sandwich? We very good. Do everything. You watch. You play. All okay."

Thomas knew he had to escape. He pushed his way towards Go Go, with one girl holding onto each arm. "I promise I'll be back. But I have to go to Go Go. I have an appointment. With my friend."

The girls giggled again, said something in Thai that Thomas assumed was not a compliment, and gave him his freedom. By the time he looked up they were already closing in on another target.

With a little regret over the path not taken, Thomas went into Lady Go Go and was immediately seated by one of the seemingly omnipresent waiters.

"Drink?"

"Yes, of course. Sure. I'll have a beer please."

"Singha."

"Excuse me?"

"Singha beer ok?"

"Um, yes. I guess so. Also, I'd like to have a girl join me."

"What number?"

"I don't know which number. I'm looking for a girl who speaks English fluently."

"What name?"

"I don't know. I haven't met her yet."

"You show me."

"Forget it. Sorry."

"No girl?"

"No girl, just the beer please."

While he waited for his beer Thomas wondered how he could determine a girl's English fluency based solely on the meagerness of her bikini. Finally he had a brainstorm: pick one, and use her to work his way up the ladder to someone capable of carrying her end of a conversation.

He later told Ian he chose #112 "pretty much at random," but that was a lie. Thomas had a thing for Asian women with long hair, an athletic body, big eyes, and a rather severe look. As #112 climbed down off the stage, gathered her hairbrush and cigarettes and made her way to Thomas' table, he had a moment of panic when he realized he had just requested a Thai Sally.

Fortunately he didn't need to spend much time thinking about the implications of that revelation, as the girl he chose was now standing right in front of him.

Thomas stood and held out his hand. "Hi, I'm Thomas," he said far too loudly. "What's your name?"

#112 took his hand, held it, and said not a word.

"Okay, then. Would you like a drink?" The girl turned to the waiter, said something in Thai, and resumed holding Thomas' hand. He was never going to climb the ladder to English fluency if he couldn't even get onto the first rung.

Thomas sat, which proved to be rather tricky with a standing girl still attached to his right hand. This is hopeless, he thought. He signaled for a waiter. "Can I see the mama-san please?"

The young man – he looked to be not a day older than 15 – said nothing, but Thomas saw him go directly to a woman who stood behind the counter, laughing with her cashier. Thomas could see the waiter pointing in his direction. He wanted to wave in acknowledgement, but his right hand remained a captive and his left was holding a drink, so he sat there quietly – hoping against hope the mama-san didn't remember him from the other night.

No such luck. Mama made her way to Thomas' table, skipped the greeting, and went straight for the jugular. "You come here before."

"Yes, I was here the other night with my colleagues."

"You don't take girl. Just ask questions."

"Well yes, that night we were working. But tonight it's just me, and I want to have fun!"

"So you take girl?" Mama pointed at #112.

"Yes, but not her."

Mama did not look pleased.

"I mean, she's very beautiful. Gorgeous, actually. But she doesn't speak any English."

"So you more questions?"

"What? No, no. Like I said, I'm here to have fun. But I want to be able to talk to the girl. That makes sense, right?"

Mama looked at him as if she could see clear through his soul and right into his insecurities, lies, and perversions. Perhaps on a busier night she would have sent him packing. But after a look around the half-full bar she nodded decisively.

"She good English."

Thomas followed Mama's index finger to a woman halfheartedly dancing in the darkest corner of the stage. She looked to be pushing 40 – and 40 was pushing back. She was pudgy and her face was covered in so much makeup when the spotlight caught her she looked like a ghost. Thomas was about to swallow hard and do what he had to do, but then it occurred to him that agreeing to take a woman so clearly past her sell-by date might set off alarm bells.

"I'm sure she's very nice, but I was hoping for someone a bit younger."

For the first time, mama-san seemed to relax just a little.

"You pay bar fine?"

"If we get along, sure."

"And you go to hotel?"

"That's what I'm here for, isn't it?"

Now Mama was truly happy. She signaled for a girl who was sitting at the bar behind the stage. She looked rather shy, and very young. "You like. She very horny. Good English. Like American."

"I'm British, actually."

"Same same. All *farang*. Good, yes?"

Thomas had to admit, she was very good indeed. And if she really did speak fluent English she'd be pretty damn close to perfect. He nodded in eager acceptance.

Mama waved her finger imperiously, and three waiters appeared out of the ether. Marching orders were given, and in less than a minute, Mama's selection was making her way towards Thomas. As she got nearer and nearer, he realized that perhaps he'd misread her level of innocence. There was something in her eyes that suggested she'd seen it all before. Twice.

"What's your name?" she asked in a syrupy smooth voice.

"Uh, Thomas," he blurted out before thinking perhaps it would have been wise to use a pseudonym.

"You can call me Lilly."

"'Lilly?' Surely that's not your real name."

"No, it's a nickname. I guess *farang* like that name."

Certainly not anyone he knew, Thomas thought.

"You're British, not American, right?"

Impressive, the young man thought. "Absolutely right. How could you tell?"

"I lived in London for almost two years."

"Really? What were you doing there?"

Lilly smiled wistfully. "I went because a customer said he loved me, and wanted me to come live with him. He said he could get me a work visa."

"And on the strength of that you went?"

"Pardon?"

"He said come and you went?"

"Yes," Lilly said, still unable to determine what Thomas found strange about her answer.

"Was he planning to marry you or something?"

Lilly shrugged. "I don't know. Then, I thought, maybe. But he was no good."

"He mistreated you?"

"What does that mean?"

"Did he hurt you in any way?"

Lilly laughed in a marvelously unrestrained way. "No, that would have been interesting."

"I don't follow," Thomas admitted.

"I got there. He met me at the airport. Took me to his house, and then straight to his bed. I was very tired, and hungry after the long flight. But I did my duty. When we finished he said he had to go to work tomorrow, but would try to be home by 7 P.M."

"Okay."

"Not okay. What am I supposed to do all day? I sat in the house, doing nothing."

"Why didn't you go out?"

"Go out where? I didn't know anything about London. I didn't have any money. It was cold outside and I didn't own a coat or even a sweater. And in those days I didn't speak much English – just enough to work in a Bangkok bar."

"So what happened?"

"He came home and asked me about my day. I said my day was no good. He said 'Did you make dinner?' Then I knew: He didn't love me at all. He just said that so I would come to London." Lilly shook her head, the wound still raw. "He was a bad man."

Thomas trod as lightly as possible. "I wouldn't say he's necessarily a bad man. Maybe the two of you just had different expectations."

Lilly shrugged as if the distinction was meaningless. "The next day he told me to go shopping, and he gave me some money. It took me a while to find the shops, but I did, and I bought some warm clothes. When he got home he was mad. 'I told you to go shopping,' he said. I did! 'Then where's dinner?' I think he meant go shopping, have fun. He wants me to be his cook."

"I can see how that might be a problem for you."

"I tried, for ten days. But every day he's angry with me. I can only cook Thai dishes, and he doesn't like spicy food. He ask me, 'Why can't you make something decent?' I said, 'This *is* decent,' though it really wasn't. I couldn't find the right chilies, and the fish was all frozen. Even the rice tasted... actually, it didn't have any taste at all. But I was cooking his food for him. Why should he complain?"

"So what happened?"

"On the 10th day he took one look at the meal, and pushed all the dishes onto the floor. Then he stood up. I thought he was going to clean up his mess, but instead he hit me. Hard."

"Did you go to the police?"

"Of course not. My English wasn't good enough to explain what happened, and I thought they might put me in jail for cheating on my tourist visa."

"So what did you do?"

"The next day, after he went to work, I packed my suitcase and ran away. I wanted to go home, but I didn't have any money for a plane ticket. There was a sign in the Chinese market where I shopped for food saying there were jobs in Soho.

Thomas knew where this was heading. "Doing what?"

"Working in a... bar."

"And you just walked in and got the job?"

Lilly folded her hands across her lap in exaggerated modesty. "These days most of the customers come from Mainland China. My grandmother is Chinese and can only speak Mandarin, so I grew up hearing it at home. I can understand almost everything, and speak okay. Plus, Chinese men think Thai girls are more sexy than Chinese girls. So it was easy for me to find a job."

"But the job didn't suit you?"

Lilly looked at Thomas with an intensity that made him shiver. "Of course not. Chinese men are pigs." Lilly's face

tightened as old memories forced their way back into conscious-
ness. "Thai men not good, but better than Chinese. *Farang* are
the best. Usually."

"So you left?"

"I couldn't, not immediately. I owed a lot of money to the bar
owner, who helped me get an apartment and some clothes for
England weather. It took two years to pay him back."

"Whatever happened to the bad man? Did he come looking
for you?"

Lilly feigned indifference. "I heard he come back to Bangkok.
Come here. Looking for me or looking for another girl? I don't
know. *Mai pen rai.*"

"What does that mean?"

"Never mind. Don't worry."

But the expression on Lilly's face suggested she still minded
– quite a bit. "Were you sad it didn't work out?"

"What do you mean?"

"Would you have been happy living in a country so far away
from your family and friends, a country with bland food and
terrible weather?"

Lilly gave the question more thought than it probably
deserved. "Maybe. He very rich man. His house has six rooms –
for one man! Very nice car. Jaguar. Just not nice man."

Thomas wasn't sure whether he felt contempt or awe. Lilly
had left behind everything and everyone she knew, hopped on
a plane, and cast her lot with a man with whom she'd been intimate but probably never had an intimate conversation. When

he didn't live up to her arguably unfounded expectations, she walked out the door and into a strange country where she had nowhere to live, no money, and no food. Yet somehow she survived, and came home a little wiser and with very good English as a bonus. It was quite a story, but what struck Thomas most was how devoid it was of any feeling. There was clearly some anger at the man who promised love when what he really wanted was a maid with privileges. Yet Lilly's last statement suggested she might have put up with that if the man had been a bit more tolerant of her cooking. She was willing to forego even the thought of emotional happiness if she could be assured of material comfort.

Thomas became so lost in his own thoughts he didn't notice the mama-san standing over him, looking displeased.

"You pay bar fine?"

"Oh, right. Yes, of course. We were just talking." Thomas pulled out his wallet, struggled to see the denominations on the unfamiliar bills, but eventually laid enough of them on the tabletop that mama-san gave her assent.

"I'll get my purse," Lilly said. That left Thomas feeling uncomfortable as mama remained by his side. She had her money; why didn't she leave him alone?

"You like talking."

"Well, yes. I like to get to know someone before, you know...."

Mama-san's eyes narrowed and lines appeared in an otherwise wrinkle-free forehead. "But you no gay, right?"

"What, no! I like women. I like them a lot. Maybe I'm just a little shy."

"Maybe," mama agreed without conviction.

Fortunately Lilly returned quickly, smiled, and took Thomas by the arm. Together they walked out of the bar looking like a happy couple rather than two people who just met five minutes ago but were now heading off to bed.

"Which hotel you staying?"

"The Four Seasons."

"Four Seasons is no good. They don't like bar girls. We'll go here," she said as she pulled his arm so hard it nearly popped out of its socket.

"Here" turned out to be a tiny unmarked hotel that was so full of people coming and going it could have been a train station. Lilly demanded five hundred baht, which she immediately handed over in exchange for a room key. They walked up a dark staircase, moving out of the way for what felt like a dozen tiny maids carrying armfuls of wrinkled and presumably filthy sheets.

The room itself was small and – fortunately, Thomas thought – dark. "You take shower first?" Lilly asked.

"Um, no. Maybe after."

A few minutes later Lilly re-emerged wearing nothing but a towel, her hair pulled up in a tight bun. She sat down next to Thomas on the bed, and placed her hand on his knee.

"I thought maybe we could talk a little first."

"Why?"

Thomas could feel the flush that started at the base of his neck and worked its way up to his hairline. "I'm not used to, you know, just getting straight into it. Back home I'd ask the girl out to dinner, we'd chat, get to know each other, that sort of thing."

Lilly smiled gently. "So talk."

"Okay, yes, thanks. Um, do you like your job?"

Lilly looked at him incredulously. "You think this is fun?"

"Of course not. I'm sorry, that was a bad question." Thomas tried to look sheepish, which wasn't difficult under the circumstances. "I ask because I knew this girl who worked in Patpong. She told me she liked having sex, so getting paid to do it was like a bonus."

Lilly shook her head in disbelief.

"Her name was Nan. That was her nickname, anyway. I could never pronounce her surname, but it was something like Supitayaporn. Did you know her, by any chance?"

"Nan is a common nickname. I must know 50 girls with that name."

"With the last name Supitayaporn?"

"We Thais don't use last names much, especially in Patpong."

It was hard to read body language in the feeble light cast by what must have been a 10-watt bulb, but Thomas was pretty sure Lilly hadn't flinched when he mentioned either of Nan's names. He decided to turn up the heat. "Unfortunately she died of a drug overdose. I was really surprised. I mean, I knew she took *ya ba* from time to time, but I didn't think she was suicidal."

"Maybe the overdose was an accident," Lilly suggested. "You should ask the police."

Again, Thomas saw no reaction other than sympathy for the departed. "Maybe," Thomas agreed, and decamped for safer territory. "Did you like London?"

"Too cold."

"It can be, sure, but it's lovely in the warmth of the summer."

Thomas thought he saw a generous serving of pity in Lilly's bemused expression.

"Would you consider going back to London, if you could find the right man?"

Lilly's response was far more thoughtful – and emphatic – than Thomas had expected. "Thai girl should be in Thailand. If man likes me, he can come to Bangkok."

"But surely most men only come here – I don't know – once a year or so? It's hard to have a relationship when you only see each other every twelve months."

Lilly shook her head. "Some men come here many times. Every month. Every two weeks. It happens."

"Well, that's certainly better," Thomas agreed. "And do they come to the bar each time? Or do you arrange to meet them outside?"

Perhaps without realizing it, Lilly shifted her body so that her shoulder was facing Thomas. When she spoke again she didn't make eye contact. "Why are you asking so many questions?"

"I'm just curious, really. We don't have anything like this in London."

"Yes you do," she countered. "I know. I was there."

So the bar in Soho served more than just drinks. "Are most of the men you meet nice?"

Still wary, Lilly waited a moment before replying. "Some men nice. Some men not."

"So is it better to have regular customers that you know are nice?"

"Not all regulars are nice. Some like me, but I don't like them."

"But you still go with them?"

"No choice."

Thomas could feel himself losing even the flimsiest threads of a connection, and decided to jump into the deep end before he lost that option completely. "I suspect the bar prefers regulars. Most businesses do. It gives them a steady revenue stream they can count on. Is it the same in your business?"

"Ask mama-san about business. I just dance."

Thomas' thoughts ran ahead to tomorrow morning, when Ian and Sally would press him for details of his solo investigation. He needed to come back with more than "ask mama-san" if he hoped to escape several weeks of mockery.

"I guess what I'm trying to say is I think you're very pretty, and also very nice, and your English is excellent. I'd definitely like to see you the next time I come to Bangkok. Can I just walk into the bar and ask for you? Or are you likely to be with another man – I mean, another customer?"

Lilly shrugged disinterestedly. "It depends."

"On what? Do you get bought out every night?"

"It depends. Sometimes yes, sometimes no."

"In an average week, how many times does a man take you out?"

"Why are you asking all these questions?"

"I'm just trying to calculate my odds. And if you get bought out most nights, how can I make sure I'll see you?"

"Come to the bar early. Most girls are there until at least nine o'clock."

"That's good advice. I'll do that, if I can. But usually I come to Bangkok with my colleagues, and we have dinner together. That makes it hard to get here much before ten. Is there any other way I can make sure you're available?"

Lilly remained wary, but lured by the prospect of turning Thomas from an unsettling and surprisingly hesitant one-off to a regular source of income, she decided to play along.

"I could give you my phone number. Before you come to Bangkok you call me. I can meet you at the airport, or your hotel. I stay with you the whole time."

"And how much does that cost?"

A little of the earlier hesitation returned. "Why do you ask?"

For once, Thomas had an answer easily to hand. "To make sure I can afford it! I mean, a beautiful girl like you for the entire day? That must cost a fortune."

Lilly's smile return. "No, I'm very cheap."

"How much is very cheap?"

Thomas was surprised to see that Lilly looked embarrassed. She hadn't batted an eye when he bought her out of the bar a few minutes after meeting her. Nor had she struggled with the concept of becoming a kept woman. It was only when they got into the nitty gritty of price that she suddenly turned shy. Perhaps she was unaccustomed to making the opening bid?

"You have to pay the bar fine, for every night. And you pay me because I can't work."

"How much is that?"

"Six thousand baht per day."

There was something in the way she said it that made Thomas think she'd inflated her initial offer, either because she took him to be an easy mark, or because she wanted some room for negotiation. But even her opening bid was only £120, still out of his league, but a mere fraction of what he was expecting.

"And is that it? Just the bar fine and six thousand baht per day?"

Maybe the word "just" made Lilly think Thomas had more to give. Maybe she just wanted to see how far her luck would stretch. Whatever the reason, she took a shot. "Good men give more, to pay for family."

"Pay for family? I don't want all of them – just you."

Lilly laughed, and Thomas got a glimpse of the carefree girl she had been before Life forced her to grow a hard shell. "Not make love with mama! I mean, give money to help family. My family are farmers, very poor. I send them 20,000 baht every month. Some men help me."

Thomas nodded with what he hoped was a thoughtful expression. The next question would be key; he needed to get it right. "And these men who support your family, do you have just one? Or could there be several?"

Lilly turned her head away, making Thomas think he'd gone too far. Fortunately, he was wrong.

"One man is best, sure. But who knows? Man says he loves you, then you never see him again. Or you see him at the bar, but he pretends he doesn't know you and chooses another girl. Men are butterflies. They can't be trusted."

"So?"

"So, sometimes a girl has to be a butterfly. Keep several men, for safety."

That, Thomas thought, was an expression he was unlikely ever to hear again.

"And if I said I wanted to keep you, would you agree?"

Lilly turned her body to face Thomas, and looked into his eyes.

"Of course."

They two sat quietly for a moment. Thomas understood that the next move was his, but he was unsure of the steps to this dance. Fortunately, Lilly took pity on him.

"So, now that we know each other a bit better, should we... get started?"

"No!" Thomas shouted. "I mean, not yet." He felt his ears getting warm. "I mean, I want to and everything. You're very beautiful, and you seem like a really nice person."

It was all Lilly could do to keep from laughing. "Nice personality!" was *not* one of the things that drunken customers usually shouted at her as she gyrated on stage.

"You want to, but... you can't? There's a Watson's nearby. I can send a boy to buy some Viagra if you'd like."

Thomas was horrified. "No! It's nothing like that. My... equipment is fine. It's just that this is a business trip and I'm here with some colleagues from work."

"I didn't see them at the bar."

"No, they didn't come to Patpong. They went to dinner together instead. But they made me promise I wouldn't do anything, you know...."

"Sexy."

"Yes! Exactly."

"But how would they know? You could tell them you went to the bar, had a couple of beers, and went home."

If I told them that they'd be mad I hadn't accomplished what I set out to, Thomas thought. What he said was, "I don't think they'd believe me."

"So why don't you do whatever you want, and tell them whatever they'll believe?"

"That's a good idea," he had to admit.

Lilly slid closer to him on the bed. "What is it you'd like to do?"

Now *that* was a difficult question. When Lilly led him into this sleazy little room there was a moment when he wanted nothing more than to tear her clothes off and bang her to within an inch of her life. But now that he'd heard her story, he couldn't see her as "just" a prostitute. She was a real person, one who'd had a hard life but somehow managed to remain surprisingly soft and sweet. What he really wanted, he realized, was to meet her tomorrow for dinner. But that was one pleasure that wasn't on the menu.

Lilly could see that Thomas was struggling, and again threw him a lifeline. "How about I give you a massage?"

"That sounds like an excellent idea," Thomas said as kicked off his shoes and lay face down on the bed – fully clothed.

Lilly frowned. "That's no good. You have to take your shirt off."

Thomas endured a moment of embarrassment, but did as he was told. Seconds later he felt Lilly's fingers gently exploring his shoulders and upper back.

"Nice body! Do you work out a lot?"

"Not as much as I should. Work's just too busy. But I played a lot of sport when I was younger."

"I can tell," she said as she fingers dug into the stiff muscles in his neck and shoulders.

Thomas' first thought was that she wasn't nearly as strong as the trainer who stretched him out before games when he played club rugby. His second thought was that this was much, much better. It was soft, sensual, almost a form of communication without words.

He felt himself grow mellow to the point of nodding off when suddenly a pair of hands started tugging at his belt.

"What are you doing?" he asked in a voice as high as a pre-pubescent boy's.

"Your jeans are too thick for my little hands. You need to take them off."

It seemed a sensible request, so Thomas stood up and did what he was told. As his Levi 501's hit the floor he noticed Lilly staring at him.

"You like the massage, I see."

Reddening, Thomas quickly flopped back on the bed, face down. The gentle kneading recommenced, starting with his hamstrings, but moving rather quickly to his inner thighs.

And then higher.

"Do you want me to release you?" Lilly asked.

Thomas didn't know what she meant.

Lilly's left hand tugged at the waistband of his underwear, while her right went exploring inside. Thomas closed his eyes, and concentrated on listing up the last 10 winners of The Ashes test cricket.

To no avail. He only got as far as 2005 – when England triumphed – before admitting defeat.

"I have a better idea," he said as he turned over, pulled Lilly towards him, and gently removed her towel.

CHAPTER 28

At 10:30 on Monday morning, Brian Cahill dropped his bag onto seat 1A on BA 10 to London. He had what looked to be a painful sunburn and dark, almost purple bags under his eyes.

"So how was your weekend of unbridled lust?" Andrew asked with undisguised glee as Brian tossed the bag into the overhead compartment and collapsed into his seat.

"There's nothing I could say that would match the sordid drama that's already flooding through the gutter that passes for your mind, so why don't you stick with what you've got, put on some headphones, and let me use the flight to catch up on my sleep."

"And what is it that has left you so tired, Young Brian? We both did the same amount of work, yet I'm fighting fit and ready for anything."

"You're telling me you didn't go to Lady Go Go over the weekend?"

"No, I went there every night. Briefly. Just long enough to shop. All that sitting around making chit-chat in a noisy bar is a distraction from the real business of showing the locals just how wonderful the act of love-making can be."

Brian thought about letting the remark pass unscathed, but he was tired and irritable, and the thought of going a round or two with Andrew was uniquely appealing. "Different girl every night, eh?"

"I fail to see why you persist in using the singular, when you know a man of my... *appetites* requires multiple lovers to satisfy his needs."

"And that makes you happy, does it?"

"Bloody delirious! You should try it."

"You never wish – oh, I don't know – you knew the names of the girls you were banging?"

"I know their two-to-three-digit numbers, which are all I need to place my order."

Brian shook his head. "I know you were a virgin until the first time we came to Bangkok. I can understand you wanting to make up for lost time. I realize most of the use-'em-and-abuse-'em routine is an act to make you look like the lothario you will never, ever be. But let me ask you a serious question: don't you want to spend *any* time with these women while they have their clothes on?"

Andrew looked at his colleague with genuine curiosity. "Let's unpack your question, shall we? You're asking whether I want to really get to know women who are with me for only one reason: to trade sex for money. You're asking whether the fact they can only speak a few words of English diminishes my enthusiasm for a frank exchange of views. You're asking whether the minuscule likelihood I'll ever see any of them again affects my thinking on this issue in any way. In other words, you're asking me whether I'm willing to join you in pretending that a prostitute is not a prostitute but a really sweet girl just waiting to meet the man who can turn her into Julia Roberts in *Pretty Woman*. And my answer is: you are quite clearly out of your bloody mind."

"Why?"

"Why what?"

"Why do you assume that just because circumstances have forced them to do something they'd rather not that they don't have feelings and ambitions like any other girl their age?"

"Because other girls their age don't have sex with strange men every night! Jesus, Brian. These aren't ordinary girls. Maybe they were, once upon a time. But they left the road to a wee cottage in the Cotswolds the minute they put on a bikini no larger than a postage stamp and hopped on stage at Lady Go Go."

Brian said nothing, staring at his warm macadamia nuts with something approaching contempt.

"Oh, wait: I get it. This isn't about me at all. This is about you. You want my blessing on *your* little tart. You want me to say that for every other guy who goes to Bangkok it's all about animal needs, but your case is different. Yours is love in the grand courtly tradition. You really do see yourself as Richard Gere."

"Is that so ridiculous?"

"Yes! *Pretty Woman* was a movie! It's make-believe. People go to see it because – and here's the important bit – *it is not real!*"

"But why can't that sort of thing happen in real life?"

Andrew looked like his circuits might overload. He started to speak, stopped himself, then started again. And stopped. Rolled his head around. Ordered another Bloody Mary. Finally: "Tell me this: do you pay her?"

"What?"

"Simple question: at the end of your weekends, do you hand her money?"

Brian reddened. "I give her some money so she can buy something nice."

"And that differs from paying for sex because...?

"Because it's not compensation for services rendered. We go away together. We have fun. I buy her something nice to remember the weekend."

"No, you give her money and she does whatever she wants with it."

"Same difference."

"Completely different. Next question: does she give you gifts of cash to remember the weekend?"

"Of course not!"

"And why not? Don't you want to remember the weekend as well?"

"I can remember it just fine. I don't need any gifts to jog my memory."

"But she does. Next question: has she ever asked you for money?"

That one stung. Over dessert last night, Nan brought up his promise to "take care" of her. It took some time before Brian worked out what she was asking, but eventually it became clear she wanted money to give her father. The rice harvest had been disappointing, and he was unable to make the payments on all his outstanding loans. Either Nan helped him out, or he'd be forced to sell yet another patch of the family farm.

Brian's first reaction was that Nan should be able to help him herself, given her apparent popularity amongst the foreign patrons of Lady Go Go. But he managed to keep that thought locked up inside his head, and instead asked how much she needed. The answer was only a few hundred pounds. For that, he thought, the lecture on fiscal probity could wait. He gave her the money.

"I helped out her father. Once. And only because the rice harvest was bad."

"Once *so far*," Andrew corrected. "And when was this instance of generosity?"

Brian was forced to admit it had just happened.

"So now you've started down the slippery slope. You've shown that, as long as Nan keeps spreading her legs, you're willing to play the role of generous benefactor."

Anger flashed across Brian's eyes. "Look Andrew: I don't pass judgment on what you do. I expect that favor to be returned. And I demand you extend the same courtesy to Nan."

Andrew's head snapped back in surprise. "I'm not sure what I said to set you off, but I assure you I meant no offense. My only point is that we're not so different, you and I. The only thing that separates us is that *I* can be honest about what we're doing."

For the rest of the flight back to London, Brian asked himself whether Andrew was right.

CHAPTER 29

The detectives had agreed a return to the breakfast room was in order so they could compare notes before meeting up – hopefully – with Nat.

"So, Commander Bond, did you keep the British end up?" Sally asked while putting her arm around Thomas' shoulder.

"Wouldn't you like to know?"

"Yes, I would! That's why I asked. And when you get to the kinky stuff, don't leave anything out. I want to know how big the whip was and which one of you got the blindfold."

"Sally, we just talked."

"Yeah, right. You paid the bar fine and took a prostitute to a skanky hotel and all you did was talk?"

"That's what I was supposed to do!"

"I know that. I just didn't think you'd actually do that. Or not do *that*, as the case may be."

"Enough, Sally," McLean intervened. "Thomas, ignore her and tell me what happened."

Relieved, Thomas threw one last glare in Sally's direction, and began his story. "Okay. First of all, the mama-san recognized me and was very suspicious. She kept asking if I wanted a girl or just to ask questions. She calmed down a little bit after I paid the bar fine, but she knows something's not quite right."

"And when your little tart returns to work with the news she never saw your tighty whities those suspicions will have been confirmed," Sally pointed out.

Thomas commanded his eyes to roll dramatically. "You were ordered to lay off, remember?"

"Bad choice of words, young man."

"Anyhow," Thomas persevered, "we talked a bit about the types of customers she gets. It doesn't seem there are any hard and fast rules – Sally, don't even think about it! – but in general a regular customer is preferred to an occasional. No surprise there, I suppose. The way it works is the girl gives the customer her number, he calls before he... *arrives* and the girl meets him either at the airport or the hotel. He pays her a daily rate."

"And they'll do this for any man who asks?" Ian inquired.

"I wondered the same thing. So I asked Lilly – that was her name, by the way – whether she'd be willing to be my mistress." Thomas grinned. "She said she would."

"Of course she did," Sally said indulgently.

"She said they get three times as much from a day hire as from someone who just buys them out of the bar. And if they're really lucky, the guys will send them money even when they're not in Bangkok, to help take care of the girl's family. That seems to be really important. Also, she said they try to juggle as many of these regular customers as possible."

"Of course they do."

"It's not like that, Sally," Thomas insisted. "Lilly said lots of guys promise they'll get together the next time they're in Bangkok, and then they turn up in the same bar the next night, completely ignore the girl they were with, and choose someone new."

"Men lie to women? Now I've heard everything."

"You know what I mean. The girls have to hedge their bets."

Sally's expression suddenly turned serious. "I can understand that with one-night stands. But a kept woman remains kept as long as the checks keep coming."

"Children," McLean interrupted, "the details of mistress keeping don't matter. Thomas was sent to find out whether, outside of the bar where mama-san can't see her, one of the girls would admit to knowing Nan. Did she?"

Thomas sighed in disappointment. "No. Pretty much the same answer we got from the mama-san: there are lots of girls named Nan. But she showed no reaction when I mentioned Nan's surname. Same thing with the overdose. Either she's a very good actress – and, in her profession, I guess that's a requirement for the job – or she really doesn't know who I'm talking about."

"Did she say anything about drug use?"

"Only that the OD could have been an accident."

"So we're still no closer to understanding why either of them died."

Thomas leaned over the table, and spoke just louder than a whisper. "See, that's why I was talking about the whole mistress thing. Like you've been saying all along, sir, the fact they were together so many times *must* be significant. Reading between the lines of what Lilly said, I'm pretty sure that's the sort of arrangement Cahill had with Nan. And I'll bet that after she felt comfortable she asked him to contribute a little extra to help her family."

"I'll grant you that's possible," McLean said. "But so what?"

"Maybe Brian thought the regular payments were buying Nan's devotion. Then he finds out she's got the same arrangement with a couple of other men, and threatens to cut her off. She flies into a rage and kills him."

"Maybe it was the other way around," Sally suggested. "Maybe she finds out he's got a girlfriend back in Blighty and that's what sends her over the edge."

Thomas was not happy about losing the spotlight to Sally. "I think that's highly unlikely. These girls aren't stupid. This isn't love, it's business."

"Do what you want with your heart but save your bank account for me?" If Sally had been expecting support from Ian she was sorely disappointed. After an uncomfortable silence, she signaled for a waiter. "There's some sort of Thai breakfast porridge, isn't there?"

"Yes. It's called *kao thom*."

"Could I get one of those?"

"With chicken or pork, ma'am?"

"Um, pork please."

Once the waiter left, Ian looked at Sally in surprise. "Gone troppo, have we?"

"If you must know, I may have had a little too much of that foul Mekong whisky last night. And *kao thom* is meant to be good for a hangover."

"Says who?" Thomas demanded.

"Says the tourist guide in the room. I had plenty of time to read it between heaves."

"And once again Sally provides us with too much information," Thomas said with a sour face as he put down the sausage he was about to eat.

While Sally and Thomas continued to trade jabs, Ian grew pensive. "Thomas, tell me *exactly* what Lilly said about the overdose."

"Don't pick on the boy, boss. I'm sure he was a bit distracted. Men get that way when there's a chance of seeing boobies."

"I wasn't distracted, there were no boobies, and I remember exactly what she said."

"Which was?"

"'Maybe it was an accident. Ask the police.'"

"I suppose we should be pleased England doesn't have exclusivity on smart-arses," Sally opined. "So basically we don't know anything more than we did before."

"Actually, maybe we do," said Ian. "'Ask the police' might simply have meant 'talk to the people who are paid to find out that sort of thing.' Or it could have meant..."

Ian didn't get a chance to finish the sentence before Thomas did it for him. "Or it could have meant the police know a lot more than they're telling us."

Ian nodded.

Sally's *kao thom* arrived. It was a fragrant soup with rice, bits of ground pork, coriander, and not a single chili. "It smells heavenly," she told the very pleased waiter.

"Well, eat it quickly. We need to get to the conference room. Nat should be here any minute – if he's not already," Ian said hurriedly.

He needn't have worried. It was 9:45 before Nat burst through the door, muttering apologies for keeping the visitors waiting for three-quarters of an hour. "Sorry I'm so late. The chief wanted an update and it ended up taking a lot longer than expected."

"Been there, done that" said Sally, even though she had yet to brief Chief Franklin on anything. That was Ian's job.

"What did I miss?"

"Breakfast, mostly" Thomas said with a slightly guilty look that the still-flustered Nat overlooked completely.

"Good, because I had a thought on the way over here. I spoke with the officer who looked into Ms. Supitayaporn's death. He admitted they didn't do much more than check whether the body was cold. Before you say anything, I know it's wrong. So does the officer assigned. But it's a fact of life that we're too under-resourced to do a thorough job of everything, so we have to set priorities. And the death of a bar girl is pretty far down the list, especially when it's obvious she died of a drug overdose."

"And all that matters because...?" Sally asked.

Ian got there before Nat could. "Because her flat should be just like she left it. With luck we might be able to find an actual clue."

Sally had purloined a glass of Mandarin orange juice from the buffet outside, and now she sipped it slowly while working her way through the implications of this development. She didn't believe for a second that this "thought" had suddenly popped into Nat's head. More likely he'd been holding onto it until he could trade it for something he needed. And that was very interesting indeed.

Until now she had seen Nat as a naïve young cop who had the misfortune to be thrown into the deep end of a very dangerous pool. She had watched him flounder with both amusement and a decent dollop of sympathy. He had been so proud of his collection of Brian Cahill landing cards, and so shocked and humiliated when he found out his own team had failed to tell him about the mutilation of Cahill's body, that her heart went out to him.

Now she wondered if she'd been played for a sucker. Maybe it was just good luck that the Nan's-apartment card had appeared at the perfect time. But maybe Nattapong Kadesadayurat was a far more skilled operator than she'd given him credit for.

Sally looked up to see her colleagues were standing at the hotel entrance, looking impatient. She increased her pace, and then followed them into the same police BMW that had picked them up at the airport. Same driver, still as silent as the crypt. This time, however, Nat was not cowed into following suit. In fact, he was downright voluble. "We're going to a suburb called Din Daeng, near the old airport. The government built a bunch of apartments there a few years ago, so it's pretty densely populated. The metro links are excellent, so it's become a popular option for people who work in the city but can't afford to live there."

"Like bar girls looking to pay off a debt," Thomas said to no one in particular.

Ian's nose remained pressed against the window. "Not a lot of English signage," he pointed out.

"Tourists don't come out this far. At least, they didn't used to. But the markets and street stalls got written up in a couple of the more adventurous backpacker handbooks a year or two ago, so you might see a scruffy foreign face roaming the streets from time to time."

The BMW pulled up next to a well-rusted bicycle with a beach umbrella mounted behind the seat. It half-covered the driver, and half-covered a rack to which dozens of bunches of small more-brown-than-yellow bananas had been tied. Sally smiled in amused approval of the creative engineering.

Nat pointed at the top floor of a three-story dwelling that sold motorbikes on the ground floor. "According to the information provided by my colleague, that should be it. I hope you're ok to walk; these places rarely have elevators."

"Thomas and I will be fine, though I can't speak for this elderly gentleman who keeps following us around," Sally said with a good-natured smirk.

Nat grinned as he led them through a narrow alley that took them to the rear of the building. There they trudged up a rickety metal staircase to a landing with four doors. "Should be the one on the far right," Nat said.

Sally grabbed his elbow, and pointed to a small crack at the doorframe. Light was coming from inside the apartment. Nat reached behind himself, lifted his shirt, and grabbed a small pistol that had been stored between his back and his belt.

"I'll bet you dinner that's not a regulation weapon," Thomas said in a soft voice.

Nat pushed open the door with the barrel of the gun, revealing a tiny but surprisingly neat room. Every surface except the ceiling was covered in what looked like bathroom tiles: large cream-colored squares on the floor, smaller shiny white tiles halfway up the wall, then yellowish slabs leading up to the ceiling. The walls shone brilliantly, suggesting they had been recently cleaned. Ian found himself wondering if that was a reflection of Ms. Supitayaporn's cleaning habits, or an attempt to get rid of trace evidence.

As in most Thai homes there was a picture of King Bhumibol placed high up on one wall. In the corner was a small spirit house on a pillar that looked like it had been stolen from a Greek temple. Nat pointed at the burning incense, and then the garland of fresh jasmine flowers that was draped over the platform on which the spirit house rested. Someone was living in the dead girl's apartment.

Suddenly a baby cried in the next room. A door flew open as a man came out. He saw the visitors, then Nat's gun, and reached for the nearest thing he could use as a weapon: a high-heeled shoe covered with red sequins.

Nat snarled something in Thai. The man snarled back. Without lowering his gun, Nat held out his left hand, and then moved it slowly towards his left pocket. He pulled out his badge at a snail's pace and showed it to the man. The shoe was lowered, but not dropped.

The man then inexplicably returned to the bedroom, a sudden departure that made the three detectives from Scotland Yard very nervous. He came back quickly, holding a wallet but no shoe. With four pairs of eyes staring at him intently, he pulled out his ID card and handed it to Nat. A conversation followed, all in Thai. After what seemed like an half an hour – but was probably only a few minutes – Nat returned his gun to its hiding place and turned to face the detectives. Ian kept his gaze on the man, alert for any sudden moves.

"His name is Jeab. He says he's Nan's brother," Nat explained. "Same last name, and he's also from Isaan. Might be a distant relative. Might be just a coincidence. But I think he's telling the truth."

"Could we ask him some questions?"

Nat shrugged. "You're welcome to try."

McLean took a minute to organize his thoughts. "Did he live here with Nan?"

Nat translated and received a nod in answer.

"For how long?"

"Two months," came the reply.

"Why?"

Jeab looked confused.

"Why did he come to Bangkok? And then why did he move in with his sister?"

A long discussion in Thai followed, leaving the detectives to wonder how the answer to two simple questions could require so much debate.

At last Nat switched to English. "He comes from a small farm near the border with Laos. It was always assumed he would take over when his father died. But the last few years have been tough, and they've had to sell off parcels of land in order to pay the bills. Jeab figured that by the time it was his turn, there would be nothing left to inherit. Since Nan was already in Bangkok, he thought he could live here for free, get a job doing construction – which pays pretty well, at least by local standards – and save enough money to buy the farm back. Once the farm was whole again, he'd go home."

"But then his sister got killed."

Nat nodded.

McLean pulled out a small notepad and a pen. It gave him something to do with his eyes while he asked his next question. "Does he know what his sister did for a living?"

Nat translated. Jeab answered with the tiniest nod of his head.

McLean had a moment's doubt about whether the next step was going too far too fast. But he'd always approached interrogations like a boxing match: when the other guy let his guard down, you jumped in close and swung as hard as you could.

"Does he know how she died?"

Ian had expected the question to stagger Jeab, but instead he treated it as nonchalantly as if he'd been asked about the weather. "Drug overdose," he replied.

Sally folded her right arm across her stomach, and mounted the left on top of it so she'd have somewhere to rest her chin. She looked at McLean quizzically.

"And how does he know that?"

Jeab appeared unperturbed. Either he had absolutely no suspicions about how his sister had died, or he was the greatest actor since Sir Laurence Olivier. Having to work through a translator made it particularly difficult to decide which.

"He says that's what the doctor told him. *Ya ba*. Enough to kill a horse, apparently."

"And how did he know that? Did he see results from an autopsy or even a tox screen?"

A lengthy discussion in Thai followed. "He's never heard of either of those things," Nat explained.

"Who found the body?"

Once again the question took surprisingly long to translate and involved several rounds of back and forth. The answer, however, was simple: "He did."

Sally grew suspicious. "That's all he said? There was certainly a lot of to-ing and fro-ing for a two word answer."

Nat couldn't keep the annoyance off his face. "If you insist on hearing the full answer, he says he came home at about two in the morning, and thought his sister was sleeping. Then he saw the open bag of pills on the night table, and got worried. He put his hand near her nose and mouth, and couldn't detect any sign of breathing. He called an ambulance, and they brought in a doctor who pronounced Nan dead on the scene."

"Of an overdose?"

"Yes," Nat replied.

"Absent any proof whatsoever," McLean confirmed.

"Except for the big bag of methamphetamines, which are known to be lethal in large quantities."

"Only if you swallow them," Sally pointed out.

Nat's nostrils flared, but he quickly got his emotions under control. "Look: we're all cops. We know there's the book way, and the way things really get done. Yes, they should have at least run a tox screen and made a few calls to check on her state of mind. But put yourself in the shoes of the investigating officers and the on-call doctor. By Thai standards this is a very nice apartment. The only way a single girl could afford to live in a place like this is if she works in the bars."

"No possibility whatsoever that she's a successful career woman?" Sally asked with an unmistakably hostile tone.

Nat shook his head. "Most office jobs don't pay nearly enough. *Maybe* if she worked for a foreign bank, but as far as I know, red sequined hooker heels are rarely part of the corporate dress code."

"Even bankers like a night out," Sally remonstrated.

Nat looked annoyed by the pushback. "Go have a look in her closet. I bet you'll find a lot more bikinis than you will business suits."

Without a word, Sally marched off to the bedroom. 20 seconds later she was back, a little flicker of the eyelids the only acknowledgement that Nat's guess had been spot on.

Ian restarted the questioning. "So the doctor comes in, takes a look around, assumes she's a bar girl, sees the pills, and decides she must have committed suicide in order to escape her horrible life. Is that about right?"

"That's it exactly," Nat agreed.

"No chance she had a heart attack. Or that someone choked her to death."

"If she'd been choked there would have been signs of strangulation around her neck."

"Unless someone held a pillow over her mouth," Thomas pointed out. "They should have checked her mouth and throat for feathers."

"For all I know, they did," Nat snapped. "I'll say it again if it will make you happy: they could have done a better job. But all of the evidence pointed to a single conclusion: Kanokwan Supitayaporn died of a drug overdose."

Sally was starting to pace. "Is that how police work is done in this country? Take a quick look around and reach a conclusion based solely on the evidence in plain sight?"

Nat looked as if he'd been slapped. "Maybe things are different in the UK, but Thailand doesn't have unlimited resources. We can't chase down every scenario that *might* have happened; we have to focus on what almost certainly did."

"Would we be having this discussion if the victim wasn't a bar girl but a wealthy businessman?"

Sally watched Nat deflate before her eyes. "To be honest, probably not. Look: I'm not saying that's right or fair. I'm just saying that's the way it is. I'm sure that if the cops had walked in and there had been blood all over the walls, they would have done a much more thorough investigation – even for a bar girl. But no sign of foul play and an open bag of pills? That's a straightforward drug overdose, 99 times out of 100."

Just like 99 times out of 100, an overweight businessman in a high-stress profession with a bottle of heart medicine on the night table next to him died of some form of heart trouble. But there was always that pesky 1% chance that things weren't what they seemed to be.

Just ask Brian Cahill.

The similarity of the two deaths was a topic that would require further discussion, but McLean was not willing to have that debate in front of a possible suspect – regardless of whether he understood a single word of what the detectives were saying. "So what's Jeah going to do now?"

Nat translated the question with obvious relief. "He's going back to the farm. With his sister dead he can't afford to stay here."

"Not even with a job in construction?" Sally asked.

Another brief exchange in Thai. "He never got one. Ever since the coup a lot of building projects have been put on hold as investors wait to see what's going to happen. Right now there are a lot more workers than there are jobs for them to do."

"And the baby?"

"She'll go back to the farm, too. Nan's mother will have to raise her."

Although Ian had never been good with children, there was something about this baby that was so innocent, so pure, he felt the irresistible urge to place his forefinger in the baby's palm so he could feel the grip reflex kick in. As the tiny fingers closed around the tip of his forefinger, he smiled so broadly it made the muscles in his face hurt.

"Who's the lucky father?" he asked.

The answer was slow in coming. "He doesn't know," Nat said.

"Whaddya mean?" Sally asked reflexively.

"He said he asked Nan several times, and all she'd say was 'it's a friend.'"

"Did he ever meet this friend?" Sally asked. "Did he ever come over to see his child? Was Nan dating someone?"

Jeab just shook his head.

"So it was some sort of immaculate conception?" Ian asked dismissively.

Nat didn't bother to translate the question. "Think about it, Ian: Nan was sleeping with a different man every night. On busy nights she might have had two. Chances are even she didn't know who the father was. Her brother didn't force the issue because it would humiliate his sister. Personally, I think that's rather noble."

Ian looked around the room very slowly, pausing to dwell first on Jeab's face, and then on the baby's. McLean was sure of two things. One was that Jeab was lying. The other was that, for a Thai, the baby had surprisingly curly hair.

CHAPTER 30

Brian Cahill found it nearly impossible to accept defeat, even in the smallest of things. That's one of the reasons he was good at his job. He was able to reimagine, restructure, and repackage a deal in stunningly creative ways.

And then his native persistence – some called it stubbornness – kicked in.

But the same qualities that made him a talented investment banker could, when applied to everyday life, make him a royal pain in the ass. This was one of those times.

"But we need to get there *tonight!*" Brian leaned over the counter as he spoke, hoping to convey both seriousness of purpose and a none-too-subtle threat.

"I understand that, sir. But the ferry for today has already gone. I can get you on one tomorrow morning."

"What good does that do me? My hotel reservations are on Koh Lanta, not here in Krabi Town." He pulled a folder out of the inside pocket of his sports coat. "See? Read that. What does it say?"

"Sir, I'm sure...."

"What does it say?"

"It says Koh Lanta, sir."

"Right. So figure out how to get me to Koh Lanta."

"Sir, I sell passenger ferry tickets."

"So sell me two tickets."

"For tomorrow's ferry, sir? I'd be glad to."

"No, you idiot. Now! Don't you get it? I want to go *now*!"

"But sir, there is only one passenger ferry a day, and it left hours ago."

For the first time, Brian looked uncertain. "Only one ferry?"

"Yes, sir. At 11 A.M."

"I'm absolutely certain I read that the ferries run every hour until 10 P.M."

"Yes, that's right."

"So sell me a damn ticket!"

"But that's the car ferry."

"I don't care. We'll stand if we have to. I'll sit on the trunk of someone's car. I'll buy a car if that's what it takes to get me on the damn boat."

"But the car ferry doesn't go from here."

"Well then, where the hell *does* it go from?"

"Aonang."

"And where, pray tell, is that?"

"About 20 kilometers from here."

"So we'll take a taxi. Or do they also run only once a day?"

"You can get a taxi out front, sir." Brian spun around on his heels, and was about to storm off when he heard the relentlessly polite clerk saying, "But I wouldn't recommend it."

Brian inhaled and exhaled as loudly as he possibly could, hoping to highlight his patience in dealing with this mental midget of a man. "And why is that?"

"Because the taxi could take you all the way to Koh Lanta in about two hours. The ferry will take two hours and fifteen minutes if it's on time, which it usually isn't."

Brian considered reaching across the counter and strangling the clerk, not least to provoke some sort of reaction from the seemingly imperturbable man. But instead he decided to chalk this one up as another Cahill victory. "Then that is what we shall do. Thank you."

When Brian turned to Nan her humiliation was painfully obvious. "What? Did I say something wrong? Was I culturally insensitive to that smart-arse?"

Nan said nothing, but started walking towards the door. Brian followed, carrying his small overnight bag and Nan's bright orange suitcase. "Seriously: if I broke some taboo, tell me about it."

"Why you angry?" she asked.

"Angry? I'm not angry. Actually, right now I feel pretty good."

"Before."

"What, when I was talking to that idiot clerk?"

Nan nodded in affirmation.

"He was just so stupid. I get frustrated with people like that."

"He no stupid. *You* stupid."

Brian was stunned. Nan had shown her disappointment with him before, but she'd never chastised him in public. And while she was doing her best to keep her anger inside, it was clear she could blow at any minute.

"Why am I the stupid one?"

"One ferry. You think many. You wrong. You should say 'I sorry,' but you don't. You pretend he wrong. All Thai people see him. See *farang* yell at him. But he can't do anything. You the customer."

"Wow. I certainly didn't see that coming." Nan let the remark pass without comment. "I admit I was wrong about the ferry schedule. But all he had to do was say there are no more ferries today so please take a taxi."

"Why he have to do?"

"Why? It's his job!"

"No," Nan said with steely determination. "He ferry man. Taxi not his problem."

Brian had to admit she had a point. "Okay, maybe I overreacted."

"You always like this. Get angry too easy. Like child."

That one hurt. "Nan, I know Thai people like to avoid conflict, but that's not how we do things in England."

"Here not England. Here Thailand."

Another point to Nan. Perhaps it was time to admit defeat. "You're right. I'm sorry."

"Don't say me. Say him."

"You want me to walk over and apologize to that clerk?"

Nan nodded once, with certainty.

Brian knew he had been outmaneuvered. Knowing that if he didn't do it quickly his brain would talk him out of doing it at all, Brian went back to the counter where the very nervous-looking clerk was preparing himself for another onslaught.

"I've come to say I'm sorry. I overreacted. It's not your job to figure out how to get me to Koh Lanta. But you did, and I thank you for it."

The transformation in the clerk was nothing short of miraculous. "My pleasure, sir! I hope you have a very good trip to Koh Lanta, and we look forward to serving you in the future."

Brian stuck out his hand, and the two men shook. As he walked back to Nan he couldn't help noticing she radiated satisfaction. However she said nothing once he arrived, just picked up her bag and headed for the taxi queue.

The long ride to Koh Lanta gave him plenty of time to think. He tried to remember a time when Sylvia had stood up to him, not for her own benefit but on behalf of a total stranger. He couldn't think of a single instance.

Then he tried to figure out why he was so quick to follow orders from a girl who was really just a paid companion, an employee. Perhaps because the incident took place in her country, and therefore her rules applied. Maybe he was bowing to her superior judgment of what was culturally acceptable. Or maybe he didn't want to piss her off before a weekend during which he planned to get out of bed only for the occasional meal needed to keep his energy levels up.

Then a very disturbing thought battled its way into his mind. It had actually upset him when Nan made clear her disappointment in him. By extension, that meant he cared, really cared, what she thought. How, he wondered, did his relationship with a whore reach this point? Had it become – he found it difficult to even think the word – *serious*?

Don't be daft, the rational part of his brain told him. How does this lovely little scenario play out? You quit your ridiculously well paid job in the City, marry a prostitute, and open up a beach bar on one of Thailand's remote islands? The ones with only a single ferry each day? Or maybe she moves to London, where the sun never shines and plum pudding is the closest thing she'll get to fruit. Despite the fact she has no friends and barely speaks the language, she's deliriously happy sitting at home all day waiting for you to crawl home drunk after yet another business dinner that doesn't involve her. And on the weekends, maybe the two of you could take in the cricket and perhaps a play; surely she could develop a love of Elizabethan dramas, given time.

No, they were Venus and Mars, except for the occasional weekend when their orbits crossed. Except planets don't cross orbits. It was a law of nature.

He turned to Nan, who had also been looking out the window. Seeing her in profile reminded him that she was a truly beautiful girl. With no makeup or artifice of any kind, she could still run circles around all of the girls he knew in London – including Sylvia.

And then there were her eyes. Black orbs resting in a field of pure white. They conveyed strength, decisiveness, and unfathomable depth. A man could get lost in those eyes. Happily and forever.

The more he thought about the strength of his attraction to the woman sitting next to him, the more uncomfortable he became. Deep feelings lead to deep trouble, and if boarding school had taught him one thing, it was that socially inappropriate or inconvenient emotions should be repressed until forgotten. A change of topic was in order.

"So, how's your father?"

"He good."

"Was he able to pay off all his debts? You know, with the money I gave you?"

It was immediately clear that Brian had once again said something wrong, but he had no idea what it was.

"Many debts. Always debts. Need much money."

This was territory that Brian understood. "Tell me about it."

Nan shook her head. "Not good. Not happy."

"Nan, I can help you. I can help your family. I *want* to help them."

She turned to face him. "You take care me?"

"Yes, I will take care of you."

He had no idea those words would cost him his life.

CHAPTER 31

Having completed his travelogue on the way to Nan's apartment, Nat was silent the entire ride back to the Four Seasons. It wasn't until a pair of bellboys, dressed in matching white uniforms with shiny brass buttons, pulled open the massive doors and welcomed them back to the hotel that Nat found his voice.

"Can we talk about Lilly?"

All three detectives from Scotland Yard froze in their tracks. McLean recovered first. "Sure. But let's wait until we get back to the privacy of the conference room."

"Whatever makes you happy," said Nat, clearly relishing possession of the upper hand.

He didn't have it for long. As soon as the conference room doors were shut and the coffee-bearing waiter dismissed, McLean went on the attack.

"How do you know about Lilly?"

Nat shrugged. "I'm a cop. We know things."

"Not this thing," Ian countered.

The detectives stared at their host with something just shy of hostility. Nat threw up his hands. "I don't know what you're getting so excited about. I told you my bosses were having you watched."

"No, you told us there was a pair of officers out in the hallway making sure we listened to your presentation. You told us you followed us to Lady Go Go when we went as a team to find someone who knew Nan. But you did not tell us you'd assigned minders to trail us after hours. And you never once suggested you'd be interrogating everyone we talked to, regardless of how that might impact our investigation, as if this were North Korea instead of Thailand."

Nat's head snapped back as if he'd been slapped. "Thomas wasn't exactly talking, was he?"

As a matter of fact, Ian thought, that's exactly what he *was* doing. So either Nat was practicing his sarcasm, or the Thai policed hadn't managed to eavesdrop on Thomas' conversation with the bar girl.

While Ian mused, Sally boiled. And then she blew. "You know, Nat, I'm really fed up with your bullshit. Two people have been killed, and instead of trying to find out what happened to them, you're having us followed like *we're* suspects. It's as if you think the purpose of the exercise is to catch us not telling you everything we say and do during every waking moment rather than finding a killer."

Nat weathered the storm with surprising patience. "Are you finished?"

Perhaps she had been, but Nat's tone reignited the spark. "No, I am just getting started. You ship us a body that's been sliced in half and don't even notice. Is there anyone wearing a badge who's really that incompetent? You don't investigate a girl's death because you think the cause is self-evident. You don't stop to consider the possibility the drugs were planted there for misdirection. You know Cahill and Nan were sexually and maybe romantically connected, but you don't bother to investigate whether their deaths are also linked. That's incompetence of the worst fucking kind. But when it comes to tailing Thomas, suddenly you're supercops? That's just... *weird*."

"You're one to talk," Nat countered. "I'd love to see the part of your training manual that says engaging the services of a prostitute is a valid method of investigation."

On a personal level Ian would have liked to see Sally get in a few more licks. But the professional part of his brain knew that if they wanted to keep Nat at least a little bit on their side, now was the time to step in between the combatants. "We needed an opportunity to talk to one of the girls at Lady Go Go without the mama-san looking over our shoulders. Thomas bought her out and took her to a hotel where they could talk without anyone listening. And that's all they did: talk."

McLean's tone had a soothing effect. Nat took a deep breath, and released it slowly. "That makes sense. I hope you can understand my surprise when I got the report."

"I can," Ian agreed.

Sally couldn't. "That's it? We're all gonna kiss and make up? Without Nat here telling us why Thomas was followed? Did you follow Ian and me to dinner as well? Maybe put a video camera in our rooms? Throw a bug in the bathroom just in case one of us started singing secrets in the shower? You want to play this clean, fine. But it works both ways. We told you what Thomas was up to. Now it's your turn. Tell us what you got up to after leaving us last night. Tell us what grand theory of the case is driving your bizarre misallocation of resources. Tell us why following Thomas was more important than investigating the murder."

"That's fair," Nat replied wearily. He ran his hands through his thick black hair and looked around the room as if he never expected to see it again. "Imagine you're sitting in my boss's shoes. You already look incompetent because your team screwed up Cahill's cause of death. Then, before that cloud has a chance to clear, you make another overly quick call – this time on Miss Supitayaporn's suicide." Nat held up his hands to defend against the punch he knew Sally was preparing to deliver. "In fact, it might not have been a suicide, but now it's unlikely we'll ever know because the body has been cremated. That's the way we do it in Thailand." The detective pulled a white plastic tube about the size of a lipstick out of his pocket, stuck it in one nostril, and inhaled deeply. The process was repeated on the other side.

Nat looked up to see all three detectives staring at him. "Sorry. That was probably a bit strange if you're not used to seeing it. I promise you it's not poppers or anything else illegal. It's just menthol. Gives your brain a bit of a jolt. Plus it helps clear the nose. Everyone in Thailand uses them. Anyhow, where was I?"

"Trying to get us to see things from you boss's perspective," Sally said suspiciously.

Nat took another hit from the inhaler, and then put it back in his pocket. "Right. So, you know Cahill and Nan were connected during life. You even have the details of their travels together. But you never stop to think their deaths might be connected as well. That's a pretty big oversight, one you can be pretty sure is making someone on a higher floor wonder whether you're up to your job.

"Then the team from Scotland Yard shows up, casting a spot-light on every single thing you and your team have done wrong. What was an internal matter that might lead to a wrist slap is suddenly being broadcast internationally. It's formal. Official. And it doesn't leave you anywhere to hide."

"Still don't see how that leads to tailing Thomas," Sally harrumphed.

"An abundance of caution. If there's going to be another humiliating loss of face, the guys upstairs want to know about it well in advance so they can prepare their defenses."

There was something about the phrase "abundance of caution" that set off alarm bells in Ian's head. "So Thomas wasn't the only one of us you followed?"

Nat shook his head almost imperceptibly. "The four guys at the table next to yours last night? All ours. By the way, they said you've got good taste in restaurants."

Ian started the counting. "Plus the two outside this room, and the relief team downstairs."

"Yes."

"That's eight. Then there's your driver, who we call Silent Sam."

"He's actually a sergeant, and not at all happy about having to serve as my chauffeur."

"Does he even speak English?" Thomas asked.

"He does. The other eight don't. At least, I don't think they do."

"That's a lot of manpower."

"Given the recent unrest, the government is particularly sensitive to how the outside world sees us. My orders were very clear: no more surprises."

McLean felt his neck beginning to tighten up. He let his head drop, first to the right shoulder, and then to the left. There was one loud pop, and a number of small cracks. But when Ian straightened his head again, the stiffness was worse. "So what would you have done if Thomas' mission had produced more than just talk? What would you have done if he uncovered – or created – another surprise?"

Nat shook his head. "Fortunately, that was something I didn't have to think about."

CHAPTER 32

For his 12th visit to Bangkok, Brian decided to make another attempt at playing house. He flew in on Wednesday morning, planning to work through Friday evening. Nan would meet him in the lobby of the Four Seasons at 7 P.M., he'd check her in as an additional guest in his room, and the two of them would have dinner at The Spice Market – the hotel's internationally renowned Thai restaurant. They would have two days and – more important – three nights to spend together before he took BA 10 back to Heathrow on Monday morning.

By Thursday he had completed every item on the agenda. On Friday his proposal for basing the cost of the acquisition on the trailing six-month share price was accepted by the target company. So it was with a justifiable sense of accomplishment that he said goodbye to Greg at 5 o'clock Friday evening and headed back to the hotel for a shower. Nan was already there when he arrived, sitting on one of the couches that line the broad entrance to the lobby.

"You're here early." He started to spread his arms for a hug, noticed the look of horror on Nan's face, and opted for a *wai* instead. As Nan returned the gesture he could see she was trying not to laugh.

Perhaps his *wai* needed work.

Brian had included Nan's name on the registration when he checked in on Wednesday, but they stopped by Reception so that a copy of her ID card could be added to the files. Then they went upstairs to the huge one-bedroom suite Brian had booked, partly to wow Nan, and partly to ensure they had a door to put between them should a weekend without the distraction of a sunny beach or a memory of elephants prove to be more than they were ready to handle. "I'm going to take a quick shower. You're welcome to join me."

Somewhat to his surprise, she did.

Equally surprising was how quickly she made herself ready for dinner. Her only makeup was a touch of light blue eyeliner and two stripes of red lipstick. She let her hair dry naturally, and then gave it a quick brush. No curling iron. No product. No artificial hair extensions.

Her dress was equally simple: an off-the-shoulder black dress that was both elegant and alluring. The material had a bit of a shine that whispered "polyester," but that thought was wiped out in infancy by how good the dress looked against Nan's dark caramel skin and well-toned limbs.

Unbidden, an image of Sylvia took root in his mind. In it she had curlers in her hair and bobby pins jammed in so many places it was a wonder she was able to recover them all. For Sylvia, makeup was a painstaking process, made still slower by frequent breaks to ask Brian's opinion on things like which of two virtually identical colors of nail polish would look better on her sadly sausage-like fingers.

That fussiness had never really bothered him before; he just assumed that's the way women are. But not Nan. She seemed more confident, more comfortable in her own skin. And so it was with considerable pride that he offered her his arm as they took the elevator down to dinner at The Spice Market. Bumping shoulders in the way only newly made couples find amusing, they walked past the courtyard – pausing briefly to admire the koi pond.

Just inside the entrance to the restaurant a woman in traditional Thai dress sat cross-legged on a raised wooden platform. With a small knife she was carving an intricate pattern into the top of a large watermelon. She used the contrast between the white pith and bright red fruit to create a half-open flower with at least 100 petals, each curved in the center and pointed at the tip.

"Jesus," Brian remarked. "That must have taken her bloody ages."

"Thai lady very patient," Nan replied. "She want, she can wait."

"Well, not me," he replied. "I'd rather poke myself in the eye than do that all night long."

As if to prove Nan's point, the hostess had been waiting patiently while the couple enjoyed the carving demonstration. When she sensed their interest flagging she guided them to their table. Brian left the ordering to Nan, giving himself a chance to reflect on the strangeness of his situation. Here he was, in a five-star hotel, sitting across the table from a whore. His parents would be horrified if they knew. Sylvia would insist he visit a doctor, a psychiatrist and probably a priest before breaking down in tears and recriminations. And yet he couldn't have cared less.

Not for the first time, he asked himself if this was just a last fling before he settled down to a life of quiet respectability. Was it an extended road trip, one in which he'd do things that could never be spoken of again? Or was he – the thought hit him like a blow to the gut – falling in love?

"I order not so spicy. For you. Can't eat Thai style."

"I think you underestimate my digestive powers. I've been known to eat the very hottest curries Bombay Bazaar has to offer."

"No Bombay. Thailand. Very hot."

When the food came it was accompanied by a small bowl of *nam pla prik* – fish sauce covered in a thick layer of red, green and orange chilies. Brian dipped his pinky in it, and sucked his finger. The pain was nearly instantaneous, followed by a coughing fit.

Nan burst out laughing. "You no eat! Too hot for *farang*. Just Thai people."

"I don't know how you do it." The fiery assault on his digestive system gave him a case of the hiccups, sending Nan into hysterics. Once the rhythm of his breathing returned to normal he asked Nan "How old were you when you started eating this stuff?"

Nan had to think about the question. "Maybe one year, maybe two."

"It's a miracle you don't all have holes in your stomachs." Brian smiled, and then helped himself to the red duck curry. It was a little spicy, but creamy and soothing compared with the *nam pla prik*. Brian figured he had the generous use of coconut milk to thank for that.

"Good?" Nan asked.

"Very," he said. "Right now everything is good. You. Me. This place. The food. It's all good."

Nan nodded agreement. "Also good news."

"Oh yes? What's that?" Brian asked the question mindlessly, his attention having shifted to the deep-fried fish topped with a chili-rich sweet and sour sauce. That's why he nearly missed the response.

"You have baby."

"What?"

Nan pointed at her stomach. "You have baby," she beamed.

Suddenly Brian found it difficult to breathe. On an earlier trip he had run out of condoms late at night, and they'd had unprotected sex. The next morning he'd been a bit worried about picking up a disease from one of Nan's customers. But after a few weeks passed with no burning or itching, he concluded he was in the clear. It had never occurred to him that the most significant reminder of that night was less likely to be a disease than a son or daughter.

He was also surprised that Nan relied solely on condoms, which have been known to fail. Given how often she had sex, she should have been using an IUD *and* taking the pill.

That thought led to a very dark place. How many men had she slept with in the past few months? One most nights, maybe two when business was good? That was 100, maybe 150 different men who could be the father. "Are you sure it's mine?"

Nan smiled, blissfully unaware of the math Brian had just done. "Sure."

"But how can you know? I mean, what with, you know, the other customers and everything."

"Customers use condom. No condom, only you."

The grammar was terrible, but the message couldn't have been clearer.

Brian wasn't at all sure what he thought about this disclosure, but he knew exactly what his reaction was *supposed* to be. "That's great news! Congratulations! To both of us! Let's get some Champagne to celebrate. Wait, no: you shouldn't drink, should you?"

"A little, okay."

For the first time in his life, Brian expansively called for "a bottle of your finest Champagne." When the cheery waitress brought it to the table she asked, "Are we celebrating something?"

"Yes," Brian replied. "We're going to have a baby." No sooner were the words out of his mouth than Sylvia appeared – at least in his imagination. She had her hands on her ever-broader hips. Her head was cocked and she was looking at him as if he'd lost his mind.

Had he?

Once again the benefits of good breeding rose to the fore. He put his concerns and his fears into a box and locked it shut. Then he covered both of Nan's hands with his own and looked into her eyes. "I want you to know that I will always take care of both you and the baby. You don't need to worry about a thing."

Nan pulled back her hands, and picked up her fork. Judging from the smile on her face while she demurely pushed food around her plate, that was exactly what she wanted to hear. But then she dropped a bombshell.

"You move Thailand?"

"Move to Thailand? What, just pick up and move? Of course not."

Brian took another immensely satisfying bite of the duck curry, then ladled some of the sauce over his rice and had a second, equally pleasurable experience. He was so engaged in his meal that he didn't notice that storm clouds had rolled in.

"Why you say 'of course not'?"

"It just doesn't make any sense. My job is in London. My house is in London. My family is in London." He managed to stop himself before adding, "My fiancée is in London."

When Nan spoke again there was no mistaking the disdain in her voice. "My job Thailand. My house Thailand. My family Thailand. And you baby Thailand."

Brian no longer had any interest in the meal. "Nan, it's not that easy. What would I do here? How would we get money?"

"You come Thailand many time. Have job here. Maybe go London business."

Despite the blunt way in which she expressed it, her point was actually well made. There probably was enough work at Cooper, Littleton & Hall to keep him fully engaged, and Greg might be willing to take him on. In fact, there was more work – and less competition – in Bangkok than in London, which had been battered by the crisis in the Eurozone. Being based in Bangkok would let him expand into Southeast Asia and maybe even China, where the real money was being made these days. Perhaps the baby was a blessing in disguise, precisely the sort of kick in the rear his career needed.

Just before the dream could be prepared for flight, reality came thundering in to crush it. Even assuming he could make a transfer to Bangkok work, would he really want to start a new life with a whore who barely spoke English? Yes, every man in the restaurant was staring at Nan with undisguised lust. But every woman was sending daggers sharpened by the instinctual certainty of how Nan spent her evenings. Perhaps he was just an aspirationally upper-class snob who cared too much about the opinion of strangers, but Brian couldn't face spending the rest of his life with lesser mortals looking down on him.

"There are other options, you know," he said as gently as he could manage.

Nan didn't respond.

"What I mean to say is, you don't have to keep the baby if you don't want to."

The look in Nan's eyes went well beyond anger, reaching a point very close to hatred.

"Why you no keep baby? You no like baby? No like Nan?"

"Of course not." Brian sighed as he realized the potential for misunderstanding the negative. "I like Nan. I like the baby. I'm just being practical."

"What means, 'prak ti kal'?"

"It means thinking about reality. Nan, you live here. I live in London. We have very separate lives, and we need to be realistic about what that means for the baby – *our* baby. But as I said, if you decide to keep the baby, I will make sure both of you are always taken care of." Brian should have stopped there, but he could never resist amplifying his language until a deal had been closed. "You and your family."

Nan dropped her fork and spoon like a rapper dropping a microphone. They clattered against her still-full plate, drawing every pair of eyes in the room. "Just send money. No see baby."

"Of course I'll see the baby. Whenever I'm in Bangkok. We'll do things together. We'll go to the park and the zoo – or whatever you do with kids here. We'll eat ice cream together. It will be fun."

"But no live Thailand."

"I can't, Nan. You know that."

"You always think money everything. Have money, buy girl. Buy Nan. Have money, send Nan shopping while you go work. Have money, just give baby. Not be father. Just rich man." She shook her head in disappointment. "No good heart."

The clipped sentences hit like bullets from a machine gun. "That's not fair," Brian said while knowing that it most definitely was. "This... *happened*. I'm trying to make the best of a difficult situation."

"No just happened. *You make.*"

They ate the rest of the suddenly tasteless meal in silence.

CHAPTER 33

Sally managed to get rid of Nat by telling him that jet lag was settling in and she needed to clear her mind.

"Do you want something to help you stay awake?"

"That's very kind, Nat, but what I really need is a trip to the gym. I haven't worked out once since we got here, and I'm not used to sitting in conference rooms all day."

"Well, if you're sure...."

Sally assured him that she was. The detectives said their goodbyes, and took the elevator up to the fifth floor – out of earshot, they hoped, of their police minders. Thomas and Sally went back to their rooms, checked for messages, switched on Do Not Disturb signs, and reconvened in Ian's suite.

Sally opened the discussion. "You buying this 'we just don't want any surprises' excuse?"

"I'm sure it's true, as far as it goes. The question is whether that's the *only* thing going on."

"Seems like an awful lot of manpower just to protect yourself from a problem that might not even exist," Thomas suggested.

Ian again succumbed to the temptation to counter every argument, even those he tended to agree with. "True, though we know Thai salaries are low. Maybe throwing bodies at it is how they solve problems here."

"I'd be far more likely to believe that if there weren't so much other inexplicable shit going on," Sally said. "Overlook a piece of trace evidence or a potential eyewitness? That's the sort of embarrassment you guard against. But overlook the fact the deceased had his heart turned into Swiss cheese? That goes well beyond 'oops.'"

Something Sally said resonated in Ian's brain. He leaned back in his chair, closed his eyes, and tried to let the thought land where it ought to.

"Sorry we're boring you, boss. You just go right ahead and have a little snooze."

The insult caused the fog in Ian's brain to clear. "We've been going about this all wrong."

Sally's expression was a mix of skepticism and hope. "Care to elaborate?"

"What's odd about this case?"

"Might be faster to list up the small number of things that *aren't*."

Ian gave Sally a look dripping with disapproval. "Less wit, more wisdom, please."

"Sorry, boss. Well, for starters, somebody cut Cahill's body open with a meat cleaver."

"Yes, yes. What else?"

"Then somebody – maybe the same somebody, maybe not – used a Thai fruit carving knife to poke holes in what was probably a no-longer-beating heart."

"But those are the obvious things. *Think!*"

"Christ, Ian, enough of the games. Just fucking tell us!"

McLean started pacing around the room, eyes focused on the point where wall meets ceiling. "You hack open a body and mutilate the heart. What happens?"

"I don't know. My hobbies run to needlework and stamp collecting."

McLean looked away from Sally and towards Thomas.

"It bleeds," the young man said.

"Precisely!" The inspector held up his index finger to highlight his growing excitement. "So where was all the blood?"

"Presumably the hotel cleaned it up," suggested Sally.

"Possible, but problematic. For starters, cleaning up a bloody crime scene isn't easy. That's why most people call in a specialist service."

"It's a five-star hotel, Ian. I'm sure their housekeeping crews have dealt with much worse."

McLean let the comment sail past unmolested. "Given the level of violence committed on Cahill's body, you would expect him to have bled out completely in a matter of minutes. There should have been blood everywhere. The mattress would have been like a sponge. Splatters on the wall. You'd probably have to replace all the wallpaper. And the carpets."

"Still not seeing the point, boss."

"Imagine how the room must have looked when the police arrived on the scene. It would have been like something out of a horror movie."

"Still nothing."

"Yet there's not a single word in the report we received from the Thai authorities that mentions any of that."

"Of course not, Ian. That report said Cahill died of natural causes. That's a tough sell if you then go on to describe a blood-soaked hotel room. They had to cover it up."

"Unless they didn't."

"Now you're just being obtuse."

"*Think*, Sally!" Ian stared at her as if sheer force of will could pull the desired response out of her brain and through her mouth. But after several moments of neck craning he gave up and provided the answer. "There wasn't any blood in the hotel because the murder was committed elsewhere."

"So why bother to carry him back to the hotel rather than dumping him in one of the canals? They're so full of crap no one would have found the body for years."

"Answer your own question," McLean demanded.

Sally's lack of confidence in her reply was evident from the gentle shaking of her head while she spoke. "Whoever did it wanted the body found."

"To what end? No, forget that. It's the How not the Why that's important here."

Sally turned to Thomas. "Any idea what he's nattering on about?"

"Actually," the young man said, "I think I do. He's saying that bringing a dead body into a hotel without being noticed isn't an easy thing to do – especially in a top hotel where you're sur-rounded by staff eager to help 24 hours a day. Think about it:

you walk in with a trash bag or a duffel or whatever you're carrying the body in, and a bellboy snatches it out of your hand
while saying 'Let me take that for you.'"

Slowly, Sally began to see where McLean was headed. "You're
saying they *knew* they could get the body inside without being
noticed. And that makes the question: what made them so sure?"

Ian pumped his fist in triumph. "Absolutely right. That *is* the
question. Now comes the hard part – finding the answer."

That silenced the room for several minutes. Ian got up, went
to the sink, and picked up one of the glass bottles standing next
to it. There was no label or explanatory neck tag, just a bunch
of squiggles printed on the bottle itself in a language that Ian
assumed was Thai. Instead of a reusable screw cap it had a pull
tab of the sort England had abandoned decades earlier. Ian had
no idea what the bottles contained, but judging from the fact
they were neatly arranged next to the washbasin he assumed
they were either mineral water or drain cleaner.

Given the downside of guessing wrong he reached for the
faucet, then suddenly remembered he'd been warned not to
drink tap water in Thailand – even at the finest establishments.
No salads or anything else raw. Be sure meats are well cooked,
and even then be prepared for a bout of Traveler's Tummy. It
was a strange thing, being surrounded by the luxury of a truly
superb suite but unable to drink water straight from the tap.

A signal flare went off somewhere deep in the recesses of
Ian's brain. He knew from long experience it meant he'd stumbled onto something important. The tricky bit was getting whatever it was to come out of hiding.

That quickly, he had it. "What room was Cahill's body found
in?"

Thomas pulled out his iPad, and quickly skimmed through the official report supplied by the Thai authorities. "Something called the Garden Terrace Suite."

"Must be one of those villas surrounding the pool," Sally asserted. "I saw them the other day when I went for a swim. They're like small houses or cottages." And then she looked up at her boss and grinned. "Meaning it's *outside*."

Ian smiled back. "Within the complex, of course, but I suspect villas like that have a separate entrance so celebrities don't have to walk through the lobby where they'd be mobbed by fans."

While his colleagues were rapidly reaching agreement, Thomas was typing and swiping. "Well I'll be damned: the Garden Terrace Suite not only has a separate entrance, it has a *private* entrance."

Ian's pacing had turned into a slow jog as the excitement began to build. "It's probably guarded, but it's a lot easier to buy off a couple of rent-a-cops than it is an entire hotel staff and a large number of guests." The inspector froze in his tracks. "Or maybe there was no need for money to exchange hands. Maybe Cahill's body was accompanied by someone who could simply order the guard to open the gate and not tell anyone about it."

"Someone like..." Thomas started.

Sally finished the sentence. "Someone like a cop."

CHAPTER 34

Brian Cahill couldn't sleep. Nan's gentle snoring had started the instant her head hit the pillow, but the chances of Brian falling off dropped with each tick of the oppressively loud bedside clock.

His first thought had been caring for the baby, but that one was easy. He made lots of money, and life in Thailand was cheap. So provided he was able to squirrel some money away without Sylvia noticing, the financial side presented no problem.

But that invited the question of whether sending checks was enough. The child had a right to know his – or her – father. And even if Brian's motivations were no more than idle curiosity, he knew he would want to see his baby grow up. As long as the Thai business continued to prosper there should be multiple opportunities for business trips to Bangkok. But slipping away at night to go to a girlie bar was one thing. Sneaking out during the day to visit one's secret illegitimate child was quite another.

What would life be like for a half-Thai, half-British kid? Did the Thais discriminate? Would both Nan and her baby be shunned for venturing beyond the tribe? Mixed race. Mixed social class. Father in one country and mother in another. Would a child like that *ever* fit in? And what happens on the day when some loud-mouthed kid points at his child and shouts, "Your mother was a whore!" The insult would be bad enough; the fact that it was true would make the hurt last forever.

As the hours crept by Brian felt his thoughts grow darker. How could he be sure the child was his? Nan had sworn it was, but even if all her other customers really had worn a condom, there was still the possibility one of those condoms had failed.

Or that Nan was lying.

Maybe the real father was some impoverished but handsome backpacker who could do nothing for the child, and Nan had made the sensible decision to award parentage to the man with the most money. For all Brian knew, the two of them could have come up with the plan together. He'd never been to her apartment. Maybe the backpacker was living there, and when he wasn't screwing Brian's girl he was eating food and drinking beer paid for with Brian's money.

Was she even pregnant? She said she was, but she wasn't showing and Brian had made a pretty thorough exploration during their shared shower earlier in the evening. Maybe they should visit an ob/gyn together?

But wouldn't that entail filling out forms in which he admitted to being the father? That would leave a paper trail Nan could use in a paternity suit. Or for blackmail. And how could he be sure that when Nan was nattering away in Thai she wasn't alerting the doctor to her deception and offering him a piece of the action if he agreed to play along? This was Asia, after all, a place where bribes are an everyday occurrence. With this much at stake, Nan would be handing them out like candy to a toddler.

Brian glanced at the clock: 3 A.M., the time when fears come out to play and hope vanishes in the mist. Had Nan really run out of condoms that night? Maybe she set him up. Maybe she lied about the condoms so he would either get her pregnant or make the claim that he had seem credible. Over the past few months Brian had realized she was a lot more intelligent than her limited English made her seem. Could she have planned the whole thing?

Nan had been talking more and more about money lately. Maybe the piles of cash he handed her at the end of each weekend were no longer enough. Maybe her father was so deeply in debt that a long con looked like the only way out.

Although thinking about it, how could he be sure the supposed father even existed? To get out of unattractive social engagements, Brian had used the "dead grandmother" excuse so many times there were enough corpses to fill the Albert Hall. Surely Nan had the nimbleness of mind to do the same?

Maybe when country girls came to the brothels of the big city one of the first things they learned was how to create fictional relatives with tales of woe. Nan admitted the girls had been trained in how to please a man; was it impossible to believe they had also picked up ways of separating a foolish *farang* from his money?

Lots of questions, zero answers. How could he possibly know what the truth was? Sure, the two of them had spent a fair amount of time together over the past two years, but if you cut out sleeping, sex and lying in the sun, they couldn't have passed more than a few hours talking to each other. And even that was constrained by Nan's English.

Although she did seem to understand a lot more than she spoke. Maybe that was all part of the plot? After all, the language barrier *did* shield her from a lot of invasive questions, and gave her an endlessly effective excuse for not telling Brian what she got up to when he wasn't around.

His mind flashed back to his first night at Lady Go Go, when Greg had described "the system." The home team was clearly better prepared for this game than the visitors. They had spent countless hours perfecting their technique, whereas he was a babe in the woods. Had they seen him coming and played him for a sucker?

With mounting horror, he remembered Greg talking about *kathoey* or ladyboys. If you couldn't trust what your eyes – and occasionally your hands – told you about someone's gender, how could you trust your other senses to tell the difference between truth and a carefully spun web of lies?

He turned to look at Nan, her chest rising and falling gently as she slept. There was no telltale surgical scar beneath her breasts, and her neck was as graceful and smooth as a swan's. But you just couldn't be sure.

Right now, Brian Cahill wasn't sure about anything.

CHAPTER 35

"Let's recap." McLean ticked off the points on his finger as he spoke. "We agree Cahill was killed elsewhere. We agree the body was brought in through a private entrance. We agree that whoever transported the body had reason to believe he or they could get past security at that entrance. And one possibility – though right now it's no more than that – is that there was a cop involved. Okay so far?"

Thomas and Sally nodded.

"Seems to me the next thing we need to figure out is where Cahill was killed."

"It could have been anywhere, you know," Sally moaned.

"Yes, it could have. But we've got to start somewhere, so let's start with the places we know he'd been."

As always, Thomas was eager to show his enthusiasm for the boss's proposed plan of attack. "Well, there's the hotel, which we've just ruled out. Then there's Lady Go Go."

"Although we don't know whether he went there after the first time he met Nan. And even if he did I bet that place is covered in so much blood, semen, spit and piss that it's completely worthless forensically." Sally punctuated her remarks with a growl of frustration.

Thomas was not to be put off. "Okay, there's also the offices of Cooper, Littleton & Hall."

"Unlikely place for a murder," Sally objected. "The security guard slash door opener in the parking garage may be a waste of space, but most of the doors inside Cooper Littleton can only be opened with an electronic ID."

Ian and Thomas exchanged a look, both suddenly reminded of one of their first cases together. A body had been found lying on the floor of Delacroix, the world's most powerful diamond company. Cracking that one had shown them that even the most advanced security systems could be compromised by just a dash of human weakness. "That would mean his killer was either an employee, or someone who had help on the inside," Thomas said.

"Unlikely but not impossible," Sally maintained.

"True," Ian agreed. "But it would have been a hell of a job mopping up all the blood before the cleaning crew arrived in the early hours of the morning."

"All right already. I'm just trying to help."

"And you are, Sally. Ruling out what it can't be helps us identify what it might." No sooner were the words out of his mouth than Ian looked suddenly energized. "Focus on the cleanup. What factors make that easier?"

Thomas ticked them off on his fingers. "A non-absorbent surface that's easily cleaned. Access to cleaning materials – especially water. Manpower. Privacy. Time."

"Exactly. And where can you find all of those things?"

"In a morgue," Sally snapped.

"Or something like a morgue," Ian said, excitement giving energy to his words. "Where have we been recently that was like a morgue?"

"That damn conference room? It's nice, but I'm getting really sick of the sight of it," Sally said. Then she cocked her head. Looked at Ian. Laughed. "Well slap my ass and call me Nancy."

Thomas had been unable to keep up. "That's okay. Don't tell me what's going on. I actually prefer living in ignorance."

Sally smiled. "It's not that hard a question. We've only been a handful of places since we got here, and most of those have already been tossed out."

And then Thomas joined the inner circle. "Nan's house! Fake marble floor *and* walls. You could hose that place down if you had to."

Ian nodded triumphantly.

"But we don't know if Brian ever went there," Sally pointed out.

"No, we don't," her boss replied happily. "But we know someone who might."

CHAPTER 36

After spending seven hours without a wink of sleep, Brian Cahill had reached a number of decisions. First, until the baby was born, Nan would get everything she needed. He'd pay for all medical costs, up to and including the moment Nan left the hospital with her new child. If she wanted to stop working – and at some point in the fairly near future she'd have to – he would replace the lost income. Plus he would provide money – within sensible limits – for her to help her family, be they real or imaginary.

The second decision was that once the baby was born, he would demand a paternity test. If someone else proved to be the father, he would have lost a not-trivial sum of money, but gained a valuable lesson. If the baby *was* his, well, he'd cross that bridge when and if he reached it.

Third, he decided that he would share only the first decision with Nan. He didn't want a replay of last night's drama, and while it was technically possible to do a paternity test on an unborn child, it was also... yucky. Invasive. And probably dangerous. So if the question of fatherhood couldn't be answered until the baby was born, there was absolutely no point in asking it now.

Feeling energized by getting all that behind him, Brian jumped out of bed and did a few gentle stretches to get the kinks out of his neck and lower back.

"Goood maahneeng," Nan said while stretching her vowels to just short of the breaking point.

"Good morning, Nan. Sleep well?"

"Yes. You too?"

Brian preferred not to tell an outright lie if he could get away with it. And given his skill at shading the truth, he usually could. "Not really. I guess I was just too excited."

Judging from her reaction, that was exactly what Nan wanted to hear.

Brian headed for the shower, and by the time he'd finished his ablutions Nan was already dressed and obviously eager to go to breakfast.

"Are you *always* hungry?" he asked.

"Now two mouth. Two stomach. Must eat two times."

Brian grinned and gestured towards the door with his head. Nan didn't need to be asked twice.

Over breakfast they discussed how they were going to spend the day. Brian had been expecting another demand to go shopping, at least partially as punishment for how he responded to the news last night. He was therefore very surprised when she suggested they do some sightseeing – "like tourists!"

Despite having been to Bangkok a dozen times, Brian hadn't seen a single one of its famous landmarks. Moreover having something to focus on other than the life growing inside Nan's belly was an unquestionably good idea. He quickly agreed, booked a hotel car, and instructed the driver to "show us around."

Their first stop was the Grand Palace, which in terms of scale, crowds and excessive use of gold leaf more than lived up to its name. They hired one of the English-speaking guides who descend on every taxi that arrives bearing foreign tourists. He proved to be extremely knowledgeable – to a fault. As his telling of the Ramayana story entered its 20th minute, Brian found his attention wandering to the many saffron-robed monks who were doing a little sightseeing of their own. While Brian was still paying attention, the guide had said that many Thai men become monks before entering the workforce, as do businessmen who think their lives need a reset. The objective was to delink from the stresses of everyday life, and refocus one's mental energy on becoming a better Buddhist.

Brian couldn't imagine that. What would you do all day? Sit around and think about nothing? Although, maybe having too little on your mind was better than having too much. He glanced over at Nan, who today was wearing jeans and a tight Body Glove shirt. Definitely not showing yet.

At the driver's insistence they had lunch at the legendary Oriental Hotel. As the weather was hot without being oppressive, they chose The Verandah, an outdoor café overlooking the bustling Chao Praya River. The mud-brown water was packed with longboats, most of which were powered by noisy, smoky engines that could be raised or lowered depending on the depth of the river. One boat caught Brian's eye for no particular reason, and he watched as a man with the feet of a monkey stood on the back edge, maneuvering a tiller that was at least six feet long.

Most of the boats were filled with passengers: camera-carrying sightseers, locals wanting to cross from one bank of the river to the other, and that rare breed of human who thinks bobbing up and down in a small boat for two weeks counts as an enjoyable vacation. But many of the boats, particularly the smaller ones, were floating businesses. These sat low in the water, filled with piles of colorful tropical fruit, some of it found nowhere else in the world. Others carried brilliantly colored Thai silk from the northeast region of the country directly to the markets of Bangkok. Brian saw the river version of the ubiquitous food carts: a woman cooking what looked to be either a thin pancake or omelet into which she ladled mysterious ingredients from one of the eight pots placed around her makeshift stove. He saw a woman in a simple, motor-free boat, picking up what appeared to be plastic garbage with a stick. Is there a market for that sort of thing, he wondered, or is she just civically minded?

Once again Nan had been left to do the ordering on her own, which she did after tutting "too expensive!" For starters they had a crabmeat and green papaya salad that was both refreshing and spicy at the same time. Grilled river prawns, and a mixed vegetable stir-fry followed. The meal ended with mango sticky rice, which Brian pronounced "bloody brilliant."

"Damn, that was good. Well-ordered, Nan!"

She smiled demurely. "My mother come Bangkok."

"What? Why? When?"

"Must talk *sin sod*."

"What's *sin sod*?"

"Money for parents."

"But I gave you money for your parents the last time I was here."

"Not same. Must pay *sin sod* before marry."

"Before marry? Nan, what are you saying?"

"Must marry before baby." She shrugged as if the statement was no weightier than a recipe.

"Nan, I can't marry you. We talked about this last night. Besides, I've got a girlfriend, a fiancée, really."

The change was instantaneous. Nan's nostrils flared and her eyes narrowed. She moved her hands under the table, but not before Brian saw them curl into fists. When she spoke the soft vowels were gone, replaced by a harsh diction that sounded like nothing so much as a machine gun. "Why you no say before?"

"It just... never came up."

"You tell her you have baby with me?"

"Of course not! Even I didn't know until yesterday."

"So you no marry Nan?"

"I'm sorry, but I can't."

"Why you say you take care – me, baby, parents?"

"Because I will. I promise: you'll have all the money you need. When you visit the doctor, keep the receipts and I'll pay you back. I'll pay all the hospital bills. I'll give you money for incidentals, and for your family. It'll work out just fine. Trust me."

"How much you send?"

"I don't know, Nan. We'll figure it out."

"Nan have baby, can't work. Can't marry. No man want girl with baby." She held her hand out in front of her stomach to emphasize how big she'd become in the months ahead.

"I know. But don't worry. I'll give you money so you never have to work." As he said the words Brian realized he was making a lifelong commitment — to providing the funds *and* to ensuring Sylvia never found out. "I'll set up some sort of auto transfer with your bank, so you'll get the money every month."

Nan shook her head furiously. "You talk big, but no believe. Maybe money come, maybe no. Get money now. Then sure."

"Nan, I'm not going to hand you a big pile of cash just because you ask for it. Be reasonable. You don't need all the money now. And when you do need it, I promise it will be there."

"Maybe I not be there," Nan said as she stood up, threw her napkin angrily onto the table, and stormed off.

Embarrassed, Brian waited for her to come back while pretending to admire the view. He even took a few pictures with his iPhone to make it look like he was happy to be on his own. But eventually it became clear that if Nan was coming back, it wasn't going to be anytime soon. He paid the bill, and left word with the maître d' – "If anyone comes looking for me, I'm back at my hotel."

Which is where he expected to find the mother of his child, if for no other reason than the fact she'd left clothes, cosmetics and a large handbag in the room when they departed for their morning of sightseeing. But when he opened the door to his suite, he saw that Nan had been there before him and cleaned the place out. Not just her stuff, but his as well.

"I think she might be just a tad vexed with me," he told the plate of sliced fresh pineapple that housekeeping had left on the desk.

For a moment he imagined coming home with only the clothes on his back. "It's the damn airline, Sylvia, they lost my bag!" As long as she didn't remember he only traveled with carry-on luggage in order to get out of the airport faster, that might actually work. And then he panicked: had the bitch taken his passport as well?

After a few seconds of furiously throwing sheets, pillows and magazines into the air, he found his passport next to the desk lamp. "Hope she didn't spit in it," he said as he flipped idly through the pages.

And then he saw it. In huge angry letters, on the photo page, she had written "BAD MAN!" In ink. And despite his anger at the damage done, Brian smiled in admiration. Nan certainly knew how to extract her revenge.

CHAPTER 37

Ian knew there was no way they'd be allowed into Nan's apartment on their own – not least because they didn't share a language with her brother, Jeab. Moreover while McLean was never short of advice for the people working a crime scene, he knew the task well enough to realize that he lacked both the tools and the skills to work one himself. So he overruled the half-hearted objections voiced by Sally and Thomas – who both still harbored doubts as to which team Nat was playing for – and asked the Thai policeman to take them to Nan's apartment with a six-man forensics team in tow.

"Have them start with the Luminol," Ian ordered, "and make sure they pay particular attention to the grout. It's incredibly difficult to clean blood out of that narrow space between the tiles."

Jeab was standing at the entrance to the bedroom, holding the baby and looking absolutely terrified. McLean couldn't blame him. The tech team was covered in plastic from head to toe, spraying unlabeled liquids on every surface and waving ultraviolet devices like lighters at a rock concert. Two men were on their hands and knees with tiny brooms and dustpans, their noses less than three inches from the floor. And then there was Ian and his colleagues, three *farang* well out of water but nonetheless quite obviously in charge.

The inspector wasn't the least surprised when the man with the UV lamp announced – in English – "found something!" Or when the chant was quickly repeated by another techie, and then a third. Whoever had done the cleanup job had been far too hasty. Ultimately the police were able to collect 38 different blood samples from the floor and wall. There were also some footprints and fingerprints which were dutifully logged, though McLean was all but certain they would turn out to be either Nan's or her brothers. The police photographer was being pulled this way and that, trying unsuccessfully to keep up with the pace of discovery.

"Wish they were all this easy," Sally said.

Ian smiled, went out into the hall where Jeab was standing, and extended his arms. "Mind if I hold the baby?"

Sally and Thomas looked at each other in astonishment. Ian was usually all business at a crime scene; often so intensely focused he didn't hear people talking to him. Now he seemed completely absorbed in rocking a baby and nuzzling its neck, leaving the technicians completely unsupervised while Nat took Jeab into the bedroom for a DNA sample and fingerprinting.

Five minutes later Ian announced, "Let's go. We're done here. The local guys can finish up." He handed the baby off to the nearest forensic technician, who clearly had no idea what to do with her. "Let's go," he said again, this time in a loud and aggressively impatient voice.

Nat said he was going to stay behind with the crime scene crew, making sure they didn't miss anything. He offered to have the police BMW take the detectives wherever they wanted to go, but McLean insisted on taking a taxi.

It required several attempts before his pronunciation of "Four Seasons" was elongated enough to be intelligible to the driver. While he was experimenting with variations of "seeezon", Sally was muttering about the ineffective air-conditioning.

"I assume you've got a good reason for putting us in this bread basket-sized sauna rather than the cool luxury of the BMW," she said.

In response, Ian held up his thumb and forefinger, which were pressed tightly together.

"What? That's how little patience you've got for my whining? You're that close to punching me in the nose? You want me to pinch my nose so I don't smell all the sweat on this back seat?"

McLean shook his head. "You've got the makings of a paranoid, you know that? If you look carefully you'll see I'm holding something between my fingers."

Sally strained forward for a better look, and the taxi hit a pothole. "Save me the neck injury and tell me what I'm looking at."

"A hair," Ian said.

"You're pissed off because one of my lustrous hairs invaded your personal space?"

"No, silly. It's not your hair. It's the baby's."

"How in the hell did you get that?"

"If you must know, I yanked it out."

Sally burst out laughing. "And here I was thinking the two of you were having a cuddle."

"We were, though admittedly mostly so I could keep the little ankle-biter quiet. And that's not all I've got. I also managed to pick up a loose tile with a blood stain on it."

"You took evidence from a crime scene?" Thomas asked in amazement.

"I'd prefer to say I'm borrowing it. I'll send it, together with the hair, to London as soon as we get back to the hotel. I want to know whether our lab guys come to the same conclusion as theirs."

"And you want to know if the baby's DNA matches Brian Cahill's."

McLean nodded in smug satisfaction.

"Plus it's a health check on Nat. Tells us whether he's being honest with us – finally," Thomas added.

"It's gross on a couple of levels, illegal on a couple more, and probably enough to get your badge pulled. But as far as detecting goes, it's pretty damn good." Sally leaned back in her seat, savoring the win. "Eww. When we get back to the hotel, this shirt goes in the rubbish."

Brian was about to do something he hoped he'd never have to do again. "Andrew, fancy a spot of lunch? My shout."

"*You* are asking *me* to lunch? Here in London, where you have other options? What the hell happened? Wait: let me guess. You're standing for Parliament. No? You need to borrow money to pay for your sex change operation. You're thinking of starting your own company, but only if I join you in a very senior and vastly overpaid position. Am I getting warm?"

"Not at all. But you are giving me a very revolting look into the twisted house of horrors that is your mind."

"*That's* my Brian! Good to have you back. Where are we going? Somewhere shockingly expensive I hope."

"I was thinking of Cecconi's."

"Interesting choice. Trendy enough to impress, but far enough into its dotage you're unlikely to run into anyone important. Mostly Persians and the bulimic girls who love them – or at least their wallets."

"Do you analyze *everything*?"

"Hey – I've got a Ferrari between my ears. I've got to put the pedal down now and again in order to keep the sludge out."

"That makes absolutely no sense. So take your finely tuned sports car and cut to the chase: coming or not?"

"Fear not: I shall be there. 1 P.M. okay?

"Yeah, great. Oh, and, uh, thanks."

"Now you've got me worried," Andrew said before hanging up the phone.

Brian arrived first and selected a table in the back corner. The maître d' looked surprised; usually people came early to claim one of the prized window seats where they could see and be seen. But this was a conversation Brian would rather not have anyone overhear. If an extended mocking from Andrew was the price of privacy, so be it.

As the clock struck one, Andrew dropped his heavy frame into the seat opposite Brian. "I would have been here earlier but I didn't realize the restaurant stretched this far back. Or did you get them to clean out a storage locker just for you?"

Brian made a face, and handed over the menu. "You choose. Whatever you want."

Andrew put down the menu. "This is rapidly approaching the point where it's not funny. In fact, you're starting to worry me. What's going on?"

"Order something and I'll take you through it."

Andrew waved his hand to catch the waiter's attention – he seemed very distracted by the 6-foot blonde in faded jeans that must have been spray-painted onto her long, thin legs – and ordered bruschetta to start, followed by crab ravioli and then the veal Milanese. "And throw in a carafe of the Gavi di Gavi, my good man."

"You're definitely getting your money's worth. Well, my money, actually."

"First of all, if I wanted to exploit the opportunity I would have ordered the spaghetti lobster – even though it's impossible to eat properly without making an absolute mess of one's hands and shirt. Second, I assumed that when you said this would be your treat, you meant it would be your name on the expense claim. If you're paying for this personally then I can safely deduce we're not here to talk work."

"You know, Andrew, if you'd just shut up for a second I'd tell you what I want to talk about and you could stop trying to be Sherlock Holmes in a badly tailored suit."

"I thought my performance was rather good, something Benedict Cumberbatch might aspire to. But have it your way. It's your party."

The bruschetta came, and Brian waited until the waiter had returned to the stretch blonde before starting his story. The plan had been to keep the pregnancy a secret, but as he spoke it quickly became apparent the whole tale didn't make sense without that critical piece of information. It took close to 10 minutes for Brian to lay the whole thing on the table, by which point Andrew had finished off all the bruschetta and a good portion of the wine.

"You are fucked, my friend."

"I figured out that much on my own."

"So, you want my advice?"

Reluctantly, Brian nodded.

"Never go back to Thailand."

"That's it? That's all you've got?"

"It's all you need. I'll take over the two deals that are still in progress. Tell Greg you've got health issues or family problems or – hey, this has the benefit of actually being true – you need to get a new passport."

Even Brian smiled at that one.

"Write off the suits and the Marks & Spencer unmentionables that Nan sniffs each night before going to sleep. Just forget the whole thing ever happened."

"But aren't you forgetting something?"

"Don't think so."

"What about the kid? *My* kid?"

"I hate to be the one to break it to you, but there's at least a small chance that Nan wasn't a virgin when you met her."

"Believe me, I know."

"So how do you know it's your kid?"

"I don't. But if it is, I just can't ignore it. I have a responsibility, don't I?"

"For that matter, are you even sure she's pregnant? Did you watch her piss on a stick?"

Brian shook his head no.

"So maybe it's all bullshit. Maybe she's just trying to get money out of you. Come to think of it, there's your problem right there: you're trying to make a very important decision before you've gathered all the facts. And we both know that rarely ends well."

Andrew put his finger over his lips as the waiter approached with two plates of crab ravioli. The instant he left, Andrew began to eat and Brian to speak. "You're right about that much. So, smart guy, how do I go about getting more information?"

"Simple: go back."

"First you say never go there again. Then you say go there again. Your clients must love the consistency of your thinking."

"Someone put on his Grumpy Pants this morning." Andrew took a long sip of wine and smacked his lips appreciatively. "You go back, say, two months from now."

"Because?"

"Because by that point she'll be showing. Assuming she's pregnant in the first place."

"And if she is?"

"You treat this like one more business deal." Andrew skewered a ravioli. "She's trying to sell you a product that you've never seen. What would you say if I brought you a proposition like that?"

"That at best I'd put up a little seed money – no pun intended. And I'd hold off any sort of major investment until I'd seen a working sample."

"Exactly."

"But I tried something like that already."

"And?"

"And she said she didn't trust me. Not in so many words, as she hasn't got that many English words to give. But that's what she meant. She also pointed out that I could do exactly what you initially suggested: disappear and never be seen again. That's why she wants the money up front."

Andrew grinned. "Smart. I'm beginning to like this girl."

"That's the funny thing: I was, too."

"So why did she steal your clothes and deface your passport?"

"I've been thinking about that pretty much nonstop for the last five days, and I haven't really come up with an answer. She clearly thinks I'm lying to her, but I'm not sure why."

"Did you?"

"Lie to her?"

Andrew, suddenly engrossed in using his fork to trace a pattern in the sauce on his plate, simply nodded.

Brian found the question surprisingly difficult. "Not a flat out lie. I mean, I didn't volunteer information about Sylvia. But I told her I had a girlfriend."

"And when did you share that little tidbit?"

"The night she stormed out on me at dinner."

"Also known as the night before she stormed out on you at lunch."

Brian shrugged. "Your point being?"

"That it doesn't take Sherlock Holmes to figure out what's going on here. Both times, what were you talking about just before she dumped you?"

"Money."

"Uh-huh."

"But I told her I'd pay for the pregnancy and even give her some money to help her family."

"You told her this."

"Exactly."

"And then were surprised when she didn't believe you despite the total lack of evidence that you're a good man and one who can be trusted?"

"I'm not in the mood, Andrew."

"I'm not either. Think about it from her perspective. You jet in, spend most of your time hanging around with me and Greg, and reach out to her only when your little soldier wants to go for a march. Yes, you've given her more money than is strictly required by the nature of your business transactions, but we're talking about something along the lines of a spot bonus rather than the sort of 'what's mine is yours' crap that a woman has the right to expect from the father of her child."

"You're saying I didn't give her enough?"

"Blimey you're thick. I'm saying that as long as you've known her, you've treated her nicely. But you've still treated her like a whore. She thought the pregnancy was going to change that – that you'd become partners. But instead you insisted on remaining a patron. A generous one, I'll grant you, but that's not what she was hoping for."

Brian was shocked. Andrew was a smart guy, as the size of his bonus checks confirmed. But he seemed to have no understanding whatsoever of human beings. Yet somehow he had managed, in a quarter of an hour, to understand more about Nan than Brian had managed in a year and a half.

"That's not all you did wrong, you know."

"Go on," Brian said without enthusiasm.

"Think back to the night you met her. You go to the hotel. You do your thing. Did she then turn to you and say, 'That will be 3,273 baht, please'?"

"No, it wasn't that expensive."

"I'm going to assume that was a lame joke told in a failed attempt to distract attention from what an idiot you are. I am *not* doing price comparisons. I am asking who set the price: you or her?"

"I'm not sure there was a price. I gave her what I thought was reasonably generous, and she said thank you."

"Precisely."

Brian waited for Andrew to elaborate, but gave up when his colleague started scraping tomato sauce off his plate with the last piece of bread.

"Why don't we pretend I don't exactly understand what it is you're saying, and you tell me straight up?"

"Because you'll never learn that way. Answer me this: when you were waxing lyrical about how you'd take care of her, what was her body language telling you?"

Brian didn't have to think hard about that one. "That she was happy."

"And when did she turn angry?"

"After I told her I'd pay for everything. All she has to do is send the invoices, and I'll reimburse her in full."

"There they are! The five little words every girl dreams of hearing: I'll reimburse you in full."

"What's wrong with that?"

"Nothing, if you're talking to me. But a woman you're going to have a child with? Don't you think it's possible that, despite the accidental nature of the baby's creation, she wants to think of you as something approaching a husband and father – and not just a banker? Or worse still, an accountant?"

Brian felt a tremendous sense of relief that he hadn't mentioned Nan's expectation that the two of them would wed in the Thai style. He was taking enough of a battering from Andrew as it was, a battering that hurt all the more because every single punch had landed.

"So what do I do now?"

"As I said earlier, you could do nothing."

"And I said I couldn't."

"You could have the baby aborted – assuming they do that in Thailand."

"What's to stop her from telling me that's what she's done, and then keeping both the baby and my money?"

"*That's* your biggest concern?"

"No, but, you know. It would mean I have to spend the rest of my life worrying that one day there will be a knock on the door followed by some kid looking up at me and saying 'hi, Daddy!' with a Thai accent."

"So go to Bangkok and hold her hand while she gets the operation. Or you take Option 3."

"Which is?"

"You go back to Bangkok. You hand her a large wad of cash."

"How much?"

"However much you like. The key thing is it's visually impressive. Better still, get a stack or two that still have the bank's paper bands around them. Push it across the table like they do in the movies. Show her you're not counting pennies on this thing; you're all in. And most important, for the first time since you met that poor girl, you're doing something for her *before* she does something for you."

Maybe it was the rare consumption of wine in the middle of the day. Maybe he was worn down by days of worry and too little sleep. But Brian had to admit that what Andrew was saying actually made sense. Despite the unexpected emergence of some strong feelings for Nan, he still thought of her first and foremost as a bar girl.

"I need to stop thinking about her as a whore, and start thinking of her as the mother of my child."

"Welcome to your final destination, Mr. Cahill," said a supremely satisfied Andrew. "We hope you've enjoyed your flight."

For the first time since Nan had stormed out of lunch at the Oriental Hotel, Brian felt the muscles in his upper back unclench. He raised a finger to call over the waiter but never took his eyes off his colleague. "You should have gone for the Gaia & Rey Chardonnay. It's 350 quid a bottle, but today I would have considered that money well spent."

"McLean."

"Guv, it's McCarthy in the lab. I've got those results you wanted."

"I appreciate your getting them so quickly."

"Well, Chief Franklin can be very persuasive – especially when he comes to the lab in person."

Ian smiled. That was one international phone call that had been worth making, no matter how much it cost the British taxpayer. "So what did you find?"

"We've got a match."

"Excellent! So both hair and blood sample matched with Cahill?"

"I said *a* match, sir. Singular. The baby hair is definitely genetically linked to Cahill. 99% certainty on that. But the blood is from someone else."

"Someone else? How can that be?"

"That's your area of expertise, guv. All I can tell you is that the blood did not come from Brian Cahill."

"Are you sure? Did you repeat the test?"

"Five times, because I knew you'd ask. 0% correlation."

"But that can't be. It must be Cahill's."

"Again, sir, it's not. I'm positive."

"Right. Okay. Thanks. You did your best."

The last comment did not sit well with Lab Technician McCarthy. "Hey, guv, it's not my fault things didn't turn out like you thought they would. I did my job and I did it right. Everything else is on you."

"Of course. I'm sorry. Just a little surprised by the results."

McLean hit End and looked up at Sally. "The hair's a match, but the blood isn't."

"How in the hell could that happen?"

The inspector shook his head. "I don't know. Either the blood is from *after* the Cahill cleanup, or I'm barking up the wrong tree."

Thomas tried to be supportive. "The blood doesn't have to be linked to a murder. Jeab's been living there on his own for over a week, and he doesn't look like the sort who does a lot of house cleaning. Maybe he cut himself, or dropped a piece of meat on the floor, or came home bloody after a night out drinking."

"We'll know soon enough," Ian pointed out. "Nat did a DNA swab of Jeab when we were there with the forensics team. Should be easy to match that with the blood samples."

"Technically, sure," Sally agreed. "But I'm not sure I'd trust Nat's reporting of the results."

"Good point. We need to get our hands on that swab – or at least the data map – so we can compare it with the blood sample I took."

"And how, dear leader, do you propose we do that?" Sally asked. "Is there a little B&E in my future? Some light lock picking followed by a vigorous round of targeted thievery?"

Ian shook his head. "I just worked out the What. Give me a minute to figure out the How."

"I have an idea," Thomas said brightly. "We ask for some of the sample to send to London so we can check it against our criminal database, just in case this was an all-England affair that just happened to be played out in Thailand. Nat's likely to agree, since if this is just *farang* on *farang* violence, his country – and its tourist industry – come out clean."

McLean's jaw dropped. "That's bloody brilliant, Thomas."

"Glad you think so. And now that you're in a good mood I need to talk to you about how I claim for the 3,000 baht I spent on my bedside chat with Lilly – and no, she didn't give me a receipt."

CHAPTER 40

As Andrew had suggested, Brian spent the next two months trying not to think about the woman who might be carrying his child.

On the first day of the third month since the lunch at Cecconi's, he started calling her.

He managed to limit himself to a single call per day for the first week. Then he allowed himself two. By the end of the month he was calling every hour on the hour from 12 to 6 P.M. Bangkok time, when he figured she'd be home and awake. The law of averages dictated she heard the phone ring on at least several occasions, but her obstinacy was in full flower and she never picked up.

The following month he started moving the calls earlier and earlier but wasn't tremendously surprised when Nan didn't answer. He hoped she was just still mad at him. The alternative – she changed phones to keep him from ever reaching her again – would have made it impossible to put Andrew's suggestion into practice.

He thought about making a quick trip to Bangkok so they could talk in person. He had enough miles that the flight would be free. Or he could figure out a reason why the business trip scheduled for next month needed to be pulled forward. But what would he do when he got there? Nan had probably stopped working as soon as she started to show. And if she was still at Lady Go Go, there was a reasonably good chance that she'd greet his unannounced arrival with a beer bottle across the face.

The girl did have a temper.

No, he had to give her fair warning. If she chose to meet him, they'd talk until they worked things out. And if she didn't? Well, that was another way for the story to end.

He spent the next three days crafting a text message. It had to be simple enough for Nan to understand, but not so brusque it sounded angry or dismissive.

Dear Nan,

I'm very sorry about how I acted over lunch. I want to do the right thing. I can't marry you, but I can take care of you and our baby. I want you both to be happy.

I will be in Thailand again May 13 – 17. Could we meet then?

Brian

A week went by with no response. Brian felt his emotions bouncing from Disappointed to Angry to Sad and back again. Maybe this was the end of the road after all. Maybe this was the only way the story *could* end. Maybe Andrew had been right from the very beginning: happy endings only happen in Hollywood movies.

Especially when there's a prostitute in one of the lead roles.

Brian tried telling himself that the baby was never real, or at least not his. But despite there being no evidence to the contrary, he just wasn't convinced. Nan's anger had been real, and what set it off was Brian's refusal to step up and take responsibility – not just monetarily, but morally. She expected him to act like a father.

And he'd failed her.

That meant he was going to fail the baby as well, a child that he would never see, a child whose existence would haunt him until the end of his days. What if Sylvia couldn't have children? What if he never met the only child he was able to produce?

Just as he was picking up the pace of self-flagellation, a ping told him he had a new message:

Come to my apartment on May 14 at 6:30 P.M. The address is noted below.

Brian found himself thrilled to get a response, then very worried by its contents. The English was perfect, down to the unprecedented use of prepositions. There was simply no way Nan wrote it without help. And that got Brian wondering who might have lent a hand.

It didn't take long before his mind showed him a vision of the aging *farang* he had seen leaving the bar with Nan over a year ago. Was that his replacement? For that matter, was he the real father of the child? Maybe the two of them had been together for years, and had planned this little scam so that Brian would unwittingly finance their growing family. Did they lie in bed together, giggling while they composed the response? Would that wrinkly old lecher be there on the 14th, coaching Nan on how to extract the maximum value from poor blind-sided Brian?

Once the dark thoughts started falling they quickly became a downpour. Maybe it wasn't some old fart who was calling the shots. Maybe it was a young stud, someone who Nan actually fancied. All muscles and no money, an Aussie surfer dude or one of those Americans raised on nothing but animal protein. Either could add the threat of physical violence to the mental bashing Nan was managing so well on her own.

Brian tried to tell himself that his imagination was running away from him, that the most likely explanation was that Nan had asked one of her customers at the bar to help her with a short text. And even if Nan's wasn't the only face to greet him when he walked into her apartment on the 14th, Brian found he was actually looking forward to the showdown. However the story ended, he needed to get closure on this sordid chapter in his life; the constant wondering and worrying was consuming far too much of his mental energy.

The past few days he'd been so distracted that his boss called him in for a very uncomfortable chat about burnout. While he'd been tempted to reveal all – just to see the man's head explode – he settled for the incomplete yet accurate "troubles in my love life" to explain his lack of focus.

"Yes, well, get them sorted and get back to work. You're not a child, you know" the old man replied, washing his hands of the matter.

And then there was Sylvia. Amazingly, the boss had noticed something was amiss long before she did. When she finally did ask, she opted for the neutral "are you feeling okay?" Brian seized the opportunity offered, and said he "might have picked up a little something the last time I was in Bangkok."

It would have been funny had it been happening to anyone else.

Sylvia ordered him to see a doctor immediately, saying, "I fear the worst." It was all Brian could do to keep himself from saying "Oh no you don't – trust me."

Yet despite all the time he'd spent thinking about his predicament, Brian still hadn't figured out how he wanted the story to end. A verdict of "no baby" would be ideal, but that possibility dropped out of the running the second Nan agreed to meet him. Could he live with himself knowing that a child, *his* child, was growing up without a father? On the other hand, could he really create a world in which any other scenario was possible?

Ultimately, the ending of the story was not his to write. His future would be determined on May 14 at 6:30 P.M. in the Din Daeng suburb of Bangkok.

CHAPTER 41

"He said what?" an outraged Sally asked.

"He said no."

"On what grounds?"

"Chain of custody regulations don't allow him to release evidence – even redundant evidence. And of course it doesn't help we're not part of Thai law enforcement."

"Plus we want to send the evidence overseas," Thomas added.

"Exactly. It's a disappointment, but I have to admit that if the shoe was on the other foot I probably would have made the same argument."

"Stop being so damn understanding and join me in being outraged."

"I would, Sally, except there's some good news to go with the bad."

"So spill."

"Nat also told me they got a match on the blood."

"Okay, I'll admit I wasn't expecting that. Who is it?"

"Nan."

"Nan who died of a self-inflicted drug overdose involving no blood?"

"One and the same. Apparently the forensics team bagged and tagged a hairbrush, which had more than enough DNA to make the match."

"Are you certain?"

"You disappoint me, Sally. I thought you'd be pleased."

"I suppose I am. I'm just being cautious. I'm not used to getting good news on this case."

"Nat said they ran the test on all 38 blood samples. All of them match the DNA from the hairbrush with 99% confidence."

"Meaning it was either Nan or a total stranger who came over to the house and brushed her hair thoroughly before being slaughtered in the kitchen."

Ian grimaced. "Possible but not likely, I'd say."

"And you're sure Nat is telling the truth?" Thomas asked.

"That's actually the question that bothers me the most. But since he won't give us access to the evidence itself, I don't see any option other than to take him at his word."

"And you're willing to do that?" Sally asked.

"On many things, no. But we're not here to investigate Nan. Our only interest in her death is how it relates to Cahill's. If the Thai authorities are still trying to sell the natural causes idea, the last thing they'd want to do is provide us with evidence that might suggest Nan had been murdered."

That silenced the two detectives, but only for a few moments. "Unless the mutilated heart made it clear natural causes wasn't going to fly, and this bit of apparent sharing is really just a cover-up being reshaped to match changing conditions on the ground." Having finished her thought, Sally suddenly attacked her right ear, scratching at it like a dog with fleas. "What are they asking us to believe? That Cahill was sliced open without leaving any blood evidence, while Nan OD'd quietly in her bed but not before bleeding all over her kitchen floor? It's like they're having a laugh."

"Maybe that's the point," said Thomas. "Distract us from Cahill by giving us a mystery wrapped in an enigma with Nan lying in the middle."

"Winston Churchill is rolling in his grave, but I know what you mean," Ian admitted.

"Well, then that's the only thing we *do* know." Sally had stopped scratching, but was now using her thumb and forefinger to twirl the complimentary pen provided by the hotel. "Two people who were involved – sexually if not romantically – die within days of each other. In both cases the official cause of death doesn't stand up. If that's a coincidence it belongs in the *Guinness Book of World Records* under the heading 'Most Unbelievable Story Ever Told.'"

Ian suddenly sat upright. "You could well be right. This *is* a story. *Romeo and Juliet* to be precise." The inspector looked well-pleased with the statement; Sally and Thomas just looked confused. "You want me to explain that?" McLean asked.

"Uh, *yeah*," Sally said.

"Brian and Nan have a fight. In a moment of passion, she kills him. Cleans up all evidence of the murder. But then she's overcome with remorse, and tries to kill herself with the same knife that carved up Cahill. Stabs herself a couple of times, drawing blood. But she discovers it's not as easy to stick a blade through your own skin as it is to slash someone else. She decides the knife isn't going to work. She cleans up, but hastily; after all, in a few minutes a little blood on the floor is not going to matter at all. She goes to the bedroom and takes the drug overdose. Fade to black."

Sally frowned. "You'll notice we're not clapping, Ian. There are a couple of flaws in your scenario. First of all, why was there no mention of any knife wounds in the police report of her death?"

"Because they didn't bother looking. Even Nat admitted they rushed to judgment after seeing the drugs. Why search for knife wounds when you've already determined an overdose was the cause of death?"

"*Second*," a clearly irritated Sally persisted, "how did Cahill get from Nan's apartment to his hotel room if she was busy slashing herself and swallowing *ya ba*?"

"Maybe all that happened *after* the body was dropped off. It actually makes more sense that way. Gives her a little time to reflect on what she's done, and start feeling horrible about it."

Sally ignored the parry. "Third and most important, you said all along it was unlikely Nan had the physical strength to put a meat clever through Cahill's chest. What happened to that logic?"

For that, McLean had no immediate comeback.

"So I'd say we're right back where we fucking started," Sally concluded.

"No, we're not." Ian stood and began pacing around the room like a caged lion. "There *is* something wrong with my *Romeo and*

Juliet analogy. There are actually three people involved in this little drama."

"And the killer makes three," said Thomas enthusiastically.

"No! Well, technically yes. Then four. Unless he didn't come home until afterwards, like he said."

"You're incoherent again, Ian. Please slow down and tell us what you're talking about."

McLean dutifully dropped onto the sofa, then immediately sprang back to his feet. "Tell me: What's the brother doing here?"

"He said he was looking for construction work," Thomas reminded the group.

"Yes, but why is he *still* here? He's no longer got Nan to pay the rent or buy food or nurse the baby. He may not like life on the farm, but he can't afford to live in the city. He needs to be surrounded by women who know more about raising an infant than he does. And think about it: would *you* hang around the apartment where your sister committed suicide?"

"Something's holding him in Bangkok," Sally summarized.

"But what?" Thomas asked.

"The same thing that brought him here: money."

"Money for what?"

"For keeping his mouth shut."

"You think he's blackmailing the killers?"

"Either that or he's trying to. Staying where he is means he controls the crime scene. If he went home he'd be inviting the killers to frame him for both deaths."

"You think he walked in while the murders were being completed?" Thomas asked.

"Hello?" said a visibly annoyed Sally. "Aren't you boys forgetting something? Nat said Cahill and Nan didn't die on the same night."

"This being the same Nat who told us Cahill died of natural causes and Nan died of an overdose?"

"Fair point," Sally admitted.

"So what are you going to do?" Thomas asked.

"I thought I'd call Nat."

"What makes you think he's finally going to be straight with you?"

"The fact I'm not going to ask him any questions about what actually happened."

"Yeah, that would just be *rude*." Sally's scratching started again.

"I'm putting the call on speaker. Feel free to jump in if you think I'm going too easy on him." McLean scrolled down to an earlier call from Nat, and hit redial. The phone was answered so quickly it caught the inspector off guard. "Oh, hi, Nat. It's Ian. McLean. And I've got Sally and Thomas with me."

"Hi, all," Nat said with what sounded like genuine friendliness.

"We're calling to get your view on something, specifically Nan's brother Jeab. We've been wondering why he's still here in Bangkok, even though it's not a cheap place to live – especially for a man with no income – and the baby would be better off surrounded by aunts and grandmothers who have experience raising a child."

The Thai policeman took a moment to consider his response. "I suppose he's putting his sister's affairs in order. Once that's done he'll probably return to Isaan."

"But you haven't spoken to him about his plans?"

"No, I haven't. And I can't see how they would be relevant to our case."

"Hmm." Ian paused for dramatic effect; only Sally and Thomas could see him counting to five on his fingers. "I won't pretend to be a good judge of Thai body language, but there was something in his behavior the other day that I can't stop thinking about."

"What's that?"

"It may sound crazy, but I thought he seemed almost *happy* when the forensics team found traces of blood."

"Can't say I noticed that," Nat replied evenly.

"Maybe I'm reading things that weren't there. But just for a second, assume I'm right. Why would he be pleased to see his sister's blood on the floor?"

There was no hiding the irritation in Nat's reply. "I don't know, Ian. Maybe he'd prefer to think of his sister as an innocent victim rather than someone so troubled she took her own life."

"Maybe," Ian agreed, "maybe." Once again Ian paused as if he was taking time to think. "It would be a whole lot easier to close this loop if we could interview Jeab in person. Why don't we meet up at Nan's apartment later today and question him together?"

The sudden change in urgency was palpable, even through the iPhone's tiny speakers. "The interrogation is a good idea, but we'll get more out of him if we bring him in. Country boys like him tend to panic inside a big city police station, and that unlocks lips. I'll have him picked up, maybe even leave him in the cells overnight to soften up his defenses. I'll let you know as soon as he's ready to talk."

Sally couldn't resist. "You can hold him without charge?"

"For 12 days. A judge can then award another 12 days – six times."

"Nearly three months to get your ducks in a row? That's amazing!" Sally said.

"You'd think, but sometimes even three months is not long enough," Nat grumbled. "The way this case is going, I wouldn't feel confident even if we had a year."

CHAPTER 42

Cahill had the hotel car drop him off at the address Nan had sent. He walked back and forth in front of the building a few times before the driver recognized his confusion, hopped out of the Mercedes, pointed out the staircase to the rear of the building, and then drove off.

Brian climbed the stairs gingerly, more than a little concerned by how much the whole assembly shook in response to each step he took. It was with considerable relief that he opened the door to the third floor, and saw a dark entrance hall with apartments off to either side.

The once-public space had been largely converted to private storage, with children's toys, a small bicycle, two strollers, an ancient microwave, four motorcycle helmets, and dog-eared magazines stacked up chest high. Brian tried to imagine his son – he had locked onto the idea that the child would be a boy – growing up in these conditions.

And failed.

Any son of his should grow up in England. Maybe not all the time; it was important that he understand and appreciate his Thai heritage, and probably learn the language. But there was simply no way that the son of Brian Cahill was going to spend his life waiting on drunk, horny *farang* at Lady Go Go, or join the 400,000 people selling food, clothing and trinkets on the sidewalks of Bangkok. The fruit of his loins deserved better than that.

Brian made a mental note to add child rearing and educational strategies to the list of topics to be discussed in the meeting that was about to take place. Then he rang the bell.

It was answered by Nan almost immediately. She was plainly, almost unflatteringly dressed. She looked tired, and frazzled, and extremely nervous.

She also looked absolutely gorgeous.

Only then did Brian notice the baby.

The first words out of his mouth were, "Is this it?"

That was a mistake. "Not 'it'. She. She name Ploy."

"Ploy? But that means a scheme or a maneuver. It sounds terrible, in English at least."

"No English. Thai."

And suddenly all the reasons these three could never be a family came crashing back. They were all too different, their worlds too far apart.

Though the baby was adorable. Lighter skinned than Brian had expected, with thick curly hair that must have come from the Cahill genes. "May I come in?"

Nan stepped aside to let him enter. This was the first time he'd ever seen where she lived, and it wasn't what he'd expected. It was tiled floor to ceiling, making it feel more like a bathroom or a locker room than a home. There were no cute feminine touches; the emphasis was on function rather than charm.

From where he stood Brian could see a little of the bedroom, and there concessions had been made to the new baby. There were pictures of elephants and puppies that appeared to have been cut out of magazines. A mobile hung from the ceiling over what looked to be a brand new crib. Presumably Nan's bed was off to the right, hidden by the half-open door.

"This is very nice," he said.

Nan shrugged. "Okay. Better than farm."

"And the baby looks healthy. Congratulations, by the way."

Cahill couldn't believe how stupid he sounded. "By the way?" That was his daughter, his flesh and blood. Surely he felt something more than "by the way"?

"Can I hold her?"

Nan debated the request for a moment, and then extended the baby towards him. Brian took her as if she were a package, letting her head dangle dangerously from her still weak neck.

Horrified, Nan grabbed Ploy and clutched the child to her chest. "You no hold baby. No good. No understand baby."

That was certainly true, Brian had to admit.

"Why don't we sit down? We've got a lot to discuss."

Nan sat, primly, and on the edge of her chair. She clearly had her defenses up and all systems on high alert. But she was already very much a mother, rocking gently backing and forth as she shushed the baby.

"Let me start by saying how pleased I am to see the baby – to see *Ploy* – is doing so well. She's healthy. She's beautiful. You should be proud."

Nan gave the smallest of acknowledgements.

"I'm proud, too. After all, she is my daughter." As the words hung in the humidity-heavy air, Brian wondered whether they were true. If he was going to ask for a paternity test, now was the time. But one look at Nan's face and he realized that question would shut the door to him having any future relationship with Nan *or* his daughter.

With Ploy.

So he moved onto safer ground. "I told you I would pay for everything to do with the birth, but then we" – Brian struggled to find the right words – "we got separated a bit. Anyhow, we're together now, and I brought the money I promised you."

He placed two stacks of crisp new 1,000 baht bills on the living room table. He'd been unable to arrange for the paper currency straps Andrew had suggested, so the piles were held together with rubber bands. Still, it looked like an awful lot of money.

Nan was unimpressed. She said nothing, while continuing to rock the baby.

"Now I know that's not enough money to take care of everything, especially if you can't work." The words were no sooner out of his mouth than his mind flashed to that horrible image of Nan walking out of Lady Go Go on the arm of a man old enough to be her grandfather. Had she slept with men like that while little Ploy was still growing inside her? Worse, was she using the mouth with which she kissed the baby to...? Best not to think about it.

"In fact, that might not be enough money to cover all your out-of-pocket expenses: doctor's visits, taxis, the hospital, the crib, things for the baby, and so on." He'd been here for two minutes, and already he was doing exactly what Andrew told him *not* to: turning a highly emotional exchange into a bloodless review of costs incurred and subject to reimbursement.

Nan said nothing.

"As always, I don't know how often I'll be able to come to Bangkok, much less when those trips would be. Maybe the easiest thing would be for me to send you the same amount of money each month? I could wire it directly to your bank account. And if it's not enough you can just tell me. Or I can bring you cash the next time I come to town. Whichever works better for you." Brian forced himself to smile. "Look, Nan, I'm trying. I've never been a father before, and I don't know what I should be doing. I don't know what your life is like here in Bangkok, much less what you need and how I can help. But please believe I really do want to make you happy."

It was clear from Nan's contemptuous expression that Brian wasn't making headway, but he was determined to soldier on. "Remember that place in Chiang Rai we went to? We could take Ploy and let her ride on an elephant. That would be fun, wouldn't it?"

No reaction.

"Look, Nan: I love our baby, and I want to make sure she's got everything she could ever want."

The dam burst. "Love? You say *love*? Why you love but no marry?"

His natural inclination to correct the careless utterings of others had him on the verge of pointing out he'd expressed love for the baby, not for her. Fortunately he caught himself before falling over the edge. "Nan, can I suggest we separate our conversation into two parts? Let's talk about the baby first. Once that's settled we can discuss what happens between you and me."

"Me, baby, same. You say before, you take care Nan. Take care baby. Take care family. Now only take care baby. You talk sweet things, but you no good." The gentle rocking had taken on a noticeable edge.

How had he screwed this up so badly? He'd rehearsed this scene in his mind maybe a hundred times, and each time it ended with the two of them in each other's arms. He hadn't expected to encounter such resistance, such anger, such... hate. "Nan, I said I would take care of everything, and I will. You have to believe that."

"You say many thing. No true. Now I no listen."

Brian felt a surge of emotion that carried him out of his seat and closer to the mother of his child. Only a fierce glare from Nan got him to retrace his steps and return to his seat.

"You say take care Nan. Then you go London. No come back Thailand long time. Ploy born. You bring money. No present for baby. You no ask is she okay, can she sleep, can she eat, am I okay. Think only one thing. Think only money."

"That's not fair, Nan! You're right, I should have brought something for Ploy. But until I got here I didn't know if my child was a boy or a girl. Can you imagine what that feels like? I'm trying here, I really am. But I don't know what to do and you're not helping."

The words came out far more harshly than Brian intended. Nan stared at him as if trying to melt him with her eyes.

"You have to be patient with me, Nan. Okay? Now, how much do you need for the baby every month?"

Nan said nothing.

"Let's say a thousand dollars a month. That's 33,000 baht. That should be enough, right?"

No response.

"Now let's talk about you. You're not going back to work, are you?"

"How can work? Who want lady with baby?" She pointed at her belly. "All fat. No good."

"I understand. Let's say two thousand a month for you. How does three thousand dollars a month sound? That's 100,000 baht."

Nan shook her head furiously.

"Not just baby. Not just Nan. Must pay mama-san."

"Why do I have to pay mama-san?" The only response was seething silence.

"Nan, I'm not arguing with you or refusing to pay. I'm just trying to understand how this all works. Why do we need to pay the mama-san?"

"Mama bring me to Bangkok. Lend money for house, for clothes. No working, no can pay back."

"Okay. See: when you explain things like that it all makes sense to me. You owe mama-san money. How much?"

Brian thought he could see various sums auditioning in Nan's brain. The winner was "50 thousand."

"Fifty thousand baht? That's not too bad. I'll take care of that for you."

Nan shook her head violently. "No baht. Dollar."

"You owe mama-san $50,000? Are you serious?"

Nan said nothing. Brian held up his hands in surrender. "Okay, I get it. You probably needed to put up first and last months' rent, and a security deposit. Then you had to buy furniture... it all adds up. Fine. We'll find a way to pay off that debt. Is that now everything?"

"Need money for family. Father sick. Heart no good. No can work. Mother not strong. Always tired. Much sleeping. No can work in field."

Brian was starting to get angry about the apparently endless list of demands. Why was it his responsibility to pay for things that happened long before he even met Nan? Her parents' medical issues were not his problem. If she wanted to take some of the money he sent her each month and spend it on her parents rather than some new shoes or a trip to the hairdresser, fine. He wasn't going to dictate how she spent those funds. But he also wasn't going to let himself be turned into a cash machine that spews money whenever someone in Nan's family ran a bit short.

"Brother no have job. Must help him."

That did it. "Look, Nan. This is getting out of control. I said I would take care of you and the baby, and I will. But I am not going to take care of your entire family."

"You say!"

"I never said I would pay for anything and everything they want."

"You say! Dinner at Four Seasons, you say you take care. I ask family. You say yes!"

Brian had never seen her this furious. Her body was literally shaking with anger. The prudent course would have been to retreat, or at least move the conversation onto less sensitive ground. But Cahill wasn't sure he'd get another chance to engage. "Nan, you have to be reasonable. I know that to Thai people all *farang* look rich. And I *am* very comfortable, I'll admit. But that doesn't mean I'm made of money."

"What mean?"

"It means there have to be limits." The phrase clearly didn't register. "It means I can't pay for everything."

"Where you stay?" The question brought back happy memories of the night he met the girl sitting before him. He smiled. "The Four Seasons, as always."

Nan bobbed her head triumphantly. "What room you stay?"

That made Brian blush. He had paid for an upgrade to the Garden Terrace Suite with his own money, thinking that if everything went well, he and Nan might end up in bed together – just like old times. He even had two bottles of Dom Pérignon Champagne chilling in the mini-fridge next to a bowl of fresh strawberries dipped in chocolate.

Only now did he realize his planning had failed to make any provision for the baby.

"I'm staying in the Garden Terrace Suite. It's one of the villas you can see from the pool."

Nan's smiled like a courtroom lawyer who has just elicited a confession. "You rich! Best hotel. Best room. Must have much money."

Brian was about to explain the unusual extravagance, but one look at Ploy and he realized it would be easier to shoot himself and save Nan the bother. "Nan, let's both calm down. I tell you what: You tell me how much money you want, upfront – which means right now – and every month. If I think it's reasonable, I'll give you the money and you do with it whatever you want. Is that okay?"

She didn't answer immediately, making Brian think she didn't understand the question. But then she opened her mouth, and when she spoke the only emotion behind her words was a steely determination.

"$75,000 now, $10,000 every month."

"What? That's outrageous! How much money do you make now?"

Nan said nothing.

"I'm asking you: how much money do you make fucking strangers?"

Every muscle in Nan's body tensed, and the rocking became so furious it was a miracle Ploy didn't wake up screaming.

"Hmm? I'm happy to give you as much money as you're making right now, so tell me how much that is. How much do you make for sleeping with men who don't even know your goddamn name?"

"You sleep Nan first time, no know name."

"Believe me: right now I wish that night had never happened."

The two sat glaring at each other in angry silence for several minutes. Then Nan repeated her demand, with a mindlessness that made it sound like a mantra. "$75,000 now, $10,000 every month."

"That's extortion and you know it. There is simply no way you make $120,000 a year. I bet you don't even make a quarter of that. You think that just because one night we ran out of condoms – and I'm not convinced that was an accident, by the way – you think you can demand whatever you want and I'll have no choice but to pay it. But you're wrong."

"No, you wrong."

"Well, either way, I'm not paying."

"No pay, no come Thailand."

Brian wasn't sure he'd heard her correctly. "Are you telling me where I can and cannot go?"

Nan shook her head resolutely. "You bad man. Tell police. Police say no come Thailand. No can work. Shame for you."

"*You* are going to tell the police about *me*? That's hilarious! I should tell the police about *you*. About how you trick men into having unprotected sex, and then claim they're the father of your child – even though there isn't one bit of evidence you're telling the truth. I should tell the police you're trying to extort money from foreign businessmen who come here to help the Thai economy. I should tell the police that you're a bad woman, a very bad woman."

Nan was now clutching Ploy so tightly Brian worried she would suffocate the child. "You want talk police? You want? Police here. You talk him."

A man came out of Nan's bedroom. He was wearing a dark grey uniform with epaulets on the shoulders and rows of medals above the left pocket. He wasn't physically imposing, but he had the dead eyes of a man who had seen everything and cared about very little of it.

Brian was so startled by the sudden appearance that only when the man reached into a kitchen drawer did Brian notice he was wearing latex gloves.

CHAPTER 43

Jeab Supitayaporn was escorted into Interrogation Room 3 with shackles on both wrists and ankles. Sally turned to Ian in surprise; they had been expecting a witness, not a prisoner.

And a completely downtrodden prisoner at that. Jeab's head was bowed, and it remained that way throughout the interrogation that followed. Thomas elbowed his boss. "What do you think they did to him?"

McLean never got a chance to answer the question. A woman who introduced herself as "the interpreter" walked confidently into the room. She was petite and on the north side of 50, with librarian glasses on a chain and a ready smile that suggested she found pretty much everything to be at least mildly amusing. She explained that most of her work came from advertising focus groups and apologized in advance for "not knowing police lingo."

Nat pulled a recording device out of his shirt pocket, and switched it on. He began speaking in Thai, which – much to the amazement of the Scotland Yard contingent – the interpreter simultaneously translated into first-person English.

"The date is May 27, 2014. I am Nattapong Kadesadayurat of the Bangkok police. The suspect is Jeab Supitayaporn, who was arrested yesterday on suspicion of involvement in the death of Brian Cahill, a citizen of the United Kingdom. Observing this interrogation are three detectives from Scotland Yard: Detective Inspector Ian McLean, and detectives Sally Chan and Thomas McMillan. The current time" – he stopped to check the time on his massive Casio G-Shock watch – is "9:43 A.M." Nat took a sip of water from the glass to his right. "Mr. Supitayaporn, where were you on the evening of May 14?"

"I don't remember."

"You don't remember the night a man was killed in your living room?"

Jeab's head sunk still lower. "I didn't realize that was May 14. Maybe I'm still in shock."

"You haven't answered my question. Before you came home to find a dead man on your floor, what were you doing?"

"I was having dinner at a street stall on Sukhumvit."

"What was the name of that stall?"

"I don't know. I don't think it has one."

"That's very convenient, isn't it? Can you remember anything about the stand?"

"It's near the Robinson's department store."

"If we went to all of the stands near Robinson's department store and showed your picture, would someone recognize you?"

"I don't know. Probably not. I usually just eat my meal and then leave."

"Do you go to this particular stand often?"

"Yes. I like their *pad ga-prao gai.*" "That's chicken stir fried with basil," the translator added.

"The Robinsons on Sukhumvit is a long way from your house. Why go so far just for *pad ga-prao gai*?"

"I was in the area looking for work at the big construction sites. I like going at the end of the day, when the supervisors are less busy and able to talk."

"And did you find a job?"

"No, I did not."

"Then you had dinner. What happened next?"

"I went to have a few drinks with some friends."

"How is a man with no job able to afford to go drinking?"

"My sister gives me money when I need it."

"Speaking of that sister, why didn't you go home and have dinner with her?"

"She asked me not to."

"Why?"

"She said she was having a friend over, and wanted some privacy."

"Was that unusual?"

"Yes. Her friends come around often. This was the first time I was asked to stay away."

"Didn't you find that strange?"

"Yes, but it's her apartment. I must do as she asks."

"Okay. What time was it when you finished drinking?"

"I think it was about 9 P.M."

"'About'?"

"I can't say for sure. I was pretty drunk by that point."

"Then what did you do?"

"I got a *tuk-tuk* home."

"Do you remember what time it was when you arrived?"

"I do not, but if I left the bar at 9, it was probably 9:30 or 10:00 when I reached my sister's apartment."

"And what did you see when you arrived?"

"Something horrible."

"Please tell me exactly what you saw."

"There was a man, a *farang*, lying on the floor. He was surrounded by blood. I have never seen so much blood. My sister was kneeling next to him. She was crying hysterically. There was a meat cleaver sticking out of the man's chest. It was covered in blood."

"What did you think had happened?"

"I thought my sister had killed the *farang*."

"What did you do next?"

"I told my sister we had to get rid of the body."

"What did she say?"

"She didn't say anything; she was too upset."

"So what did you do?"

"I told her I would take care of it, and that she should go take a long, hot shower to get rid of the blood."

"And did she?"

"Yes."

"Then what happened?"

"After she left the room, I grabbed an empty plastic bag and covered my right hand so I wouldn't leave any fingerprints. I went to take the chopper out of the man's chest, and noticed his body had been split open like a fish. I knew this was a big problem. It would prove the man's death was murder, not an accident."

"How did you know that?"

"I watch a lot of American police shows. We have satellite TV."

"So what did you do?"

"I looked at the hole in his chest. It was very big. I could see his stomach and other organs. The hole was so large I worried that if I just picked him up, all of his insides would fall out."

Nat pretended to make a note. "So what did you do?"

"I tried to think of ways to close the body. On TV they talk about sewing up the body. I was going to ask my sister for a needle and thread, but then I realized that wouldn't be strong enough to hold the body together. So I went into my bedroom and got some fishing line and a hook."

"Why did you have these things?"

"Sometimes I go fishing in the Chao Phraya so I don't have to take money from my sister in order to eat."

"I see. What did you do next?"

"I straightened the hook so I could use it like a needle. Then I sewed up his body as best I could."

"And how good was that?"

"Not very good. It's difficult to do. The skin is very tough. The hook kept bending. And by that point I started to panic. My hands were shaking."

"But you never thought about calling the police?"

"I couldn't. I knew they would arrest my sister."

"What happened next?"

"I knew we had to get rid of the body. I wanted to throw it in the river, but when I told my sister she said that was a bad idea."

"Why?"

"Because he was *farang*, and had lots of money. She said the police would keep looking for him until they found a body."

"Did she have a better idea?"

"Yes. She said we should take him somewhere the police could easily find him."

"How did you do that?"

"I had a large duffel bag which I used when I moved from our family farm in Isaan to my sister's place. We put the body in it. Then we got a taxi and asked him to take us to the Four Seasons Hotel."

"Why there?"

"My sister said he was staying there. She also said he was staying in a very expensive room that had a private entrance.

I think it was called the Garden Terrace Suite. She told the taxi where to go, and had him drop us off in front of the entrance."

"Then what happened?"

"There was a security guard at the gate. My sister said she was staying with the guest inside. He asked the guest's name, which she told him. He asked what was in the bag. She said it was her clothes, and that she was planning to spend several days with the man."

"So he let you in?"

"No. First he called the room, and no one answered. That made him suspicious. But then my sister said that he was working late, and had asked her to wait for him in the room."

"Did the guard believe you?"

"I don't think so. He asked my sister what the name of the guy's company was."

"Did she know what it was?"

"She did! I was very surprised. But still the guard didn't believe us. He said if my sister was really staying there, she should have a room key. She reached into her handbag and pulled out a plastic card with the hotel name on it."

"Where did she get that?"

"She told me later she kept it from a stay several months ago, when she spent a weekend with the man. But she told the guard the man had given it to her so she could let herself in."

"Did the guard check the key?"

"He said he would ask someone from the front desk to come pick up the key, and take it back to the main lobby where they could put it in some kind of machine that would read it. I said the duffel bag was really heavy, and offered him 100 baht if he'd just let us in."

"And did he?"

"Yes."

"Then what?"

"We went into the room – it was more like a house – and put the man in his bed. We had taken his bloody clothes off at our apartment, and washed off all the blood. Now we dressed him in some gym clothes we found in his suitcase. My sister went into the bathroom and found some medicine in his travel bag. She said he had a bad heart, and the medicine would make it look like he died of a heart attack. I don't know about such things, but I believed her."

"What happened next?"

"We took a *tuk-tuk* back to the apartment and cleaned everything three times. We checked it very, very carefully to make sure there were no traces of blood left."

Nat leaned back in his chair, lifting the front legs off the floor. Then suddenly he propelled himself forward so that he was inches from the crown of Jeab's head. "So you're saying that your sister killed Brian Cahill?"

"Yes."

"And that you helped cover up the crime?"

"Yes."

"Why did she do such a thing?"

"She said she showed him baby Ploy and told him he was the father. The *farang* became furious and called her a dirty whore and other terrible names. He said she screwed so many men it was impossible for her to know who the father was. He accused her of lying just to get money. I asked her if he hit her, but she couldn't answer. She was crying too hard. I decided to save the questions for another day, when she had calmed down."

"But she never did calm down, did she?"

"No."

"The next day she took her own life."

"Yes. An overdose of *ya ba*."

Nat let that sit in the air for a bit, then moved in for the close. "Do you swear that everything you have said here today is the truth?"

"Yes."

Nat nodded his head, stood up, and left the interrogation room. He then opened the door to the viewing area where the Scotland Yard team was waiting. With considerable pride Nat said, "What did you think of that?"

Ian smiled. "I thought it was complete and utter bullshit."

CHAPTER 44

"What? You just heard him confess!" Nat was livid.

"No, I heard him read lines that someone else prepared for him. And his story just doesn't stand up."

"He explained everything!"

"Not everything. Not even close. For starters, how big was Nan?"

"I don't know. Maybe 5'4", 5'5"."

"Weight?"

"What does it matter?"

"Just humor me, Nat."

"Probably 110 pounds or so."

"And you're telling me this slip of a woman managed to drive a kitchen knife *through the breastbone* of a man close to a foot taller than she is, then drag that knife through skin, muscle and bone until she'd split his chest open – what was Jeab's phrase? – 'like a fish'?"

Nat could no longer maintain eye contact. "People sometimes find superhuman strength when in a fit of rage."

"We'll come back to that. So, Jeab comes home to discover his sister has just slaughtered someone on the living room floor. He doesn't panic like a normal human being. No, he calmly sews up this still-warm corpse that has been hacked in half, somehow manages to rinse off the victim *so that there is absolutely no blood left in or around the body,* and then stuffs the exsanguinated corpse into a conveniently available duffel bag."

Nat was trying hard to look relaxed and confident. "That's what he said."

"Let's think about that for a minute, shall we? You've got a little girl who just committed murder, and a brother who comes home from a night out with the boys to discover a man he has never seen lying on the kitchen floor with his chest cracked open. These two shell-shocked amateurs have the presence of mind to drain the body so thoroughly there's no telltale trail of blood dripping out of the duffle bag."

"Maybe they wrapped him in a plastic sheet."

"Maybe, though you'd think Jeab would have included that in his story if that's indeed what happened, as it's a pretty important point. And even if they used plastic, it wouldn't have helped them once they unwrapped him at the hotel. As far as we know, based on what you've told us, there was not a single drop of blood anywhere in that hotel room. Do you really think a freshly stabbed body wouldn't ooze at least a little?"

"That's more a question for the coroner than for me."

"One that I look forward to asking him. But for now let's talk about how they broke *into* the Four Seasons, a five-star hotel that frowns on bar girls in the rooms of male guests. Do you really think they just let an unaccompanied, unidentified girl into one of the most expensive suites in the hotel so she can lie in wait until the guest returns?"

"That may not be what the training manual says they should do, but that's what they did."

"In which case it will have been recorded by the security cameras. We can check that later today. But I'm willing to bet that a guard isn't going to put his job at risk for a 100 baht bribe. What is that, anyway? About 2 quid?"

"A little less," Thomas confirmed.

"But she had a key," Nat reminded everyone.

"No she didn't. She had a piece of plastic. That in itself means nothing; I forget to turn mine in all the time. What's more, I'm willing to bet that private entrance comes with a little guardhouse, and somewhere in the little guardhouse is a computer screen or a log of some kind that would have shown Brian Cahill was the only guest *registered* for that suite. And that brings us back to the No Girls In Rooms policy."

The lower lid of Nat's right eye began to twitch. "I'm told that it's different in the villas and suites. Those are used by VIP customers, who can pretty much do what they want."

"I have no doubt that if Brian and Nan had walked up arm in arm, the guard would have saluted and wished them a good night as he opened the gates. But Nan wasn't accompanied by the registered guest. She was accompanied by a Thai man carrying a duffle bag that could have been filled with guns or drugs or God knows what else. No security guard with half a brain is going to wave something like that through. It's a disaster waiting to happen."

"That's why Jeab bribed him."

"For less than the price of a cup of coffee at Starbucks."

"I can't explain why the guard did what he did."

"Then perhaps you can explain something else. Jeab's story left out something very important."

"Oh yeah? What's that?"

"The heart."

"What about it?"

"You've read the coroner's report from the UK. You know Cahill's heart had been punctured eight times."

"Yeah, so?"

"So why didn't Jeab mention that?"

Nat did his best to look disinterested. His best wasn't very good. "Possibly because I didn't ask about it." The Thai policeman suddenly sat up. "He didn't know about it because Nan did it *before* he arrived. And there was so much blood everywhere he didn't notice the puncture wounds."

"Maybe not the wounds themselves, but what about the fruit carving knife using to make them? Where did that disappear to?"

"How should I know? Maybe it got left inside the body."

"Yet it was gone by the time the coroner at Scotland Yard had a look inside."

"Maybe Nan kept it."

"As a souvenir? And how did she manage to keep her brother from seeing it?"

"He probably had a few other things on his mind at that moment. Besides, a fruit carving knife is so small Nan could have hidden it in one of her pockets."

"But why bother? She left the meat cleaver sticking out of Cahill's chest. That alone would be enough to convict her. Why put so much effort into covering up what we're told was a post-mortem injury?"

"How the hell should I know? Besides, it's just one small detail."

"Perhaps, but it's one of several either missing from or incon-sistent with the picture we had drawn for us this morning. And then there's the question of motivation."

Nat didn't rise to the bait. He simply glared.

"Think about it. Someone you had been sexually intimate with, *the father of your child,* is lying on the floor in front of you in a bloody heap, split open like a fish. It must have been an abso-lutely horrific scene. Yet Nan goes rifling through the kitchen drawers until she finds a suitable knife, then sits down next to the still-warm body and starts punching holes in its heart. There are psychopaths who don't have the nerve for something like that."

"Cahill had hurt her. She wanted to hurt him back."

"Almost certainly, though I think the meat cleaver in the chest made the point."

"But it makes a *general* point. It says she was angry, angry enough to kill. But it doesn't say *why* she was so furious. She wanted to send a message that Cahill had a bad heart."

"A message that she promptly covered up when Jeab stitched the corpse back together."

McLean scratched the back of his neck, a pivoting tactic he suddenly realized he'd stolen from TV's Lieutenant Columbo. "Of course, all of that assumes Jeab was actually there on the night."

"You just heard him say he was!"

"Well, someone certainly was. And that brings us nicely to the question of who actually killed Brian Cahill."

"Jeab just told us it was his sister! What is wrong with you people? Didn't you hear what the man said?" He turned to the interpreter. "What were you doing back here?"

She sat straight up and locked eyes with Nat. "I translated absolutely everything that was said, and I did it accurately. I know how to do my job."

McLean quickly intervened. "It's not a translation problem, Nat. I heard Jeab place the blame on his sister. And I agree it's possible – even likely – that Nan struck the first blow. I'd even accept the notion that she was so filled with rage she found superhuman strength."

"It happens," Nat said quietly.

"It does. But that sort of anger tends to burn itself out very quickly, from physical exhaustion if nothing else. Yet somehow Nan managed to land enough blows with the cleaver to kill or at least incapacitate Cahill, each blow struck with enough force to cut through bone. Then she continues whacking until she's got the chest open. Then she gets her fruit knife and goes to work on the heart. That's a very long time to maintain a homicidal rage."

"I believe the legal description of that would be 'relies on facts not in evidence,'" Nat said through clenched teeth.

"Perhaps you're right," Ian said breezily. "In fact, let us assume – temporarily – that Nan somehow managed to do all the hacking on her own. She finds her favorite carving knife and makes eight holes in Cahill's heart without so much as nicking any of the nearby organs, even though she's still in an uncontrolled rage. Her brother comes home, and tells her to go wash off the blood on her body and clothes. While she's doing that, he's figuring out a way to get all the blood out of Cahill's body so that it doesn't leak during transport. That's no easy task. Given the sloppy stitching job, Cahill's chest is still more open than closed and his heart is full of holes. I've been around corpses my entire adult life and I haven't a clue how you'd prevent a mess like that from leaving a blood trail."

"I told you: that's why they wrapped him in plastic."

"Which is fine if we're talking a couple of drops of blood from a cut on your fingertip. But we're talking butchery. Maybe if Nan just happened to have one of those vacuum sealers big enough to handle a guy nearly as tall as I am they could have packaged him up nice and tight so that no blood would leak out. But if you simply roll up a freshly mutilated corpse in a plastic sheet? Blood is going to come pouring out of both ends like an overstuffed tortilla. What happens if Jeab and Nan get in a cab, and the duffle bag starts leaking? The driver is going to know something's up."

"So maybe they dumped Cahill in the trunk."

"Could have happened that way. But it's still pretty risky. At some point the cabbie is going to notice the blood stains in his trunk, and he's going to remember the couple with the man-sized duffle bag. If he takes his suspicions to the police, there's physical evidence combined with a description of the perpetrators."

"Not to mention the driver would know both their pick up address and drop off point," Sally added.

Nat was feeling the pressure, but was not ready to buckle. "They were panicked, not thinking clearly."

"Actually, one of my concerns with this story is it's far *too* clear. Everything ties up neatly, and that rarely happens with a spontaneous crime of passion. No, what I think is far more likely is that a professional supervised the bloodletting. Someone who would know exactly how much blood is in the human body and where it's likely to settle unless forced out."

"Someone like a coroner," Sally said.

"Exactly. Maybe a mere morgue attendant, but certainly someone with more specialist knowledge than a farmer unable to find a construction job in the city."

Nat's eyes were filled with storm clouds. "They don't just farm in Isaan. They also hunt. Killing animals and killing people aren't that different."

"I'll take your word for it. And, to show how open-minded I am, I'll give you that one, too. But that brings us to the next gap in the story. No security guard is going to open a private entrance for a bar girl."

"I already explained how that happened."

"No, Nat, you just said that it did – even though you weren't there. Now, is there anyone who *would* be able to order a gate be opened? Maybe even order the security camera be turned off or the footage erased?"

"A police officer," Thomas said with obvious pleasure at having been the first to answer what he failed to realize was a rhetorical question.

"Excellent answer, Thomas! Yes, a police officer. A male police officer. Someone who also has the strength to cut open a man's chest. Someone who can call in an expert on handling blood-soaked bodies, or possibly possess that information himself. Someone with the strength to lift a dead body – which, if you haven't done it, is far harder than it sounds. There's a reason they call it dead weight, you know. Where was I?"

"Police officer," Thomas prompted.

"Right. Now, throw a bloody body bag into a taxi and you risk discovery. Throw that body in the back of a police car and you can clean up the trunk at your leisure, knowing the chances of it ever being inspected by a forensics team are close to zero. Which leads me to the next flaw in the theory.

"Cleaning up a crime scene isn't easy. I've seen pictures taken at locations where a crime had been committed as much as ten years earlier, locations that have been in constant use – and thus cleaned regularly – ever since. But spray the Luminol around and voilà: enough trace evidence to satisfy even the most demanding prosecutor. Yet somehow Jeab and his on-the-verge-of-suicide sister managed to get every single bit of Cahill's blood off the floors and walls – and given the way he was hacked up, there must have been blood everywhere."

"Unless the lab technicians *did* find traces of Cahill's blood, and covered it up by saying it was all Nan's," Sally contributed.

"That's certainly a possibility."

Nat grunted. "Or maybe they just worked very, very hard at it. After all, they were trying to cover up a murder. Jeab said they cleaned the place three times, just to be sure. And they had almost two days until the police came to investigate Nan's suicide."

"Thanks for bringing that up. Don't you find it strange that the pair of 'em did an absolutely perfect job of cleaning up after Cahill, but missed quite a bit cleaning up after Nan?"

"There were two of them for Cahill, just Jeab for Nan."

"I'm not sure how you know that, given that we have no idea how or when Nan's blood got there in the first place. Did Nan try to kill herself with a knife, fail, half-heartedly clean up her mess, and then try again with methamphetamines instead of stainless steel? Or maybe she tried the knife, failed, ran straight into the bedroom and swallowed a bunch of pills."

"It could have happened that way," Nat insisted.

"No, it couldn't. If it did, there would have been blood in the bedroom as well as the living room. But your report said there were – quote – 'no signs of a struggle', which would presumably include blood. Moreover, for that theory of the case to be true, you have to believe that Jeab comes home to a living room full of blood, walks through to the bedroom, sees the drugs, and then – instead of calling the police or, more helpfully, an ambulance – he gets on his knees and starts scrubbing the floors and changing the sheets under his dead sister. Why would he do that? Wouldn't it have been safer to get rid of the *drugs*?"

"Maybe he thought the blood would incriminate him."

"Incriminate him in what? Knife or pills, it's still a suicide."

"Unless he forced her to take the pills."

"Why would he do that, Nat? She was his meal ticket. Killing her leaves him with no money and a baby to take care of. Jeab doesn't strike me as the brightest of sparks, but I'm pretty sure he's not *that* stupid.

"Now I'll grant you there's a lot we don't know about this part of the story," Ian said before holding up one finger to silence the comment Nat clearly wanted to make. "We don't know whether Nan tried to slit her wrists, or any other part of her body. It's certainly possible that she got hurt while killing Cahill, and bled in random spots without noticing it. In either of those scenarios one would expect to see bandages or traces of Betadine. Yet because the cause of death was quickly determined by looking at a corpse lying next to a bottle of pills, we don't know if either of those things was present."

"I've already admitted – at least twice – that that was a mistake on our part."

"Yes," Ian said dismissively, "you did. But you didn't explain how the doctor knew she was dead. Did he take her pulse? Wouldn't he have seen scratches or bandages on her wrist when he held it in his hand?"

"Maybe he felt her neck instead."

"Another maybe. Doesn't it strike you, Nat, that there are quite a lot of maybes in your version of events? And that *all* of them would have to be true for the story to track the way you want it to?"

"Unlikely doesn't mean impossible."

"True. But there are other things bothering me. I realize that different cultures act differently, and that the Thai people are generally shy and arguably submissive. But I find it somewhat odd that during your entire interrogation, Jeab never once raised his head. It's almost as if – I don't know – he didn't think he could lie while staring someone in the face."

"Pure speculation."

"As is this: Again, I realize my perspective may be distorted by working through a translation." He turned to the interpreter. "And I mean no offense by that. You did an incredible job. But it seemed to me that there were no pauses to think, no verbal stumbles. Except for his surprising yet endearing inability to remember the date he discovered a dead *farang* on the kitchen floor, it was as if Jeab were reading a script."

"A script you're accusing me of writing?"

"Nat, that's one question I'm still unable to answer. And one that I've been asking myself since the first hour we met you. The only other cop we've been allowed to come into contact with is your driver, and he never said a word in our presence. All of our meetings were held in a conference room far away from where the case files are kept. We haven't met any of the investigating detectives, the policemen called to the scene, or the forensics teams called out when the bodies were found."

"They don't speak English."

"But this lady does, and very well. Yet the only time her services were felt to be necessary was today, when there was a performance you wanted us to see for ourselves."

"So you're accusing *me* of killing Cahill?"

"Actually, no." That came as a surprise to both Sally and Thomas. "You may have had a hand in the cleanup, but I suspect you were dragged in only once there were *farang* to be dealt with in person. But I could be wrong."

Nat folded his hands on the table in front of him with forced calm. "So if you've got everything worked out, Inspector McLean, tell me this: If I'm not the killer, and Nan's not the killer, who is?"

CHAPTER 45

Jeab was led back to his cell, still in chains. Nat stared hard at the still-silent McLean, shook his head, stood up, and walked out of the interrogation room.

"Guess we're not getting a lift back to the hotel," Thomas said with a wry grin.

Ian flagged down a taxi, and Thomas put his much-improved "Fooah Seeezons" to good use. No one said anything for a full 10 minutes, as though they were actually worried that the Thai police had bugged this random taxi.

"That was quite a performance you put on in there. Give any thought to letting us see the script before the curtain went up?"

"Honestly, Sally, it didn't fall into place until I watched that parody of an interrogation. It was so clear they were trying to pin the murder on a dead girl, bringing our investigation to a convenient and immediate close. But they did it badly. Jeab keeps his head down the whole time so we can't see his eyes when he's lying. Nat doesn't put a single foot wrong. No dead ends. No hesitation while he thinks about what he's going to say next. No unclear or ambiguous answers. And every single question hits pay dirt. When have you ever had an interrogation that went that smoothly?"

Sally fell easily into the role of devil's advocate. "Maybe that's how it works here. Maybe the whole conflict avoidance thing applies just as much in a police station as it does in daily life."

"Yeah, maybe. And maybe it's a cultural thing to ship home a dead Brit without noticing his chest has been cut open. Of course, there's another possibility that I think you'll agree is at least equally feasible: someone in the police department is in this up to his eyeballs."

"It's not Nat," Thomas said. Ian and Sally looked at him in surprise.

"What makes you so sure?" she asked.

"Maybe I should have said it's not *just* Nat. But come on: he's so far down the ladder he's got to hold it for everyone else. No way he's got the clout to make all this happen. No way is he allowed to handle Scotland Yard on his own. I mean, the higher ups didn't even trust him to be in the car without a minder. He didn't write today's script; he just performed it."

Traffic had come to a halt, and when a pointless light turned red, the driver switched off his engine to save fuel. The detectives waited until he switched it on again and at least partly covered the sound of their conversation. "I think he's right, Ian."

"So do I, Sally."

"So who? And why?"

"I've been thinking about that."

"What – while we were stopped at that signal?"

"For a couple of days, actually. But until some of the other pieces of the puzzle fell into place, I couldn't quite put my finger on what I was thinking."

"Which was?"

"Your mother's worst nightmare."

"That I marry a cop?" Sally laughed – and then recognition arrived. "You mean Marey, the pickled Aussie. Why were you thinking about him?"

"Because I keep remembering your question; you know, the one about why Nat dragged us out to get information from Marey he could have easily given us himself."

"And did you come up with an answer?"

"Maybe a partial one. I think the Bangkok police were trying to keep their fingerprints off this case for as long as they could. If they led us down a dead end we'd start getting suspicious; far better for us to get it wrong on our own."

"Are you saying Marey was just like Jeab: a bit player in a performance conducted solely for our benefit?"

"That's precisely what I intend to find out." Ian leaned forward over the seat and said "Patpong, please."

The driver's head snapped around several times, but he said nothing. Ian decided to try an alternate pronunciation. "Pat poooong," he said.

The driver laughed. "Most of the bars aren't open yet."

"You speak English?" Thomas asked.

"A little. I have a side business as a tour guide."

"I wish we'd run into you a couple of days ago." Ian thought for a moment. "In fact, what do you charge for a day?"

"Exclusive use?"

Ian shook his head at the surprising fluency of his driver, before suddenly panicking about how much of their earlier conversation he'd been able to follow. "Yes. All day, and probably part of the evening."

"How about 3,000 baht + gas."

Thomas did the math. "About 60 quid."

"It's a deal. For now, can you take us to Pat's Bar in Patpong?"

"There are a lot of better places to have a drink, my friend."

"The name's Ian. This is Sally and Thomas. And we're not looking for a drink. We're looking for a drunk."

They found him. Marey was at his usual table. As with most alcoholics, it was hard to tell how much he'd had, and therefore how coherent he was likely to be. But he recognized the detectives instantly and called them over to his table by name.

"I'm glad to see you're the sort of sophisticates who can appreciate the true charm of Bangkok."

"Getting drunk in a seedy bar in the middle of the afternoon?" Sally asked.

"Not *a* seedy bar. *This* seedy bar. Where else is a man free to be himself, without pretense, just watching the world go by?"

"Looks to me like you're watching soccer."

Marey stared over his glasses at Sally. "Nothing gets past you, does it, detective."

Sally grinned. "So don't even think about trying."

Marey turned to Ian. "This younger generation has an inexplicable inability to handle compliments. It's sad, really. Why bother having two sexes if a little harmless flirtation is off the table?" His wrinkled face suddenly turned serious. "But I suspect you didn't come to this luxurious establishment to hear my views on the current state of the human condition. What can I do for you?"

The direct question made Ian realize he should have put together a game plan on the way over – as he would have if the shock of discovering an English-speaking cab driver hadn't sidetracked him. Well, no choice now but to wing it. "The other day, when Nat brought us here: did you speak to him before we arrived?"

Marey tried to hide how much the question shook him, but the color draining out of his face gave him away. "He did call to see if I was around and willing to talk."

"I see," said Ian. "Do you remember what time it was when he called?"

"Not exactly, no."

"Morning, noon, early afternoon?"

"Definitely morning. Bastard woke me up."

Meaning he'd called well before suddenly having the idea during the tense discussions in the Four Seasons conference room.

"Did he give you any idea of what he wanted to talk about?"

"He mentioned three detectives from London were here working a case, and wanted a brief tour of the underbelly of the beast that is Bangkok."

"Did he give you any guidelines, any points he wanted you to emphasize or avoid?"

"He may have done. I can't say I remember exactly."

Ian took that as a yes. "Does he do this sort of thing often? Bring you visitors to educate?"

Marey took his time formulating a response. "I can't remember a specific instance, but my memory is pretty well shot by this point in both the day and my life."

"So let's agree to call it the first such instance you can remember. Did you find the request a bit strange?"

"Strange, how?"

"Well, a policeman – a *Thai* policeman no less – calls you up out of the blue and asks you to meet with some detectives from overseas. He doesn't tell you *why* he wants you to lead the briefing, which presumably he is fully capable of doing himself."

"Maybe he thought *farang* find it easier to talk with *farang*."

"Even though Nat speaks English as well as I do."

Marey shrugged. "If you want the man's actions explained, ask the man."

McLean ignored the suggestion. "Then we get here and it quickly becomes apparent we're not looking for an introductory course in Thai culture. We're investigating the death of a British national in what are increasingly suspicious circumstances. Did that surprise you?"

"Nat said you worked homicide, so I figured it would be something like that."

"Did he mention the specific case we were working on?"

Marey shook his head. "No, but I guessed. Not likely you were here for a dead Thai."

"And when a foreigner dies, word gets around."

"Yeah."

"Even though the official cause of death was listed as 'natural causes.'"

Marey snorted. "Always is, mate. Murder's bad for tourism."

"So you knew we were here about Brian Cahill. Did you also know he was seeing Kanokwan Supitayaporn, a bar girl at Lady Go Go who went by the nickname Nan?"

"Might've heard something about that."

"Yet when we showed you her picture you said you'd never taken her out and you would have remembered if you had because she was very beautiful."

"Not a word of a lie in that."

"You missed your calling, Marey. You should have been a lawyer."

"You don't live to this ripe old age by saying more than you have to."

"Did you know that Nan was dead?"

"Word gets around."

"And that's *all* you knew?"

Marey pulled out his threadbare handkerchief, and rubbed it around his nose. As a way to buy time, it was an obvious but nonetheless effective gesture. "They said it was a drug overdose. Usually is. A lot of those girls can't get through what they've got to do every night unless they're completely out of it. Eventually they get addicted, and then it's only a question of time until the *ya ba* takes over their lives – and ends them."

"So because this is a common story you were ready to believe it was true about Nan?"

"No reason not to."

"You didn't find it at all odd that less than two days after Cahill's death under questionable circumstances, his girlfriend dies of a drug overdose?"

"If you're asking me if I wondered, yeah, I did. Maybe she committed suicide because of a broken heart. Maybe both of 'em died of an overdose, just on different days. Maybe a bad bunch of pills bumped 'em both off. There's no shortage of possibilities, but that's *all* they are."

"Why didn't you mention any of this the last time we were here?" Sally challenged.

Marey spread his arms wide in a "Whaddya want me to do?" gesture. "I answered your questions. Maybe if you'd asked me to speculate about those two deaths, I would have shared some of this with you. Maybe not. It's the sorta thing that belongs in a drunken chin-wag at two in the morning, not in a so-called conversation with homicide detectives."

"So let's move the clock ahead" – McLean looked at his watch, and was stunned to be reminded how early it still was – "12 hours. We're a bunch of friends sitting around shooting the shit. We've had a couple of beers and are feeling relaxed."

"It would be easier to imagine this scenario if you had a beer sitting in front of you."

"Fair point," Ian replied as he signaled the bartender for a round. "So we're just talking, comparing theories. I say I think Nan's death was no accident, that someone else probably killed her. Got any thoughts on who that might be?"

Marey shook his head violently.

"You have my word I'm not recording any of this. I won't call on you to testify in court. I won't put your name in my report. You strike me as a smart guy who knows how the world works, and I just want to hear your thinking on what *could* have happened."

"I'm not shaking my head because I'm refusing to play your little game. I'm shaking my head because you're going about this all wrong."

"So put me right."

Marey finished off half his beer in one heroic gulp. "What was that line about Nixon and Watergate? It's not the crime, it's the cover-up?"

"Something like that. I can't remember for sure. Why?"

"*If* Nan's death wasn't a suicide or accidental overdose – and remember I said *if* – why hasn't there been an investigation?"

Thomas took the question at face value. "Because the police don't think a crime has been committed."

"Nah, son. It's not that simple. There's been no investigation because someone with influence doesn't want one."

"Who?" Sally asked.

The old drunk wagged his head. "This conversation is playing out very much like an interrogation. It takes at least two – and preferably four – to play this game."

"Fine," said Sally. "I nominate the mama-san. A death – accidental or otherwise – is bad for business. Makes the other girls think they'd be better off working at the place next door. Scares off customers who don't need any more drama in their lives. And once the police start looking around who knows what other shit they might find on the bottom of someone's shoe."

Marey slow clapped in response. "That's actually very good. Logical. Plausible. But you didn't go high enough."

"Who's higher than the mama-san?" Thomas asked. "I thought she ran the place."

Marey seemed rejuvenated by the question. He downed what remained of his beer and called for another. "And a plate of chips would be nice, Pat." The handkerchief came out again, though this time it was put to good use as Marey gave his nose a loud honk. "Damn pollution. It's better than it used to be, but it still wreaks havoc with a man's sinuses."

"You're pretty awful at stalling for time," Sally said with a gentle grin.

"Right. Bangkok Night Life: Lesson 2. Your average girlie bar has, what, 50 or 60 girls? Every single one of them will eventually get old – by which I mean late 20's. Guys stop calling her over, her requests for a Lady Drink are ignored, and it can be weeks between finding someone willing to pay her bar fine. She realizes the game is over, and it's time to move on. But the only things she knows are backbreaking slave labor on a farm upcountry, and working on her back. After a couple of years surrounded by the bright lights of Bangkok, there's no way she's going back to shoveling shit in Isaan. Besides: how hard can it be to run a bar? Ask a couple of your friends to join you and bring their friends with them. Offer the one honest bartender more money to jump ship. Smile back at that sleazy bar supplier who thinks you haven't noticed him trying to stare up your skirt while he stocks the under-counter fridge. What else do you need?"

"Start-up capital," Sally said with a confidence that came from having spent most of her career in Vice.

"Also known as cash. And that's something none of these girls have got because they piss away all their money on tarty clothing, hair salons and mobile phones. But there's money everywhere if you know how to find it. The other requirement is much harder to meet. Any guesses?" Marey didn't wait for an answer. "Apologies. That's an unfair question in present company. Answering it would require you to piss on the Thin Blue Line."

This time Sally's voice was cold and rather ominous. "You're saying they need a protector in the police."

"Ta-da! There you have it, ladies and gentlemen, boys and girls."

"Explain," Ian demanded.

"A place like this doesn't have to worry much." Marey waved his hand around Pat's Bar as if he were a white-gloved tour guide. "Most of the customers know each other, and we're all too pissed to mix it up. But in a girlie bar? A drunk German sees a drunk Brit lusting after the girl he's planning to buy out, and the next thing you know it's a replay of World War II. You need the cops to show up before the bar gets trashed, or someone gets seriously hurt and writes all about it in a damning review on Trip Advisor. You need cops who are very good at making problems disappear and very bad at filing paperwork. You need cops who can keep *other* cops from dropping by to demand a free drink or a blowjob. And to get all that, you need someone high enough up the ladder he can give orders and have them followed."

"And such people exist?"

"Of course they do, Ian. I suspect you lot think you're under-paid, but trust me when I tell you that what Thai police are paid is an insult. There is simply no way they can live on what they make legitimately. It's as if the HR department assumes every-one is on the take, and the pittance they get in their pay enve-lopes is just a bit of icing on the cake."

"So they take backhanders."

"For riding a motorcycle without a helmet, sure. But like I said, Lady Go Go's needs are a lot more complicated than that. Backing by law enforcement can make the difference between success and failure for a high-profile establishment. You don't buy that sort of cooperation with a couple of tattered bills hid-den in a handshake. You buy it with an equity stake."

"You're saying senior police are part owners of these strip clubs?" Sally was taken aback.

"Don't act so shocked. I'll bet you a night of passion that some of your colleagues in London are part-owners of seedy bars or clubs, even though they won't admit it until the day after they retire and maybe not even then."

Ian steered the conversation back to Thailand. "I don't see what cops owning bars has to do with our two deaths, at least one of which was a murder."

"Sure you do. Girls getting knocked up are bad for business. They remind the customers of what can happen if they're not careful. And outside of a few fetishists, no one buys drinks for a girl with a baby bump. Eventually the girl has to stop working, meaning you have to hire a replacement. After the baby's born she wants to – she *needs* to come back but you no longer have an opening. Drama ensues. Or you do take her back but she's constantly leaving customers with their hands in their pockets while she goes to answer a phone call from the baby sitter."

"So fire girls who get pregnant. I assume there's no law against that here?"

"Wouldn't matter if there was. Patpong isn't exactly a paragon of civic virtue. But you're missing the revenue opportunity."

"Which is?" Ian asked eagerly.

"Babies have fathers. Fathers have money, especially if they're foreigners with a Judeo-Christian guilt complex, a wife who terrifies them, and the sort of high-profile job that sends them on business trips to Thailand."

Ian leaned back in his chair, causing it to wobble dangerously. "And the bar and its protector want a piece of the action."

"Pays a lot better than turning the other way from traffic violations," Marey pointed out.

"I understand what you're saying, but I don't see how it gets us to two dead bodies."

"Neither do I. That's the bit I believe is called 'detective work.' But what I can tell you is that sometimes the baby daddy is reluctant to pay up. And in such cases it's not uncommon to bring in some heavyweights to help shore up the argument in favor."

Now that, Ian thought, was interesting. A visit from "the man upstairs" has been in the career criminal's toolkit since the beginning of time. No reason the same shouldn't be true when the criminals involved also wore a badge.

"How high up the ladder are we looking?" he asked.

"High enough to get things done."

"Can't you give us a hint?"

"Not if I hope to live out the week."

McLean wondered if Marey was as responsive to financial incentives as the Thai police appeared to be. And then he remembered he had another pressure point to work with, one much closer to the heart of the matter.

"Thanks, Marey, that was very helpful." Sally and Thomas looked at him in bewilderment. It was not like the boss to leave with questions still unanswered. He must, they thought, have a plan in mind.

As it turned out, so did Marey. "What have you got for leverage?"

"Leverage?" Thomas repeated.

"You're not going to take down a respected member of the Royal Thai Police with just the mental meanderings of a well-known lush and deviate. And I'd be surprised if you had any evidence – given the fact you don't have a name to pin it to. So I'm assuming you've got some pretty significant leverage you haven't told me about."

Ian smiled and called for the bill. "You're a wise man, Marey, and we appreciate all your help. He pulled out one of his cards and laid it on the table. If you're ever in London, give me a ring. We can go out for a curry together – unless you'd like to take a break from spicy food and have something traditional like Spotted Dick."

Marey burst out laughing. "You Poms really do eat some shite. But a good Spotted Dick story should earn me a couple of free rounds from mates old and new. Consider it a deal."

They all shook hands, and the detectives walked out into the humid heat of a Bangkok night.

"We have a plan?" Thomas asked incredulously.

"We most certainly do," McLean replied. "Call Nat and tell him we're taking him out to dinner."

CHAPTER 46

Saying the only restaurants he knew were the ones he'd already visited, McLean asked Nat to select the restaurant. His brief was a difficult one: somewhere with lots of tourists who don't speak English. Thai food preferred but not mandatory. Hopefully not more than £20 per head before drinks.

Nat chose Praeng Kaeow, an unimpressive looking place that had a surprisingly extensive menu. Every table was full, but as Ian looked around all he saw were Japanese expats and their young families. The only language he could hear was – he guessed – Japanese.

"Perfect," he said as he extended a hand to the clearly wary Nat.

"I'll admit it was a challenge. And I'll also admit I'm very eager to know exactly *why* that particular combination of factors was important."

"I'll be happy to explain, just as soon as you order us some dinner – if you wouldn't mind. It's been quite a revealing day, and I confess it's left me famished."

Nat made one more attempt to read McLean's body language, gave up, and turned his attention to the menu. Two minutes later he'd ordered the meal and dismissed the waitress. "I asked her not to interrupt us except to bring the food."

"Excellent idea. Thanks."

"Are you going to start or should I?" Nat asked.

"I'll go first, if you don't mind. I'm going to tell you what we know, what we think and can't prove, and what we only suspect. Then I'm going to give you a choice. And I'll close by telling you what happens after we get back to London, which – you'll be pleased to hear – will be tomorrow."

Nat tried unsuccessfully to hide his relief.

"Brian Cahill was killed, not by Kanokwan Supitayaporn – I hope you're impressed I finally remembered her full name – but by a man strong enough to put metal through bone and tall enough to hit Cahill's collarbone with a downward strike. Remember that Cahill was over six feet tall. Nan might have been able to reach that high if she'd stood on her tippy-toes, but she wouldn't have had enough leverage to break skin, much less bone.

"However that doesn't mean she's completely innocent. While it's possible that the killer also made the holes in Cahill's heart, I strongly suspect this was Nan's doing. If the killer wanted to mutilate Cahill's internal organs, he could have done a fine job of it with the bloody meat cleaver he already had to hand. Why go to the trouble of rummaging through the kitchen drawers in search of a fiddly little knife? And why focus exclusively on the heart rather than spreading the punctures around a bit? No, the post-mortem savagery has all the hallmarks of a woman scorned.

"That leads to the theoretical possibility that Jeab and Nan were in it together. To be honest, if you'd gone that route with this morning's performance, we might have believed you. Trying to put all the blame on someone no longer living was just a tad too greedy."

Nat started to object, but Ian held up a hand. "Let me get through this and then we can discuss any points you find unclear or objectionable."

Nat nodded reluctantly.

"I've also been troubled by the cleanup."

"What about it?"

"Brian Cahill is killed in Nan's apartment and there isn't a trace of him to be found. No matter how careful they try to be, amateurs always make mistakes. Whoever cleaned up after the butchering of Brian Cahill knew what he was doing.

"Then Nan is stabbed or slits her wrist in the very same place, and your tech guys walk away with – what? – 40 blood samples? How did a cleanup team that was so good suddenly get so bad?"

"We've been over this. Nan was there to help with the first one. For the second Jeab was on his own, and men aren't as meticulous as women."

"As a glance at any man's fingernails will prove," snapped an obviously irritated Sally. McLean ignored her.

"Assuming Nan was dead before he started. That's possible, but not very likely. My guess is that the B Team was assigned to the second body."

"What B Team?"

"I'll get to that in a minute, but first let's return to Cahill. What was he doing in Nan's apartment? And, more to the point, who was there with him?"

"How the hell should I know?"

"That is indeed the question, and the reason we asked you here tonight."

The waitress arrived with three spicy salads and four beers. As soon as the plates touched table, Nat waved her away.

"One of the things we know for certain is that the baby who was living in Nan's apartment until you arrested her brother is Brian Cahill's."

Nat's eyes were the size of saucers. "How could you possibly know that?"

"DNA test on the baby's hair. 99% match."

Nat pushed his plate away and folded his arms protectively across his chest. His face, however, conveyed a different emotion: contempt bordering on hatred.

McLean pressed on, unperturbed. "What we can't prove but are reasonably certain of is that Nan asked Brian for financial support. As I said, we have no evidence – but there are a couple of reasons we believe it to be true. First, a bar girl can't work when she's pregnant, and even if she returns to the bar after giving birth she's got lots of new expenses for babysitters, doctors, and so on. It would make sense for a working girl like Nan to request financial support from the father of her child, especially if she believed he was a wealthy foreigner who could easily afford it.

"Second, Thomas has kindly put together this chart" – Thomas leaned across the table and placed his iPad in front of Nat – "showing the frequency of Cahill's visits to Thailand. They get closer and closer together until the 14th visit. Then the 15th and 16th come more slowly. But what's of primary interest to us is the six-month gap between visits 16 and 17.

Nat shrugged to show that he was unimpressed.

"Now, in this next chart" – McLean swiped his finger across the iPad – Thomas has added the details of where Cahill stayed: location, room grade, and whether Nan was with him. It's a bit small, so you may want to expand the relevant bits with your fingers."

Nat's fingers didn't move.

"Right. What you can see is that on the 14th visit, Nan and Brian stayed together in a suite. On visits 15 and 16, Brian stayed alone in a deluxe room on the Executive Floor. And on the last visit, he sprung for the Garden Terrace Suite."

"Is that supposed to tell me something?"

"'Tell' might be too strong a word. 'Suggest' is probably more accurate."

"Either way, I don't see what you're driving at."

"Nothing more than a possibility I'll grant you. But if you check the calendar you'll see there were exactly 10 months between visit #14 in August 2013, and visit #17 this May. That time line is a perfect match for the theory that Nan gave Brian the news in August, the baby was born in March or April, and Brian was killed in May following a discussion about caring for the child long-term."

"A lot of that's just speculation," Nat grunted.

"The ice gets even thinner from here on in. Now, one possibility is that Nan called her brother in from the farm to help her put pressure on Cahill. As far as I know Jeab speaks no English, and he's not the least bit imposing physically. I suppose we all have to work with what we've got, but there are a couple of other possibilities I find more intriguing."

"Do tell."

"It started with thinking about who else loses when a bar girl gets pregnant. Mama-san is one, as she's down one girl."

"Replacements are everywhere."

"That's what we thought, too. At first. But that's because we were focusing on the loss of revenue from a girl who can't work in the bar. What we *hadn't* considered was the potentially lucrative new profit stream from a girl able to work from home."

The waitress returned with *pad Thai*, a yellow chicken curry, ground pork stir-fried with chili and served with a fried egg, and a wing bean salad. She took one look at the faces around the table, and disappeared as quickly as she could.

"Where was I? Oh, right. The new profit stream. Brian Cahill was a wealthy man. High-paying job on top of family money. Now, Nan may not have been familiar with the details of Brian's financial situation but she did know he stayed at one of the best hotels in Bangkok – in its finest rooms. Sally checked with the front desk before we came here. The Junior Suite goes for 14,730 baht, and the Garden Terrace 23,350 – though that includes breakfast. I'm assuming tax and service is extra." The last set of details was so entirely superfluous that even Thomas had to suppress a smirk.

"Again, she may not have known the rack rates, but a girl in her profession has probably seen a number of local hotel rooms. And one look at the luxury of Brian's accommodations would tell her he was well past comfortable."

"Don't forget the weekend getaways," Sally reminded Ian.

"I almost did – thank you. On most of his visits Brian took Nan somewhere really nice, the sort of trip that most foreigners would be happy to have once every couple of years, and most Thais can presumably only dream about. That's another pretty obvious clue to his financial wherewithal. Plus, we're assuming he tipped rather well, which is why she was always available when he was in town."

McLean was so busy talking his plate remained empty. Sally and Thomas were wolfing down their meals, adding to their enjoyment of the show. Nat managed to serve himself some of the wing bean salad before the discourse began, but now it sat untouched on the plate while he glared at McLean. "What's the point of all this?"

"I'm getting to that. Someone, somewhere along the way, realized that Brian could be good for a lot more than child support. He could be the gift that keeps on giving, at least for the 22 or so years it would take his daughter to graduate from college. The cost of living in Thailand is cheap. Cost estimates could be heavily padded and still look reasonable to someone used to London prices. Fictional expenses could easily be created. Made-up customs and religious festivals could justify requests for large piles of cash. The opportunities are truly limitless. And almost endless – unlike the career of the average dancer at Lady Go Go."

"Cahill wouldn't fall for that sort of scam. He was an investment banker. They're neither stupid nor naïve."

"Exactly!" Ian shouted with enthusiasm, before being stared down by the couple at the next table. "That's why Nan needed someone to put some teeth into her demands, or should I say some muscle – someone whose very presence would make Brian think that paying up was the path of least resistance, not to mention the safest as far as his life was concerned."

"You're saying he was blackmailed."

"That's certainly a possibility. But there may not have been a quid pro quo. My guess would be this was really about intimidation."

"And who is this mysterious person?"

Ian smiled again. Thomas wondered if Nat found the grin as unnerving as he did. "That's where you come in."

"*Me*?"

"One of the things we've struggled with since the beginning of this case is whether you were a pawn or a queen. And to be honest, I'm still not sure, but I'm leaning towards pawn. No offense intended, of course. You certainly have the physical strength to open Cahill's chest with a meat cleaver. You're the perfect height for putting a knife through his collarbone. You've got enough crime scene experience to supervise a cleanup. You seem like the sort of fellow who is loved by all his coworkers – coworkers who can be counted on when a problem needs to disappear. And your English is flawless, so you could have bridged the linguistic gap between Brian and Nan at the same time you added a little threat of your own."

Nat banged his fist on the table, causing his fork to bounce against the plate and then fall to the floor with a loud clatter. "You invited me to dinner to tell me you think I'm a murderer? Here, in a public place? With absolutely no hard evidence and just some... *fairy tale* to support your accusations?"

"I'm not accusing you of anything, Nat. I am simply saying that you *could* have done it. But so far we've been unable to find any connection between you and Nan."

"Maybe I bought her out of the bar one time, and we fell madly in love."

"Possible. But there's something else that makes us think you weren't calling the shots."

"This little fantasy of yours is absolutely nuts, but it's fascinating in a twisted sort of way. Please proceed."

"Your driver."

"My driver?"

"Hmm," Ian said as he absent-mindedly used his fork to pull some meat off the drumstick in the yellow curry. "He was clearly your minder. As were all the cops stationed inside the hotel. Somebody else, somebody much higher up, wanted to keep an eye on you."

"And who was that?"

"Now that, *that* is what tonight is all about. You see, we know that many of the bars in Patpong are protected by a senior police officer that most likely has a share in the place and thus is committed to maximizing its profitability. Most of the time that's a rather mundane task – ensuring that other officers don't try to drink at the same well he's gulping at, and sorting out the occasional fight or other disruption that every bar encounters. But when a big fish like Brian Cahill comes along, the rewards are lucrative enough that the protector might decide to get personally involved."

Ian paused to give Nat a chance to comment, but whatever was running through the young man's mind had no chance of getting access to his mouth.

"Imagine you're Cahill, heading into the forbidding Bangkok suburbs to have what you know is going to be a difficult conversation with the mother of your child. You're worried, but not too much. After all, you hold most of the cards. At least you think you do. She can ask. She can beg. She can even threaten to expose you. But you know the chances of a bar girl who doesn't speak much English tracking down your family, your girlfriend, your boss – those chances are nearly nonexistent.

"So you walk in feeling mildly confident. But then you see a policeman with epaulets on his shoulder and handcuffs hanging off his belt, and the game changes. Abruptly. He could arrest you just for the hell of it, and throw you in some dank prison where all kinds of unimaginable horrors occur before your embassy manages to get you out. He could have you barred from returning to Thailand, the country that propelled your highly lucrative career for the last few years. Or he could go old school and find a packet of white powder in your pocket. Compared with those scenarios, sending regular checks to a girl you should be looking after anyway seems like a more than reasonable deal."

"So why didn't they all shake hands and part as friends? How does Cahill end up dead?"

"Excellent question! Unfortunately I'm not sure we'll ever know the answer, unless the man who killed Brian decides to tell us. Pumping Nan full of methamphetamines ensured that *she* would remain quiet forever."

"So, you have no evidence. No motive. Not even the name of the supposed perp."

"Not until you give it to us."

Nat laughed. He looked at Ian, who was beaming as though he'd just become a father. Sally and Thomas were more serious but their expressions were a long way from worried. Nat laughed again.

"You must be out of your goddamned mind! Why would I give you the name of a senior Thai police official on whom you have absolutely nothing?"

"One word: leverage."

"What" – Nat spat out the word – "leverage could you possibly have? Effectively you're just... *tourists* here."

"Absolutely right." Ian turned to his colleagues. "Didn't I tell you he was smart? He's either right there with us or one step ahead."

Ian calmly ate some noodles, drank some beer, and had a heaping tablespoon of the stir-fried pork with chili. "Wow, that is hot."

"Still waiting, Ian."

"Oh, right. Sorry. You are completely correct that we have no leverage. Here. Which is why we're going home tomorrow. But back in London, we've got plenty of leverage. Thomas, would you mind telling Nat how much?"

"£486.83 million worth."

"What in the hell does that mean?"

"It means that the UK accounts for 1.7% of Thailand's exports. If you look at the chart Thomas has on his ever-useful iPad, you'll see that a category called 'Meat, Seafood Preparations' is the top export to the UK, and was worth £486.83 million in 2013."

"So what?"

"It comes down to a question of how much one man's job is worth. I'm sure the man you're protecting has many friends in government – assuming he was on the right side of the coup. But would they see protecting a killer as being worth nearly £500 million in exports – a cost that would be have to be paid in full, every year, for many years to come? Somehow, I think not."

"You must be a lousy poker player, Ian. There's no way your government is going to start a trade war over one unfounded allegation."

"Nat, Nat, Nat. In leverage, as in life, timing is everything. With the Russian sanctions in place, Europe is awash in unsold meat and seafood preparations that used to go to Moscow. Shifting suppliers from distant Thailand to our overstocked neighbors would be a highly popular move for our government; getting some justice for Brian Cahill is just the cherry on top."

Ian attacked his meal again, and ate with the relish of a man who'd been without food for days. Nat sat silently, brow furrowed, watching. After several minutes he crossed his arms and spoke. "What about me?"

"If you help us nail the man in charge, you'd come out of this as one of the good guys."

"And if I don't?"

"You might have to become the scapegoat."

"I need to think," Nat said as he stood up from the table on which his food sat untouched.

"Take all the time you want, as long as you call me before 10:30 tomorrow morning with your decision. After that we'll be boarding our flight to London, and the offer will be withdrawn."

Nat left the restaurant without looking back.

"What do you think? Sally asked.

"50:50 at best. His colleagues are going to know he was the snitch, since he was the only person who had direct contact with us. That means his career as a cop is over. And that's the best case scenario."

"What's the worst?" Thomas asked.

"That the same guy who thought nothing of putting a meat cleaver in Cahill's chest would have no problem putting a bullet in the back of the guy who ratted him out."

Sally looked around the restaurant, seeing nothing. "And you're okay with that?"

"I'm not happy with it. But I'm also not happy with Cahill's killer getting off scot-free. And let's face it: Nat hasn't played straight since he met us at the airport."

"May not have been his choice. And even if it was, does he deserve to die for it?" Sally's voice resonated with concern.

"Of course not. But I think the odds of the worst-case scenario are pretty low. It's one thing to kill off a *farang*, quite another to kill a colleague on the force."

Thomas had been listening, but his mind was clearly else-where. "Do you really think you can get Chief Franklin to go along?"

"Honestly, Thomas, I have no idea. But I will recommend we put the idea to Cahill's father. He's a former minister, and under-stands the politics of what I'm suggesting. If he's determined to get some sort of justice for his son, he'll take the lead and push the plan through. If he thinks we're attacking an ant with an atom bomb, he'll thank us for our efforts and give us permission to let the mat-ter drop. Either way, Cahill Senior gets the result he wants."

"That's some cynical shit, Ian, even for you," Sally said. "And for it to have even a hope in hell of working, we need Nat to give us a name. Without that we've got nothing."

CHAPTER 47

The team from Scotland Yard gathered in the breakfast room one last time.

"I'm going to miss this place," Sally said as she surveyed her glass of fresh Mandarin orange juice and her bowl of *kao thom* – with chicken this time. "Sure we shouldn't hang around a day or two and wait for Nat's response? I'm telling you: the pool here is really, really nice."

Ian smiled. "Nat said I'd make a lousy poker player, and he's probably right. But I do know a thing or two about bluffing. The longer we give Nat to think, the more holes he finds in our story. The more escape hatches he uncovers. The more support he lines up. If he's going to jump ship, he'll do it this morning."

Thomas looked at his watch. "He's cutting it pretty close. Only three hours left before the deadline."

"My bet is he rings at 10:29. Makes us sweat a bit and gives the impression the decision could have gone either way. If he looks too eager he gives away too much power."

"Didn't think he had much left after last night," Sally said with a tinge of pity.

"If you're going to feel sorry for anyone," Thomas said with surprising sharpness, "feel sorry for Jeab. He comes to Bangkok

423

looking for work, and finds a dead body on the kitchen floor. Next thing he knows he's being fitted up for murder."

"Do you think he was involved at all?" Sally asked while looking at Ian.

"At first I thought that part of his story was true – that he sewed up the body and helped move it to the hotel. But now I wonder if that was just a very clever move by the real killer."

"A misdirection," Sally clarified. "The fishing line and shoddy workmanship make it look like the work of an amateur, rather than a cop, a coroner and/or someone from the morgue."

"If that was the plan," Thomas replied, "it was a good one. Until this moment it never occurred to me the sloppiness could have been intentional." He pushed a small mound of scrambled eggs around his plate. "What about Nan? Did she just sit back and watch the whole thing unfold?"

"Absolutely not." Sally's anger bordered on the defiant. "The mutilated heart? I'll bet a month's pay that was her handiwork."

"What makes you so sure?" Thomas asked.

"It's the only answer that makes any sense. If hacking Brian open left the killer wanting more, he could have lopped off a limb or two with the cleaver he had in his hand. Why would such a violent man suddenly switch to a fiddly little fruit knife and start poking holes in a dead man's heart?"

Thomas shrugged.

"He wouldn't," Sally continued. "But Nan would. The murder was someone else's handiwork. She wanted to make a statement of her very own. It's no accident that every single one of the punctures was made in the heart. Brian hurt her emotionally, and she wanted to hurt him back."

"How can you be so certain?" Ian asked hesitantly.

"I get angry women," she replied.

The rest of the meal passed in silence. The detectives went upstairs to pack their bags, and then back downstairs to check out. Ian thought there was a slight chance Nat would have sent over the police BMW with the mute driver, just to maintain the fiction that all was normal with the investigation. But Ian confirmed with the safari-ready doorman that no policemen had pulled into the hotel's wide driveway that morning.

The detectives took an ordinary metered taxi to the airport, and checked in without incident. As they stood in the 25-deep line at Immigration, Ian found himself wishing that Nat were there to whisk them through the VIP lane.

That's what happens when you burn your bridges, he chastised himself.

Eventually their passports were stamped, and their carry-on luggage searched for explosives. Sally was selected for a more thorough body search; Ian couldn't help thinking the choice was no accident. As soon as she was cleared, Sally rejoined her colleagues saying "Why is it always me who gets the pat-down?"

Ian and Thomas shared a smile. Then the detectives split up to explore the seemingly endless retail outlets that filled the Departures floor. Never one to spend more than a few minutes shopping, Ian quickly settled on a box of purple and yellow orchids – each stem in its own test tube of water – for his wife Edith. Thomas bought green mangoes and half a dozen rambutan, a Thai fruit that tastes like a lychee but looks like a red porcupine and had no chance of being allowed into the UK. After smelling every bottle on the shelf, Sally bought some lotus oil – "for headaches," she said.

All three checked their watches almost constantly.

Finally, there was nothing left to check. "They're calling our flight," Thomas announced.

Ian shrugged, picked up his bag, and headed for the gate.

"It was a good play, Ian. It just didn't work out."

"She's right, sir. Police involved in both a murder and the cover-up? We never stood a chance."

McLean knew they were both wrong, but appreciated the attempt to lighten his load. He smiled as he handed his ticket to the lovely young woman standing at the entrance to the Jetway. Then his phone rang.

Ian checked his caller ID. It was Nat.

"Colonel Somchai Charoenkul. C-h-a-r-o-e-n-k-u-l." With that, the call was cut off.

Ian flashed a thumbs up and rushed to rejoin his colleagues.

CHAPTER 48

Chief Franklin looked in turn at each of the three detectives sitting before him. "I'm sorry it's taken so long to get the band back together. As you know, Ian dumped his homework on my desk, and I've been rather busy shuttling back and forth between the various ministries involved, sorting out all the loose ends."

"And did you succeed, sir?" Thomas asked eagerly.

"I did. We did. The Foreign Ministry informed me this morning that Colonel Charoenkul is no longer employed by the Royal Thai Police force. He's been pensioned off."

"Well, that's a win, isn't it? Sally asked. "I mean, I'd rather see him in a prison cell for the rest of his life, but under the circumstances this is the best we could have hoped for."

McLean wasn't ready to pick up the pom-poms. "What does Cahill's father think?"

"He's actually very pleased. Told the prime minister that while formal commendations would probably be inappropriate given the sensitivity of the matter, he would be happy to – and I'm quoting here – 'invite the men responsible to dinner at my club.'"

Sally frowned. "I'll go wearing my shortest skirt and hooker heels. With any luck I'll give the sexist bastard a gentle heart attack."

"Hmm. Perhaps we shouldn't push too hard to finalize the date, Miss Chan. Instead, I thought I might offer you three a little toast of my own."

McLean expected Chief Franklin to reach into his bottom drawer and pull out the bottle of Lagavulin he kept for emergencies. But to the inspector's surprise, the chief had a bottle of Champagne on ice, and four proper glasses.

"So *this* is what you do when you come up to the chief's office," Sally said with a devilish grin.

"Most of the time Ian is lucky to get out of here with a mild whipping, Miss Chan. This is a special occasion."

The chief filled the glasses, and passed them around. "I know that for a policeman it never feels like a win until you hear the cell door slam shut. But that measure of success isn't relevant to Mr. Cahill's case. This was more about diplomacy and the ability to quickly find your way around unfamiliar and frequently hostile territory. Criminal involvement by the Thai Royal Police could easily have turned this into a bugger's muddle, but you got your man and did so in a way that kept our nation's good diplomatic relationship with the Thai military government intact. On behalf of a grateful father and a well-satisfied prime minister, I thank you."

The four clinked glasses and drank deeply.

"That's very good Champagne," Sally said after lowering her glass. "A girl could get to like this sort of thing."

"Keep cracking difficult cases and I'm sure you'll be back here. Perhaps next time I'll really push the boat out and order a cheese plate. I find the bubbles always make one feel rather peckish."

Split four ways the bottle didn't last long. The chief shook hands all around and then sat down at his desk in a way that made it clear the party was over. Ian drained the few drops still clinging to the bottom of his glass, and returned to his office feeling at peace with the world.

An early night would be just the thing, he decided. Have a chat with Edith, a meal that wasn't booby-trapped with unassuming but fiery hot chilies, and then a good long sleep. He started gathering his things and noticed something unfamiliar on top of his desk. It was a rarity in this electronic age: an actual letter. Addressed by hand. And sent Special Delivery from Thailand. He tore it open eagerly.

Dear Ian,

I trust that you, Sally and Thomas have returned safely to London, and have some happy memories of your time in Thailand. I will certainly never forget meeting you.

I have taken the liberty of enclosing an article from Thai Raht, *Thailand's leading newspaper. It's in Thai, I'm afraid, so let me give you a few of the key points.*

The story concerns a lieutenant colonel in the Royal Thai Police named Somchai Charoenkul. He was behind the wheel in a drunk driving incident in which an eight-year-old girl was killed. Colonel Charoenkul was also injured, and has been in the hospital for the last three months with two broken legs and a ruptured pelvis.

The article concerns the surprising news that, rather than press criminal charges upon his release as had been indicated earlier, prosecutors have agreed to drop the matter in exchange for Colonel Charoenkul taking early retirement – on a full pension.

No rationale was given for this decision, and police spokesmen had no comment other than to say the matter is now considered closed.

In other news, I have been promoted and given a surprisingly generous raise. Moreover, the owners of Lady Go Go were so pleased that we were able to resolve this matter quietly that they gave me a small equity stake in the bar.

If you ever return to Thailand, know that at Lady Go Go the drinks will be on me. It's the least I can do, given how much you've contributed to my own quality of life.

With warm regards,

"Nat"

"That bloody bastard!" Ian yelled.

Sally and Thomas came rushing into the boss's office. "What's wrong?"

In response, Ian slammed the letter down on the table. Thomas grabbed it, read it once quickly and then again carefully. Shaking his head, he handed the paper to Sally.

"You must be seeing something I'm not," she said once she'd finished reading.

Ian was so angry it took a moment before he could speak. "How long was that guy in the hospital?"

"How should I know?" she replied.

"It's right there in Nat's letter!" He banged his forefinger in the general vicinity of the critical information. "Charoenkul has been in the hospital for three months."

Sally's expression clouded, and then cleared. "Meaning he couldn't have been there on the night Brian was killed."

McLean scowled, then nodded.

"So while he could have ordered Cahill's death, he didn't cause it."

The inspector crossed his arms and squeezed.

"So the real killer goes free."

"Looks that way," McLean admitted.

"Charoenkul gets a pass on the little girl killed in the car accident, a pass on Cahill, a pass on whatever happened to Nan, and a full fucking pension."

"That's about the size of it," McLean agreed.

"And for *his* role in all this – which remains a mystery – Nat gets a promotion, a raise, and a slice of a girlie bar that's going to be printing money until he's old and gray." She began pacing the room like a bear in a cage. "That little bastard played us. All that 'I'm just here for my English ability' bullshit. He was just covering up his true involvement."

"Which was?" Thomas asked.

"Which was... how the hell should I know? Maybe he was the mastermind all along, calling the shots from behind the scenes. Maybe he was there on the night, and gave the order to kill. For all I know, maybe he was the one who picked up the meat cleaver and started hacking at poor Cahill." Sally paused for breath. "Honestly, I didn't think he had all that in him. But I also didn't think he'd send us a letter that is pretty close to a written confession."

"No it isn't," Ian replied. "Read it carefully. He walks right up to the line, but never crosses it. The letter is highly suggestive, but it's not proof of anything. And even if it were, we still couldn't get him."

"Why not?" Thomas asked.

"Have you forgotten? We already solved this case. And then we pressured our own government to threaten a trade war with Thailand, telling them that was the only way to get justice for Brian Cahill. We can't go back to them now and say 'oops, wrong guy.'"

"So because we're not willing to admit we got outplayed, a killer walks free?" Sally fumed.

"I don't see any other way for this story to end," Ian admitted. Then he froze, cocked his head, and closed his eyes. When they reopened, he was smiling. "Thomas, go online and see if you can find out the name of Nat's father. There's a pint in it if you can also figure out where he works."

The young man stared at his boss, hoping an explanation was to follow. After a few moments he gave up, returned to his desk, and started banging on his keyboard.

CHAPTER 49

It took nearly 30 minutes, but when Thomas came back to Ian's office – a visibly curious Sally in tow – he was grinning from ear to ear.

"How did you know?" he asked as he showed his boss the information on his iPad.

"I didn't," McLean admitted. "I guessed."

"There must have been more to it."

"If you insist," Ian said coyly, "we have the University of Iowa to thank."

Sally's head swiveled back and forth between the two men. "Did you guys come up with some sort of secret code so you don't have to talk about me behind my back? What in God's name are you on about?"

McLean relaxed into his chair, savoring the tale he was about to tell. "This case has been about a lot of things. Love. Sex. Power. And money. Money above all. Money and the things people will do to get it."

"You've just described about 90% of our cases, boss," Sally observed.

"Touché. But it got me thinking: American colleges are ridiculously expensive. How could Nat afford it?"

"A rich father, I guess."

"That's a possibility. But would a rich father let an expensive US education be wasted on a career in the police? He'd want his son to take over the family business, or enter the professions, or do something that makes a lot more money than a cop ever would."

Suddenly Sally understood. "Unless the family business was being a cop."

"And it generated a lot more money than their paychecks," Thomas added.

Ian beamed. "Precisely."

Sally held out her right hand for a high five, then slowly withdrew it before Ian and Thomas had a chance to react. "So maybe they were in it together. Maybe Dad ordered and Nat did. Maybe it was Nat's plan and Dad cleared the way. But it doesn't really matter, does it?"

"Why not?" a wounded Thomas asked.

"Because there's not one damn thing we can do about it. Like Ian said a minute ago, this case has already been solved."

Once again the inspector had drifted off into his own little world. Thomas looked at him, then at Sally, and then shrugged. They tacitly decided to wait it out.

It was worth the wait. "A few years ago a disgruntled employee took a list of HSBC Switzerland's private banking clients, and turned it over to European officials. If I remember correctly there are something like 100,000 names on that list.

Thomas, can you do some digging and find out if Police Senior Colonel Thanakorn Kadesadayurat is one of them?"

The young man was out the door before the sound of Ian's voice had faded.

Sally smiled at her boss. "And what do you plan to do if it is?"

"I plan to write a reply to Nat's letter."

CHAPTER 50

Dear Nat,

Thank you for your kind letter. I'm delighted to hear that things are going so well for you, and congratulations on your promotion!

I'm sure your father is very proud of you, and pleased that you are following in his footsteps with a very successful career in the Royal Thai Police.

You never mentioned your father during the time we were together, but in the internet age it's easy to find out pretty much anything about anyone. I went online hoping to learn a bit more about his history and hobbies, and was very surprised to see he was on the leaked list of private banking clients served by HSBC's Swiss arm.

As I'm sure you know, HSBC was recently fined $1.9 billion by the US Government as a penalty for their involvement in money laundering. That incident left them both slightly poorer and significantly more sensitive to their public image, particularly on matters related to potentially dirty money. Consequently we weren't surprised when they immediately agreed to freeze your father's account until such time as our investigation into the death of Brian Cahill has been satisfactorily concluded.

At the time the freeze was applied, that account contained £2,305,214.16. That's a phenomenal sum for a police officer of any rank, and your family is to be congratulated on their frugality and commitment to regular savings.

Of course, it wouldn't be appropriate for Scotland Yard to single out HSBC for special treatment. Consequently we are searching for the Kadesadayurat name in the records of all offshore UK banks, a process that will undoubtedly be completed by the time you read this letter. European banks have also been most helpful.

The Cahill case will remain open until we are able to obtain forensic evidence proving beyond – as they say on American courtroom dramas – a shadow of a doubt the involvement of Colonel Somchai Charoenkul. If you have access to any relevant materials, I would ask that you forward them to us so we can close this case as speedily as possible and restore your family's access to its truly impressive life savings.

I sincerely hope our paths across again. Until then I remain,

Wishing you all the very best,

Ian

The End

ACKNOWLEDGEMENTS

Hidden from view by the memory of elephants are several people without whom this book would not have been possible.

One is my dear friend – we've reached an age where calling someone an *old* friend could be seen as insulting – Iain White. Ian lived in Bangkok for many years, and was a wonderful host during my many stops in the City of Angels. We traveled together to Chiang Rai (well worth a visit!), Hua Hin, and Koh Lanta, and I'm pleased to say that at no point during any of these trips did I shout at an innocent clerk at the ferry counter. We sweated our way – admittedly me more than him – through countless spicy meals, including some truly fantastic dishes at The Spice Market where Brian Cahill learned he was about to become a father. Iain was the first person to read a finished draft of the book, and provided invaluable assistance with everything from the price of a drink in a Patpong bar to recent Thai political history. He also rejected an earlier, weaker ending to the story.

As did my indefatigable editor, Ed Sikov. He's very light on the bull hook – a wooden stick with a metal spike used to control unruly elephants – but still manages to shape my meanderings into something approaching coherence. He also patiently endures an endless stream of emails during the editing process in which I question the logic of grammar rules I should have adopted half a century ago, and defend bad choices in a hapless attempt to get a point on the scoreboard. I've said it before but it bears repeating: Every writer should be so lucky as to have an Ed.

Thanks also go to Jim Weeks, a former Reuters correspondent, an unsurpassed lunch companion, my authority on All Things British, and a wonderfully sharp proofreader.

I raise a glass of *blaak sodaaah* in toast to the many men – and even a few women – who shared their stories about life in the bars of Patpong. Some of the tales were gut-wrenchingly sad, others were thigh-slappingly funny, but most were more than a little embarrassing for the person doing the telling. For that reason all of these critically important contributors shall remain nameless, but that does not diminish in the slightest my admiration for their honesty and my thanks for their help.

A clumsy *wai* and an all-embracing hug to the people of Thailand – especially those in Bangkok. I made my first trip to the country in 1981, when the airport didn't have Jetways and deplaning involved a very long walk across the tarmac in the excruciating midday heat. Exit the terminal building and you were mobbed by street urchins – barefoot, undernourished, and smiling like today was the best day of their lives.

During the late 80's and early 90's I was based in Hong Kong, but traveled to Bangkok every few weeks on business. It is there I began my love affair with the Four Seasons, previously The Regent, and before that the Peninsula, and now the Anantara Siam Bangkok Hotel. I once tried to figure out how many nights I'd spent there over the years, and gave up at 150. It is an extraordinary hotel, and one of the great pleasures of my life as a road warrior was being greeted at the entrance with the entirely appropriate "Welcome home!"

I've been in Bangkok just before a coup, just after one (before the bullet holes had been patched up), and in the middle of street protests. Yet I never, ever felt afraid. While there is no denying the complexity of the underlying issues, I remain confident that the Thai love of harmony and peace of mind will ensure the country remains a top tourist destination for many decades to come.

As always, I close these acknowledgements with a huge hug and kiss for the two most important people in my life: my wife Kaoru and my daughter Julia. Many times during the writing of this book my mind flashed back to the good times we had together in Thailand, from my daughter's first encounter with an elephant (tearful) to her first visit to the inside of a bar (wide-eyed). Without their love, their laughter and their endless love of adventure this book would not have been possible.

Made in the USA
San Bernardino, CA
03 August 2015